PRAISE FOR

Finding Father is a great read... the steps of two men, who are searching for their roots in modern-day Vietnam. Glick's vibrant writing style transports readers to the streets of Saigon, the lush rubber and tea plantations, and to the mysterious mountain tribe hamlets. The poignant and romantic stories of the two men and the intelligent and powerful women, and other characters they encounter, reveal much about the soul of the Vietnamese people.
— *Anthony O. Tyler, PhD. Retired Chair, Department of English, SUNY, Binghamton*

Finding Father is a tour de force. Peter Glick, with uncommon insight, has written a brilliant father/son book in the literary tradition of Philip Roth's *Patrimony* or Alec Waugh's *Fathers and Sons*. The style is lyrical, the plot well framed and articulated. The writing is fluid, and accessible. He vividly paints scenes of beauty interlaced with horror, inter-racial marriage, devastating inhumanity and incredible romance.
— *James D. Zirin, esq. Author, The Mother Court. Plaintiff in Chief, a portrait of Donald Trump in 3500 lawsuits*

Finding Father is a deeply moving story of a man looking for his roots in Vietnam where his father lived an important time of his life. His father's presence in Vietnam was by accident of history, but what he found there and did there became an act of love for the Vietnamese people.

It is an excellent story, truly authentic and mesmerizingly beautiful. It broke my heart because I was there in those years, living them and what the story tells. This is not a war story; it is a human story.
— *Nguyen Duc Cuong, former official of the South Vietnam Ministry of Economy a former resident of Ngo Thoi Nhiem Street*

Recapturing the past in a way that vividly speaks to both the young and the old, American and Vietnamese, is a tall order. Deeply influenced by his own experiences in South Vietnam from 1965-75, Peter Glick has written a superb work of fiction.
Like Graham Greene's *The Quiet American*, *Finding Father* powerfully captures a time in history and the timeless complexity of relationships across cultures.
— *James McAllister, Fred Greene Third Century Professor of Political Science, Williams College*

FINDING FATHER

Vietnam 50 Years After

By Peter S. Glick

FINDING FATHER: Vietnam Fifty Years Later

Peter Glick

Copyright © 2020 by Peter Glick

2020 Sixty Degrees Publishing Paperback Edition

Finding Father: Vietnam Fifty Years After, is work of historical fiction, sometimes using well-known historical and public figures. All the action, dialog and character depictions are products of the author's imagination and are not to be considered real. All the situations, actions and conversations within are entirely fictional and are not intended to change the fictional definition of this book. In all other respects, any resemblance to persons living or dead is completely and entirely coincidental.

10 9 8 7 6 5 4 3 2 1

Library of Congress Cataloging-in-Publication Data is available
Peter Glick

    Finding Father: a novel /Peter Glick – 1st ed.

    p. cm.

    1. Contemporary fiction – Vietnam   2. Vietnam – romantic fiction
    3. Fathers and sons   4. Historical fiction -- Vietnam

978-1-7334321-2-2

Sixtydegreespublishing.com

To Mom and Dad

No child could have asked for better

*Time present and time past
Are both perhaps present in time future,
And time future contained in time past.
If all time is eternally present.
All time is unredeemable.*

*What might have been and what has been
Point to one end, which is always present.*

> T.S. Eliot, Burnt Norton
> The Four Quartets

*In my beginning is my end...
In my end is my beginning.*

> T.S. Eliot, East Coker
> The Four Quartets

FOREWORD

Wars don't end when the shooting stops or when the last casualty is counted. They endure for decades, as their impact on the warriors, nations involved, families and even children yet-to-be-born, is worked out and resolved. Now, some forty-five years removed from America's war in Vietnam, attitudes have changed and memories have softened. We are gaining, perhaps, a fairer perspective on that war and its lessons, and beginning, at long last, to know and respect the courage and humanity of our allies in that war.

This book emerged from the ten years I spent in Vietnam, 1965-1975. I left only a few days before the last evacuation helicopter took off from the roof of the US Embassy in Saigon. While in Vietnam, although an independent businessman, I became close to many Vietnamese government officials and deeply involved in economic, rural and education development. I traveled extensively, working in the cities and in mountain tribe hamlets. I developed a deep respect for the Vietnamese people, their history, their culture and their challenging character. I went from being an outsider, ignorant of the culture and people, to being an integrated part of the life of the country. This transformation was facilitated by my ability to speak, in addition to English, French and Vietnamese, the two most common languages among older Vietnamese in positions of importance and influence.

Over time I built close friendships with many Vietnamese, several of whom were key factors in political, economic or military events of the time or had been key participants in important moments of Vietnamese history dating from 1946. In private conversations, they shared with me their personal memories and experiences of those times and events. My understanding of and fondness for Vietnam was cultured by these conversations.

A trust grew between us to the point where, when I was in a group of Vietnamese speaking among themselves, the conversation flowed as if no foreigner were present. In one case, a Vietnamese man told a story. The punchline was a dig at the Americans. We all laughed. Then the speaker stopped and put his hand over his mouth. Another of our group took in the scene and said, gesturing towards me, "You're worried about him? Don't worry. He's Vietnamese!"

I am fortunate to have been so accepted. This book shares my love for Vietnam and my respect for its suffering in those years. And, although many of the stories are based on real people, events, and outlooks, it is a book of fiction. Further, although much of what transpires is based on my own experiences, it should not be considered as autobiographical.

I have written these pages because I had to, for myself and for my respected and admired Vietnamese friends, and because I lived some of its events and came to know the spirit of the Vietnamese. I hope that in reading Finding Father, you may get a fairer sense of the people and the country than what was available during the cauldron of the war years.

In the end, though, this book is about something that transcends all cultures and nations, and that is family. Different as each culture around the world may be, each is based on that same elemental building block – family. Regardless of cultural background, we can figure out who we truly are only by understanding family — our own family. Then we can begin to plot a true course in life and find fulfilment. This is a story of one such journey.

Chapter 1

I have avoided the house. I have been living in a small apartment near the beach since my father's death a year ago. I love the house where I grew up and where he died, but I haven't been able to face it. It's a light-filled Hawaii house that sits on the side of a ridge looking out on an extraordinary panorama. From the deck my father built I can gaze across green valleys and lava cliffs at Waikiki, Diamond Head and the Pacific. I can see westward all the way to the far end of the island. I never tire of the view, but I doubt it will ever be for me the miracle it was for him. There was something between him and this place. They fit together, understood each other. Maybe that's why I have stayed away during the past year: fear that I would be poaching or that the house and I would not find our own fit.

Dad always said the house would be mine when he died, but I could never imagine such a thing. It bears his mark. He personally redesigned the space and labored to renovate it. It rings with his presence, and here, I can always feel his loneliness, scholarship and love of the sun. I reflect on these things as I walk tentatively through what is now, my house. It is so familiar, but without my father, it is strangely foreign. Still, my old room remains as it was when I lived in it until leaving for college twenty years ago. It has new carpet and a fresh coat of paint, that's all. Dad made many changes to the house over the years, but my room was sacrosanct – even though he never expected I would come back to it for anything other than a visit.

I stand in the doorway of the room and peek in like a tourist sneaking a glance at the off-limits areas of a national shrine. Memories are everywhere. I lived my entire childhood, boyhood and adolescence here. I cross the threshold and am immediately pulled back in time. My old trophies, books, vintage movie posters, tape cassettes, stuffed animals and even a few newspaper clippings have not been moved. The Bar Mitzvah gifts from my dad's best and oldest friend, are still here too. They meant a great deal to me because they came from a man who was so important to my father. I touch them and have an immediate vision of the two men together. There was total ease between them. To me, my dad never looked so happy as when he was with Uncle Tony.

The sight of my bed all but turns me into a little boy again. My father would read to me, faithfully, every night. My childhood bedtimes were often wonderful moments. They were poignant too, in many ways – especially given what followed between us in later years. My Dad was a great reader, so we went to the library and to the bookshop at least once a week. He encouraged me to pick out books I liked. These we would take home, and he would read them to me before bed. There were mysteries and fantasies and sports stories and adventures. We read Momotarō and James and the Giant Peach and Issun-bōshi the Inchling. I especially liked the Hardy Boys stories and *In the Year of the Boar and Jackie Robinson*.

Dad never did all the reading himself. He always had me read, at least a little, and he praised me as I conquered hard words and got better over time. When he did read, I loved his voice. He imitated accents and sounds. He sped up or slowed down as appropriate. He was nervous, or happy, or excited, or frozen with fear. He was sweet, or open, or scheming. His voice was an instrument and a paintbrush all in one. Most of all, though, I just loved the sound of it: deep, steady, strong, reassuring. I look at the bed and remember us as we were: me, lying back in the pillows, just so happy to have my father's complete attention; him, sitting on the bed, reading and switching his gaze from the page to me and back again. And always there was his wonderful voice. I can hear it still. In the silence of the house now, I wish, with the intensity of a praying child, that I could hear it just once more, from him directly.

I think I never loved him more than at those bedtime moments, and it may well be that he distilled all his love for me to its purest form each night before I went to sleep. Sometimes I would cling to him just because I loved him so much then. Other times he could tell that I needed more than just a story and his love, and he would become Field Marshall Von Tickle, a Prussian officer, complete with appropriate accent. He would tickle me everywhere and banish, for the moment at least, my fears or concerns. Sometimes these were about monsters under the bed or threats from a rambunctious classmate, but looking back, I am sure my greatest fear was that Dad would leave me, just as my mother had. I needed his reassurance at bedtime more than at any other. The reading and his voice and the Field Marshall all gave me this. I would fall asleep smiling, believing, as if by magic, that everything really was OK.

That was all so long ago, but it is here, as fresh as when we lived it. I stand in the room, and I realize that preserving this place was an expression of my father's deep love for me and of his iron commitment to the family he and I were. I turn to leave my room. I prepare to face his.

In the hallway between the rooms I encounter still other memories, but these are of harsher times, of anger and discontent – emotions and experiences I never resolved. As

I walk the hallway, I look down into the bright, open living room. In memory, I can see my father sitting on the couch reading, as he did every night while I did my homework. He is waiting to talk with me if I take a break, help me with my schoolwork or get me a snack if I wish. On this night too, he is waiting, waiting for me, to "get it." He has hardly spoken since picking me up at school. A teacher phoned him during the day and gave him a report on my failure to turn in homework assignments and to meet other work obligations. Now he is angry, about lies I have told and test corrections I said I had done but actually had not. The anger is layered on top of still other anger about the homework I have not turned in and about the fact that I just don't seem to care about my studies and the opportunities my wonderful school offers. In his mind this is getting to be an old story for us, for me, and he has become increasingly frustrated each time I repeat the pattern. He is so angry now that he is beyond yelling at me. His solution is to freeze me out, give me the silent treatment. He will do this for days, or even longer, do it until I "get it," until I say I will be a good boy and do things his way and never sin again. I am only ten years old, and I have no other parent to turn to, and no way to seek a friend's support because my phone privileges are suspended. The only person in the world who I have has withdrawn himself from me. Do I "get it?" No, I don't get it. How can I? I am ten years old. "Daddy… Daddy? Daddy, I love you." But he sits like a statue. When I can gather my courage, I actually dare to go into the living room and stand in front of him and tell him again, "Daddy, I love you." He is silent. It is all I can do not to scream or to break down and cry. I am ten years old.

The sun is setting beyond the wonderful picture windows in the living room. I am standing by the couch, with no memory of how I got down here. My shoulders are cramping, and I am breathing hard. The clock on the ancient VCR beneath the television tells me that two hours have slipped by. I had no idea. I sit down on the couch. The dining table is where it has always been. The bookcase too stands in its place filled with the books my father loved so much. The tension in my neck and shoulders eases a bit. I begin to recall stopping in the hallway above and feeling drawn towards the stairs and the living room. I remember taking a few steps down. Then, it was as if I had slipped through a portal and no time at all had passed between my school days and now. I became lost in anger and resentment and in memories and emotions I have not experienced for years. But just a walk through the hallway was enough to re-ignite them. I had thought them dead, but, God help me, they are not.

I look up into the darkness, towards where I was headed, my father's room. More than anywhere else in the house, he will await me there. I don't know if I can bear that. I am almost physically afraid to go up. In his room, I will have to acknowledge the finality of his being "gone," not here, not coming back – ever. I will have to recognize all the opportunities that ended for me with his death. That's what this is all about, what staying away from the house was about: putting off this moment. But, the time has clearly come. What will my father say to me when we meet in his room; when I have to admit that all the relationships of my life have somehow lacked balance; that they can trace their defects to this house and the mismatch my relationship with him became? How can I ever, now, redeem that relationship? He is gone. How can I ever redeem myself?

The master bedroom, my room now, or is it? Quiet, neat, as it has always been. The house settles around me, simple, open, with no attic or dark places where secrets might lurk – or so I think. I absorb the room. The hard-mattressed, king-size bed reminds me that I am about to sleep where he slept. I have not done that since I was a child and he let me creep into his bed because I was afraid or just terribly lonely. I can almost see his outline in the slightly disturbed cover of the bed. I touch the comforter. A tear comes unbidden. "Dad. Oh, Dad." The words escape, out loud. I just can't stop them, and in a moment I am crying. Things flash before me: the phone call telling me of his death; the task of informing friends and relatives; the funeral, the legal hocus-pocus, my sudden awareness that, in the French term I had once heard from him, I was an "orphelin de père" (orphaned of my father). I never shed a tear then. People thought I was stoic. They were wrong. I was hollow. I look again at the bed. I can't bear it. I turn off the light and leave the room. For tonight, Dad, I will sleep in my boyhood room, and you in the bed you loved so much. One last time, I will be your little boy, and you will read to me and tickle me to sleep.

* * * * * * * * * * *

I am awakened early by the sound of a radio tuned to NPR. The room comes into focus. My childhood trophies stand on the bookcase. A water polo ball from our state championship and a medal from our national championship are at the center of things. The radio begins the news, and for a moment I believe that the death never happened. "Dad... Dad!" I am sure he turned on the radio, so he must be here. Against all reason, I go to look. Of course, there is no one. The house is quite empty, but in my father's room I discover that the radio, untouched since his death, has continued to awaken itself each morning at 6:00, as it did when he was alive. I am reminded of the last line of a French poem my father liked: "Le dernier clocher resté debout/ Sonne minuit " (The last clarion left standing, tolls midnight.) The human race has destroyed itself. Only its works remain, and these, no longer serving any purpose, nevertheless toil on in senseless consistency.

This thought focuses me. My father, after all, is gone. The house, indeed, is now mine, as he intended it should be. It has been a year since his passing, high time that I establish my occupation of this place. So be it. Today I will bring my clothes and belongings up from the apartment by the beach. I will shop for my food. I will claim the home.

* * * * * * * * * * *

It's late afternoon. The fridge and pantry are full. My clothes lie on the bed. I open the closet to hang them and am startled to find my father's clothes waiting as if he has done nothing but step out for a walk. It's not only his presence but his being that is everywhere. His closet is arranged exactly as it has been for the past thirty-eight years. Trousers, each hung from an individual pants hanger, are lined up on the right. Next to them, to the left, are his aloha shirts, neatly pressed and on wooden hangers.

It's better not to put them in a drawer. This way, when you put them on, they have no creases. (His mantra)

Then come the polo shirts, then the dress shirts and finally, in zipped garment bags, his sport coats. On the floor, his shoes wait at attention like soldiers, arranged by color and smart in their shoetrees.

I have to take a minute. How could he live like this? He had a sense of humor, loved jokes, fun and adventure. But this side of him, the order and iron discipline, defined him, at least in my eyes. It was the essence of him, perhaps the quintessence. It is what enabled him to live alone all those years and still believe he was happy. It's what enabled him to be Field Marshall Von Tickle one minute and to freeze me out the next. It's what he wanted of me and for me, and there lay the difference and the distance between us. I was not him, am not him, never would be, never will be. I am damned if I would ever even think of consenting to such a thing, to living such a soulless existence. Who the hell did he think he was anyway?

I take his clothes from the closet in great armfuls. I hurl them to the floor and set about hanging my things in *my* closet in any order that I choose. When I am done, I feel as if I have won a victory. I am going to end his reign of terror over my life, my way, my being.

My determination is momentarily banked as I notice the closet shelf that sits above the clothes bar. It is almost chaotic, strewn with a collection of what he would normally have called junk. I look through things and begin to take items down, opening bags and boxes at random. I find many things, some of which I recognize and others that are alien; but I realize that these pieces are of a life he had before I was born, before he had even met my mother. There is a Montagnard chief's shirt from Việtnam, a peach-colored towel that he told me was from his boyhood home, one of the last things he had that his mother and father had touched. There is a camouflage fatigue cap that he wore for years in the jungle. It is stained with sweat and mud. There is a strange pipe shaped like a check mark. I smell it. There is no hint of drugs, just a stale tobacco odor. And there are old black-and-white photos of him with strange-looking small, dark-skinned men. Some are in military fatigues and carry assault rifles. Others, older, wear loincloths and carry crossbows. One of the men is smoking a pipe like the one I have found. The pictures bespeak affection and camaraderie. My father is the only Caucasian.

The bedroom has become dark. It seems filled with the spirits of my father's past, spirits I cannot name, spirits that almost threaten to become incarnate. If they do, I know they will demand of me that I be the kind of white man they knew in my father: someone evidently at ease with them, sharing their fight, happy in their forest. What will they do when I cannot?

I put the fatigue hat and most of the other things away, but I leave the pictures aside so I may study them more later on. I gather up my father's clothes and realize I must decide what to do with them. Perhaps I will give them away. Perhaps I will keep some, to have an item that he had touched, just as he kept the towel. For now I put them on my old bed and leave the house.

Chapter 2

I have been transported, beamed away like some cadet in a Star Trek landing party. The terrain I'm in is every bit as alien as such a group might encounter. I am among strange beings, funny brown men in primitive garb but carrying strangely modern weapons. It has happened. The spirits from the photos are alive. I am with them, but they seem not to know. They pass by me, even through me. I am somehow in a different dimension. It hits me that this is a dream. If I want out, all I have to do is wake up. I try, but my greatest efforts change nothing. I am vapor-locked, stuck in some limbo whose boundaries I cannot locate.

The men are moving through a jungle. I follow. We come to a village, more a hamlet, perhaps. There are several buildings on stilts, longhouses. They have structural frames of heavy timber. Their walls are made of woven matting or bamboo. The roofs are of thatch or mat or corrugated metal sheet. There is a whole, socialized life here. I begin to become caught up. The people appear tribal. If they are indeed the folk from the photos, they are tribal. But they are not primitives out of a National Geographic photo essay. Old men in loincloths, smoking those strange pipes and shaping slender arrows from bamboo. Young men in combat fatigues, carrying loads, cleaning guns, even stringing crossbows. Old women, wizened and ugly, their ancient, shriveled breasts concealed in black cloth twisted in an X across their chests. Young women in black sarongs with bright lines of color woven at the bottom. Above they wear blouses fastened to the neck with large silver buttons. I am excited by some of them. A few are beautiful, and many have large round breasts impressively visible through their fitted tops. Their bottoms are molded into their sarongs. In spite of myself, I move towards one in particular. She does not see me. I am disappointed.

Evening falls. I watch as food is prepared over small fires. Young boys use bamboo sticks to usher water buffalo under the houses. The tribe's dogs snuffle up to the men squatting around mats where food is laid. They are waved off but eventually extort a bone or a scrap for themselves. Chickens strut. The women talk. The men smoke and suck what must be a potent wine through a reed placed in a large earthen crock. Like a voyeur, I watch people as they go to defecate, and I spy as young women, to me unusual in their aggression, make obvious their interest in the young men. My favorite, of course, has a beau. I am jealous.

It is night. The hamlet sleeps. In the darkness several dogs are sniffing the air and pacing about. Under the longhouses the buffalo sleep in a twitching animal stupor. The jungle is not silent. There are noises from the wind and the moaning trees and an occasional animal. Regardless, I am filled with a sense of calm. In a moment that is shattered. Roused by something, the dogs have begun to howl. I am scared. The jungle goes alive. Men have broken from the tree line and are racing across cleared ground towards the longhouses. The tribe's livestock is in motion, the chickens squawking and fluttering, the buffalo trying to heave their bulks up from the ground. They are the first casualties of this attack. The invaders carry flame-throwers and are blasting at the houses with them. The buffalo are caught by the fire and are massively burned. Too huge to die immediately, they wallow or stagger around, their hides burnt off, their flesh burst and smoldering. They bleat in agony as chunks of the longhouses, now fully afire, crash upon them. The noise and confusion are immense. Mixed with the cries of the animals are the shrieks of the women and children. The huge timbers that hold the houses together snap and pop in the heat. The rattle of gunfire is both incessant and intermittent. I hear hoarse voices calling out. The words are laced with glottal clicks. I see women herding children towards the safety of the jungle. The attackers cut them off and begin a murderous carnage. The hamlet is chaos. Men spill from the sides of the burning houses. They are cut down by deadly fire.

I cannot stand it. I race into the fight. The tribesmen have managed to form a perimeter behind the carcasses of the dead buffalo. I retrieve a gun from the grasp of a dead man. I rush to the women. I point them towards their men and try to cover their flight with a wall of fire. A miracle. They reach the safety of the strong point. The battle rages, takes on a shape. The tide turns. The attackers withdraw to the jungle.

It is daybreak. I am standing in the midst of a ruined world. I count nineteen dead. There are many children among them. There is one young woman who was pregnant. I am crying. The hamlet headman stands by me. Something must have happened when I joined the fight. From that instant he could see me, as could the others. I cannot understand what he says. I can guess. I feel like one of them. I feel I have lost friends.

We bury the dead with only brief ceremony. There are many, and we have much to do. We try to put order in the hamlet. We repair what we can of the houses. The women salvage much of the food supply. By evening it seems that life will indeed go on. We eat a quiet dinner. I have become an accepted guest. It is dark. The women and children drift away. The men remain.

We are seated around a campfire. The place seems to have ceremonial significance. Communal drinking begins, once again by reed from large crocks. I am offered a drink. Cautiously I take a swallow. It is a rice liquor. It tastes like lighter fluid, slightly sour, very bitter. I nod, grin and pass the reed back to the headman. He shakes his head, gestures that I am to drink more. I take several large swallows. I feel instantly dizzy.

Perhaps I have dozed off. All at once I am aware that there are captured men at the edges of our circle. By dress they are from last night's attack force. I understand. The time for grieving will continue, but now is a time for revenge. The captives are not tribal people. They have been badly beaten. They are disoriented, afraid. I too am afraid. I watch as one is led into our midst. An old man appears before him wielding a primitive, angle-shaped knife. The captive is held still as the man weaves in front of him, circles him, makes the knife dance at the extreme edges of his vision. The man, his head held tightly by a tribesman, struggles to keep the blade in sight. After what seems a long time, it ends. His head is swept backwards. The old man slashes his throat with a single quick stroke. The body drops. The headman stoops to collect the spurting blood in a wooden bowl. The executioner turns to the other two captives.

The same scene is repeated with the second man. He is petrified. His eyes are huge, as he tries to keep the knifeman in view. Towards the end of the torment, the pattern changes. The executioner disappears for several minutes. The captive, held tightly, struggles to turn and find him. All at once he appears. Holding out his empty hands, he smiles. A look of complete terror crosses the captive's face. His head is swept back. Another man now holds the knife. He delivers the death stroke from the rear. The body drops. Its face wears an expression of surprise tinged, I think, with relief. The headman again collects the blood. The third captive is left tied and alive to consider his fate.

A ceremony takes place. The headman chants and sprinkles the blood on each man. I am included. I have heard about such things: purification rituals. I feel important and different than I ever have. The headman holds his arm out in my direction, displaying me to the men. They murmur approval. As they turn to leave, I become aware of a figure in the shadows. It is a woman, my favorite. The headman smiles. He nods in the direction of the girl. She waits. I go to embrace her.

Chapter 3

*I*t is 4:03 AM by my old clock radio. I am disoriented. The wonderful, exotic girl is gone. She was real, I know. I ache for her. I search for her in the pre-dawn shadows. There is no one. The interlude has ended, abruptly, unconsummated. I fume with frustration. I know something real has happened but that I have lost it--perhaps through the same wrinkle in the time-space continuum that allowed the dream itself, or maybe my father has somehow played a trick on me from beyond the grave. Slowly I begin to see that the landscape has changed. I notice the photos on the nightstand. I lapse backwards into the pillows. It has all been a dream.

I resist the day, allow it to come upon me only slowly. I am unprepared to re-enter this world. The dream has been so vivid. It takes an act of will for me to subside, to come down to my old plane of existence. Everything seems pale. In the dream I was vital, needed, involved. I recall one of my father's favorite quotes: "A man must participate in the agony and passion of his time, lest he be judged not to have lived." I can't help it. My pulse is racing again. The exhilaration of the dream goes on. I have never even thought what it would be like to live such a life. The quote, until now it was just my father, something he would say at odd times.

I pass the day at work, living in my life. I have never been especially unhappy in what I do. Securities law is hardly high drama, but it requires a close knowledge of the law, foresight, planning and attention to detail. I entered the practice because I had a mentor in the field. He encouraged me and made it clear he would groom me for partner and eventually to replace him. It seemed like a good idea: money, job security, prestige. Then too, while the practice is not rocket science, most laymen are cowed enough by it to see it as the greater and lesser arcane all rolled into one. Clients don't question me much. Even their counsels tend to cede the high ground of knowledge to me.

Sometimes I think I am regarded in the same way as the medieval wizard in robes and a pointed hat. This has not displeased me. There is none of the messiness of family law, none of the ugliness of criminal law, none of the posturing of torts or personal injury. If one does it right, the practice can be neat, intellectually challenging and unemotional. Entities are involved; in a way, human beings are not. No one wakes me up at night to appear at the jail or to complain to me about what an estranged spouse has just done. All in all, not bad.

Now, however, something is wrong. I am appalled that the jungle, the men, the fight, the girl, the entire episode, has turned out to be just a dream. I know that I cannot let this chimera color my existence, but it is doing so. Before, I reveled in the isolation of my practice. Now I see it as lacking something I never even knew existed. I am so disturbed that I seek out my mentor and tell him the story. Over five years of working closely together, Tom Jackson has become a friend, advisor and something between a big brother and a father surrogate. His wife Carol has strengthened this relationship by her fondness and big-sisterly care for me. Tom suggests that I have been working extremely hard and may just need a break. He speaks vaguely of Freud and offers the idea that the sheer romance of my father's early life is a titillating counterpoint to the demanding routine of my own. "You're looking at this as if it were an adventure film in which the hero fights the forces of evil, against considerable odds and danger. You've tossed exotic places and exotic women into the drama. Who doesn't dream of that? You fight by day, make wild love to dusky women at night and live to have a calm life later. Come on. It's time to get real again."

He consoles me a bit more, pointing out how successful I am – far more so, he dares say, than my father was – no offense intended. Finally, he wonders about the detail of the dream: how I could know such things; what agency could possibly have whispered them to me, when I insist I did not know them before the dream. We ponder this for a few minutes but reach no conclusion. Two lawyers, we laugh at our foray into the insubstantial world of the supernatural. He nods, glances at his watch. I am being dismissed. We are friends and colleagues. I'll get over this. All will go back to normal. Of that I am not so certain. As for the "no offense intended," I am certain. He has gone too far. My father, whatever his faults, was successful in his way – a way my mentor may not be capable of understanding. And Dad was never on the clock when hearing my concerns. I am offended.

I go back to the house, unwilling, for today at least, to work my normal, long hours. I prowl the rooms. I remind myself that this is my place, my home now. It bears nothing of me, no imprint of who I am. It will take time for me to put my mark upon it. It is still my father's home. I look at the books in the bookcases, the art on the walls, the framed citations. These last, there are two of them, commemorate medals presented to my father by the government of South Việtnam, years ago when there was such a thing. They recognize his service to that nation. He was an American who made its cause his own. I can't read Việtnamese, and my father never said specifically what they were for. Almost for the very first time, I wonder about them. Surely, they were not awarded to a man "less successful" than I.

I go to the bookcase and look over the titles. Typically, Dad has arranged the books by category. One small section contains old, yellowing, Việtnamese-language paperbacks. I take them down. The corner of an onionskin sheet juts from the edges of one. I slip it out. It is a letter in French addressed to my father. This I can decipher. It is from the book's author. He has also inscribed and signed the flyleaf, but that, again, is in Việtnamese. The letter in French is friendly, almost intimate in tone. The author knew my father well and was very fond of him. He thanks him for his support and assistance over the years, his foresight in understanding that such a book was needed. The letter says my father's research help was "precious." It concludes, "No matter what happens in this war, our book will tell a bit of what we Việtnamese jurists attempted and accomplished."

Is this the kind of declaration one makes to a man who did nothing but fight by day and make love to "dusky maidens" at night? I don't think so. I know I am being unfair to Tom. He was just trying to help me. Then too, over the years we have known each other, I may have conveyed to him a sense of cynicism about my father. If I did that--and honesty, a trait my father labored to instill in me, requires I admit I did indeed--then I was being unfair. I know Dad saw action in Việtnam, but I had no idea that he had had any contact with the legal community there or with the scholarship of its members and the efforts of its jurists to improve the legal environment.

I leaf through the other volumes. Each contains a dedication to my father from the author, each a letter to him acknowledging, I assume, his help or support or input. There are twelve books in all. Some are in French, some subtitled in French, others in Việtnamese only. The subjects are eclectic: Việtnamese traditions, taboos and magic; the musical tradition in Việtnam; an annotated copy of Kim Van Kiêu (a long poem, perhaps an epic); the Complaints of an Odâlisk (a poem in translation); a history of the Catholic mission in the tribal highlands; traditional medical practices in Việtnam; the diplomacy of Việtnamese independence. The very last book I find stops me cold. A letter inside, in French, gives its title as Ethnic Minority Policies of the Việtnamese Government. The author, like all the others, was close to my father. He was Minister of Montagnard Affairs when the book was published. I flip the pages. There is an index. I need no foreign language ability to pick out my father's name.

For the second time in as many days, I am reminded that my father had a life before I was born, and that I know almost nothing of who he was in that life. The house he created is noticeably quiet now. It waits around me. The silence is filled with questions. I begin to wonder if I knew my father at all.

Chapter 4
Sydney, Australia

*J*J flips through the pages of the letter. There are five sheets, all written in his mother's flowing script, ever showing the influence of her youth in the French-stream schools of Việtnam. Her solicitor and confidant, an elderly Việtnamese whom he has always called Bắc (Uncle) Thu, motions that he should read the document. He glances at the envelope. It is addressed: "To my dearest son." Tears come over him. She has always loved him so much. That should have made up for his not having had a real father. It has not. He is angry and conflicted and uncertain of who he really is. His mother has responded to this by assuring him that her husband, Malcolm, is his father. JJ does not believe it. The man is a surrogate, a poor one at that.

He is in no hurry to read the letter. He has waited this long. A few minutes more won't hurt. He thinks of his mother. She has remained silent to the grave. The letter he holds speaks for her, from beyond the grave, in a way. He thinks of that. This is her version of Mémoires d'outre-tombe, without the melancholy, he is sure. Words from beyond the grave. They can span the divide and reach the living. But no flow can be sent back. It's a one-way communication, unsatisfactory unless all questions are answered. He knows without looking that they have not been.

Bắc Thu cuts in on his thoughts: "Will you read it?"

"No rush."

"Now, no rush? You have been demanding answers for years."

"Ones I could discuss with her. This may create more questions than it settles."

"So, read it. You may be surprised."

"No chance. I have caught a few key things already. She says: 'There are things better left unexplored. What I have not revealed here is in that category. I warn you, no good will come of pursuing such information. Some sleeping dogs must be let lie'."

"Many things happened back there in those years. There are ghosts in the past. She did not want to let them loose to do harm in the present."

"Too late. She let the genie out of the bottle a long, long time ago. It will not go back in. Believe me, the ghosts are loose, and they have already done their harm. Obviously, she forgot that the sins of the father – the mother, in this case – are visited on the sons."

The old man shakes his head. JJ looks at him for a long moment. He reflects. He has loved his mother deeply. Her death leaves a great void. He is so sorry she is gone. Still, he cannot let go of some things. At age forty, he regards himself as stunted, undeveloped somewhere inside where there is the deepest need to be complete. He has never belonged. His life has never been right. Malcolm and his three children, his "brothers", have tried to love him. They have never known how to reach him. He does not know how to reach himself. Even his profession as an engineer allows him to remain apart from close human relationships. He relates to numbers, not to people.

There is a strangeness around him. People feel it. If the letter he holds indeed lacks melancholy, he can supply all that is needed. He is a displaced person, ignorant of the geography of even his own soul. How can he expect to find home, or recognize it if he does?

Chapter 5

I am living from day to day. With small steps and even smaller touches I am changing the house, making it mine. I sleep each night in the master bed now. The memory of the Montagnards and of the wonderful girl lingers. Perhaps in time it will pass entirely. Perhaps not.

In the living room the books I have taken down remain on the floor. The moment to put them back has not come. I sense this. It is not my normal way. There are other, like changes in me since the dream. Something is happening to me. The books. I now believe them to be alive. I am convinced they breathe. They whisper. I have been trying to hear them, understand them. The photos, the framed certificates, my father's clothes, everything breathes. Everything whispers. There are stories all around me. I am beginning to believe in spirits. I do believe in spirits. I start to sense them everywhere. I tell no one.

I have begun to read my father's book on Viêtnamese traditions, taboos and magic. It speaks of geomancy. I am intrigued. I roam the house wondering if my father chose it and redesigned it with these strange principles in mind. There is serious talk of white dragons and blue dragons that lie beneath the ground. It is possible to anger them, even to harm them physically. If such a thing happens, ill fortune follows.

The beasts must then be placated. I am thinking. My father was at peace in this home. I have never felt the same. Must I change things to match my beingness? Must I change myself? Can I?

I spend hours roaming the property, lying on the ground, trying to feel its soul. I study the shape of the plot, the placement of trees, the orientation of entrances, furniture, windows. I enter and leave the property many times trying to sense an influence from coming onto or going off the land.

I am becoming withdrawn. My friends complain. They kid me that I am living in my dream with my "dream girl." I do not even protest. They are right. Something is happening, has happened. I do not understand. All my certainties are softening.

Days pass. I am content to be led by cues from what surrounds me. I begin to sense a hidden nature in things, to believe in it. I am shaken. This is not me. I am going off. I believe now that there is a life behind life, an energy that flows in the background. It is what gives knowledge to seers and adepts. I want to access it, to touch it. I fail.

The time comes to pick up the books. I return them to the shelves. They feel different to me now. Each has a distinction about it. One by one I hold them, caress them, touch them to my face. They whisper. The ethnic minorities volume catches me. It has some words in the title that appear in one of the citations on the wall. I make the connection. I stare at the framed certificate willing it to speak. I know it has a story to tell.

Reflecting what may be the greatest change in me, I sit still and silent on the floor before the certificate. Time passes. I am almost oblivious. Attention is required. I know this, though how, I cannot say. It occurs to me that I have not lived my life with attention. I have missed much that has been. I sink almost into a trance. The way I have lived – inattentively. It is like being deaf and not even knowing that sound exists. You have no idea of missing anything, no sense of the richness available.

After a time, hours perhaps, I am absorbed into the certificate. I am aware of its texture. I see the life of the man who wrote my father's name on the paper. An insignificant, underpaid man. His calligraphy gives life to the document. His attention to detail, his care, make him more a part of this, perhaps, than the minister who signed it. He signed so often, one act among many. But the calligrapher, the writing was his life.

The certificate hangs in the house. I know now that it was very important to my father. In the silence, in my "trance," attentively, I understand. It is not the paper. It is the relationship with a whole people. There is no one act he performed. There must have been many. He was attentive to them and so earned their attention, trust, perhaps even love.

I am deeply moved for my father, for what he no longer had when that part of his life closed. I take the certificate from the wall. I want to touch it. Surprise. Taped to the back of the frame is a large, brown envelope. It opens easily. Inside are a medal, a citation, its English translation and a photo of my father, the medal being pinned on him by a smaller, tribal-looking man in a neatly pressed military uniform.

I know. Everything in the house is the same. It represents my father's attention to some part of his life. The books. They represent his attention to the beleaguered people of the Việtnam of those years. Almost nothing escaped him. All those books he assisted, on all those subjects. For once – is it the first time – I am proud of him.

Chapter 6

There is no question. The entire house is a resource, a repository, an archive. If I mine it properly, I may learn still more things about my father that I never knew. I begin to plan a search. I am excited about what I may discover. Even thinking about this charges my system, sparks my pulse. I feel again like a little boy, enthralled by the sound of Daddy's voice, wide-eyed at his stories. Wistful, I remember such moments. They were long ago, and I was very little. In the memory is a thorn. I realize that as I grew my father told me less and less about himself. At some point he simply stopped. In an instant I am sad. What happened? Did he just cut me out, or did he, perhaps, think I had no interest in hearing from him anymore? How could he? I was his boy. I adored him. Honesty, conscience? Something unsettles me. *Did* I adore him? Might he have seen or sensed something different? I admit to myself that by the time I was twelve there was a clear distance between us. But that was his fault.

Restless, I prowl the house with my thoughts. I come upon the room to which I have consigned his clothes. They lie in a jumbled heap. I recall my attack on his closet – not the act of an adoring son. I sit down in the room. To have treated the belongings of any deceased in such a way is wrong. My father, he set such store by neatness and order. To have treated him and his things this way is an insult. I remember but cannot recapture the passion and anger that justified this. More than being sad, I am ashamed. I stare at the clothes for a long time. I become aware of tears. Then, I am crying deeply. "I love you, Dad. You know that, don't you? You knew that."

The crying goes on. Finally I am exhausted, cried out. I go to wash my face. Looking at me from the mirror is a sad, hurting man. I can't quite place him. It is not me. I am fine, have been fine for many, many years. I go back to the room. Quietly I untangle the heap of clothes. Carefully I hang the garments in my old closet. I smooth them, take care to arrange them as my father would have wanted. I have decided. These, I will not give away.

* * * * * * * * * * * *

In the living room, behind the couch, there is a long, koa-wood table. In its position, it is sheltered from the bright sunshine that fills the room for six hours a day. The tabletop is covered with photographs of me and of the children of my father's friends. Prominent are the daughter and son of his oldest friend, but there are many others. He has always kept this place for this purpose, adding to it over the years as photos would come to him. I don't believe he ever removed any picture from it. I look at the array and realize that it is a kind of time machine. The pictures have remained fresh and vivid, but their subjects have grown and been aged by the years. The most recent shots were taken at least fifteen years ago. The majority date back twenty-five years. Some of the children in the photos, adults now, sent me condolence notes on my father's death bespeaking deep affection for him. Others actually came to the islands to attend the funeral. They stood on the beach and smiled and cried as I joined a ceremony that had been proposed and organized by a group of Dad's unlikely friends: men from the Longboard

Surfing Association. Many surfed only rarely or not at all in view of their age, but they mounted their boards in my father's honor. We all paddled out and spread his ashes beyond the reef, on the waters of the ocean he loved so much.

This memory reminds me of my father's Protean nature. He seemed able to transmogrify under the influence of the societies he experienced. The friends of his youth have remained, to my eye, what he and they were all those years ago: East-coast, prep-school, ivy-league, establishment types. Brooks Brothers, Saks Fifth Avenue, Hickey Freeman, very much buttoned up and button-down. How did my father move so easily beyond this? Who was he in his other and various incarnations?

I go back to the bookcase to begin seeking the answer. I leaf carefully through every book. It is a long process. By the end I have assembled a stack of some fifty business cards. Vietnamese, Chinese, French, Americans, even a few names that are Thai, Malaysian and, possibly, Danish. The cards appear very old. Some contain business and personal information, others only one or the other. I have also extracted eight photographs from between the pages of various books. These are old but in excellent condition. All but one show my father with either a single Việtnamese man or in groups of people. The sole exception to this rule is a blurred picture of a chubby baby. There is no context for the picture. Only the infant and the hands holding it are visible, and not clearly so. Who is it? Like all the other photos, this one has writing on the back. It says: Cúa ai?...26/11/72. Undoubtedly the child of yet another friend.

Chapter 7

*T*he children of friends. I used to think my father paid more attention to them than to me. Perhaps I was wrong. It is clear that he had many attentions and that he tended to all of them. I have always seen his life as flat: going to work, caring for me. I know now that there was far more to him than I was ready to see. I have been learning. When he was my age, his life was charged with a vitality, excitement and meaning that mine has never known. How did he do that? How does anyone go about constructing a vital, dynamic life? Where have I gone off? He was my father. I saw him only that way. I never did him the courtesy of seeing him as a man, until recently, until he died. The truth is, I am surprised. I have hated and loved him as a father. As a man, I have learned – too late perhaps – that there was much to admire in him. As peers we would have been good friends--if he had wanted me as a friend. The thought hangs in my mind.

I am beginning to look at my life. My normal, perfectly acceptable life is neither. By any measure it is unchallenged, unchallenging. I am reminded of my dream, the exhilaration of it, the thrill. The wonderful girl therein has all but slipped from my memory. She bubbles to the surface now. Is there anything to do about her? I have gone from wanting to believe she exists to thinking, hoping, knowing that she does and that I can find her somewhere. I have ever refused to permit my father to define me, or to define myself in his terms. Now I worry that I have no course but to seek myself and my dream in the land where he found his own personal meaning. I have never been tempted to far-off places. That was his way. It was not mine.

Something comes over me. My breath is coming quickly. My jaw is set. For a moment, I am swearing that no matter what has changed, I will not be tricked or trapped into living his life. My God, it is still so easy for me to rise in rebellion against him. He is dead, irretrievable and in truth asking nothing of me. Perhaps after all, I have not learned a thing. I make a conscious effort to slow my breathing, to regain control. This is not who I want to be. It is not who I am anymore. New thoughts and new perspectives have been engulfing me. I so want them to be part of me. I remember my father would sometimes say: "Assert who you are – not who you aren't. How do you prove a negative?"

Chapter 8

*M*y father was an orderly man, meticulous to a fault. On the wall in the kitchen is a tube-shaped plastic holder with a wide opening at the top and a smaller opening on the side towards the bottom. We would stuff plastic grocery bags in the top and pull them out at the bottom when needed. My father had a ritual. He would fold the bags in thirds, first across the width, then from bottom to top. Only after the compulsive folding and creasing would he place them in the holder. It drove me nuts. Why do this for garbage bags? He never ceased the practice. It was his way. One day, probably after I had carried on about this beyond reason, he told me that he and his best friend had both been like this, even in prep school. They would arrive for class with sharpened pencils and color-coded notes. It was such a fetish with each of them that other friends began by saying the behavior was typical of them. They finished by using the word as both a noun and an adjective; any behavior involving excessive neatness, organization or preparation was "typical". My dad and his friend (I have always called him uncle) were each called "Typ" from time to time.

It becomes clear to me as I search for information that my father's mania has its advantages. He has records of everything. He was the kind of man who actually mailed in the warranty cards that came with every appliance in those days. I find an archive box in his study that contains complete records of all the work done on the house. I file through the contents quickly. There are bills from tradesmen, receipts for materials purchased. A large, folded sheet of tracing paper catches my eye. I open it and am almost stunned to find the plans for the deck he added to the house when we first moved in. He drafted them himself. Dimensions and construction notes are entered in his own neat hand. For a moment I am eight years old again. I relive the busy activity of the construction. I am almost overcome with nostalgia. In those days I truly did believe he could do no wrong. He took pains, I remember with perfect clarity, to include me in the work. He assigned me tasks that I could do and coached me as I did them. Finally, I remember sitting on the partly completed structure, happily and patiently driving large nails to set the planking. The memory is so real and immediate I almost believe I can go back and begin my life again from that moment. If I could, I would do much of it differently. Most of all, I think, I would find a way to make sure he and I did not become so grievously estranged.

There is a second sheet of tracing paper. It contains details of the railing and of the attachment of the deck to the house. Stapled at one corner of this sheet is a picture. My God, it's me. I am sitting just as I have remembered, hammer in hand, absorbed in my task. I didn't even know this had been taken. I can do nothing but stare at the image. Unlike the memory, which plunged me back in time, into the moment, the picture draws me away. I regard things from a long perspective. On the back of the photo my father has written: "the little carpenter." At this remove and this age I understand what the caption really means. All his love for me, all his pride in me, all his hope for me are bounded in those words. The intensity of those emotions, the burden they place upon their object, is daunting. This I understand with the benefit of the long look back I am taking. I do not believe my father intended any burden, just love.

Slowly the work of raising the deck and the work of raising a child become related in my mind. You cannot do either casually and do it well. My father, he was attentive to all his work, to all his relationships and especially to raising me. I am thinking now that I wanted his love and attention on my terms only – dessert without having to eat my veggies. Does this explain his frustration and disappointment with me? It strikes me that all my life he tried to tell me something but did not know how. The lesson was so basic, perhaps, that it beggared his ability to express. Being loved is a responsibility.

* * * * * * * * * * *

The last item in the box is an accordion-style folder with several pockets. I take it out and discover more plans. These are marked, Renovation 2000. I am not the technician my father was. I have a difficult time reading them. Slowly I understand that they chart the major changes he designed in order to take better advantage of our magnificent view. One sheet shows the additions laid against the original foot print of the house. I have actually forgotten the way things were when we first moved in. At that time, my father walled off an L portion of the living room and joined the space to his bedroom by knocking out a wall and putting in a small stair. This was his study in the early years. It was little more than a cubbyhole. It has disappeared.

I continue to leaf through the drawings, more out of curiosity than expectation. After the pages of major design, construction and floor plans come several detail sheets. I force myself to look at them. I am not good at this. The initiated can read these things in the blink of an eye. My father understood them easily. I stay at it, if only to prove to myself that some of his blood flows in my veins. I begin to understand – not in depth, but enough. I may never execute something from such a plan, but I will know what is pictured. One sheet seems simplicity itself. It describes a section of floor which, I think, raises like a trap door. There are details of what must be a lift system for this and its lock and release mechanism. I struggle through notations on the preceding construction and floor plans before I realize what this is.

Chapter 9

*J*J holds his mother's letter. He is waiting for Bắc Thu. In the months since their last meeting, he has read it many times. It is all as he had feared. The letter tells him much but leaves out more. His mother has smothered him with detail. The real information, the name of his father, is missing. The old man emerges from his office and motions JJ in.

"You have been silent for months." It is a reproach.

"I have been thinking," JJ says. "This," he waves the letter in the air, "is useless."

"It tells you all about him."

"It does not give his name, his whereabouts. This is ancient history and not very pretty at that."

"It tells you what she considered necessary."

"It tells me she threw herself like a whore at some man she lusted for to get him into marriage. It tells me he had such little regard for her that she failed. It tells me I was a strategy that failed. She never wanted me. She wanted him!"

"Read it again. You have obviously missed 'the good parts'."

"There are none."

"She loved you more than anything…"

"She didn't have a choice did she? It was that or admit that her family's scorn was well placed."

"In this life," continued the old man. "She married Malcolm, even though she had to mother his children by another woman, so she could give you a father. She worked and succeeded so you would never have to be dependent on anyone but her. She had you finely educated so you would take a place among the elite and respected. She cut herself off from most Việtnamese so you would never be tarred with the brush of their Việtnam snobbish scorn for those of mixed blood. Everything for you, and you don't get it."

"What I get is that from the night she decided to seduce that man, my father, my nameless, faceless father; from that night, it has all been about her, not about me. I was her badge of courage; the thumb to her nose; the finger in the eye of everyone who ever looked down on her."

"You should know better than that."

"I know what I know. What I don't know is the kind of man my father was or is. What kind of husband was he? What kind of father? Am I like him? Would he have liked me had he known me? How could she have thought these things were secondary to her own needs? And then, to try to pass off Malcolm and his band as my father and siblings; it was noxious. Look at me. Look at my life, all because I couldn't imagine why I felt so different from them. All because I was tortured that I did not fit with them."

"You are a man, JJ. If you want to lay blame, blame yourself. Your mother was beyond reproach."

JJ stiffens at this. His shoulders slump. He turns to leave.

"What?"

"I had thought I would get through to you; that you would tell me the whole story."

"I will respect your mother's desires. To the end."

It dawns on him: "Because you loved her."

"Yes."

"I mean really loved her."

"Yes. Since I was fifteen and she was twelve."

"Then why?"

"It's in the letter. My family. We were too good for her 'class'."

"All these years. It must have been torture for you."

"I loved her. Being close and a trusted friend were enough."

"You could have married her, had children with her."

"She would not."

"All of this. It could have been so different. You might have been my father."

"Never. You are the unique product of that man and your mother. She and I would not have had a JJ."

"Then you see how important it is for me to know."

"Yes."

"Tell me."

JJ knows it is useless. The old man offers only a sad smile.

"A moment ago," JJ says, "I meant that you might have served as my father. That would have been so much better for me – for her too."

Silence. Bắc Thu seems lost in a reverie. JJ wonders if he is regretting what might have been. He tries again: "Please. It can't harm anything."

The old man shakes his head. "I thank you for thinking kindly of me. I am touched. But your approval only confirms the validity of my commitment to your mother. I have done what I have had to, and I will do what I must."

"I am afraid the same goes for me."

"Meaning?"

"I have to find out what I can. There are clues in the letter."

"Please, she asked you, warned you, not to."

"I'll start with old news stories in the American papers. She mentions that."

The old man has tears in his eyes. JJ looks directly at him. He softens for a moment and then says, "If that fails, I'll do what I should have done years ago. I'll try to find the trail of this in Việtnam."

Chapter 10

I have found the old study. The floor over it is perfectly balanced. It raises at a touch of the mechanism my father devised. I feel as if I have opened the burial chamber of a pyramid. The old stairs are still in place. I descend into a time capsule. The room is a treasure trove. Every document my father ever touched, every photo he ever owned must be here. There are files of correspondence, newspaper clippings in Việtnamese and French as well as English, maps of exotic places, old passports filled with visa stamps – some from countries that no longer exist – mimeographed issues of Việtnam Presse that seem complete for 1965-1975, an extensive collection of the Bulletin des Amis de Vieux Huê, a row of photo albums and a series of leather-bound books marked, Journal, on the spine. I look around wide-eyed. I touch things just to have contact with them. This seems an almost complete record of my father's adult life. I sit down on the stairs and close my eyes. The aura of this place is powerful. My father's presence is palpable. I am thinking: if the soul is immortal and goes to rest somewhere after death, his has surely come here.

* * * * * * * * * * *

Plei Mrong, Việtnam

> We were hit last night. It is bad. Many dead. There was a breakdown somewhere. They should never be able to take us

by surprise. Did one of ours betray us? Unthinkable. These are Montagnards. They are fiercely loyal within their groups. Still, very strange.

The tribe lives in longhouses. I have the honor of living with the headman and his family group. I sleep on the Emperor's bed. It is a beautifully worked and polished piece of hardwood, dark and smooth. In the old days, every hamlet had one, reserved for the Emperor's use should he ever visit. Here the tradition still holds. People who come to help, who stay and become part of the tribe are sometimes given this honor. Several of the dead are from our house. That hurts particularly, but the hamlet is so small, and we are all so close, even one death is terrible.

We are laying out the dead. The Montagnards have rituals they like to observe. Y'Prun says there is no time. We make what observance we can. By nightfall order is restored to the hamlet.

I read on fascinated. The journal describes an attack all but identical to the one in my dream. Seated in this forgotten room, I am surrounded by the spirits of the past. It is cool in here, but the chill I feel is one of awe and not of cold. How could the story of this attack have been communicated to me? My father never spoke of it.

Once again I am aware that something is happening to me. I am being taught or trained or made aware or – dare I say it – enlightened. What has transpired since the death, since I moved into the house, cannot be normal. Then again, perhaps it is, and the world which does not receive these perceptions is the one that's flawed. I turn pages in the journal I am holding and come upon this:

The old man has adopted me. He is a shaman and has decided that I am the incarnation of some long-dead adept, or at least that I possess qualities that destine me to be a leader of the tribe. He has discussed all this with Y'Prun who is helping me to understand it. My tribal dialect knowledge is still weak.

Here's the substance of it: the Montagnards read qualities in people. Some bear special signs. They are referred to as being destined for greatness. Y'Chorn, the old man, sees this in me. He wants to teach me all his lore. He says I am able to receive such knowledge and to become a shaman like him. I would dismiss him as nuts, but I've seen too much since I've been here to ridicule anything.

There was that thing a few months back when Han was killed in a fire fight. K'Sor said he had been done in one of our own. He knew because the shirt Han always wore into combat made him invulnerable to harm by an enemy. I must have looked skeptical because he stretched the shirt on a frame and asked me to shoot it. I played along and put two rounds into it – or thought I did. When we looked, there were no marks on the shirt. K'Sor nodded and smiled at my confusion. I know I hit the shirt. It jumped with the impact, but it showed no sign of a hit. The day after this demonstration, he presented me with the shirt and instructed me to wear it. I am touched and a bit awed. It was meant for a Montagnard chief. I wear it now often, and without fail when we go on patrol.

This must be the shirt I found in his closet. I'm surprised that he kept it so close over all the years. Perhaps he believed in its power. I'm surprised too that he never told me its story. I begin to wonder if the shirt communicated the attack dream to me. I promise myself I'll get it out and see what I can learn from it – see what it tells me. I am being drawn into a way of seeing things I have never before imagined – drawn, in the same way my father describes being drawn in his journal. And now, at once, I am hit by the strangest of all my recent thoughts: is my father speaking to me through these objects and his belongings across time, across the gap between life and …? All of a sudden I can't form the word, "death." It becomes conceivable to me that there may truly be no such thing.

Chapter 11

*R*eading my father's journals in their entirety was to have been a project. It turns out to be an adventure. They are a revelation. He has been all over the world: to Europe, South America, Asia, the Karakoram dessert, India, the South Pacific, Oceania. In each place he seems to have sought out, been drawn to or merely stumbled upon pockets within society that have resisted modernization and that hold to traditional ways of living and believing. There are encounters with rainforest shamans in Brazil, village adepts in Siberia, swamis and sadhus in India, witch doctors in New Guinea, and, of course, the Việtnam Montagnard shaman. These are worlds that should be utterly foreign to me. Somehow now they are not. As I read the various passages that recount his experiences, I identify fully with his excitement and his sense of being admitted to what he calls "the level of true reality". This is the first time I have felt so akin to him, so in tune with who he was, so absolutely accepting of the way he saw the world. In one of his Vietnam journals I find this:

> For weeks, the old man has appropriated any free hour I have. Although Y'Prun is always at hand to translate if needed, the old man has been speaking very slowly and clearly. He wants me to understand on my own. It is a great effort for him to explain these things which, in his world, are instinctual. There is no common knowledge or culture base

between us. Still, he seems undaunted. At the beginning I was tolerating his desire to teach me. It was harmless, interesting and, above all, a way to understand the tribe and better cement the trust it bore me. That attitude was patronizing. It has long since disappeared. I have come to take the old man's lore very seriously.

Our last two sessions have been about geomancy. At least that's what I call it. Y'Chorn has explained that there are tigers and dragons that reside in the earth. These are either blue or white. The way they are disposed can protect a site from harm or make it a place that fosters ill fortune. The beasts can be injured or aided, angered or propitiated. Other, more obvious, physical features affect the character of a place also. The location of hills, streams and distinctive rocks is important. Above all, the land has a soul. He tells me that if I can harmonize my soul with that of the land, it will always support me and protect me. There will be a bond between us. I will always hear the land when it speaks or calls out to me. At this point he nods and looks at me expectantly. I glance at Y'Prun. He is silent, expectant also like the old man. I am blank. There is great significance here. I am not getting it.

At this point there is a crude asterisk and a note squeezed in above the line saying: "see pg. 67." That is more than twenty pages further on. I skim the intervening contents. It tells of war along with its story of the shaman's teaching. There are patrols, fire-fights, ambushes, struggles to bring crops through a dry spell. My father's main job is to organize and assist these people. The goals are two-fold: interdict the movement of men and supplies by the communists and keep them from winning the loyalty of these tribesmen who have no natural affinity for the Viêtnamese. Finally, at page 67 he writes:

Our current mission is to observe the status of the trail where it passes through Cambodia close to our area. Four of us have hiked two days to get here. The stories are correct. The trail has been greatly improved in the past ten months. We see no significant movement now, however, and determine to remain overnight. This is a mistake. A large force of North Viêtnamese regulars moves in after dark. It camps to the East, blocking our way home. We are well concealed, but we know we must move immediately.

The withdrawal is tricky. It is pitch black out. We cannot make a sound. We move southeast at first hoping to avoid the main force and any pickets it has set. Ultimately we are successful, although we suffer injury to one of our number. This we learn only when we dare to group together some forty minutes from where we started. K'Broi is the one missing. He is young and very brave. Better he is dead than captured. We all fear for him.

We backtrack with great caution. There is only slim hope of finding him. Miracle. We come upon him, wounded but alive. He has happened on a roving picket and had no choice but to attempt a silent kill. Imperfect result. Before finishing the job, he is stabbed in the side. Still, he has prevented alarm by the sentry, killed him, hidden the body and distanced himself from it. This is not a miracle. It is courage, training, determination. The last undoubtedly continues to serve him. He remains alive and alert despite considerable blood loss. I am the medic. I stabilize him. Then we begin the task of getting clear of this dangerous place and of getting him home alive.

Little remains of the night when we finally stop to rest. I stay by K'Broi, much moved by his courage and by his faith in me. "You will get me home," he says. "You are special." In this last declaration he uses a tribal word meaning something like charismatic. The meaning is very particular. It is a word Y'Chorn uses. This is no coincidence. I am stopped on the spot. What did I think was going on all the time the old man was instructing me? He told me I was destined to be a leader of the tribe. He is not a frivolous man. I should have understood. This weighs on me. I am afraid that in accepting instruction from Y'Chorn, I have in a way given my agreement to remain with the tribe forever. I ponder this as we trek, as I, like the others, yearn to be back in the hamlet, to be "home."

It is night again. My mind has been grinding all day. Now, in the inky darkness, it seems that its work is done. I understand, finally, what Y'Prun and Y'Chorn wanted me to see so many weeks ago when they looked at me expectantly: a man's bond to the land is his bond to his place in the cosmos. If you don't know where you are from; if you do not understand that place, you cannot know who you are. You will suffer constant turmoil. You will not know peace. In my case, no matter where I was born, the Montagnards believe my spirit has always been of their tribal home.

I close the journal quietly, wondering as I do so about the turmoil of my life, its failed relationships, its lack of peace, its absence of balance. I wonder too about my dream, my future and my own place in the cosmos.

Chapter 12

I look out the window. Below me stretches the Mekong delta. I am seized by feelings of awe, calm, clarity, wonder. I have never been here, but I have a sense of returning home. For just a moment, I see my father's funeral again. Had the war turned out differently, his ashes might have been spread here on this land that once took such deep possession of him. I have wondered whether it was wise to make this trip. My motives for it are so mixed and confused. But now, in this instant, it is clear: nothing could have been more right.

The countryside is flat, amazingly so. It consists of little but flooded padi fields. Rivers snake their scrawny arms everywhere. We are dropping slowly, preparing to land in Hồ Chí Minh City. My father could never call it that. To him it was always Saigon. Unaccountably, I too cannot think of it as anything other than Saigon. Details appear as we descend. I see people in conical shaped hats and baggy black trousers, sampans being sculled along the waterways, boys ushering bored-looking water buffalo down the berms that define the padis. It seems as if time has forgotten this place. I spot the occasional rototill machine, but mainly buffalo drag ancient-looking plows through the muck. Men and women, their trousers and sleeves rolled, are planting sprouted rice plants in the flooded fields.

The plane crosses over a large city and banks out over the South China Sea. This must be Cần Thơ. One of the letters my father had was from the first Rector of the university here thanking him for his support during the university's formative stage. There are photos of my father at the inaugural ceremonies. I am thousands of feet up, but I am being touched by the land. My father's life is coming alive for me. These are, all at once, real places. There are real people down there, just as there were when he would drive back and forth between here and Saigon. Just as there were when he lived through an attack on one of this area's first strategic hamlets.

I am but minutes from setting foot on what I have come to consider as holy ground. I remember Yeats: "And therefore I have sailed the seas and come/ To the sacred city of Byzantium." The plane continues north. The delta recedes behind us. And then, almost without warning, Saigon.

In a certain way, the airport is familiar to me. I have my father's photos of it, and although there is a new modern terminal building, I can still see the geography of the airport of those old days. I realize that I am going to experience this trip as if I were two people living in two separate eras. The greeting signs on the terminal buildings are, of course, completely different from those of my father's time. I see them for what they are today, but a part of me remembers that fifty years ago, thousands of young men experienced this place with feelings of fear, wonder, curiosity and excitement. I walk towards the parking lot and see, not the busy modern area, but the old, poorly paved, rough terrain of my father's photos. In one of those there is a scrawny, lonesome-looking pole bearing a sign that says, "MACV Transport. New arrivals form up here."

I feel as if I am in a time warp. This place, Tân Sơn Nhứt airport, was the site of a sprawling American and South Viêtnamese base. It was the headquarters of Air Vice Marshall Nguyễn Cao Kỳ who became Prime Minister of South Viêtnam in 1965. It was the location of the Việtnamese General Staff. It was even the location of the UTT, America's first armed helicopter unit that flew out of here in 1962 and 63. Today there is little evidence of any of this, but it is all here, if one knows how to listen for it.

    I am in a cab. We head for the exit gate and the road to town. My driver is using his English on me. He is a young man. He assumes I am a simple tourist, that my only baggage is the canvas carry-on beside him on the front seat. I have photos of a cemetery near the gate of the airport. I ask the driver to point it out when he can. He turns to look at me and asks if I have been here before. I shake my head but show him yet another of my father's photos. In it a few head stones are visible off to one side. The center shows a whitewashed stone marker that says, in English, "The noble sacrifice of allied soldiers will never be forgotten." The driver is silent. After a few minutes, he pulls off the road. We both step out of the cab. He points saying that this spot must be where the picture was taken. I can see the gravestones. There is no marker bearing a message of appreciation.

    We exit the airport. I am alert to everything. I have studied my father's journals almost as a guide. I know what sites I will pass as we head into town. The Third Field Hospital was out here. A former Vice President of South Việtnam died there in 1974. No Việtnamese hospital wanted the stigma of his expiring on its premises. There used to be a cluster of two-and-three story buildings just beyond the airport exit. That is gone now. I should have expected such changes. Still, I hope I will be able to find the key places his journals speak of.

    We are getting up some speed. The roads are filled with bicycles, many being ridden by stunningly beautiful young girls. Some wear the distinctive Việtnamese conical-shaped straw hats to keep the sun off. Their long, shiny black hair is arrayed on their backs. Some have clamped the flowing back panel of their white áo dàis lightly under the bar of a spring-mounted book carrier on the rear of their bikes. The wind billows it gently. Riding in a group they look like a flock of beautiful birds. My father was very taken with the women here, and he was not alone. He reports that one awed comrade, seeing the young girls as I am seeing them now, sighed and said: "My God, I've died and gone to heaven."

We are riding along a wide road. One of the old maps I found in my father's study shows it as going straight from the airport to the Saigon River. For a while he lived on a cul de sac off of here. I am trying to spot it as we go but suspect that will have to wait for a special trip. A street sign catches my eye: Đại Lô Xô Viết Nghệ Tĩnh. My father's map identified this as Đai Lô Cách Mang, Ngày 1 Tháng 11, 1963. He was fascinated by the changes in Việtnam's street names and wrote many pages on the subject. There was clear irony in some of the changes. When Ngô Đình Diệm became President here, he renamed this road in honor of his dead older brother whom he considered a national hero: Boulevard Ngô Đình Khôi. The Cách Mang name meant: Boulevard of the November First Revolution – the one that overthrew Điểm and in which he died. It's easy to tell that the name now refers to the Nghệ-Tinh Soviets, an early experiment with communism in Northern Việtnam around the 1920s.

We cross a bridge. There is irony here too. In 1965, American Secretary of Defense, Robert McNamara, visited. Of course he had to travel this road into town and cross this bridge. Although heavily guarded, the bridge was discovered, only a short time ahead of the Secretary's passage, to have been rigged with explosives. It came to be known as the McNamara Bridge. I ask my driver if he ever heard that story or if he knows what the street name was before its current incarnation. He answers no to both questions, but I have caught his attention. How do I know these things? What else do I know about those old years and the American war? Why am I staying at an old hotel instead of the new one on the river?

We pass in front of the old presidential palace (rebuilt from scratch not long after a renegade Việtnamese air force pilot dropped a bomb on part of it in a 1963 attempt to get Ngô Đình Nhu and his "Dragon-Lady" wife) and turn left. A right turn by the Saigon cathedral and we arrive at my hotel, what the driver has called, "an old hotel". If he knew nothing of Boulevard Ngô Đình Khỏi, how can I explain the ghosts and emotion I expect to find here at the Continental Palace? The old, colonial era building has been cleaned up and painted, but beneath the fresh paint, it remains the wonderful building that witnessed so much of Việtnam as Cochin China in the days of the French and so much more when Americans replaced the French colonials.

He puts my bag on the curb, accepts the fare and a tip and asks my name. His name is Phùng. He would like to visit me and learn about those old years. We make an appointment to meet. He leaves me standing in front of "the old hotel." I turn around to face the square. The ornate façade of the old Indochina Opera House looks down on me. I know this place from my father's journals and photos. The reality of it is deeply moving. I catch my breath. He used to take early morning coffee in the café across the street. He watched years ago as two French protestors climbed a statue in the square and unfurled a large Việt Cong flag. He marveled as the angry noontime crowd of that day was stopped from beating the men severely when an old man shouted: "Don't. We are Việtnamese. This is not our way." And he met often on the terrace of "the old hotel" with great reporters like Robert Shaplen, Keyes Beach and François Sully. Shaplen kept a room here filled with notes and files. He used it as an office and a home on his many visits. Philippe Francini, owner of the hotel, made sure that the room was kept vacant and security was assured. Even I can understand how special these relationships were, how they became dear friendships and how our times no longer encourage such closeness. I will explore this place, walk the halls, stand in front of the door to Robert Shaplen's old room and listen for the walls to tell me all their stories. Perhaps, among the voices, I will hear my father's, speaking as it did when he was just a young man, before I was born. Perhaps it will help to light my way. A boy from the hotel appears and asks if I want to go inside. I nod. He takes my bag. I draw a breath and follow him in.

Chapter 13

*I*t is evening. I stand in the entry of the hotel. Nighttime does not make the city more beautiful or cooler or less humid, but the mood is different. The pace has slowed. This suits me. I want to go slowly through this area, to wander, to absorb the city, to experience if I can the feelings it produced in my father long years ago. I feel almost like a time traveler. Some of the buildings around me were part of my father's years here. Current reality seems to mesh somewhat with his recorded memories, but the city is undergoing major changes. Had I delayed my trip, I might well have missed seeing any of the buildings of his era.

  I walk toward the river along what was Rue Catinat under the French and Tự Do Street under the anti-communist South Việtnamese. I am well aware of how the names of many Saigon streets were changed when the city became Hồ Chí Minh City. Catinat was named for a French warship that played a major role in the French takeover of Saigon in the 19th Century. The ship in turn was named for Nicholas Catinat, Marshall of France in the late 17th and early 18th centuries. Tự Do means freedom and was the name given the street when Việtnam gained independence from France. The street is now Đường Đồng Khởi (Total Revolution), but it remains a bustling business and entertainment center where several top quality hotels offer fine dining and night club venues. I search in vain for the girlie bars that lined the street in the war years until I notice that a side road is heavily shadowed. I turn into the street and see that there are darkened bars along its length. In front of several are groups of men talking with exquisite young women, some in miniskirts and revealing tops, others, to my eye even more alluring, wearing the traditional Việtnamese áo dài.

I am almost stunned by their beauty. Several beckon to me. I mean to ignore them, but they are compelling. I enter one place and go to sit at the bar. A young woman brushes herself sinuously against me, slips her arm in mine and guides me instead to a booth in the depths of the establishment. Up front, where I was permitted only a moment, there is a bar running lengthwise. The lighting there is subdued, but adequate. My companion, however, has hustled me into a dark, deeply shadowed area. It is wider than the front section and contains high-backed booths covered in black vinyl. The walls are hung with paintings done on black velour of impossibly sensual and buxom oriental women. We slip into a booth. In no time the girl has a drink in front of her. Her hand is on my knee, and she is speaking softly, breathily into my ear. The atmosphere pulses with sexual energy and erotic promise. I struggle to remind myself that this is all a game.

The girl downs her drink in an instant. Another appears in its place. I have a thought about refusing this, but she has moved her hand to the inside of my thigh and is kissing me deeply, thrillingly. It is as if I have been drugged. My will is in place but does not quite operate. We sit entwined for some minutes. I feel the heat of her body. She is stroking the inside of my leg, higher and higher up. She leans against me and gives me a dreamy look. Then, strange alchemy, the reality around me is transformed. It is no longer the twenty-first century. It is 1968. I am not me. I am my father. The girl next to me is her grandmother, and the bar is filled with young GI's, boys just out of high school, scared, away from home for the first time. They may miss their blue-eyed, corn-fed high school sweethearts, but they are stunned by the beauty of these exotic girls who seem to offer gentle female companionship. The boys are lonely, trying to appear in control, running their small-town-America cool-guy act on these women, many younger than they, who have, nevertheless, heard and seen it almost all. It is a hard act to keep up, and behind the façade, the boys are wondering if they will ever see home again.

The girl next to me whispers a promise: she will make me happy, very happy, tonight. But I am no longer present. I am hearing music from my father's time: "Young girl get out of my mind..." "Sweet cream ladies forward march..." "Honey I miss you, and I'm bein' good..." "Fighting soldiers from the sky..." "As they lay me 'neath the green, green grass of home."

My God. No one got it right. The movies and books and documentaries somehow never conveyed this aspect of things. Young men – incredibly young – their adolescence truncated, forced to grow up in unhealthy haste, in a world where nothing made sense anymore. Their souls, seared in combat, were not at all salved by these strange, non-combat interactions. They did not understand the politics, the war, the Việtnamese, the dynamic, anything! How could they have returned home untainted? How could any of them ever have lived the lives they would have, absent the war?

The girl with me has gotten up, aware, I think, that I have not been with her. She promises to come back in a minute and enjoins me not to "butterfly" to another girl in her absence. I nod, but I know, as does she, that the spell is broken. It was an easier sell to the boys during the war, in the days she never knew.

I can imagine my father in such a place, but not often – not at all when he came back to Saigon after his tour here with the military. Even then, on that combat tour, he was not as young or naïve as the boys of my vision. It is all over his journals that he knew why he was here, and that is why he eventually returned. He believed that serious threats must be met head-on, regardless of any personal fear or risk. I am reminded that there is a name for this quality that sees its duty and then does it. It is called integrity.

It's not such a big thing, this realization. I should have known it all along, but I didn't. Now, I look at it closely, examine its shape, feel its texture, run my fingers along its edges. After a while I find the place for it and fit it into the puzzle I have been assembling since that first post-mortem night I spent in my father's house, my house, in Honolulu. It's a strange puzzle. There were no box and no pieces at first. Then, as if welling up from the past on their own initiative, the pieces began to appear. Later, moved perhaps by some living property within them, I began to fit them together. There is still no box, no photo of the finished product, no finite number of pieces. But then, how many pieces make up a life lived? How many make up the subject of this puzzle? I thought I knew. I had no idea.

* * * * * * * * * * *

The bar is behind me. I have reached the end of Đồng Khởi where it joins Tôn Đức Thắng which runs along the river. To my right is the Majestic Hotel, once the Grande Dame of Saigon hostelries, updated and renovated now, but competing with the numerous recent luxury constructions. To my left is one such modern hotel. It stands on the former site of a colonial-era building that interested my father very much, the old offices of Denis Frères, the French trading group. He writes in his journals of its wide arches facing the river. He imagines these, which in his time framed large windows, as being open to the cooling breezes from the water, when there was no air conditioning. He had a nostalgia for those times. I pause for a moment to try to capture a sense of Việtnam's colonial past, but I do not have the gift. My father loved these old buildings and was able to imagine Việtnam of the French era as if it were present with him even in the 1960's. I turn right and walk a block. There I turn right again and enter Nguyễn Huệ Boulevard. The communist rulers of the country, who have changed many street names, have seen no need to change this one. I have done some reading. I can guess why. Nguyễn Huệ was a patriot – of sorts. In a time of turmoil and national division between contending emperors in the north and south, he and his brothers struggled to bring stability back to the country. The parallel of contending emperors resonates. In the 1780's it was the Trinh in the north and the Nguyễn in the south. In the 1950's it was Hồ Chí Minh in the north and Ngô Đình Diệm in the south. Ultimately, Nguyễn Huệ won a great and defining military victory over the Manchu Chinese. It had been considered the greatest feat of Việtnamese arms until the Việt Minh defeated the French at Điện Biên Phủ. The communists may appreciate the historical symmetry, but more, they doubtless note that, like Ho, Nguyễn Huệ came from Nghệ An province – the cradle of all of Việtnam's revolutionaries. His place in history, even that written by the communist victors, is secure.

Nguyễn Huệ's boulevard is wide with islands on either side that create narrow, shaded lanes so different in feel from the broad roadway that is the central avenue. Far down, the street ends at a park, which stands in front of yet another colonial building, Saigon's ornate City Hall. My parents began their married life in an apartment just next door. I will go there tomorrow, but for the moment, I stroll the boulevard and remember my father's description of it at Tết when it became the city's flower market. He speaks of virtually "wall-to-wall" flowers, all for sale to brighten houses for the coming of spring. Crowds of people came to buy and just to see and be seen. The Street of the Flowers. It was a haven, a spot of beauty and--given the cease-fires declared yearly at Tết by the Việt Cong--a moment of calm and respite from all the other times of year when gatherings of large crowds might have invited a terrorist to toss a grenade into the mass.

Most of all, my father tells of the hundreds of vendors selling what he first saw as scrawny branches with yellow flowers. These were bông hoa, the flower that is the very symbol of the coming of spring, of the birth of a new year. He did not understand the marvel of the branches until he had his own villa where the garden held many of these bushes. About six weeks before Tết, in his first year in the house, his maids invited him to pluck all the green leaves from the branches. The result, of course, was bare, ugly bushes. But, almost miraculously, on the very morning of Tết, the glorious golden flowers of the plant burst forth.

Saigon, January 1967

This year I feel a bit strange. I am no longer segregated from the population by my uniform and the kind of extraterritoriality the American military has. In the past Tết was an oddity, a curiosity, part of "the host country culture". Now, I am in it. There is no mess hall to serve my meals and no buddies in a BOQ to pal around with. Last night, after dinner with Việtnamese friends, I visited the flower market with them. I keep thinking that this is now my holiday too. For the Việtnamese it is steeped in history, tradition, ritual, religion and cultural practice. Every home has an altar for the ancestors. Today, both rich and poor will offer food to the dead, burn incense at the altar and make visits to and receive them from dear relatives and friends. I will, at least, make my visits. These will be to close friends and also to distinguished people who have befriended me. I look on this as a duty. I wish I could see it as a pleasure, but I have yet to get Tết into my blood.

This time of year is cool, even chilly, in Saigon. Today follows the pattern. The air has a distinct edge. It feels unusually fresh. My maids have the holiday off. I am alone to contemplate the day, and I admit to myself that the crisp feel of the air does make me think I am unwrapping a new moment, perhaps even a new year. I step out into the garden to enjoy the sharper and less-languid-than-usual atmosphere. The air smells sweet, scented, no doubt by the flowers of my garden and by the hundreds bought from the flower market by my neighbors. I have at first looked up, rather than around. My gaze lowers to the garden, and I am stunned. Along one wall the bong hoa have burst into bloom. These glorious golden blossoms must have been making their way into being ever since we plucked the leaves six weeks ago. I have never noticed. Today they are in full flower, and my heart jumps. For just a moment I know I have experienced what the Vietnamese call, "tân xuân", the new spring. The entire garden now seems miraculous and rejuvenated.

Later in the same journal entry, my father reports that something has changed for him. He embarks on his round of visits with a smile and looks forward both to paying his respects to friends and to seeing the flowers that will fill their homes and the beauty of their family altars. It was always so easy for him. He just fit here. But when this was no longer available to him, he managed to fit in Hawaii. I have never had that facility. I have never truly fit anywhere.

Back in the present, I continue my way up the street. The Vietnamese both stroll and bustle. There are small shops and street vendors selling everything from electronic goods to toothpaste. I look at the crowd. The women are exquisite: small in stature, delicate, beautiful. The men strike me differently. Some are handsome, but often they too are small in stature and a bit delicate in appearance. It is not unusual to see two walking together holding hands. This jars me, though I have been told it is a common sign of friendship. I remind myself that these "delicate" males have, over the centuries, fought and defeated some of the world's most powerful armies: Chinese, French and most lately, American. The Việts are the only one of the 100 yueh, a numerous, widely-dispersed, non-Han tribe of China, not to have become Chinese, but to have endured as a distinct people and culture and to have hewn out and asserted final control over their own nation.

As I walk I am surrounded by these extraordinary people. Their blood flows in my veins, but I have never related to them or seen myself as one of them. Now I am seeing their smiles, watching them pass their time. Part of their life, their suffering, their history comes to me, suffuses me through my father's memories and wonder and is made real to me by my presence here. I stop to watch and listen as a man bargains with a vendor selling dried squid from a cart. I try to dredge from deep memory my elemental knowledge of the language. When the man has completed his purchase, he turns to me and offers a strip of the fish. I laugh.

"Dựng mô cả," he says. I shake my head. I can't quite catch the words. "An đi. Don't be shy. Go on and eat." He has a strong accent, but his English is good.

"I couldn't."

"Sure you can. Try it." I don't know what to say. I just stand there grinning so he adds: "It won't kill you." I accept the morsel. It's salty and good and takes a lot of chewing to get down. He offers another piece, this time dipped in a red-colored sauce the vendor has spooned out with the fish. I take that too. He nods and looks at me critically for several seconds: "See? Still alive!"

"Cảm ơn." I try out my Việtnamese. He nods: "Không có gì, You're welcome." We stand in silence for a minute. It feels awkward. "Xin lỗi," I say, "Tôi fai đi."

He ignores my comment. "You know a little Vietnamese."

"A little. My mother is Vietnamese."

"And your father?"

"American."

"And you? American, I suppose."

"Of course, um, yes. I grew up there." It sounds like an apology.

"Excuse me. I'm not trying to be rude. My name is Ngọc." I give him my name. After a moment he says: "Do you have a Việtnamese name? Did your mother at least give you that much?"

"It's a long story."

"I have time. Unless you really 'fai đi'," he says, making reference to my lame, I've-got-to-go excuse.

"No, I can talk. I just felt awkward before. Do you drink beer? You bought the squid…"

"Mức," he interrupts.

"Mức," I say. "I'll buy the beer."

"Bia. That's easy to remember."

We laugh together. The ice is broken. He leads me to an outdoor stand surrounded by folding tables and distinct little stools with wooden seats and folding metal legs. He buys more squid. I buy bottles of 33 Beer, a brew that appears in my father's journals as being famous for its high formaldehyde content. I mention this to Ngọc and ask if he has heard such stories. He shakes his head but tells me that the beer has been brewed in Việtnam by a French company for almost one hundred years. "It is drunk in the villages and in the cities from one end of the country to the other. If your American soldiers drank it in the bars with the girls of that era, you can bet that the French soldiers of the Corps Expéditionaire drank it too and that it followed them all the way to Điện Biên Phủ."

For a moment, my vision from the bar returns. In an instant it mingles with the sudden idea that there is a collective, universal memory of all the beer ever brewed or consumed since the dawn of time by men facing boundary situations or pursuing women out of loneliness or gripped by fear in anticipation of combat or trying to reconcile being alive in its wake. I worry that my brief episode in the bar down the street may have slipped me dishonestly into this stream of memory, and I make a silent apology to my father and to all the men of any race who served here in any war.

Briefly Ngọc and I sip our beer in silence. "What did you mean," I say, "when you asked if my mother gave me at least a Vietnamese name?"

"She seems to have given you nothing Vietnamese, almost

to have tried to ensure that nothing of her land or culture touched you."

"As I said, it's a long story."

"As I said, I have time."

Ngọc sees my hesitation and so begins to tell me a bit about himself. He is an English teacher, born just outside of Saigon 42 years ago. His wife works in a government office. They have five children. He remembers nothing of "The American war" but has learned about it in school. His father, still alive at age 85, worked for the Americans for some years. He was sent to re-education camp after the communists took the South. He survived three years of the harsh, sometimes brutal, treatment and the incessant political harangue. It is only in recent years, Ngọc says, that his personality has begun to return to what it had been prior to the camp experience.

"My father was here for many years during the war," I say.

"I assumed that. He met your mother here?"

"Yes, and when the end came, he went to great lengths to get her entire family safely away. One thing I know is that although he and she were long divorced, he always loved her family and made consistent efforts to remain in touch with my grandmother, my Bà Ngoại."

"So you should know some Việtnamese, then, and maybe something of history and culture too."

"Well not as much as I should, and a lot of what I do know I learned only recently."

"Ahh," he says, "we have come to the beginning of 'the long story'. I'd like you to try to tell it to me in Việtnamese."

I say that this is impossible, but the teacher in him coaxes me forward. He lets me use liberal sprinklings of my rusty French to support my rudimentary Việtnamese, and he anticipates certain parts of the story supplying the correct Việtnamese word here and there to cover my huge inadequacies. In the end, he has a sense of things and says: "So your mother decided when Vietnam fell that there was no sense in teaching you the language or anything else about her country; and if she ever changed her mind, it was too late because she had moved away after the divorce, ordered by the court to leave you with your father. But didn't he think you should know your mother's language and culture?"

"He tried, but my mother did not support him, and in the end, just raising me was a full-time job."

"Still, it seems that he gave you more of the language and history than you knew. And now you have come here to learn more."

"No. That's not really it."

"Then what?"

How can I possibly express to him everything that I hope to get from this trip? I am silent.

"A voyage of discovery, perhaps," he says.

"Dạ vâng, a voyage of discovery."

Ngọc looks at me. "That is excellent Việtnamese. It is the way the people speak."

"Idiomatic," I offer.

"Yes. You have a gift for making the sounds and tones of my language, but there must be more. That phrase. It is the Việtnamese in you coming out. You see, you have discovered something already."

Chapter 14

*J*J has been as good as his word. He has labored through hundreds of news articles on micro-fiche. It has taken weeks. The results are at best inconclusive. The process has been wearing and discouraging. He has reached Việtnam with far less to go on than he thought he would have, and the magnitude of the task is beginning to daunt him. His arrival itself is inauspicious. He looks almost purely Việtnamese, in spite of his very mixed blood. The immigration officials insist on speaking to him in Việtnamese. They are offended when he can offer only a few words of the language that is their own, and which they believe to be his. His Australian accent and passport seem to anger them more. He is singled out for closer inspection.

The passport control officers wave him to the side and keep his documents. He protests. They pay no attention. He refuses to move from his place at the head of the line. The officer reaches around him for the papers of the next passenger. JJ steps in the way, loudly demanding to be permitted entry. He gets nothing but a bland look. Moments later he is seized by two policemen who begin to hustle him from the line. At first he resists and is treated roughly. In an act of will he regains his control and permits himself to be led away. The crowd of tourists is upset. There is considerable talk and milling around in the line until a passport officer casts a displeased look at the group. The processing then continues in uneasy quiet.

JJ is led to a small office. He is told to empty his pockets, turn over his baggage claim check, go behind the flimsy curtain in a corner of the room and undress. He does not show his dismay. He does not resist physically. His sole act of protest is to try reason. He explains that he has come to Việtnam to find traces of his father – whom he does not know, even by name – and for no other purpose. The ranking officer betrays no understanding or reaction. He merely gestures towards the curtain. JJ moves forward to comply.

Behind the curtain he is stricken with fear and anger and uncertainty and self-loathing. How could this have happened? Why do so many of his interactions go awry? He didn't do anything. Is just looking Việtnamese enough of a crime to merit this treatment? Is his inability to speak the language cause for such persecution?

A hefty Việtnamese steps in behind the curtain. JJ is not yet nude, and the man gestures impatiently that he should get his clothes off. JJ is nervous and now also afraid. He can't unbutton his shirt. The man has a broad nose and a flat face. If JJ had the understanding he should, he would recognize the man as a North Vietnamese and would know there will be no easy end to this episode. The man carries a baton and a holstered gun. He does not look like someone you would see on a tourism poster. He waits with thinly veiled impatience. JJ gets his shirt off. His hands are shaking. The man draws the baton from its holder and gestures with it at the trousers. JJ fumbles with his belt. The policeman grabs the pants by a pocket and rips hard at the fabric. JJ is pulled off balance. The officer shoves him upright, slamming him into the wall. At the noise, the original two officers are behind the curtain in an instant. One slaps JJ hard. He falls and cowers on the floor understanding at last that he may be severely beaten. He is seeking a way to show submission, to not offend, while yet maintaining some shred of his dignity. Nothing works. He is yanked to his feet and jabbed with the baton. The pain is shocking. He stands absolutely still, as straight as he can manage. He is now naked. The policemen proceed with their strip search. It is rough, humiliating, excruciatingly invasive. Each man takes a turn. They find nothing. Perhaps they expected this. They leave him just as he is and lock the door.

JJ staggers to a chair. He hesitates. Sitting, if he is caught at it, may provoke another and perhaps more savage beating. He decides to remain standing. He is nauseous, naked, gulping for air and in more pain, he thinks, than he has ever experienced. His rectum is tender. It feels torn inside. He begins to imagine that he has been violated in the manner of anal sex. The humiliation is enormous. He starts to cry quietly. He curses himself for having thought to come here, his mother for not just telling him the truth, Bắc Thu for compounding her secrecy, the Việtnamese in him for what it seems to have provoked.

Outside he can hear the public address announcements in Việtnamese and English. More flights are arriving. He reflects bitterly that the tourists coming in for the first time would be wiser never to have come at all. Then, with more bitterness, he acknowledges that they may be all right if they do not bear the stain of being an overseas, non-Vietnamese-speaking Vietnamese. He feels lost and adrift and rejected as he has for most of his life. Now, however, he is also keenly aware of how powerless he is; of how he truly could disappear for good without anyone knowing at all what had happened to him. He makes himself a promise: if he is ever released, he will do what he can to find out about his father, but he will leave this place no matter what after ten days; and he will never return.

* * * * * * * * * * *

They have taken all his belongings. He has no way of knowing how much time has passed. It seems hours. When they do not return immediately; when their absence becomes prolonged, and when he simply cannot remain standing any longer, he slumps to the floor. He is there now. The door flies open. He jumps to his feet, ashamed of the fear he feels. The hefty man enters alone. He carries JJ's bag. He throws it at him and barks a command in Vietnamese. JJ does not understand. He manages to say so in some of the long-forgotten words his mother has taught him. The officer gestures. JJ opens the bag. The officer performs a search every bit as thorough, violent and intrusive as the one he had committed on JJ's person. At the bottom of the bag he finds something: JJ's file of news-article printouts. He brandishes it: "What? This what?"

"News articles, old ones, about my father."

"Who? You father, who? Name!"

JJ is still naked. He is trembling and cannot hide it. He did not think he could be further humiliated. He was wrong. "I don't know," he says, almost mumbling.

"What? You don't know you father name?" The officer is incredulous. "Bastard," he sneers.

* * * * * * * * * * *

They have let him get dressed but have not returned his watch or other belongings. He remains in the room alone. He has no idea of the time, only that it must be hours since he was detained. He thinks of it that way. He won't use the term, arrested. "Hefty" enters the room accompanied by two new officers who clearly outrank him. JJ wonders if this is good or bad. He is more in control of himself now. The long isolation has let him find a footing. He tells the new officers he wants to see an Australian consular representative. They ignore him. It is as if he exists for their purposes only. He is still afraid, but over time, the fear has been turning to anger. He has had enough. He asks again. Hefty shoots him a warning look. JJ stares back. Hefty smirks and fingers his baton. JJ is beyond caring.

The officers confer for several minutes. Hefty then turns and indicates that JJ should repack his bag. JJ shakes his head. Hefty takes out the baton and gestures with it at the heap on the floor. "Up yours, mate," says JJ. "You screwed it up; now you pack it." Hefty lashes out with the baton and catches him just above the elbow. His arm goes limp. He doesn't care. He stands his ground and gives Hefty a defiant look. The two glare at each other. In a moment, the taller of the newly arrived officers has slipped between them. The shorter is trying to lead Hefty away from the encounter. There is a brief scuffle. "Stretch" turns and shoots a tense order at Hefty. He leaves the room accompanied by the other officer, but looking at JJ with absolute hate.

Stretch draws a breath. "Please pack," he says quietly.

"I want to see my consul."

"That is not necessary."

"For you, maybe. I've been beat up and detained and isolated and, yes, scared, for…how long? And all for no reason. No sir, mate, I want my consul."

"It was a misunderstanding."

"No, I think I understood just fine."

"A misunderstanding about your behavior."

"Right on that. Hefty there misunderstood that I wouldn't take his crap forever."

"Hefty? Oh, I see. You should understand him. He is a North Việtnamese. Northern people are very tough. Southerners are more easy-going. Also, his father and uncle were killed during the war by Australians – perhaps by your father."

"Not bloody likely. My father was American."

"American? I don't understand."

"Yeah, well, ask Hefty. He has an opinion about my parentage."

"Try to understand. He has a job to do. He must control the entry to our country of potential troublemakers. You were certainly troublesome."

"Not until you people made trouble for me. No, mate, I don't want to understand. I think it's time for the Australian consul."

"We are not detaining you any longer. I am to take you to your hotel."

"Why?"

"As I said, a misunderstanding that we regret."

"What about my things?"

Stretch points to the desk at the opposite end of the room.

"They better all be there. My passport, my money – all of it." JJ takes inventory. All seems in order. Then, just as he notices its absence, Stretch says:

"We are keeping your file of articles. You can pick it up tomorrow at the address on this paper. It is a receipt."

JJ does not want to fight anymore. "Yeah, sure, for all the good it will do you." He looks at the paper. "What is this place?"

"Ministry of Interior. It's on Dong Khoi Street near the cathedral and the post office. You'll see. It's not far from the hotel named on your entry form."

"Ministry of Interior! Christ this is still a Soviet-style police state, isn't it? No matter what my birth says about me, it's all of you who are the real bastards. I hope you and this rotten place all sink into the bloody sea."

Stretch is quiet for a few moments. He looks sadly at JJ. "I regret this misunderstanding, but you have much to learn. You are a visitor. Keep quiet. Don't be insulting. We don't respond well to that. Nobody does. We fought two modern wars and many in times before that because foreigners wanted to dominate us, wanted us to be something not Việtnamese. You look Việtnamese, but there is no Việtnamese in you. What are you anyway?"

JJ is silent. The question echoes.

Chapter 15

*I*t is the morning of my first full day in Saigon. I awake feeling energized, as if my wanderings last night and my conversation with Ngọc have worked a change in me. Only twenty hours ago I regarded Việtnam as an alien planet. Now, I feel a kinship, a sense that I can be here, that somehow there are attachments waiting for me. I cannot say why, but I am no longer a stranger. The city seems to accept me with a sense of familiarity, as if I have walked its streets for years. Is it possible that it confuses me with my father? Does it somehow sense the DNA in my cells, or is it, as Ngọc said, "the Việtnamese in me coming out?"

I go for breakfast in the café across from the hotel where my father took morning coffee so many years ago. I look out on the crowd. I know I do not see it with his eyes. Although a foreigner, he was one of them. I am only beginning, but I have learned something. My meeting with Ngọc has put a human face on what I think of now as the "real" Việtnamese – people who were not only born here but who have lived their lives here. I know from my experience of my mother's family that being Việtnamese means many things. But I think there is something particular about being a Vietnamese in one's own land. Ngọc, for example, earns a pittance but is not bitter, and he seems to have no thoughts of seeking a better life elsewhere. He appears centered, someone who, while hoping and striving for better, feels anchored in his context and in his country.

My Việtnamese grandfather died in the United States shortly after fleeing Saigon in 1975. Grandma outlived him by more than thirty years. She seemed to find comfort in America, but upon her death, the family contributed money so my mother could bring her ashes, along with those of grandpa, back here. It was the final wish of each. Their ashes remain to this day, side-by-side on a family altar in Grandpa's childhood home in the Mekong Delta village where both were born. This kind of commitment to the land assures a people its place in eternity. The Việtnamese of my mother's generation, those who left this country as children or youths when the communists took over, seem not to feel the same need to be buried here. I never thought about such things, but this strikes me now as a significant alienation – one my mother, along with many others, suffers from. Perhaps it explains her lack of balance. Perhaps, in some way, it explains my own.

I look out on the busy crowd beyond the windows. There are large numbers of old men on bicycles. They pedal placidly through the mass of people and motorcycles and cyclos and cars. They seem to be present only within themselves, untouched by the rush around them, tapped in, it seems, to the elemental forces that underlie the universe. Words from my father's journals come back to me: "A man's bond to the land is his bond to his place in the cosmos." Do the old men know this instinctively? Does Ngọc know it? Did my grandparents? Do all the peoples who live close to the basic elements of life know it because they stand so inescapably on the land, because there is so little distance between them and it?

I pay my bill, exit the café and go in search of the apartment where my parents lived when they were first married. It is a short walk. The old, stone building still bears the French-style blue and white, enameled number plaque. I enter a cavernous, high-ceilinged lobby. It is cool and dark, almost dingy. I am seized by a chill that has nothing to do with the ambient temperature. I am at the source, the place where it began for my parents and, although I was not conceived here, for me. The floor is done in very old tile, small, once-white squares for the most part, with a border around the perimeter of the hall in yellow. There are stairways and elevators to both the right and the left. I know to go to the right. My father devoted many journal pages to this place. I have a sheaf of photos, but nothing has prepared me for being here. The wooden staircase rises five floors in a squared-spiral form. In the middle of the hole created by the stair is the open shaft where the elevator runs. I can reach out and touch the ancient cab and cables. My father used to dash up the stairs, unwilling to wait for the slow and unreliable elevator.

I begin my climb. In the darkness I can feel his presence. He is young, so young, so vital. On the third floor I pass an apartment that used to be home to one of his friends. The man had a Việtnamese wife whom my mother looked down on. She enjoined my father to steer clear of this lady whom she considered promiscuous. Standing here, I have a sense of my mother as she was: very young, but suspicious, watchful, judgmental, with no joy in her that I can detect at the moment. I hear her voice. It is harsh, threatening. I sense the unraveling of the marriage, almost at its inception. What was it like for my mother to have such doubts from the very beginning? What was it like for my father to be the object of these? He always insisted – and I believed him – that my mother's jealousies were unfounded. I listen in the darkness for evidence of his frustration or anger. I hear nothing. Perhaps, at the time, he was still too much in love to believe her doubts could play a role in breaking the marriage. Perhaps he was too optimistic or perhaps just too young. I know well what the end was. I am here to experience the beginning. I continue my climb.

On the fourth floor I stop to collect myself. I stand before the door to their apartment. I know this door. It is made of a wood the Việtnamese call, sao. My father marveled at it. The wood is so dense it has virtually no grain. It is slightly yellow in color, very smooth and almost impossible to drive a nail into. It is used in making ships' hulls and as pilings for docks – virtually indestructible according to my father. I knock. An elderly lady opens the door a crack. She gestures that I should wait. After a minute or so a man comes to the door. He looks to be my age. He asks what I want. I hold up a photo. My father, age thirty-four, is dressed in a blue suit, white shirt and wine-colored tie. Smiling broadly, he strides along the hall that is on the other side of the door. He carries my mother. She too is smiling. Her hair is up; she holds a bouquet, wears a magnificent white-silk áo dài. She looks beautiful and very happy. The man looks at the picture for a moment and then turns and looks down his hallway. Without a word he steps aside and makes room for me to enter.

I cross the threshold, past the wonderful door made of sao. Once inside, I can only gasp. In a reflex the man reaches to help me. I am transfixed. It is all here. They are here. They have never left. I watch their progress down the hall towards the living room where the family awaits "les mariés," the newlyweds. There is a tall Việtnamese man, my grandfather. He beams. Around him are my grandmother, my uncles and several of my father's friends who were in the wedding party. Someone is pouring champagne. Everyone stands ready to toast the happy couple. My mother jokes that she is too heavy for my father. "I love you," he says; "I can carry you forever." She laughs happily, like the girl she is.

The hallway is long. I proceed as if in a dream. Near the end, on the left, is the kitchen. Opposite is a casement. There is no window, just shutters thrown wide. I look out. My host is ahead of me. He hands me a photo from my pile. It is the exact view I am seeing now: Đồng Khởi (Tự Do in those days) shaded by tamarind trees, the old Ministry of Economy in front of me, the Ministry of Interior ahead to the right, and farther still, the Saigon Cathedral standing in the center of its square.

Beyond that runs Lê Duẩn Street. In my father's time it was Thông Nhút Blvd. It begins at the old presidential palace and proceeds, straight and wide to its end at the Saigon zoo about two miles away. I know this view. It became very important to my father as the communists approached Saigon.

Saigon, April 10, 1975

Thuy has gone. Her exit visa was finally approved today, and I managed to get her on the Air France flight to Paris. The scene at the airport was scary. While almost no Americans have their families here, all the French do. They have likely been shipping the wives and children out for weeks. Tonight I saw it all first-hand. The departure hall was packed: husbands seeing off their dear ones, saying good-bye to wives who fear they may never see their men again. It was strange. Many of these people have been married for years. To all outward appearances they have forgotten the love that brought them together at the start. More than a few have had frequent public quarrels. Tonight all that had been forgotten. Wives clung to husbands reluctant to let them go. Women in their fifties, no longer young, no longer fit, no longer burning with the passion of their youth, discovered again the depth of their attachment to the husband who may have cheated on them, who had taken them so far from their homes in France, who had played a role in the disappointment of their dreams, but who had been and was the father of their young and the companion of their lives. The small children seemed oblivious to the moment, like those under age who are not concerned with the second coming because they are still too young to bear the stain of sin. The teenagers hugged dear friends or enacted passionate scenes with romantic partners. They knew things would never be the same between them again.

Indeed, perhaps that is the theme for tonight's moment and for the coming days: things will never be the same for any of us – Việtnamese and foreigner alike – again. This is a melancholy moment. I am even more aware of it upon return to the apartment. Thủy is not here. While the furniture remains, the place is empty. "Un seul être vous manque, et tout est dépeuplé." I now understand what Pascal meant.

In the hallway I stop and look out towards the cathedral. Although I cannot sit and gaze at this vista, for me it is a feature of our home. The scene is the essence of Saigon:

tamarind trees shading the street, colonial-style buildings, women in conical hats, old men and young girls on bicycles, a pace more leisurely than one finds just a few blocks off. In recent weeks, this spot has become a focus for me. Brandy would lie here, just below the casement, cooling herself by holding her belly against the tiles. When the vet could do nothing for her, he let me take her home. Sweet dog, she would wait patiently for me to return and made no complaint as she eased towards her end. Whenever I passed she would wag her tail, although the effort was undoubtedly a strain. She died on this very spot, looking gently at me while I stroked her head.

Now I look at the view and focus myself beyond the cathedral, as I have for many days, as the NVA draw up towards the city. The communists will surely parade on Thông Nhút. They will break through the palace gates with their tanks. They will run them down Tự Do right at my house. I remember the old palace which this one replaced. A renegade VNAF pilot destroyed part of it on a bombing run intended to kill Madame Nhu. I have seen the widening of Thông Nhút to make it suitable for an embassy row. I have watched the new US embassy rise at its intersection with Mạc Đĩnh Chi. I drove down it on the morning of January 31, 1968 as the communists struck the city in the Tết attack. Unaware of what was happening, I was going to the embassy to pick up Allan who had been the duty officer that night. On the way past the cathedral I picked up François Sully of Newsweek and Jim Pringle of Reuters. Parked by the embassy, we watched as the 101 Airborne landed on the roof, sallied out of the chancery and shot to death the seventeen VC trapped in the garden because the courage of the Marine guards had kept them out of the building.

I am deeply moved, but much more awaits me. I catch sight of the living room and turn towards it. It has a very high ceiling. To the right is a large wall with doors in it at either end. The entire wall is painted blue. I never expected this feature to have endured. My father mixed the color over forty years ago. Similarly, the divider he designed and installed to give the room some definition remains in place. I am staggered.

My host motions for me to sit. He looks concerned. He calls to a maid. I understand that she is to bring tea. He smiles at me. I introduce myself and begin to explain why I have come. He nods, still leafing through my photos. "I can see," he says. "I understand. These are your parents?" He has no need to wait for an answer. "When?" he says. I reply and continue to look almost goggle-eyed at the room. He knows I want to see the rest of the apartment. He is gracious.

Opposite where we sit is a small balcony. I cross to it, step out onto it. This is the one. It overlooks the city hall. The man hands me yet another photo. My father, wearing chino pants and a white T shirt, stands smiling on this balcony. There is a bougainvillea behind him. He looks like a college student, but I know he was at least thirty-three when the picture was taken. I am sure my mother took it. He looks so happy, so fit. I become aware that he and my mother were indeed young at one time. Looking at him I know that they had a romance, loved each other, were happy in those early days of the marriage. And I now know the context of that joy. I am permitted into what was their bedroom. It is spacious. Photos in my pack show how it was arranged. The furniture my father designed and had built for it is long gone, given to my mother's aunt when my parents left before the communist takeover. But everything of them and their time here peoples the space. I can hear them, see them, experience their young lives in those days when their love was new and the future, briefly, looked bright.

I think of my father. He was young, handsome, vibrant, successful in his own business and married to a lovely local girl. He must have felt as if he had the world on a string. He must have thought he knew what the road ahead would be. He was wrong. The string broke; the country fell; the road ahead took a vicious turn; the end came. Standing here, feeling the youth of my parents, I touch the tip of a new understanding. In my mind I drift back towards the hallway. I gaze out through the casement. I feel the menace gathering on the outskirts. I hear the daily reports of communist advance and ARVN disintegration. I have a growing sense of the inevitability of the end. I see thousands of people preparing as best they can to escape, if it comes to that. But I also see them trying to deny that it will come to that. In his journals my father appears matter-of-fact about things, with only a modest sense of how historic the moment was.

> Saigon, April 27, 1975
>
> Things have now become grave. No one pretends any more that there is any real hope of stopping the communist advance. President Thieu has stepped down and left the country. A three-man directorate has replaced him: Dương Văn Minh (Big Minh), Nguyễn Văn Hảo and Vũ Văn Mẫu. It is a group calculated to appeal to the communists, but I think it is just a joke. Big Minh was an ineffectual leader when he was Chief of State. He is popular with the Americans and the locals and is supposedly seen as "acceptable" by the communists. Hảo is an economist and former Minister of Commerce and Industry. He is bright, a Southerner who should appeal to the VC – as if they will have any say in matters. I think people believe he will be an effective negotiator whose abilities as a planner will help the future of any newly configured country. Mẫu is a professor, a politician, a lawyer, an intellectual and an outspoken neutral with views that appear "soft" on communism. The thought is that he lends stature to the group and will be trusted by the communists. As I say, a joke. The NVA are advancing on the city with thousands of troops. Our guys scatter before them. In Nhatrang a few weeks back rumors that the communists were on the way turned the city into a ghost town. The ARVN evaporated. When someone went back to look a few days later, no North Vietnamese military was there. They finally invested the place without a fight. All they had to do was shout, "Boo!"
>
> Thieu bears a lot of responsibility for this, but so do the Americans – we and our phony peace deal. What really gets me is what this is doing to the good people of this land who believed in us and what it will do to this country in the future. Since I got Thuy out and then located her family and got them out, I have been focused on saving friends, acquaintances and employees who want to leave. My days are crazy. Rumors are rife. Panic in the Việtnamese community is only millimeters beneath the surface.

I am trying to pack the house up and get it out. I am destroying office files so people who worked with me don't get into trouble. In spite of the insane numbers of people I see during the day begging for my help, when the curfew goes on at 8:00PM, I am alone. Then I have time to think, and that's not good. I can hear the artillery booming in the distance. It gets closer each night. When the city was being rocketed with 122's back in 1968, I was never really scared. You can't aim those things too well, and they hit where they will. But the artillery is different. Good gunners can drop a round down one chimney among hundreds, and the range of this stuff the commies have is rumored to be over 20 miles. That means they can lay out by Bien Hoa and hit us right downtown. I admit to being somewhat scared for the first time in all my years as a civilian here. A friend said to me yesterday that it would be insane for me to have gotten Thùy and her family out and then to get killed myself or stuck here after the fall. He's right. But I have obligations as a leader of the American business community and to so many people I have known.

I would never tell Thuy, but I see a constant parade of old girl friends who beg for help. I have been most touched by Nicole and others like her. She has a half-American child whom she adores. She knows the communists will hate the child – they make no secret of their disdain for the métis – and she knows too how they will use her because she has so clearly lain with the foreigners.

In the end, we are all just doing what we must. We are so caught up in this, we fail to see that each day we are living will eventually appear in the history books. I can't allow myself to wait too much longer before leaving. The noose is being drawn. I and thousands like me must be ready to make new lives.

I have read that entry many times. Standing on the very spot where it was written, however, gives it an utterly different impact. I see a man looking directly at the loss of all he had built, of the friends he had made, of the country he had adopted, of the future he had planned. I see him as I never saw him in life, never dreamed him to be: a man doing unusual things in an orderly way in extreme circumstances; a man focused on meeting his responsibilities to his family and others before – even in dangerous times – he would meet his obligations to himself. This is not history. It is life--my father's life--one he never spoke with me about. I stand in silence. He provided me comfort and safety and permitted me a prolonged adolescence. It has taken me so very long to grow up. At age thirty-four, I am just getting there. My father who loved me, withheld these stories from me because, I am sure, he felt me unworthy of them, incapable of understanding. Yet, he was worthy and capable at half my current age. I have so long focused on what he denied me. I now see some of what I denied him. And I understand something he tried and tried to tell me: that the debts of honor I owe, I owe not to him or to others but to myself and to the children I may someday have.

I thank my host for the tea, for his patience, and for his willingness to permit me to see and experience the apartment as I have. He smiles. "People leave parts of themselves in the places where they have lived. I hope you have found something of your parents here." I nod. Indeed I have. As I rise to leave, he walks ahead of me and leads me through the kitchen to usher me out by way of a servant's entrance. I am surprised but say nothing. He opens the door. We are standing on an open-air walkway, almost a catwalk, that runs across the back of the building. The walls here are whitewashed. The color is a faded, pale red. He hands me the stack of photos I had given him when I entered. On the top is a picture taken where we stand. A beautiful young woman laughs happily out at the camera. She is wearing jeans and a blue T-shirt with red piping around the scoop neck and the sleeves. She is winding her long, lush hair into a chignon. She is still more girl than woman, and she is as graceful and lovely as anyone I have ever seen. She is my mother, caught, by my father, I am sure, in a moment of openness and joy, before her jealousies and insecurities poisoned her happiness and put an end to the fulfillment of her childhood fantasies and to her ability to believe in dreams.

I take the elevator down. As it descends in the dark, I remember my dream and the girl so central to it.

Chapter 16

I leave the building in something of a trance, perhaps even a mildly altered state of consciousness. My father is so close to me now that I can close my eyes and almost slip into his skin. My mother is present too. I am experiencing her as I never thought to, as a young man excited by a beautiful young woman, attracted, slightly uncertain of himself, so enthralled as to be teetering on the edge of falling in love. She is a girl, smiling, playful, behaving the way young women do before the young men they are "deciding on." I am poised, I think, but inwardly, I am almost breathless in her presence. The years fall away. The two of us stand on the spot I am standing on now, but it is 1972. We have argued, and I honestly do not know why. The problem arose out of nowhere, like a summer storm. This has happened before between us. She has walked a few steps away from me in the direction of the cathedral. I don't know what to say or do. I don't want her to leave, not when she is angry with me. "Will I see you?" I am grasping at straws.

"When, why?" She is abrupt, almost dismissive.

"Tomorrow night..." I want it to be a statement, but it is more like a question.

She pauses and for a moment gives me a smile that is mischievous, almost sensual. "We have a date, don't we?" I get no chance to answer. She has turned on her heel and is already receding up the street. Her ponytail swings smartly. I look after her.

People pass around me. It takes a moment before I am back in the present, back in my own skin. I cross the street and decide to get coffee in a shop called, Là Pagode. It is on the ground floor of a building in which my father once had an office. I sit and look out. Diagonally across the street is a small park. Directly across is a series of two-story shop houses. One used to be Jimmy's Kitchen, run by a French couple, Georges and Jacqueline. My father wrote of spending evenings there with friends, among them the German Military Attaché, Hermann Koch, a Lieutenant Colonel and former Wehrmacht officer. The irony of this friendship was not lost on my Jewish father – nor on his father, who had met Hermann on a brief trip he made to Việtnam. At first put off by the very Prussian-appearing Hermann, who came complete with wavy silver hair and a dueling scar, my grandfather soon began to enjoy the man's sense of humor and irony. A year later, when my father wrote to tell his father that he had been unharmed in the Tết Attack, he mentioned seeing Hermann standing in front of his villa. The attacks had begun the night before, and my father's home had been hit. Hermann waved him down and made a sincere offer. My father reported it to grandpa saying, "Guess which military attaché is offering me the protection of which house and which flag!" Grandpa wrote back noting that "It was the least Hermann could do."

Hermann was romancing Jacqueline, a forty-plus lady with an almost cherry colored rinse in her hair. Georges seemed not to mind, as he himself had a weakness for very young Việtnamese girls and was actively engaged with a few who met him daily after school. It was not a marriage that would last, but that was fine with Hermann. He had a weakness for very Gallic women of "a certain age". Indeed, my father's journal notes that Hermann was licking wounds inflicted in his pursuit of another forty-plus French woman – this one a petite métisse. She had finally discouraged Hermann by declaring that she "feared his Germanic violence and how it would no doubt be reflected in his love making." Jacqueline, apparently, had no such concerns. She began by tolerating his attentions, laughing them off and letting my father know that she would never have "a Boche". In the end, my father relates, there was a replay of World War II, and Germany laid France low for a second time.

Next to Jimmy's was a florist's shop named Linh. Before a law passed during the Nguyễn Cao Ky years that required all shops to display signs in Việtnamese, it had gone by its owner's French name, Lynne. When my father knew her, Lynne was an elderly lady who lived alone except for the company of her tiny Chihuahua, which she would walk in the nearby park several times a day. She had come to Việtnam almost as a girl and had taught in the French school system. With great nostalgia, she talked to my father of the old times: 'Ah, Monsieur qu'est-ce quê j'étais belle ces jours-là.' (Oh, Monsieur, how beautiful I was then.) She told him stories of the grand balls held by diplomatic missions, at the rubber plantations, by the great trading houses and even by the military. She danced the nights away in lovely gowns with dashing young officers but, alas, never found a husband. By the time she felt that she must choose, all her suitors had stopped asking. With no family to speak of in France, she had opted to remain in "l'Indoche". It had become her home. She would have been lost without it. The French community supported her by patronizing her shop extravagantly. "And so," my father notes, "she passed permanently into the company of les Français d'outre mer without ever intending to."

He had a soft spot for the French of the Indochina era, and his journals contain much musing about what it must have been like here in those days. He imagines the sweetness of the life for the old colonial masters, the ability of these people to live well in this lovely country, when they might not have been able to do so back in "la métropole." He mentions talking with old legionnaires who so loved this place that, like Lynne, they stayed forever. They too told him stories: of the village girls they encountered in their rural postings, playful, flirtatious, sexually curious and, "môn Điều," more beautiful than any other creatures in God's creation; of disdain for the undersized Việtnamese men; of fighting "les Việts" and coming to respect and admire what they had first derided; and of the siege of Điện Biên Phủ.

"It was war, mon Vieux, war, you see. What did they know, our generals. They thought that basin was an ideal spot to draw the Việts into a definitive battle. Our superior ability to fight as a massed force was supposed to lead to their destruction. We were not far from Hanoi; we would supply over land. Well, what they didn't know was that some Chinese strategist centuries earlier had said never to defend ground that looked like a tortoise turned on its back. Giáp knew that. The Việts did the opposite of everything we had counted on. They disassembled their field pieces and humped them a hundred miles on bicycles through thick jungle, on trails hacked out by guys with machetes. They dragged them up the mountain on their backs, reassembled them, bunkered them in, camouflaged them and sat looking down on us and waiting. They supplied themselves without using exposed roads, and finally came at us, not over the open ground, but through trenches. They dug miles of trenches, like ants, like groundhogs, and we didn't know until they popped up right at the edge of the wire and bit-by-bit overran us. I remember. Piroth blew his own brains out when he understood that his arrogance had resulted in our artillery being destroyed in the first few days of the battle. De Castries became increasingly depressed as things got worse. Only the doctor and Bigéard seemed to be able to face things day after day. I remember.

"Above all, I remember les gars. They never quit. I am proud of them. We got chewed up, but we fought. And I remember the young guys, raw volunteers, who came to us as the siege got worse. They would sign on for duty, as if more men could change the inevitable. What did they know? But they signed on. They would drink in the bars of Hanoi for a few last days, love the beautiful women of this country one last time, and come to us to face their deaths. They had to be flown in. The Việts had cut the roads. Like our supplies, they were hauled in a bunch of old Douglas Dakotas. The planes that landed were increasingly blown up on the ground. The Việt artillery had our range. It was bad enough that the supplies got blasted, but the young troops, lots of them were dead before they ever got a chance to be brave. The planes that didn't land parachuted their men and supplies. It was no good. More and more – of the men as well as the supplies – landed outside our shrinking perimeter. The supplies lay out of reach. Only a few of the men escaped death, capture or crippling wounds.

"At the end, when there was just no chance left, Bigéard led a breakout. I went with him. Well, I'm here, so you know we succeeded – at least a few of us--and maybe you know too that in spite of that beating, I love this country, the women. I don't love the men, but I admire them. They are tough. That was my last battle. Even, it was the last of war in the grand style, swashbuckling, raw courage, devil-may-care, le beau geste. Oui, actually it was that. Do you know what Navarre's instruction to Cogny was? 'Prière monter opération spectaculaire avec maximum publicité and minimum de pertes.' (Please mount spectacular operation having maximum publicity and minimum losses.) Now you're here. There's still plenty of courage and heroism, but it's all mundane, no longer war in the grand style, no longer heroism that is acclaimed at home, just young men dying and a sense of futility. The more things change, the more they stay the same. You know?"

My father knew. He had seen the NVA use the old Viet Minh trenching tactics at Khe Sanh, and he had been in Vietnam during the battle at Ia Drang. But like the legionnaire who shared those memories with him, he had been conquered by Vietnam. He loved the women, admired the men, believed in the effort his country was making. He lived his war here, became a man here, made his commitment here but in the end, could not remain as his legionnaire friend had. He just took his impressions and memories and lessons of this place and consigned them to his journals, which he then never even told me about.

Reading those journals at home was moving and informative. In them my father writes that an awareness of the Vietnam of the old days, what he sometimes thought of as "legionnaire days," was never very far from his consciousness and that he was often reminded of those times as he walked down some of the graceful, tree-shaded boulevards here. For me, being in this place is powerful. Experiencing this, with my father's life here and reactions to it as a shadow-presence, is almost transformative. I am at the beginnings of an understanding that, for my father, Vietnam was not a country, Saigon not a city. Each was a state of mind, a place in the heart.

I have left Là Pagode. I am back in the street. I look around, more than half expecting to encounter my father. This, of course, is impossible, but as I wander through my moments here, I am surely meeting parts of his spirit. One day, I shall meet it in all its colors. On that day, I will welcome it, invite it for a drink, talk with it and listen to it as I never did when it was incarnate. And if it asks me, as the legionnaire did my father himself, "Do you know," I hope I may in truth say at least, "I am beginning to."

Chapter 17

*I*t has been only a few days, but I am falling into a pattern. My regular Saigon breakfast is strong Việtnamese coffee, croissant and orange pressé, which I take here, on the terrace of the hotel. I wonder and even marvel a bit at how the city seems to have suggested a way for me to organize my life. Each morning, and each evening also, I come here. It is a place of reflection for me, a place where I can draw some perspective on my day, either in anticipation or in retrospect. And always, Saigon is the context of my thoughts.

I am enthralled by the city: the gracious architecture of its colonial-era public buildings, the evocative beauty of the colonial villas in its residential areas, the busy energy of Cholon, its Chinese section, the old-Asia feel of scrawny coolies patiently traipsing up and down bouncing board-gangplanks to unload hundred-pound, jute bags of rice from barges that have come up from the Mekong Delta. I reflect on these things, and I am thrilled to be here. I never expected this. The trip was to help me discover more about my father. Instead I am engaged myself as I have never been. Further, that part of me that was central--at least until I moved back into the Hawaii house and began the process that has brought me here – is beginning to feel strange. It senses the degree to which I may actually be slipping into my father's Vietnam patterns. Now, as I await Phùng, my airport cab driver, and his grandfather, I am yet again divided between the present and my father's time.

I am imagining how things might have been in the days when people who are now part of history sipped drinks here and discussed the latest political rumor or military challenge. I let my glance wander off into the middle distance. The noise of the present recedes a bit, and I can almost believe that I have been transported back to that time. I imagine the thrill of returning to this terrace at day's end to tell friends of a battle lived through, in the mountains or perhaps the delta, earlier that same day. They each have their own stories or contribute the latest gossip: the editorial assistant at AP or UPI is believed to be a Viet Cong; the Ambassador is angry with one of the President's personal appointees to his staff; the Buddhists are going to try again to overthrow the regime; Thieu and Ky do not get along. In the middle of this, a young pilot joins the group. He is fresh from a series of bombing runs over Hanoi and from dodging SAM missiles. Everyone admires his courage. He shrugs. This is his business. It's what he does. In my reverie, I can actually feel the thrill of being young and full of life that is tested and put on the line daily. I can almost believe that I, like my father and the friends of his days here, am special, different from those who did not serve, who did not experience this place at that time.

The power of the reverie is overwhelming. The line between now and then is all but lost, between my identity and that of my father, hopelessly blurred. His emotions, awareness, sensitivities and prejudices sweep through me. I too now feel sad that marvelous old French street names, rooted in the history of Indochina or World War II or both, have had to disappear. Boulevard DeLattre de Tassigny, Boulevard de la Somme, Boulevard Bonard, Place Joffre and Boulevard Pigneau de Behaine are gone. They have been renamed, mainly for Vietnamese emperors or heroes: Công Lý, Hàm Nghi, Lê Loi, Chien Si and Hòa Bình. But there are other changes. Boulevard Norodom, which became Thống Nhut Nhứt is now Boulevard Lê Duẩn; and Boulevard Mayer, which became Hien Vuong, is now Boulevard Điện Biên Phủ.

There are of course more such, but I am stuck on Lê Duẩn. He was Communist Party Secretary in the 1970s. Early in his career, he served as head of the Viet Minh in the South and laid the groundwork for the eventual corruption and overthrow of an independent, non-communist South Vietnam. Even to me, naming Saigon's most central boulevard after him is an insult, an abomination. This street had its name hopefully changed in 1954 from Norodom, a Cambodian dynasty, to Thông Nhứt, Reunification. What need did it have of becoming Lê Duẩn? What need did Hien Vuong, named for a seventeenth-century Emperor, have of being renamed for a communist victory, and what need did Saigon have of becoming Hồ Chí Minh City! This is imperialism pure and simple. Almost out of nowhere I begin to understand why my father hated the communists and saw them as smug and duplicitous. And something within me, to my great surprise, vows that the name changes shall not stand; that this country will yet see the day when Saigon is again Saigon, and when the communists recede into the perspective of history and the eternal Vietnam reasserts itself.

* * * * * * * * * * *

Phùng arrives, and I am forced back into the present. There is no time for me to adjust before his grandfather, a neat, smallish man, trim and fit looking, steps forward. He has a full head of gray hair and a strong face. He looks remarkably young for someone who must be close to ninety. I stand, smile and find that I have clasped my hands, raised them to the middle of my chest and am bowing slightly to the old man. Phùng makes the introductions in English. His grandfather, Mr. Nam, smiles broadly, acknowledges my gesture and offers his hand.

"That is quite a greeting," he says. "I have been thinking of you as an American. I did not expect you to know the proper Vietnamese way of acknowledging an elder."

I am still struggling to shake off the emotions of my reverie. "My father taught me that when I was very young. He required that I greet all Vietnamese elders that way. I haven't thought of it for years."

"But you remembered, almost as a reflex, I would say. It tells me that your father cared enough about your Vietnamese half to want to nourish it and that the Vietnamese in you has not died."

"I wish I could accept the compliment. It's true that my father cared and that he tried. But my mother, for the short time she was with us, was so hurt by the loss of the country to the communists that she discouraged my father's efforts. In the end, he had enough to do just raising me, and I was not interested at all in being Vietnamese."

"Ah."

"But that seems to be changing."

"Now that you are here, in the land of your ancestors?"

"Now that I am here and can see and feel and touch and experience a bit of what my father bonded with in Vietnam. Now that I can meet a few 'real' Vietnamese – not refugees in America. Now that I can begin to get outside the person I have been for all these years of my life."

I stop abruptly, embarrassed by my emotions and what they have prompted me to pour out. There is an awkward silence. I draw a breath. A waiter hovering nearby reminds me of my manners. "Excuse me," I say. "Would you like something to drink?"

Mr. Nam orders hot tea. Phùng and I get cold beer. After a bit more silence, Mr. Nam asks: "Are you finding disturbing things here – things that are different from what you expected?"

"The truth is that I came almost without expectations. You speak of my being half Vietnamese, but I really am not. I am an American who happens to have a Việtnamese mother. There is a difference. I know, knew, nothing of this place, and I didn't care. I grew up as an American and had all the benefits and problems people of my generation in America had. Now I get here, and I begin – just begin – to get the flavor of this place. Maybe more importantly for me, I am seeing where my father's war took place. It is very strange to me, but that war in a way provided a context for his life. Because of that, and for other reasons too, I never understood him. I guess I never really wanted to. But now, being here, it's as if this man, who raised me, is being opened to me like an unfolding bud – hidden mysteries slowly revealed."

"And that is upsetting to you?"

"No. It's surprising. I find myself feeling some of the things my father felt. In some of my reveries, I almost become him. For years, he was incomprehensible to me. Now I am understanding, through my own experience, at least some of his emotions. I seem upset because just before you came, I all of a sudden felt in my bones the same distaste for the communists that he had."

"How so? You can't know very much about them."

"I know they are smug enough and hold the South in sufficient disdain that they dared to name this city for Hồ Chí Minh and one of its main streets for Lê Duan."

"Ah. So, you must be Việtnamese after all, if you are able to feel so intensely about that."

"My father wasn't, and he felt strongly about it."

"Perhaps he was Việtnamese, in the way that counts most: in his heart."

I have no reply to this. The statement stands as its own value. Immediately I wonder why I never thought of my father that way. I was well aware of his ability to fit smoothly into a number of very different contexts, with very different people. It never dawned on me that his heart may have had many chambers, each a space for complete acceptance of and identification with people different from whom he was, or at least who he was at birth and by upbringing.

Phùng has been listening to the conversation, but he has also been eyeing the thick stack of black-and-white photographs I have had on the table. He begins to look through them. I am silent for so long that Mr. Nam looks quizzically at me.

"Sorry. What you just said…it kind of opened a door for me. I'm here because I want to understand my father. This place was so much a part of who he was that I decided I could never really know him without coming here. He's dead now, so I have to rely on my memories of him, on the diaries he kept, on people I might find here who knew him, and on what I can learn by being here and feeling what it was like--might have been like--when he lived his experiences here. You have just added something I never thought of."

"What you are trying to do is not easy."

"Maybe, but I have actually been making progress. And I do have his journals and old photos." I nod towards the stack that Phùng is looking through.

"Yes, Phùng told me about the picture of the cemetery by the airport and about the McNamara Bridge. Your father seems to have written details, maybe mostly anecdotes even."

"Anecdotes, sometimes almost actual reports of events, sometimes his thoughts about what was going on or what he experienced. He wrote about what impressed him. I don't think he was trying to create a story, just recording an important time of his life. Based on his photos and his reporting, I find sometimes that I can actually almost dream myself back into the Vietnam of his era. Before you came, I was remembering that he and many of his friends often met right here and discussed the politics of Vietnam and swapped stories of combat engagements they had experienced maybe during the day itself."

"Yes. This was a popular place back then: for journalists, spies, businessmen, even our politicians. Things were intense. Everybody took everything so seriously. There was a very great sense of drama. Your father would have felt that. Well, it was a time of war. We all thought we were fighting for our very survival."

"Weren't you?

"I guess we were. From what we knew then, yes. The South lost the war, but its survival, I don't think so. Seeing things now, it looks a lot like we won after all. The nation today is much more the way we envisioned it than the way the communists did."

"My father would be glad. He hated the communists. He refused to return to Vietnam after 1975. He said he would never return for as long as this was a communist country run by the original, old-line communists. He said those people killed his friends. He loved Vietnam, but he hated what he thought of as the smugness of the original communist crowd. He always refused to call this city Hồ Chí Minh. If he were alive now, he would never agree, for example, to use the street names the communists have put in place."

"That's an interesting thing to say because the French colonials who stayed here after 1954, even those who came here after that but had never been here before, insisted on using the old French street names."

"It wasn't like that for my father, I don't think. He just didn't see the communists as legitimate somehow."

"Many of us did not. Those of us who have lived long enough are over that because the eternal Vietnam has reasserted itself. That, I think, is what your father bonded with when he was here. He was a young man, feeling things intensely. I am sure those years were a defining part of his life. They were for so many young people on both sides. They had to have been for him."

I am silent. I have surely known this, but hearing it from Mr. Nam, actually here on the ground in Saigon, and in the context he has given it, all at once I see not my father, but myself. My own life has been distinctly lacking a Vietnam, a watershed moment. Nothing has yet spoken to me with such a compelling voice that I understand – at last--who I truly am. Perhaps it is that nothing yet has forced me to be who I truly am.

Mr. Nam continues: "And after Vietnam, what did he do? How did he live the rest of his life?"

I have to consider my answer. The best I can produce is, "Quietly."

"Quietly?"

"Yes. My mother divorced him, and he settled down, I guess, to the job of being my father."

"In Vietnam, traditionally, men have been more powerful under the law than women. I understand that America is different. Was it normal for a father to get his child after divorce?"

"No."

"So he had to try hard to win you. I think you became his next passion, the commitment that replaced Vietnam for him. You were his next battle, the next thing he was going to fight for; the next cause for which he would give his life so that you could have the freedom of unlimited choice and the tools to succeed."

Mr. Nam has a way of putting things that upset the views I have long held. Of course it has dawned on me before that my father was ferociously committed to me, but I saw that as a bad thing, a burden. Only now do I understand that there were other ways to see it: as a challenge, as a chance to rise to an occasion. In facing up to being a single parent, both mother and father, as it were, perhaps he heard life telling him that he now had a second chance, the opportunity to continue to be faithful to his duty – if he had the courage to do so, if he was willing to accept the challenge, to make the hard choice, to give up a piece of his future for the good of mine.

Phùng has been looking through my father's photos, and now Mr. Nam picks up some of the ones Phùng has laid aside. I am silent, perhaps for too long, as he glances through them. He says to me, "You are thinking."

"Yes."

Mr. Nam gives me a long look. For a moment he seems about to say something but, apparently, decides on silence. He returns to the pictures. I watch him. He smiles at some and looks closely at others, occasionally nodding and remembering, it seems, some of the scenes or the people in them. I wait expectantly for him to comment, but he just keeps moving through the stack, although now his face tells me that some of the shots bring back living memories to him. "You recognize places and people?"

"Almost all the places and several of the people. This one, for example. This man was very important here back in those years. He was the chief judge of what we called the cour de cassassion, an incorruptible man in a system that had much corruption."

I grab the pile of old business cards I have brought and file quickly through it. I find what I want and hold it out to Mr. Nam. "Is that Judge Đao?"

He looks surprised. "Yes," he replies slowly and takes the card. "Choi oi (My God). This must be fifty years old. But that is his writing." He reads the brief note: "'Sincere thanks for your help with our project on the Code Commerciale.' Your father knew him. He is still alive. Would you like to meet him?"

"Very much."

"I'll arrange it," he says and then returns to the pictures.

It is my turn now to take a long look at my companion. He has not moved on to another picture. I begin to wonder about him, his life, even his relationship with Judge Dao, as he seems moved by the photo. He feels me looking at him, turns to me and smiles. "Please," I say, "tell me a bit about yourself. Are you a lawyer? I mean if you know the judge…"

"Well, I do have a law degree, but I never practiced law in a 'cabinet judiciaire.' I know the judge because we studied law together in France at Montpellier."

"And he practiced and you did not?"

"Đao and I went to France at the same time. Actually, I met him on the boat. It was a great adventure for us, although maybe more so for me. I was from the Delta, kind of what your GIs here called 'a farm boy.' Đao was from a mandarin family in Hanoi. They came south when the war, la deuxième guerre, ended. He always knew he wanted to be a lawyer and hopefully a judge. I just wanted to get some experience, some polish and a credential that might get me into government, maybe even diplomatic service. We sailed to France on La Marseillaise, a Méssageries Maritimes ship. The voyage was a thrilling adventure for each of us. Đao knew all about the great vessels of that company that sailed from France to Indochina for so many years. He felt he was living in history. I was just awed by everything."

"So what was your career?

"I was born in the delta in 1930, a village near Cần Thơ. My grandparents were rice farmers. My father saw that the real money in that business was as a rice trader. He managed to develop a small business as a middleman between the Việtnamese growers and the locally-based Chinese who worked for the big traders. The Chinese controlled that business completely so my father never got to grow his business very big, but he earned the trust of the Chinese, and by that he made money. His good relations with the rich Chinese resulted in local Viêtnamese functionaries wanting to be on his good side so they could be in touch with the power that money conferred. My father was always modest. He never tried to eclipse anyone and so he rose. He foresaw the time when we would have independence, and he sent me to a French school in Saigon. From there I got on the road to studying in France. That is my early life."

"Then what? You returned here and went into a government office?"

"No. Things were not quite that simple. I met a girl in France. She was so beautiful, blue eyes and blonde hair and rounder, fuller, if you know what I mean, than our Vietnamese girls. She was so alive and open. Our women are taught to be quiet and modest – at least during the early moments of courtship. Hugette was...I think your word is 'irrepressible.' She seemed to enjoy everything in her life. I fell in love with her from a distance and never thought she would have anything to do with an Asian boy from the French colonies. But she knew I was smitten with her. Well, anyone who looked at me could tell. She spoke to me one day after a lecture, and we just drifted off to have a student lunch together. After that I was lost, and our relationship grew. I had almost two years left in my studies, and we lived that time like a couple."

"But you did not marry her."

Mr. Nam is thoughtful, nostalgic too. "No. We had expected to marry, and I looked forward to bringing her back to my family and my beautiful Viêtnam."

"What happened?"

"Well, Vietnam was unsettled. The Viet Minh under General Giáp and Hô Chí Minh were mounting hit-and-run attacks against the French soldiers in Việtnam. France wanted to try to hold on to its place in Indochina. Things looked very scary from 8,000 Km away. Remember this was France's former colony, and the challenge from its former subjects was seen as an affront to national power and honor. Hugette was a bit frightened but willing to return with me. Her father forbade it. He asked me to remain in France and make a career there. He could help me get placed in a law firm. I had never considered this. I had always planned on going home.

"Can you imagine my choice? Stay with my wonderful Hugette. Have a life in France. Become a *Frenchman* and perhaps never see my family or my Việtnam again."

The memory of this has brought tears to Mr. Nam's eyes. He is miles and decades removed from the current moment. I met this lovely gentlemen only an hour or so earlier, but I am now thoroughly involved with him. I can hardly hold back tears. "What did you do?"

"Đao was now my best friend. I trusted him like no one else I knew in France, and he had lived through the stages of my romance with me. I asked for his advice. Do you see? We were two boys – *Việtnamese* boys – who had left home as barely more than children. Who had, in effect, come of age far from our families and our land. What did we know?

"But Đao knew, and he knew that I did too. I remember the moment as if it has only just passed. He put his hand on my shoulder. There was a deeply sad look on his face. He gave me a sad smile and said, 'I'll be downstairs having some tea,' and he left my room. When I joined him some time later, we talked of our country and our responsibilities as French-educated Việtnamese. We did not speak about Hugette. The next time I saw her, I must have looked very different to her. She threw herself into my arms and cried deeply. She knew. I promised to love her always and never to forget her. She promised the same. A few months later, it was June of 1956, Đao and I left France to return home."

"And Hugette?"

"I have been fortunate to see her several times over the years. The last time was eight years ago, just before she passed. She had grown children and a devoted husband, but I could always see in her face the love she had for me. I love her to this day."

"That's quite a story."

"It's my story, but I think the most fortunate people confront such a decision in their lives. The ability to choose one's duty over one's convenience can be empowering. Of course I don't know, but I think it was so for your father. He may have had doubts on occasion, but the choice he had made reassured him as to who he was. At the end of it all, I am sure he was happy."

"He always told me he was."

Mr. Nam nods and then continues his story. "I returned here in 1956, two years after Điện Biên Phủ fell, and at the time that Ngô Đình Diệm made his bid for real power."

"I don't know anything about that. I am sorry."

"Well, the Geneva peace agreement that came out of Điện Biên Phủ, formalized the division of the country at the 17th parallel and required that there would be free and fair elections in two years to elect a national leader. Hồ Chí Minh and his victorious Viet Minh controlled in the North and were very powerful. Emperor Bảo Đại was to control in the South, but he did not want to return from France where he had lived for many years. He named Diệm as his Ministre Plénipotentiaire, and in the two years after Điện Biên Phủ, Diệm worked hard to build a power base in the South. Hồ had been working too, and he expected to win the election required by the Geneva peace accords. Diệm knew that he would likely lose in a nationwide election, so he declared that "free and fair" elections, as called for in the Geneva accords, were not possible in the North. He held a plebiscite here in the South, instead. The ballot question was essentially: who do you want to rule in the South, Diệm or Bảo Đại? And so he frustrated the plans of the Viet Minh and seized power in the South. Hồ Chí Minh had expected something of the sort and had, as I said, been building his power in the South. When Diệm blocked his plans, our civil war, the one your father served in and found so compelling, was born.

"One of the things Diệm did was to require that anyone doing business involving a number of basic commodities: rice, cement, steel, fertilizer and several others, must have Việtnamese citizenship. Each of these businesses was controlled by our local Chinese, almost all of whom had Taiwan or Hong Kong papers. If they were Việtnamese citizens, Diem could better control them. The Chinese had their sons take Việtnamese citizenship but maintained other citizenship within their families. Still, the Chinese needed Việtnamese they could trust. As my father's son, and having a law credential, I was an ideal candidate. I went to work for a Chinese group. To protect me and increase my stature, they secured a place for me at the new Việtnamese National Institute of Administration. My law background legitimized me as a teacher there. From that point, my career unfolded as I became known for my teaching. I was invited, in the manner of such things, into one government job after another, and again, in the manner of such things rose quite high in our administration. I retired more than twenty years ago, never expecting to live this long."

"As a long-time government servant, were you sent to a re-education camp by the communists?"

"Of course, but I was lucky. At first things were very hard. Our camp was in the highlands. We lived in open-sided, thatched shelters. It was very cold at night. We were worked hard during the day and, of course, lectured on our sins by political cadres. One of the cadres who came was an old student of mine. I was shocked to see him in such a role.

I could tell that he was embarrassed when he saw me. In his lecture he called me to stand beside him and shouted insults at me. Of course I did not care, but when the lecture was over, he held me by him and whispered that he would get me better treatment. I asked him not to, but it became clear that he had.

"A communist major ran the camp. He spoke with me about my background and permitted me easier duty. He would also talk with me in the evening sometimes and eventually certified me as suited for return to Saigon."

We have been talking for quite a while. I ask if Mr. Nam would like a cold drink. He smiles: "Hot tea, please." Phùng wants a beer. I signal the waiter. We sit for a while in companionable silence. Finally I say, "That's quite a story. For a hardline Communist to show you such consideration, he must have seen something very special in you."

"Not really. I think he just saw that I am Việtnamese."

"But everyone in the camp was Việtnamese, right? And he did not favor them."

"Well, you know, we spent many years under French dominion, and many of us – of our people – became perhaps more French than Việtnamese. The convinced communists, rebelled against France, French control, even against the *'Frenchified'* Việtnamese. Some of our top military commanders were French citizens when Diệm became Bảo Đại's representative in 1956. Generally, the communists were able to tolerate Việtnamese who they saw as 'true' Việtnamese, even if they were not committed communists."

"Just that? Being Việtnamese?"

"Being Việtnamese is quite a lot. It is everything to me, just as you were, I think, to your father. You can take away my law degree, my service in the Việtnamese government, even my reputation, but at the end of all, I am left with my identity as a Việtnamese, our history, our culture, our determination, even our courage. That is how I know who I am.

"Going back to the beginning of our conversation, I will say that there is a power, a clarity and an understanding that comes with commitment. I believe your father discovered who he was, first in representing your country in our war here; then in his commitment to our people, and finally in his decision to devote himself to you. He understood who he was. And because we are on this subject, let me ask you, who are you?"

He has spoken gently, but I am stunned. There it is, I now realize, the real question I came here to get answered. Mr. Nam smiles. It is as if he has understood this almost since we met.

The waiter serves us. As he turns to leave, he passes a young man at another table but does not stop. He signals that he will be with him in just a minute. The man lets out a frustrated hiss. Then, under his breath, but loud enough to be heard, he says, with a heavy Australian accent, "Sure, no hurry. I could just as well have stayed in detention at the airport the other day." Mr. Nam, Phùng and I look at each other and shrug our shoulders. Phùng returns to the photos he has been leafing through and leans forward to share one with Mr. Nam and me. The man at the other table seems to take this personally. "Don't worry about me, any of you, he said in a loud voice. "I'm just a statue, a parked car. Don't need anything, really, just to be ignored."

We all look at him.

"What?" he says, clearly distressed.

We look at each other and then back at him. He gives us an embarrassed smile. "Sorry, mates. It's all been just a bit much since I got here."

After a moment, Mr. Nam gestures that he should join us.

Chapter 18

We are driving north from Saigon, along the stretch of highway that will soon take us to Bien Hoa and then onward to the cities and outposts that must have seemed out of reach to many in the days when the VC could set up roadblocks at will, pluck people from their cars and march them off to their deaths. I have been waiting for this moment. Saigon has been a revelation, but it was out here, in the countryside, the hinterland, the forests of the highlands and the jungles below them that my father came of age. Something happened here, an alchemy that made him the man he would not have become without such experience – the man whom I loved, hated, resented, never understood, resisted and now find myself giving in to.

I look back in the direction of the city. We have only just crossed the bridge that separates Saigon from this portion of Gia Định province. Just before the bridge I caught sight of a house that my father's journals speak of fondly: 47 Phan Thanh Giản

St. It was rented to the US Embassy and occupied by four young Foreign Service officers, the exact occupants shifting with assignment changes. From 1966 through 1973, it was the site of a huge New Year's Eve party, one that everyone who was anyone--American, French, Việtnamese, or other--wished to attend. The tradition started in 1966, when the original group, only about twelve people in all, calling themselves, "The flower people of Saigon," sent out an invitation that asked guests to "come see the light at the end of the tunnel." From there, the party and list of sponsors grew steadily, the latter to the point where it included well known journalists, ambassadors, and even the Baron de Tourane, the house dog. I grin at the memory. It's not my own, but it speaks of the feeling many had back then, that it was ok to scoff at the baroque statements US leaders sometimes made about the war. Like the one attributed to General Westmoreland. He could not predict an end date, but he could see the light at the end of the tunnel.

As has happened so often recently, I lose myself in the person I imagine my father to have been at this time of his life. Policy was made by older men, but the young guys were the tip of the spear. As only young people could, they developed friendships with their Vietnamese peers that told them more about the true feelings in-country than the bureaucrats would ever know. They were the ones who faced the enemy in battle or who dug out crucial intelligence. They did their work on the ground, not in air-conditioned meetings. It begins to make sense. Where else could very young men feel so involved in a historic moment? Where else could they feel that they mattered in an important way? To those fortunate enough to have had this perspective – instead of the one that, sadly and understandably afflicted many of the disaffected, conscripted combat GIs – serving in Việtnam was an opportunity, a defining moment, a test of manhood in its way, a challenge that one rose to and claimed and was transformed by.

Phùng's cab rattles and shakes as we gather speed. For a moment, I slump a bit in my seat. My father had this chance, and he took it. So far my life has lacked such a clear imperative.

I wonder if it will ever have one. I wonder too how many lives ever do. Again it comes to me that life cuts furrows between people, always defining them or giving them the chance to define themselves. One of those things that I have only ever considered as a silly, "Daddy saying" looms in my memory: "The sin lies not in failure, but in never trying. A man must participate in the passion and agony of his time, at the risk of being judged not to have lived.'"

For a few minutes, the scene along the side of the highway is a blur. I am back at 47 Phan Thanh Giản hearing the thumping beat of the bands, talking with ambassadors, pursuing and being pursued by beautiful Việtnamese women. We speak of the war, of what may happen, of the cease-fire declared for the holiday, of bombing Hanoi. There is beer and liquor and wine and heat and humidity and food and only a casual eye on the hour. The new year will come, and it will unfold, and so many of us will be here again next year, and so many will not.

Phùng breaks hard. The jolt knocks me out of my reverie. He has reacted to avoid a child who has wandered onto the highway. I am not surprised. Although this is a fast road, its edges meld into shoulders and then into rice paddies. There are bus stops and food stalls and barber shops and scooter repair stands and sugar cane sellers and people hawking gasoline put up in old liter bottles, just about anything one can imagine. To me there is a virtual carnival along each side of the highway. Where it interfaces with the rushing, chaotic traffic, there is great danger. In my father's day, the road was equally crazy, but it was traveled by heavy military trucks, as well as civilian traffic. My father used to come out this way to go to the US Army Property Disposal Office (PDO) at the huge American base in Long Binh. His journals say that it seemed as if the US had just thrown a fence around some huge tract of Vietnamese land and turned it into a semi-sovereign piece of America. He mentions with amusement the "LBJ" (Long

Binh Jail – a military brig), and he remembers the days on which bids were opened at the PDO. To him the jail seemed somehow inappropriate, the idea of imprisoning a man here to fight for his country making an uneasy match in his mind. He does tell, however, of driving through the base one day to get to a meeting. He stopped to pick up two black GI's who were hitchhiking. He wore no uniform at the moment, and they took him for a civilian. They chatted briefly with him, mentioning that they had a new lieutenant who was riding them hard. They allowed as how they were "gonna frag the honky fucker," if he didn't get the message soon. That impressed my father, and he decided that the LBJ was needed, at least for some reasons.

He writes often about the myriad of ways different men experienced the war: from the LRPs (long-range patrol guys, out virtually on their own for weeks and always on the edge of ambush or disaster), to the fire-base crews who lived often under constant enemy bombardment and rotted in bunkers that filled with water during the rainy season, to the Special Forces guys living in remote hamlets and training Montagnards and having only a few of their own, along with their hosts, to help them fight off sudden attack, to the sergeants who administered a club or a commissary and who sometimes became commercial kingpins. Vietnam had just about every kind of experience for our troops, most of it horrific, but as far as the Long Binh base went, Dad did find a little humor.

Bid-opening days at the PDO often took on the aura of a Miss World contest. Rapacious old crones brought their beautiful young daughters, nieces, cousins, or even bar girls, whom they paid to accompany them, on the occasion. The girls were provocatively dressed and on display to the young American contracting officers who awarded the bids. Nothing was implied. Everything was explicit: treat me right and this is yours. Some of the girls seemed ashamed, but the crones were not. Dad actually saw one woman pull down the smocked bodice of her niece's dress, revealing a most impressive bosom, which was arrayed only inches from the surprised eyes of a young JAG officer. The journal entry ends with Dad noting that the officer glanced at the photo of his wife and very young baby and observed that "war is hell."

In this direction too lay the university village of Thủ Đức, housing for professors and staff of the University of Saigon. This was a project begun by Ngô Đình Diệm, who envisioned a kind of reservation, a walled development in which lovely villas with gardens would be made available to the professors and where they could raise their children and return to spend quiet or collegial evenings away from Saigon and its bustle. My father reports this as a worthy idea that, like so many others in Việtnam, was overcome by events. Dangers on the road at night, and in the village itself, which was surrounded by jungled areas, finally made it an impractical place for university professors to live. The villas were variously sold or rented out to the brave souls who wished to be there. One such was a Frenchman, a friend of my father's, named François. The journals do not mention his last name. François was a barrel-chested man in his late forties back then. He worked for a US construction conglomerate but had been in Việtnam for years before the Americans arrived. He lived in a kind of rough-edged-but-grand style in one of the villas, which he owned. François had no fears – of the communists or of what any resolution to the war would bring. He was going to live out his days in Việtnam, and enjoy every one of them. He had a grand scheme for getting rich: there was a US military photo lab on the air base at Tân Sơn Nhứt. Miles of film were developed there, and the chemicals used in doing the job, contained silver. The waste was simply poured into the ground. François figured that the soil could be mined for what he believed would be large amounts of the precious metal. No problem. A happy retirement.

When I first read about François, I tried to imagine what might have become of him. Now, I somehow feel certain that, even if he never got his silver, he remained in Việtnam and reached a successful old age. The journals report that my father would have dinner with François a few times during the year. He would drive out to Thủ Đức in the early evening, but François would never let him drive back at night unescorted. The same scene was enacted at each departure. François and a few guards jumped in one jeep and took the lead. Dad followed in his car, and another jeep-load of guards brought up the rear. The mini convoy, bristling with weapons fore and aft, raced down the highway to Saigon. François would execute a sharp U turn just before the bridge we crossed only a few minutes ago, wave, fire a few rounds into the air, and head back to Thủ Đức. Perhaps he is still alive. If so, he will surely still be in his villa, irrepressible, more a spirit than a man. Being here, on this road, makes him real, and again I wish I had lived the days my father had. The car is moving at speed now. A sign flashes by on the left. Ahead and farther to the left I can see a number of villas. I know what this is. In my mind, I wave a greeting to François.

Mr. Nam tells me that Biên Hòa, the site of one of the first US air bases in Việtnam, is along a road that exits the highway on the left. Farther on, he points to the right. The old, buff-colored pre-fab buildings in the distance were part of the American Long Binh base. The road splits. We can either bear slightly left or turn right. Phùng pulls off the highway. We climb out of the car, and he goes to get some cold drinks for us. It is dusty, hot, humid, and the noise from the traffic is huge. No one seems to notice. This, like virtually any other spot on the side of the highway, is almost a formal rest area, although there is nothing permanent about it. In reality, it is a kind of encampment where people have established their tables and stands and shade canopies in spots that appear to have become "theirs" by a kind of

105

adverse possession. Mr. Nam says they appear early every morning and melt away not long after dark, entire lifetimes passed by the side of the road, children raised in the dust and the heat and the fumes.

Phùng asks if I want to head directly for the highlands, or if first I prefer to visit Xuan Loc and the rubber plantation where my father used to spend weekends. He explains that Xuân Lộc is about 35 km to the East and that we can get there in about half an hour. The trip to Ban Me Thuot is much longer, and in any case we will not reach there by tonight. I opt for the plantation.

Phùng pulls into traffic, and we follow the road East, to the right. It is not long before the clutter at the edges of the highway thins a bit. We pass a church. Mr. Nam points it out and tells me that there will be several more as we go along. He is right. In the space of just a few miles I count seven churches. It hits me: "Ho Nai, " I say.

"You know?"

I nod. "My father used to come out here to get furniture made."

Mr. Nam smiles: "That would be correct. These people are very good woodworkers. As the churches indicate, they are Catholic, and very serious about their religion. They were originally from the North but came South after the Geneva agreements of May 1954. They were very strong anti-communists, and they formed a kind of bulwark for Ngô Đình Diệm when he came here as Bảo Đại's Minister Plenipotentiary."

"My father writes about them in his journals. One of the stories is frankly very scary. He says that these people live kind of like a tribe – or they used to when he was here. They keep to themselves, and they tend to be hostile to outsiders, sometimes openly. I get the idea that the priest is kind of the principal authority in these communities."

"That's right. They really are kind of a strange bunch of people. Even now, they conscientiously isolate themselves from everyone else, and they still speak a Việtnamese that is peculiar to the North alone."

"Yes, I remember my father saying something like that. The first time he came out here, people gave him nasty looks. Only when he spoke to them in Việtnamese with a northern accent and using some words that, I guess, are special to the North, did they become a bit more welcoming. His journals say that going back into the sort of village areas that are away from the highway was like going to another world, not only because of the sound of the language and the words used, but also because of the way people dressed."

Mr. Nam smiles: "Do you notice anything about how they dress?"

"A little old fashioned," I ask more than say.

"Maybe, but you see that many of the women are wearing brown ao dais with black pantaloons. That color combination is very typical of dress in the North. More men than you see in Saigon are wearing very traditional Việtnamese men's clothing, the black turban-like head wrap and the black, man's version of the áo dài. And, although you can't see it as we drive by, many of the women will have their teeth lacquered brown-black."

"What? My God, why?"

"It was a tradition in the North for many, many years. I think the truth is that it was done to render the women less attractive and thus less troublesome. Remember that men dominated Việtnamese society for the longest time."

I shake my head. "Việtnam, is it such a complex place? I always thought, not that I thought about it often or almost at all, that it was straightforward: one country, one people – well, except for the Montagnards."

"Hardly. Didn't your father make any mention of the regional differences in his journals? The northerners are seen as very tough people. They often have distinctly different features from the southerners (flatter faces and broad noses). We consider them poor also. They do not have the large acreages of excellent farmland we have in the south. Traditionally it has been hard for them to scratch out a living. We joke about the northerner who keeps a small wooden fish in his kitchen. He may be able to afford rice and fish sauce to put on it, but he can only rarely afford real fish to have with it. So he puts the wooden fish in the bowl and then says his dinner was fish with rice."

I laugh, but Mr. Nam insists that this is true. "But the northerners have things they say about the southerners too – and about people from Central Việtnam for that matter. Southern girls, for example, are said to be not serious enough, to like to have frivolous fun, to dance and flirt. Southern men are pictured as lazy. Even the French Bishop of Adran, some two hundred years ago, wrote in his journal that God in his infinite wisdom had caused the rattan palm to grow *next to* the Annamite."

"And the central Việtnamese?"

"Shifty, untrustworthy, shrewd, very good at business, but devious. And the women: beautiful, very beautiful, alluring. They know this and trade on it. I think every Việtnamese male, as a young man, has had a fantasy about spending a night of love in a sampan on Huế's Perfume River with a Huế girl, looking out on the beautiful imperial city."

We are now entering an area of rubber plantations. On either side of the road I can see the orderly groves, each tree bearing a thick band of scoring marks with a cup at the lower end of the girdling to catch the latex as it runs down the cut. The trees nestle close to the road. I am struck by a strange feeling, a sense that I am at the edge of a truly different, truly foreign environment. Thus far Việtnam has had an air of the exotic, but now I feel that I am about to pass through a portal into a different universe entirely.

"What is the common fantasy of young men in America?" Mr. Nam asks.

I smile. "That's a tough one. I kind of doubt, though, that it would be one single thing, as you described. We don't have an imperial city with a romantic river and sampans. Maybe that's one of the drawbacks of a very modern, fast-moving society."

Ahead there is a break in the trees. I tell Mr. Nam that my father loved this area; that he was friendly with the managers of the SIPH plantations and used to weekend there often. Mr. Nam says something to Phùng. He slows and then turns left into the gap in the trees, which turns out to be a wide, paved road. We proceed along this in the shade created by the trees on either side. Then we break out into an open area of manicured lawns, old, colonial-style houses and low buildings. It is beautiful. The houses are far apart, and the various buildings are inconspicuous against groves of rubber trees and other wooded areas. Mr. Nam tells me this is the very plantation my father frequented. He asks if I have my pack of pictures. I hand him a small flight bag. Phùng pulls over. After a few minutes, Mr. Nam produces several photos. One is of a building that looks like an office. Another is of a beautiful, outdoor pavilion. We continue on the road, turn off down a narrower path and stop in front of the building in the picture: Institut International de Recherches en Hévas (International Rubber Research Institute, Mr. Nam tells me).

We get out of the car. I am almost overcome with the sense of having stepped into a part of my father's life that was especially precious to him. The feeling here of old Indochina, of peace, of a place almost unchanged since the early twentieth century, a place that could have been the focus of a 1920's black-and-white documentary film, is profound. This is someplace special. I think of the pavilion, and my mind conjures pictures of wonderful weekends, of formal balls and houseguests visiting from Saigon, of French dames proud in their gowns, tailored locally to Paris fashions selected from magazines brought in the mail by one of the Méssageries Maritimes ships, and of young gallants mixing with the planters. From this it is an easy switch for me to the stories told in my father's journals of the weekends he spent here – almost fifty years ago. I imagine the company: the Director of Air France in Việtnam, the General Manager of the Plantation, the Minister of Economy, doctors from the French, Grall Hospital, the head of the Michelin plantations in Việtnam, the Director of the Union of Paris Insurance Companies, wives, girlfriends and companions of these. It is all so real to me that I have to remind myself of what year it is and who I am.

A man emerges from the building. He goes to speak with Mr. Nam. Phùng comes to me, concerned, apparently, by how distracted I seem. After a minute or two Mr. Nam nods in our direction, and we go over to him. He introduces the man from the plantation, the General Manager, Emile Richard, part French, part Việtnamese. M. Richard says he is intrigued by the tiny bit of my story Mr. Nam has told him. He suggests a short tour of the plantation. I am delighted.

We drive around what is almost a campus-kind of area with well-kept lawns and beautiful trees. There are individual villas for the plantation senior staff. In another area there are various workshops, garages, sheds, for the emergency power generators and the small maintenance equipment, and storage hangars for the baled raw rubber. We pass the pavilion that is so familiar to me. I ask to stop, but M. Richard suggests that we can return there for lunch and a swim after we finish the tour. We continue. He tells me how the plantation suffered during the war. Its dense groves were often used by the Việt Cong either to mask their movements or to mount ambushes from. The Americans forced the planters to cut the trees back from the highway by almost one hundred yards on either side so ambush would be difficult. They also began the use of agent orange, a chemical defoliant which was intended to cause the trees to lose their leaves but not to kill them. The stripped trees would provide far less protective cover for guerrillas. The chemical did kill some of the trees. It also stunted their production for a period of time, and, of course, it impacted the health of people on whom it fell when sprayed from aircraft. Because the spray could not be strictly limited, it often killed small vegetable plots kept by Viêtnamese in the area. It was a devastating measure for both the people and the plantation.

After a while we pass a long, single-story building. M. Richard says it is the hospital, and immediately more memories hit. My father was good friends with the plantation doctor and used to spend weekends in his house here. I ask if today's doctor occupies the same residence as the doctor years ago. The answer is yes. M. Richard turns and begins driving away from the hospital. After several minutes we pull up in front of a lovely, colonial-style villa. I know at once from my father's descriptions where we are. I am permitted inside and then to walk through the rooms. On the second floor, the master bedroom is easy to spot, and I am virtually certain that I have properly identified the room my father used on his visits. It is on the second floor also, but it is to the back of the building and overlooks a sprawling lawn and garden area. I lean out the casement-type window and look directly down. Sure enough, there is a cement walkway about three feet wide running the length of the back of the house. The lawn abuts it and flows off towards a large copse of trees. I can see no other houses or any lights from my vantage point. My Dad's story unfolds in my mind.

He was spending the weekend at the plantation. On Saturday he and the doctor turned in towards midnight. Around two in the morning there was a pounding at the front door. The doctor was up quickly, but he lit no light. He opened Dad's door and handed him a ring heavy with keys, telling him, in a hushed voice, to toss the keys out the window to the lawn below. Dad was to be careful not to be seen, to note as best he could where the keys landed and to remain in the room, pretending to be asleep if anyone came up. There was no more explanation than this. The doctor shut the door. Dad could see a light go on down the hall. There was more pounding at the door, and he heard muffled Việtnamese voices demanding the "médecin". Dad carefully checked out the window. Seeing no one, he tossed the keys out, tried to mark the spot of their fall and returned to his bed.

Downstairs he heard voices, clearer now that his friend had opened the front door. He listened. There were several men. They were demanding medicine and medical supplies. Dad assumed them to be Việt Cong. He thought about how to act if "awakened" and questioned. The conversation downstairs was getting a bit heated. The doctor's voice was low, but one of the Việtnamese was insistent that he must provide everything they wanted. There was moving around and then steps on the stair. Doors began to open along the hall, and in a minute the door to Dad's room flew open. He sat up in bed and could see two armed men silhouetted in the doorway. One entered and pointed an AK 47 at him, telling him in Việtnamese to get up. Dad turned and sat on the edge of the bed. The man by the door turned on the light and looked around the room. He fingered through Dad's overnight bag and asked where his "papers" were. Dad had hidden them under the mattress for fear of being identified as an American. "Văn phòng (in the office)," he replied.

"Tại sau dó (why there)?"

"An ninh (security)," Dad gave him a terse reply, a bit abrupt in tone, if I can believe the story as it reads in the journals.

"Noi tiêng Việtnam ha tôt (you speak Việtnamese pretty well). Người Mỹ, ha (American, right)?"

"Pháp (French)," said Dad.

While one was talking, the other was nosing around the room. He looked at Dad's clothes and some of the labels. Fortunately everything had been tailored in Việtnam or purchased in Việtnamese shops. Even his under shorts had a French label, but his toothpaste was Colgate. The guy searching the room held up the tube. Dad said nothing.

"Mua ở đâu (where'd you buy this)?"

Dad gave the name of a black market street in Saigon. He had no idea if the men would know, but both were a bit more sophisticated than just a rural VC conscript. The one standing closest to him poked him with the barrel of his weapon and gestured toward the stairs. They went to join the doctor below.

There was a quick exchange in Việtnamese. Then, the man who had been talking to the doctor, and who was clearly in command of the group, spoke to Dad in Việtnamese: "Tell your friend that we have to have what we demand."

Dad spoke with the doctor in French. The doctor said he had already explained that, as a matter of security, the keys for the pharmacy were in the safe at the office – and he did not have the combination, security again. He could give what he had in the house. That was all.

While the doctor gathered everything he had at home, several of the men searched upstairs and down for the keys and anything else of use. They found nothing. When the supplies had been gathered and handed over, Dad and the doctor were taken outside and told to kneel on the lawn. Before Dad could comply, the doctor stopped him and said he should tell the officer in no uncertain terms that they would not do that. Dad hesitated. The leader of the group laughed, more like snorted, my father said in his journal, and motioned for his men to leave. He himself walked off a few feet and then came back. In clear French he said: "We don't have time now, and we need you, doctor, so don't worry. I don't need your friend. He's just lucky I don't want to wake anyone else by shooting him." Then, looking at Dad, he said: "Người Pháp, ha (French huh)?" and went on his way.

This story was high drama to me when I read it. Now I am standing on the very spot where it played out. I can see it all, and I feel it so immediately that I now have to make an effort to relax the tension that has crept over me. M. Richard has come into the room. Perhaps he notices something about me, and he asks if I am all right.

"Fine," I say. It's just a memory from my father's time here."

Back downstairs, I walk out the front door and try to imagine standing on this spot in the silent dark fifty years ago as a Việt Cộng squad leader tells me he has been onto my charade but that he won't kill me because it's not worth making the noise involved. Then, followed by M. Richard, I turn to go to the rear of the villa. I walk around a bit just to get a sense of where the keys might have fallen. He asks if I am looking for something. "Sort of," I reply.

He looks at me for several seconds. "And can I help you?"

"You already have, very much."

"So, you have found it."

"Finding it," I say. "It's a process."

Chapter 19

As Monsieur Richard had promised, we had lunch at the pavilion, a beautiful, large, covered structure, open on two sides. One side was the broad entrance and sat on one of the manicured, rolling lawns of the plantation campus. The other gave onto a swimming pool and deck, which sat below the pavilion on its own terrace. Beyond the pool terrace, lawns stretched outward to where they joined large groves of rubber trees, all aligned perfectly when looked at from any angle. I was moved by the beauty of the spot and by the feeling it gave me. There, perhaps for the first time on this trip, I got caught up in things, not only by empathy for my father's feelings and experience, but by a personal sense of somehow "belonging". I had just never felt touched by any place the way I did at the plantation. I could actually close my eyes and imagine living there for the rest of my days. I know that would never happen, never be possible; yet, the feeling was so strong, so unusual, that I wonder if it means more than just being a kind of daydream.

The moment brought me back to something that struck me as very strange when I read it in my father's journal. He told of going into the jungle, the rain forest of Việtnam, for the first time; and he told of his feelings of belonging. There was great heat and humidity, but he didn't mind. All he could think of for a few brief minutes was his childhood in the city and the way the sidewalk looked after some of the ice and snow from a storm had cleared. The sidewalk was dry, except towards the edges where snow and slush were piled. Crusted along the pavement in spots and strips was the dried, caked remains of rock salt that had been strewn to melt the ice. He hated those sterile white patches as they stood in the raw and bleak cold against the gray of the pavement. To him, this was the worst of winter: its leaching out of everything warm and life-giving. He relates that he often had a vision when he would see this: he was in a warm, tropical place, surrounded by exotic trees and vines and plants, hearing strange birds and seeing strange animals. He loved this imagined place and hated where he was. And one day, it came to him that he would, sometime, go to his lush, dream rainforest and remain there forever. I don't know how he could have had such thoughts, ideas and visions when he was so young, or maybe he could have them exactly because he was so young. Now, as I recall his days with the Montagnards, I realize how close his vision came to becoming reality.

So, for a while, since we have left the plantation, and as we ride north towards my father's mountains and forest, I am having my own vision. I am still back at the pavilion, feeling that magnetic sense of peace and relatedness, imagining myself there forever, and wondering if my daydream has emerged from something DNA-influenced at my core; if I am doing nothing more – or less – than living a prophecy, and if my daydream too will become reality.

These musings are nurtured by the isolation of our route, the hum of the engine and the rocking of the old car as it pushes along. Mr. Nam and Phùng are in the front seats. I am in the rear, inventorying everything that has happened since I arrived in Việtnam: new sights, new realities, new perspectives, new understandings, the unexpected and almost-impossible empathies with my father's ancient experiences and the emotions I have divined behind them. I have been drawn closer to him and, I see all at once, to myself also. I recall James Joyce: "Welcome, O life! I go to encounter for the millionth time the reality of experience..." I shake my head. For me, this is not "the millionth time." In truth, it may well be only the first. And, as for forging something in the smithy of my soul, like Joyce, I have no such pretension – just a feeling of possibility.

* * * * * * * * * * *

JJ looks at the display on his cell phone. It's 2:43 AM. He can't get back to sleep. Light from the busy square beyond his window leaks through the drapes, but that is not his problem. He is awake because he hurts badly from the beating and savaging he got thirty-six hours earlier. If he doesn't lie completely still, if he moves in his sleep, pain shoots through him, and he wakes up. Now, as he tries to ease back into his pillows, his muscle memory reminds him of a nightmare that has, twice since his arrival, tormented his sleep. It is years old. It started when he was just a child. As he has this thought, he drifts off into the dream, and, as always, it is so real that he disappears into the unrelenting ache of the past.

He is eleven years old. It is a brilliant weekend day. JJ watches his mother scurry around with her last-minute preparations. She has made herself into the perfect Australian wife. Without being asked, she has planned and prepared a picnic. The family, all six of them, climb into Malcolm's aging Holden and head off to Royal National Park. It's not a very long drive, but to amuse the kids, Malcolm begins to sing Waltzing Mathilda, a song they all know. JJ grimaces as his mother, Danielle, continues what he considers her masquerade of being the happy Australian "Sheila." She knows the words, of course, sings them almost exactly as an Australian would and, to his disgust, is belting them out at the top of her lungs. He nods to himself: "Of course, she's just as happily absorbed as can be." He feels a sourness in his throat and actually gags. He is not singing and has no intention of doing so. He just looks out the window from his perch between the parents. In the back seat, his three siblings are rowdy and bellowing away. Malcolm becomes aware of JJ's silence. He elbows him jokingly in the ribs and says, "Come on lad," and he leans over a bit, "Once a jolly swag man..." singing loudly into JJ's face to stimulate his participation.

JJ feels sick. He wants to climb out of the front seat but knows if he does, he will only fall in amongst his boisterous "brothers," something he can't stand. One of them shouts at him, "Hey, JJ, you got a voice. I hear it enough when you grouse about things. Use it to sing." The other two laugh derisively. JJ shrinks in the front seat.

They find a picnic area at the park. Danielle sets about unpacking the food and setting things up. The three older boys begin roughhousing on the grass. Malcolm cracks a beer and wanders around a bit. JJ takes a walk, anything to get away from this "family." He is strolling off along one of the park's many winding paths when he rounds a curve and comes upon a broad stretch of lawn. He watches as a group of boys, mostly about his age, play a game of cricket. The bowler is a big kid who throws a very fast ball. JJ has gotten caught up in his motion and unconsciously has begun to mimic it. After a while, the players notice and stop to stare at him. They notice that he is not pure Aussie. They notice too that his movement borders on the pathetic. JJ is unaware of all of this. He thinks he is just off by himself and not bothering anybody.

The big bowler walks right up to him and stops just a few feet from getting directly in his face. JJ stops suddenly. He can read the disapproval coming off the boys in waves. He's not surprised. It has all happened before – many times. He turns away from the bowler and tries to walk on. The bowler blocks his path and runs through his pitching motion so that his arm swings overhand and finishes brushing right by JJ's face. JJ keeps walking. These situations almost always end in fights that he loses because he is smaller than most boys his age.

The bowler is, all at once, infuriated. He baits JJ. "What's the matter, shrimp? Can't play cricket?"

JJ tries to ignore him, but the bowler gives him a shove. "Don't walk away from me!"

JJ is afraid, humiliated and fuming with impotent rage. Just for once he wishes for the courage to put this Aussie kid in his place. To make him a stand-in for all the others who have insulted him, picked on him and beaten him. Before he knows it, he glares at the boy and says, "Fuck off, shithead."

In the next instant, he is punched in the face harder than he has ever been hit. His nose is bleeding and maybe broken. He hears someone crying and knows it is him, but it's all too much. He kicks his tormentor and then is snowed under by the other cricket players. There is a furious melee. JJ rolls into a ball. He doesn't even try to get in a punch. He just wants to survive.

He has no idea how long the beating lasts, but all at once there is a familiar voice. It's Malcolm, and he is breaking things up, literally tossing kids off of JJ. There is a great deal of yelling and cursing. Malcom gently tries to unclench the balled-up JJ. "Come on, son. No worry now. It's me, dad."

JJ is relieved, grateful and humiliated all at once. He gets up and pulls away from Malcolm in shame. Malcolm goes to put an arm around him, but he is interrupted by a man who has come running to the scene. He pushes Malcolm away and says: "Who the hell are you to attack my boys? I oughtta bust your ass."

Malcolm is ready for a fight, but he draws a breath and says, "They were beating up my son."

"Really! YOUR son. You'd never know. He's just some shrimp Chink creep."

Malcolm belts the man. There is a brief fight. The men square off, and the stranger tags Malcolm on the jaw, giving him a split lip. The man's wife breaks them up. After more angry words, Malcolm looks around to find JJ, who has wandered a distance off and been watching things as best he can with his head bowed. Malcolm gestures him over, and the two head back to their picnic.

Danielle is shocked. She runs, hugs JJ, coos over him and wets a cloth to wipe his cuts. She tends to Malcolm, shaking her head. "He's just a boy, but you should know better." Malcolm starts to explain, but JJ's three "brothers" say, "Tell her, dad. You got that guy good, didn't you? Like all the time, you had to save JJ. He's keeps getting into fights. He's a half…"

Danielle screams, "Shut up all of you. That's enough. He's just…"

The dream ends. JJ emerges from its mists and realizes, as he always does when waking from it, that he should not be sweating and breathing hard. He says so to himself, "It's ok. It's just a dream." But the self-reassurance doesn't help, not even here, 8,000 miles and 30 years from where it started. It never helps, and, lying alone in this strange bed in this strange land, his mother irretrievably dead, he is finally clear on why he has come. Either he will discover his true father and complete the end of his mother's unfinished scream in the dream, or he will ever be alienated from himself and from the world, until he dies and… And what? Discovers that death does not answer all questions? And live on for eternity in an afterlife of ignorance? He begins to cry silently.

* * * * * * * * * * * *

Mr. Nam turns in the front seat so he can face me. He says we have a long way to go to get to the hamlet where my father lived for 20 months. Right now we are just north of Xuân Lôc, about three hours from Bao Lôc and four and a half from Banmethuot. I pull out my map and begin to search for these places. Mr. Nam leans towards me, scans the map and taps a spot. "We're just about here. You can see the road. Follow the road (he traces its route with his finger), and you can see where we are going. We have entered the Central Highlands. We Việtnamese used to love to travel up here for weekends and brief vacations to get away from Saigon and its heat. But during the years of the war, travel by road could be dangerous. The Việt Cong would set up road blocks and kidnap, kill or extort money from people. So travel by Air Việtnam became very important. Of course the Americans had their own airline, Air America. It moved people and cargo that did not qualify as military. It became very popular for Việtnamese to try to use their American friends and contacts to get a free ride. That worked until the flights began to fill up with the Việtnamese girl friends of the Americans. Because so many of these women were bar girls, the Việtnamese said, in private, that the airline was part flying brothel."

I laugh, but I am certain that if anything, Mr. Nam has understated things. "My father never wrote anything about that."

"He would not have. He would have had access to military flights."

I look out the window. I notice that the air is cooler now and that I am seeing a few evergreen trees. I look at my watch. It's just past 2:30 PM. "If Bao Lôc is three hours away, we should make it before dark. Is it a good place to spend the night?"

"Oh," says Mr. Nam. It's wonderful. Cool, beautiful, views that sometimes look like they are from another world."

By late afternoon we have arrived in Bao Lôc. There is a small, centrally situated lake, and the entire city is surrounded by highlands. The scenery is indeed wonderful. We drive around so I can get an idea of the area. After a while we come to a large field which is filled with row after row of what I think of as bushes. Without being asked, Phùng stops the car on a small rise that gives us a panoramic view of the fields. From our vantage point at the southern edge of the fields to distant hills that rise in north, all is these green plantings set in ordered, parallel rows. Working between the rows are numbers of colorfully dressed women with woven baskets on their backs and colorful headdresses, evidence, Mr. Nam tells me, of their mountain tribe background. "They are likely Koho. Perhaps a few are Ma. The women in the conical-shaped hats which we call, non, are Việtnamese. They are all plucking leaves from the bushes. Before I can ask anything, Mr. Nam adds, "This is one of Bao Lôc's famous tea plantations. B'lao tea is much sought after."

Phùng shuts off the engine and asks me if I have my packet of pictures. I dig in my bag, find it and hand it to him. He shuffles quickly through the pile until he comes to one of the few color photographs. He hands it to me. It is a snapshot of two men standing side-by-side in what might be this very field. One man is my father, the other has his arm draped companionably over my father's shoulder and wears an enormous smile.

Mr. Nam looks closely at the picture. "I think that is François Sully. It must be. When he first came to Việtnam, he worked as a tea planter. It was only later that he became a journalist."

I recognize the photo and turn it over. Written on the back is, "Au bon vieux temps et à encore de nombreuses années d'amitié. Tu as dû être français. (C'est un compliment, ça.) Ton grand ami, François."

Mr. Nam reads over my shoulder. He looks at me. "Do you understand that?"

"Kind of," I say.

'It says, 'To the good old days and to many more years

of friendship. You should have been French. (That's a compliment.) Your great friend, François.'"

We are both silent for a moment. Then, Mr. Nam says, I knew Monsieur Sully. He could be sarcastic about people, especially Americans. He had a warm eye for us, the Việtnamese, the children in particular, but even the French did not escape his disdain when warranted. Your father must have been a special man to have struck such a friendship with him."

Mr. Nam looks at the picture again. "There is no date. It would be interesting to know when this was taken."

"Why?"

"I am just wondering, that's all. You know, don't you, that François died here, and not a natural death? He had gone to the west with General Đỗ Cao Trí, the Commanding General of what we called the Third Corps Tactical Zone. That was mainly the area between Saigon, Tây Ninh province and the Cambodia border. General Trí was one of our great fighting generals so maybe that explains what happened."

"What did happen?"

"The General's helicopter blew up in mid-air just after taking off from Tây Ninh. Our military said it was sabotage. There were eight aboard. Seven were killed in the explosion and resulting crash. Only François survived. He jumped from the stricken plane and fell some 70 feet to the ground. The Americans rushed him to their hospital in Long Binh. The date was February 23, 1971."

Mr. Nam hesitates. He has noticed how quiet I am and also, perhaps, that I have a tear in my eye. "You are upset," he says.

"I am remembering something in my dad's journal, an entry that was prominently dated. I can't remember the date itself, but since dad was not conscientious or consistent about dating things, this item caught my attention and made a deep impression. It said, 'François died today. I was supposed to go see him again this afternoon. Now, he is gone. When I visited yesterday, he was in bad shape. He asked me to take care of his files. Of course, until you come home,' I said. I did not know who François was, only that his death had saddened my father greatly."

We are all quiet. The mood is somber. "Do you know," I ask, "where François is buried?"

Mr. Nam thinks for a bit and says, "He was in Mạc Đĩnh Chi Cemetery in Saigon. Many Việtnamese notables and heroes were buried there, but in 1983, the Communists decided that the cemetery was an insult, an unacceptable remnant and reminder of the colonial past. It was originally built by the French for those of their soldiers and sailors who died in the battle of the Gia Đĩnh Citadel in 1859. If you wish, we can visit the site when we get back to the city. It is now a park. All the graves have been destroyed, every remnant, even the great mausoleums. All plowed under. Relatives were allowed to move their loved ones, but I don't know what happened to François."

We decide to stay the night in a hotel a bit farther up the hill where we currently are. It has magnificent views of the tea estate which lies at the bottom of the basin formed by the surroundings uplands. I spend a wakeful night thinking about François Sully, his violent-but-courageous death and the exciting, absorbing life he had here. He is buried here, in Việtnam, in a cemetery among many famous Việtnamese. He is not buried in France, his native land, and which, Mr. Nam has told me, he served as a resistance fighter and soldier in World War II.

I think about what this might mean. I sense that even if he had family that would repatriate his remains to France, it was his wish to be buried here. Mr. Nam has told me also that he left the proceeds of his life insurance policy to benefit Việtnamese orphans. Somehow the life he lived in Việtnam and the people here were dearest to him and the most meaningful of all his commitments.

These thoughts lead me back to my father and how very much Việtnam and his life here meant to him. I see the photo of him and François in the tea field, two peas in a pod, smiles of friendship, pleasure, shared experience and understanding. I am sure, as Mr. Nam suggested when we first met in Saigon, that my father would have remained here but for the communist takeover. I think too that he, in his time and turn, might have wished to be laid to rest in Mạc Đĩnh Chi Cemetery among people who, known personally to him or not, meant so much to him. I begin to doze off, but my mind is not yet still. As I drowse towards sleep, I recall the moment of belonging and connectedness that seized me at the rubber plantation, and I drift off wondering.

I am awakened by a knock on my door. It is not yet morning, but the room is noticeably lighter than at night. I shake off sleep. Mr. Nam is at the door and asks to come in. I smile and make way for him. He goes to the sliding doors of my balcony, pulls aside the heavy drapes and gestures toward the view. We go out onto the spacious deck. I catch my breath. Dawn has now lightened the sky. A dense mist that obscures the tea fields far below us, fills the basin. The surrounding hills poke skyward above the mist, illuminated by the glow of the slowly rising sun. The colors are extraordinary. They form a halo above the tops of the hills, around the entire basin. The scene might be what presented itself to the nascent world when God said, "Let there be light."

* * * * * * * * * * *

JJ has gathered himself after a restless and painful night that has left him feeling exhausted. He remains shaken by his experience at the airport, but he has promised himself not to let that throw him off his mission in coming here. He is determined that Việtnam will give him answers and that these will, at long last, change the constant misfire his life has been.

He is preparing to find the Ministry of Interior and reclaim his file of papers and clippings. They are the only clues he has. He needs them, even though he only half hopes that they will put him on the trail of his father, the man whom his mother lured into bed one night when she knew he was vulnerable, hoping, he is sure, to leverage him into a marriage. He doesn't know this for certain, but he has overheard enough bits and pieces over the years, from his mother's chats with a few of her close friends, to get the idea. If he's honest, he admits that it's all vague and largely conjecture, but since piecing things together, he has always thought of himself as a failed strategy – not as a desired child, and certainly not as "a love child."

He rummages in his carry-on until he finds the packet he prepared to start him on his quest. It holds a tourist map of Hồ Chí Minh City and several pages, copied from the internet, that comprise a highly detailed map of Saigon made by an American military survey team years ago. These pages will be vital once he has to venture beyond "downtown" and into the rabbit warren of small streets and alleys that make up substantial areas of the city. With all in-hand, he still does not leave the room immediately. He takes a moment to square his shoulders and gird himself for what he is sure will be yet another trying day.

His first challenge is breakfast. With some misgiving, he ventures out onto the hotel terrace, the scene of yesterday's frustration. He finds a table, sits and prepares to call a waiter. Before he can do anything, his "enemy" from the previous day is at his side and smiling. JJ almost does a double take. The waiter executes a small bow and stands attentive, ready to take his order. "Right," says JJ. "How about some coffee, mate?" The waiter nods. "And maybe some eggs and toast while you're at it, ok?" Another nod.

JJ takes a moment to consider the change in attitude. "Now I've got a big OK sign on me. Wonder if that's because he's seen me before or because Marc, that American guy, and his local buddies put the seal of approval on me? Well, they were nice to invite me over, and they all seemed a right lot. Especially Marc. He was open and tried to bring me into their conversation. He did say we'd get together when he gets back to town. I hope he'll have time, but I know he's got a lot on his mind."

The food arrives. JJ digs in, watching the frenetic traffic and pedestrian crowd as he eats. He wonders if Việtnam was like this when his mother was a young girl. In his file, he has an address for the office she worked at in those days and also another that he found in her effects after she died. He thinks it might be for home she lived in throughout her years here. The idea that either could be a place to start his search galvanizes him. He finishes breakfast quickly and signals for the check. The waiter, ever attentive now, appears promptly. JJ signs the chit and, on a whim, decides to give the man his tip in cash. He offers 20% of the bill. The waiter smiles, gives JJ a partial bow of thanks and steps back so he can get up from the table. JJ hesitates. "What's your name, pal?"

The waiter looks blank for a moment, so JJ repeats, "Name?" Then he sees the badge that says, "Trân," and he says, "Ah, OK, Trân." The waiter smiles and nods and says, "Name... yes, Trân." Then he adds with exaggerated emphasis, "Tôi tên là Trân." It sounds to JJ like the man said, "Chun," so he tries to repeat: "Chun?" The waiter laughs and enunciates his name twice. JJ can hear a small difference between his version and the waiter's, but he just assumes that as an Aussie, with no ability in languages, he's already done his best. The waiter then asks, "Tên ông là gì?" (What is your name?). JJ struggles for a moment and then gets it. "Me? Oh, my name? Right, JJ." The waiter looks a bit lost so JJ tries again: "Tên me is JJ."

The waiter nods, smiles and repeats, "JJ." Then he brandishes the tip money and says, "Ông JJ, xin cảm ơn." (Mr. JJ, thank you.) JJ understands and tries to repeat the thank you part. Trân nods enthusiastically, but JJ knows he is very wide of the mark. He smiles and goes on his way.

Out in the street, he checks the address for the Ministry, discovers it should be just up the block, and starts off, practicing his newly learned Viêtnamese. "Couldn't hurt to ask for a name or say thank you, both in the local language," he thinks. He likes the idea and nods to himself. "Right. Ease off a bit. Might help." The thought brings a smile, and he walks ahead with a slight spring in his step. He reaches the square where the Cathedral stands and looks around. To his right is the central post office, but he can't spot the street number he needs. He starts to walk around the square and decides that he is lost. He heads back towards his hotel and stumbles on his destination, an old colonial era villa that looks as if it is now a police station.

JJ checks the address against his notes. This is it. He walks past the iron gate into a small yard that might once have been green space. Now it's just ugly cement, but it leads to a stone stairway. JJ climbs the few steps and enters the building. He finds a man in police uniform at a desk and asks him in English where he can pick up papers taken from him by the airport police. All he gets is a blank stare. He raises his voice a bit and says, "papers, file?" The desk officer shakes his head and returns to his work. "Oh, great," mutters JJ. "The information man speaks no known language." As he says this, another officer is passing. He stops and asks in poor English, "You, help?"

"Yeah, um right. Great. I need to pick up some papers…"

The officer cuts him off. "You come," and he starts off towards a different room.

JJ runs to catch up. They enter a large, open space filled with desks. Each is stacked with files, and behind each sits a bored looking officer. JJ's guide stops by a desk at the rear and gestures him to sit in the visitor's chair. He then says something to the man at the desk, whose badge indicates him to be of officer rank. His name plate says, Đại Úy

(Captain) Nguyễn Thien Vien. Vien looks at JJ, extends his hand and makes a gimme gesture.

It takes several seconds for JJ to react. Vien frowns at him. JJ says, "I came to get back a file taken from me at the airport yesterday." Vien says nothing but makes the gimme gesture again, this time evidencing some impatience. JJ digs in a folder he is carrying and produces the receipt he was given. Vien takes it, raises his glance so it encompasses some of the nearby desks, and snaps out a word. Another policeman, jumps up from his place and comes to stand respectfully by Đại Úy Vien. There is an exchange in Việtnamese as Vien hands the receipt to his underling. The man salutes and scurries off. Vien looks at JJ and says gruffly, while shooing him away, "You sit there. Wait." He then returns to his papers.

JJ is a bit stunned. His good mood slips a notch. "God," he thinks, "the police just seem to hate me." He looks back in the direction Vien has indicated and sees a long wooden bench against a windowless wall. Several Việtnamese, lower class or office boys for businesses, are seated there. He hesitates. He doesn't want to get on this man's bad side. He smiles and says, "If it will be long, I can come back."

Vien's head snaps up. He scowls. "You sit. You wait."

"JJ's good mood takes another hit. Oh great," he mutters. Vien gives him a hard look. JJ goes to the bench. The people there make some space for him, and he sits. He has no idea how long things will take, but he figures it can't be too long. He checks his watch. It's just past 9:00 AM.

JJ feels strange sitting in this Việtnamese police office as the only foreigner amid a number of local errand boys. He tries to ignore them, but they are curious about him. One tries to start a conversation. JJ, uncharacteristically, attempts to reply. But the two have no common language, and the effort fails. JJ sits and eyes the goings on. He scans the room for the officer who ran off with his receipt. He doesn't see him. He looks over at Đại Úy Vien, who is deeply absorbed in something that JJ decides must be more important than nuclear secrets. He shakes his head. As he does so, Vien looks up and sees the gesture. He glares back.

After a while, Vien signals to one of the Việtnamese on the bench. The man gets up and goes to the desk where he makes an obsequious bow, clutching his hands at mid-chest level. Vien says something, his mouth working fast. He wears a stern look. The Việtnamese nods and bows several times. Vien taps a spot on a paper. The man takes a proffered pen and signs. He then produces what must be an identity card. Vien nods, stamps the paper and shoos the man away.

JJ has watched the scene and checks to see what time it is. He is surprised to find that it is almost 10:00 AM. He fixes his gaze on Đại ÚyVien, hoping that the man will just do the simple task of getting his file. Vien feels the scrutiny. He gives JJ a disapproving look and returns to his doings. The bench begins to feel hard. JJ gets up, stretches and paces around a bit. He wants to wander among the desks, maybe even to remind Vien that he can return later if the wait will be longer, but, somewhat as he was yesterday, he is cowed. He sits back down. More time passes. An office boy is going among the seated policemen and changing the cold glasses of tea on their desks for fresh hot ones.

JJ is suddenly thirsty. He looks around for a water cooler. There is nothing. He gets up and timidly paces in the room thinking that there must be a soda machine or something. One of the men from the bench comes up to him and gestures back in the direction from which JJ originally came. He walks to the doorway and points. JJ joins him. Following the man's guidance, he sees a short hallway ending in an open door. His new friend nods. JJ walks down the hall, peeks through the door and finds a courtyard full of food vendors. He goes out and somehow, between gestures, grunts, nods and proffering piasters, manages to buy himself a croissant and a glass of tea.

He has a thought and doubles his order. It won't hurt to thank his guide.

The entire operation has taken a bit of time. When he returns to the room, the bench by the wall has been cleared of a few of its occupants. JJ offers the tea and croissant to his helper, saying cảm ơn (thank you) or as closely as he can approximate. The man accepts gratefully and pushes JJ towards Đại Úy Vien. JJ reluctantly approaches the great man and stands quietly before his desk. At length, Vien looks up. "Where you go?" he demands. JJ brandishes the food. Vien misunderstands. He slaps an empty spot on his desk. JJ puts down his snack. Vien says, "You wait," and shoos him back towards the bench. JJ is too scared to protest. He sits down and looks at his watch. It is nearly noon. He can't believe it.

The room is almost empty. Only two people remain on the bench with him, and all the police officers but Vien have gone off for the noontime siesta. JJ is about to leave when Vien gestures him over. JJ recognizes his folder. Vien proffers a pen and taps a spot on a form on his desktop. JJ signs and reaches for his papers. "Passport, ID Card," says Vien. JJ has not thought to bring any ID. His shoulders slump. Vien understands. He shows a glimmer of humanity. "OK, you come back lúc ba giờ'," he says, holding up three fingers. "You come take papers."

JJ nods and says, "Cảm ơn."

Vien smiles. "Không dàm." JJ looks blank. "It means you are welcome," says Vien.

JJ tries to repeat the phrase. Vien laughs. "North Việtnam man say, không dàm. It mean, I no dare to accept thank you for such small thing. Southern man say Không có gì. It mean, what I do be nothing."

JJ smiles. He did not expect this from the forbidding Vien. His mood goes back up a notch, and he clasps his hands in front of his chest, as he saw the man do earlier, makes a small bow and turns to leave. "Wait," says Vien. He hands JJ his file of papers and gruffly waves him away.

"Maybe there's hope," thinks JJ as he heads back to the hotel for lunch. But he is not paying attention to the dense traffic generated as hundreds of civil servants and office workers, in cars, and on bicycles and small motorcycles rush home for the siesta. He steps off the curb and a motorcycle runs over his foot and snags his pantleg. He spins around, trying to keep his balance but fails. He throws his arms out to break his fall and drops the file he has just spent hours waiting to retrieve. Traffic rides over the papers that are blowing loose from the folder. He screams at the loss. A few bicyclists try to chase down the papers, and two help JJ to his feet. He is shaking with frustration. The men usher him to the sidewalk and stand with him. A young man comes over and hands him a few of the lost papers.

"Cảm ơn. Cảm ơn," says JJ. But the man says something in Việtnamese. JJ looks blank. One of his rescuers translates: "He is sorry. He tried, but a few of the papers blew down a sewer before he could get them."

Chapter 20

We are going to continue our trip. Since we're up early, Mr. Nam suggests an early start. It is, he points out, a five-hour ride from Bao Lôc to Banmethuot, even longer if we want to stop through Dalat, which lies to the east of our most direct route. I am anxious to get to the village where my father served most of his early years in-country. That lies well to the north. He also worked in a hamlet east of Banmethuot. If we detour to Dalat, we will not reach Banmethuot today. I am a bit torn. My father did work with mountain tribes in the Dalat area, and he lectured on occasion at the University of Dalat. He became good friends with two professors there, one of whom served as Minister of Labor under Nguyễn Cao Ky. The memory makes me smile.

"What is it?" Mr. Nam asks.

"Nothing really. My dad's journal reports on time he spent in Dalat, on his work with tribes there and his friendship with two University of Dalat professors."

"Well, we can stop there, either on the way up or the way back. What do you think?"

"Let's save it for the return trip and get to Banmethuot today."

"Ok, but what was that smile about?"

I start to chuckle. "One of the professors served for a time as Minister of Labor under Nguyễn Cao Ky when he was Prime Minister."

"I remember. That was Professor Long."

"Yes. It seems he and my father were good friends. The journals relate that Long had quite a sense of humor and that he, his wife and my father would often have dinner together. My dad records that Long, or more exactly, his wife told a funny story. After the Tết attack in January of 1968, General Ky decided that all the girlie bars in Saigon should be closed because having Việtnamese girls carousing with foreigners was bad for the morale of Việtnam's fighting troops. The closure lasted for maybe ten days. That, it seems, was hard on the livelihood of the working girls."

Mr. Nam is smiling. "I remember this very well. The girls got together, formed a committee and asked to meet with Long, the Minister of Labor."

"Yes. My dad relates that Prime Minister Ky knew the meeting was coming and called Long to tell him that he was to refuse absolutely to permit the girls to go back to work. Long's wife picked up the story and said that on the day set for the meeting, Long spent a lot of time in the bathroom. It seems he emerged smelling of some French, He-man cologne and impeccably dressed in his best suit. She said she couldn't help but laugh at him and told him, as he left in great haste for his office, 'Long, no dates!'

"Long himself then continues the story saying that the girls had selected the most beautiful of their number to meet with him and that each was provocatively dressed, either in western attire or Việtnamese áo dài that was form-fitted from the neck to the waist. When he entered the conference to meet with them, he says, he surprised himself by actually giving out a small gasp. 'It was like a Miss Universe contest,' he said.

'And the mingled perfumes honestly made me dizzy. I began to sweat.'

"The girls made their case, with two of those closest to him, touching his hand gently from time to time. Dad notes Long saying that he took a deep breath, swallowed hard, thanked the ladies for coming but informed them in no uncertain terms, 'Don't even think of going back to work'.

"At this point, Long's wife again takes up the story and says, 'Poor man. He got nothing for his heroics. But the girls took their case to the PM himself. There is no record of that meeting, but the ladies were back at work before another week had passed.'"

Mr. Nam is chuckling, clearly absorbed in the memory and having a good bit of fun. Phùng looks at him curiously. Mr. Nam says, "He has never seen me like this."

Phùng replies, "No, I have not. You look twenty-five years younger."

Mr. Nam nods. "I'm enjoying these memories. They take me back to a Việtnam that no longer exists. So many of these people we are talking about have died that thinking of them reminds me of my early years and the moments of my own life. Those times can never be recaptured. They are part of Việtnamese and American history, but to me there is a strangeness there. I lived that history. It still maintains an air of the present for me. To your generation, Phùng, it is dusty and exists mainly in books. For me, it exists here, in my heart."

We finish our breakfast and sit for a while looking out on the fields and sipping the fragrant, bracing Blao green tea. Phùng tells his grandfather: "Maybe before this trip, the stories, memories and events you two have been speaking of were just dusty facts in dusty books. But I have fallen into living the stories with both of you. I am beginning to understand my country as I did not before."

Mr. Nam smiles and speaks to him lovingly in Việtnamese. He translates for me: "You are a wonderful boy. I am glad in my heart that you are here with us and learning of and experiencing these moments and memories. In this way, history becomes human, alive." He smiles at me, as if to say, *"Isn't that right?"*

I take another sip of the tea. It is slightly bitter on my tongue, and it carries with it this morning's glorious sunrise, my first sight of the green tea fields being harvested by hand, as they have been in this basin for generations, a sense of timelessness and, once again, the thought that perhaps I *belong* here. That here, I really could fill those voids I have always felt in my life. I shake my head, trying to break that spell, to tell myself that it just can't be that simple. I raise my cup to Mr. Nam in a gesture that says, *a last sip, and then it's time to go.* He raises his in reply.

"Yes, let's get started. In Banmethuot you can experience another Việtnamese specialty, our highland-grown Robusta coffee."

* * * * * * * * * * *

JJ is too stricken to speak. He just stands there, on a street corner in Hô Chí Minh City, seeing in his mind's eye, the last hope of finding his father circle a drain and disappear. He becomes aware that the roaring noise of the noontime rush has dulled. He looks around. It's true. The nearby traffic has all-but stopped. People who have witnessed the moment sit on their small motorcycles and look sadly, questioningly at him. Several others stand by his side, expressions of concern on their faces. A few of these are speaking to him, trying to console him, offering to help if he will tell them what he needs. He realizes that he is the recipient of kindness and concern from strangers. It's a new experience. He fights back tears of frustration and, in his newly learned Việtnamese, thanks these foreigners for their generosity. "Cảm ơn, cảm ơn." No one even so much as grins at his awkward pronunciation. His effort is appreciated and has broken the tension.

A few of the by-standers ask him, in passable English, where he is going; can they help him? He points towards the hotel, just a block away. Two young men, friends apparently, say they will accompany him. He nods, smiles and once again says, "Cảm ơn. Cảm ơn." He laughs to himself. *Who knew the words would be so helpful so quickly?* When they reach the hotel, JJ invites the two friends to the terrace for a drink. They look at each other dubiously for a moment and then seem to make a decision. They nod. He gestures towards the terrace. It is crowded. The three of them stand awkwardly just beyond the entrance. JJ says, "Can we wait a minute? Maybe a table will open up." The men smile, understanding.

It's taking longer than JJ had expected. He is holding an uncomfortable conversation with his benefactors. A couple at a table gets up to leave and another waiting group steps forward. JJ wants to pre-empt them but also doesn't want any more arguments. He hesitates. Trân, the waiter, his new "waiter-friend" appears, holds up the other group and leads JJ to the empty table. He is almost shocked by the kindness. "Ong Trân," he says, "Cảm ơn ông."

"Không dám," says Trân with a huge smile. He fetches a menu and asks, "Ong muôn an gì?" JJ looks lost. His new friends translate. "He wants to take our order."

JJ realizes it's siesta time and that the Việtnamese usually have a big meal and then nap. He says, "Is it ok if we have lunch here? I don't see Việtnamese food on the menu." The men smile and nod. Then they introduce themselves as Binh and Thien.

JJ is overwhelmed by all the Việtnamese names that have come at him this morning. He wants to remember the names of these kind men and not confuse who is who. Each man is wearing black slacks and a long-sleeved white shirt, like many others JJ has seen in the street, but he notices that Binh has on Nike trainers. *Ok, he thinks, Binh is "Nike."*

"The food is no problem," says Binh/Nike. "We just want to help you if we can. It seems like you lost some important papers back there and also maybe got hurt."

JJ has almost forgotten getting dinged by the motorcycle. "Nah, I'm not hurt much. My leg'll be ok. But, you're right. The papers were very important. Losing them hurts."

"Hurts?" asks Thien doubtfully.

"I mean, it's something that might ruin my whole reason for coming here."

"Where are you from, and why did you come here?"

JJ tells a bit of his story. Binh says, "But you don't look Australian. To me, to us, (he nods to Thien) you look even, Asian. Maybe a little Việtnamese."

"Right," says JJ. "My mother was part Việtnamese, and my father, my *real* father was Caucasian. Maybe American. I don't know. My mother would never tell me. She died, and I came here to see if I could find out who my father is… or was."

Binh and Thien look at each other. They are considering what they have just heard, and they seem to be confused by it. Thien says, "You mean you grew up not knowing who your father was? Many people here lost a father during the American war, but that was different. At least they knew. So, you had just a mother?"

"Yes, well, and a man who my mother *said* was my father. He acted that part, but you can tell about these things. He tried hard, was a good man, but nothing was right. My mother, she seemed to want to forget about Việtnam. She made herself into an Australian. She adopted the Australian way of behaving, Australian attitudes and changed her French-accented English to Australian . She seemed so completely happy in being like that. But I saw how she was different when she met with her few Việtnamese friends. And she had a lawyer who was Việtnamese and who she trusted like no one else. It was confusing. It was like she would take off one personality and appearance and put on the other whenever the situation demanded."

"But you grew up in Australia. You really were, um, are, Australian. I am sorry to ask, but why was it hard for you."

JJ looks at Binh, at both of his new friends. He is embarrassed. He has said too much--to strangers. He wants to scream, but in a moment he is thinking, *what the hell,* and he finally says out loud to another human, what he has kept inside for forty years. "It was not authentic. I was not authentic. No one knew who I was, even I didn't, still don't. I kept thinking that I had to wear a false personality, like my mother did. But she was a grown-up, and I was a little boy, and I never knew what was the real me and what was not. And I got so afraid of not knowing when to change the me I showed to people, that I guess I gave up. And everyone could tell that there was something strange about me, and nothing was ever right." He stops, out of breath and with a feeling he has never known.

Binh and Thien don't know what to do or say. As Việtnamese they would never make such a declaration, such a confession, to anyone but their most intimate friend. But they understand too what JJ has just suffered, along with the pain he built up over many years. They swallow their embarrassment at having heard all this. Thien tells him: "We just want to help you, and we will do that if you still wish."

JJ does his best to smile. He overcomes the humiliation that would have crushed him in all the years before this moment. "Yes," he says. "Cảm ơn. I want your help very much." Then, after a pause, "Can you excuse me for a minute? Please order whatever you want. Order this for me." He points to a sandwich on the menu and then hurries away.

He finds the public restroom, enters and secures himself inside one of the stalls. He collapses onto the commode and erupts in tears and sobs. He struggles to stifle the sound and to control his breathing, but it is all too much. He cries, deeply, wrenchingly, until there is nothing left in him.

* * * * * * * * * * *

We have arrived in Banmethuot. It is early afternoon. The city is quiet. Siesta has not yet ended. I ask Mr. Nam if we can take a quick run around. My idea of this place has been based on my father's photos. In his day this was a dusty provincial town, although it was the capital of Dar Lac province. It has changed greatly, from what I can tell, and I am disappointed. I looked forward to seeing it as my father lived it: miles of dirt road, a fine coating of red-brown dust on everything, a central market consisting of wood buildings and indeed, a majority of wood frame structures all around. There are still plenty of these, but modern hotels and concrete buildings, even a few monuments, are the norm. This is no longer a "frontier town". To me, it's as if someone has stolen the outpost that was here and replaced it with something that wants to deny the past. I say all this to Mr. Nam. He nods agreement. "I have not been here since the war ended. I too liked it the way it was. I did not expect time to have stood still but nevertheless...

"You just mentioned Dar Lac province. The communists can't keep their hands off of names. Now this is Dak Lak province. And, yes, they have built a number of modern buildings and seem to be well along in wiping the old wooden structures off the face of the earth. They think that by changing names, they erase forever the pre-communist soul of this place and all other places in the south." He shakes his head. "We have a history and an ethos. The communists know they can't change the oldest narratives of that, but they are very much interested in picking away at our more modern eras to adjust things they find inconvenient.

"Do you know that the largest percentage of our population now was born after your father's war? They have grown up learning the history of that time from the communists, who, as the victors, write the history. They see Saigon and think it is Hồ Chí Minh City. They see Banmethuot and have little or no idea of its past. I did some research before starting this trip. I think you will be surprised by some of what I found."

I look at him questioningly. I am a bit surprised by his intensity.

"The wartime population here was around 150,000. About 30% were Montagnards. Now the population here is almost 400,000, and the tribal people make up less than 15% of that. The math says that their numbers have grown by 15,000 or 30% of their wartime complement. But for Việtnamese, their number is three times what it was in the early 1970s. Do you see what is happening? These indigenous people are disappearing."

I am quiet, thinking about what this means. The analogy that comes to mind is the extinction of a species in nature. I say, "It's like the orangutans in Malaysia and Indonesia or the white rhino. One day they will disappear completely. We will read about them in books and see them in film, but they will be gone forever. The farther in the past that they recede, the less the emotion that will attach to their loss." I have regretted this kind of extinction in the animal kingdom, but when I think of it happening to *humans*, I actually get a chill. "So, maybe our children, grandchildren, great grandchildren and so on will stumble on photos of Montagnards in a museum somewhere and perhaps see a latter-day anthropologist's diorama of their villages."

"Yes, and the truth is that their decline is the result of assimilation, to some extent, but more significantly, it is the direct consequence of Việtnamese government policies. We, the Việtnamese, have always looked down on these tribal peoples. Often, we call them, 'moi', which means 'savages'. Yet, their ancestors surely inhabited this area before the Việts began their southward emigration from the Red River delta. If anything, we are the interlopers. But our governments, first Ngô Đình Diệm, then Nguyễn Van Thieu and now the communists, have always intended to force the tribal people to extinction."

I think of what I read in my father's journals, about the integrity and bravery of these people, of his profound affection for them, of their belief that he had been one of them in a previous life, of those moments when he was tempted to remain with them until the end of his days. The emotional impact of this takes my breath away.

"Where did these people come from originally? They surely do not look Chinese. How did they get here, to these highlands, and why did they isolate themselves?"

"I am no anthropologist, so I am not a reliable source. But I am not sure, even to this day, that there are settled answers to your questions. Over the years, I have heard that they are of Sino-Tibetan, Mon Khmer and Malayo-Polynesian origin. Maybe some of them came from the area that includes Malaya, the Philippines and Indonesia, as traders back when Việtnam was beginning to develop as a society. They have a long history in these highlands, but whether pressured by the Khmers, the Chams or the Việts, they have always had a hard life. It was only the French colonial administration that gave them a bit of consideration by allowing them an autonomous political status.

"The Americans of your father's time were perhaps the best non-tribal friends they have ever had. Your Special Forces lived with them, trained them and came to respect and admire them. They brought them into the war on their side, and they protected them from much of the abuse the Việtnamese intended for them. You have said that your father was part of this effort. But everyone else, Hồ Chí Minh, the Ngô Đình Diệm administration, the Nguyễn Van Thieu administration and now the communist masters of this country have all dealt with them harshly.

"When France disappeared as a colonial master, Hồ Chí Minh, who had promised them special status, abolished the autonomy the French had granted them. Then Diem banned the teaching of Montagnard languages, burned Montagnard books and documents, and forced them to take Việtnamese names. South Việtnamese from the coastal regions, often at government prodding or with government blessing, streamed into the highlands. In many cases they seized ancestral tribal lands while providing no compensation to the Montagnards. Tribal courts were abolished, and Viêtnamese law was imposed, even in matters involving Montagnard custom.

"The tribes came together and formed a resistance movement. First it was referred to as *Bajaraka*. The word was created from the letters of the names of the main highland tribes (Bahnar, Jarai, Rhade and Koho). Later the movement became known as FULRO. That was an acronym of its French name, Front Unifié pour la Libération des Races Opprimées, United Front for the Liberation of the Oppressed Peoples. In 1958, Diem crushed the movement. Crippled it, more accurately, but it continued to be a pressure factor representing the desires of the tribal people. The Americans essentially *obliged* the Thieu government to respect the former leaders of FULRO and the desires of the tribal peoples. It was never a comfortable situation, but the Viêtnamese did create a cabinet post, The Ministry of Ethnic Minority Affairs. It was headed by a former FULRO chieftain named Paul Nur, and its top leadership consisted of prestigious 'former' FULRO fighters like Nay Luett, Y'Bham Enoul and Colonel Ya Ba, among many others. Ultimately, our government kept it from accomplishing very much."

"Some of those names sound familiar. Actually, I think I found a book by Paul Nur in my father's library. There was a signed dedication to my father."

"Yes. I mentioned the names thinking that one or two might ring a bell."

"All of this is very moving to me. I am anxious to visit the hamlet where my father lived."

"We'll go tomorrow."

* * * * * * * * * * * *

Binh and Thien sit talking quietly together. They are worried about JJ, his state of mind and by what has happened to him. Binh says, "This man has had a lot of trouble in his life. I don't think there is much we can do, but I want to try."

Thien nods. Then he has a thought. He takes out his cell phone and dials a number. "I will call Thuy to let her know neither of us will be home before dinner. She can tell your mother."

"Maybe we should tell her what happened and see if she wants to join us when we try to help JJ."

"Good idea. A woman will surely get information that we can't." They both smile.

Thien sees JJ's file on the table. After a glance around, he opens it and begins to read some of the old newspaper clippings. "These come from several different newspapers. There are things from The Saigon Post, The Việtnam Guardian, Agènce Việtnam Presse and some translations from Việtnamese language papers." He quickly scans several articles. "They mostly talk about certain Americans who worked here in those times. Maybe he thinks one of these is his father."

"Are there any Việtnamese authors of those articles? If we could find one who is still alive, we might get some information."

"I recognize one name. He is very old now. There are also some addresses here in the file, but I don't know what they mean, and I don't think I have ever even heard of some of these street names."

JJ returns. He apologizes for his absence and is glad to see that the food has been delivered to the table. He smiles at his two new friends and says, "bon appétit." They give him a blank look. "Oh, sorry. That's French. It means kind of, 'eat up, I hope you enjoy it.' You never heard that?"

Binh and Thien offer slightly embarrassed smiles. "It has been many years since French language was common here," says Binh. "Our parents once told us that right after the communist victory, the Russian language tried to gain popularity. It never really did. They said people didn't like the Russians. They called them, 'Americans without money.' To us, it is kind of funny that after years of war against the Americans and then years our parents' generation spent in re-education camps, our generation likes the Americans, and even tries to go to the US for study. The schools here teach English as the main foreign language. Thien and I are very curious about Americans, foreigners in general, especially ones who speak English."

"So," says JJ with a broad smile, "Am I a kind of science project for you?"

"The men laugh. "No," says Binh, who is emerging as the spokesman. "But we think we can make a new friend, learn and help you all at the same time. While you were away, we looked a little at your clippings."

"What do you think?"

"I'm not sure...we're not sure. It looks like you are paying attention to Americans who worked here during the war."

"Right. I am. I mean it's one of the only leads I can start with."

"Maybe those names won't lead anywhere."

"I know." He shakes his head.

"What are the addresses you have?"

"One is for the office where my mother worked. Another is for her parents' home. The few others are just things I found in her papers after she died."

"Well, there are two things. We might find someone at one of the addresses who can give us information. Also, maybe one of the journalists who wrote these articles in Việtnamese papers is alive. If we can find that person, it could be another useful lead. There is a problem, though. Neither of us recognizes some of these street names."

"Anything we can do will help. I didn't have much hope anyway, but I had to try."

"Thien and I have to work, so we can't start this afternoon, but we're free on Saturday in the afternoon and on Sunday too. Also, if you agree, we will ask a lady friend to help us. She knows a lot about those years, and sometimes people speak more freely to women than to men. What do you think?"

"That's wonderful. I would be lost without your help. Where and at what time can I meet you?"

Binh and Thien confer. Binh says, "How about this. Let's have dinner tomorrow. We can go to a local restaurant, show you a bit of the city and discuss plans for Saturday. We'll meet you here tôi mai at 7:30."

"Tôi mai." JJ struggles with the pronunciation. "What is that?"

"Tomorrow evening," says Thien. "Now you have another new Việtnamese phrase. What do you think?"

JJ smiles broadly. "Cảm ơn."

* * * * * * * * * * *

I must have been exhausted because I slept so late that Phùng had to wake me by knocking loudly at my room. I'm still groggy when I open the door. He gives me a big smile and says in English, with some difficulty, "Rise and shine, lazy man."

I laugh. "Is that what your grandfather told you to say?"

His smile fades a little. "Oh, how do you know that?"

"Because it's not something you would have learned in school, and I would guess he said to call me 'lazybones.'"

Phùng looks mildly embarrassed. "Oh, yes, yes. Lazybones. Are you angry?"

"Not at all. Just maybe a little ashamed of wasting our chance to get an early start."

His smile returns. "Oh, it's not very late. Just 7:30. Grandpa wants to meet you downstairs at 8:00. Is that OK? He says to dress in something you can get dirty."

"I'll be there."

We rendezvous as planned, leave the hotel on foot and begin to walk the short distance to the central market. The streets are crowded with small motorcycles, cars and trucks of all kinds and even a number of war-vintage jeeps. Boys and girls in school uniforms walk on their way to class among groups of beautiful young girls in white Viêtnamese dresses riding bicycles, and numbers of Montagnard men and women. The men are roughly dressed, headed, perhaps, for work which will likely be in farming or labor. The women all wear the distinctive Montagnard woman's dress: most commonly a blouse of heavy, village-loomed cotton over a sarong of the same material. Both garments are usually black but highlighted by horizontal stripes of vivid colors. In general, the people walk in small groups, but the Montagnards are distinguished by walking in a single line, one behind the other. Mr. Nam points this out and says, "Jungle file, the way they are used to walking in the forest." It, along with their rapid pace and steady, purposeful progress leads me to believe that I am seeing something cultural and all but hardwired.

We reach the market and in an older, less central section, find an unoccupied, weathered table with several wooden stools. When we sit, a Montagnard boy comes to take our order. Mr. Nam handles the formalities. 8:30 AM may not be "late" for us, but the market has clearly been alive with activity for quite some time. I am amused by the difference between this provincial market and the urban intensity of Saigon. After a few minutes, the boy places chipped mugs of steaming coffee on the table along with a small plate for each of us and a basket with croissants. The coffee is very strong. I sip it slowly.

"Robusta," says Mr. Nam.

"What?"

"Robusta. That is the variety of coffee we grow here in the highlands."

"Boy, it's sure strong. I had better be careful, or I won't sleep for a week."

He laughs. "It does have more caffeine than the Arabica-bean coffee you are used to, but it is also less acidic and higher in what you call, anti-oxidants. We do export the coffee, but it is usually blended with Arabica beans to make instant coffee and less expensive grades of packaged coffee."

I nod, thinking that there is so much I don't know. It tells me that I have indeed had a sheltered life and that knowing the complexities of American securities law is no measure of "knowledge" at all. I look around as we talk, taking in the fact that few people here are dressed in office attire. I let my glance roam over the area, breaking off several times to pay attention to my conversation with Mr. Nam. Finally, I notice an older tribal man who arrived after we did. He is sitting at a nearby table with a younger man. He is dressed more like an office worker than the other Montagnards. There is something distinguished in his demeanor. Each time I glance around, I think he is looking at me. This time, I see him gesture in my direction to his younger companion. I mention this to Mr. Nam.

"I have noticed," he says.

After a moment, he smiles deliberately in the man's direction. There is a brief conversation at the other table, and the older man rises and comes towards us. He stops and nods politely at Mr. Nam, who gestures that he should join us. The man sits. "Excuse me for staring at you, but I believe you are Truong Van Nam." Mr. Nam nods and raises an eyebrow. "I was a student in your classes at the National Institute of Administration, many years ago."

Mr. Nam smiles broadly. After a bit of reflection, he says, "K'Sor Brui, the senator?"

The man laughs happily. "You have an excellent memory. I am so happy to see you." He turns and gestures back towards the man at his table to join us. "This is my son, Sénac. Will you introduce us to your companions?"

"Oh, I apologize. This is my grandson, Phùng." He turns towards me, but before he can say anything, K'sor Brui starts to speak.

"And this man, he is American?" Mr. Nam nods. "I apologize for interrupting you, but I am very anxious to meet him. He has some Việtnamese blood, I think."

At this, I introduce myself. Most people do not read me as being Eurasian. "My name is Marc, and yes, I am part Việtnamese."

K'Sor Brui now wears an enormous smile. "Forgive me. I am so excited. I am sure I knew your father. He lived in our hamlet many years ago. Am I right? You look so much like him. He and I were dear friends. How is he? Is he here with you?"

I am overwhelmed. Notes from my father's journals come rushing to mind. "Yes, you are right, but I am sorry to tell you that my father passed away almost two years ago."

"And your mother. I met her only once and very quickly. Is she well? Did she come with you?"

"She did not come with me, and she is getting old. Thank you for asking about her."

"Well, I knew her family much better than I knew her. Her parents had coffee plantations here. Her oldest brother is still in Banmethuot, on his plantation, but you must know that."

"Actually, my parents are long divorced, and I have been distant from my mother. My father raised me. Sadly, after my father-in-law and mother-in-law died, I have had very little contact with the family, even though I love them all. It's just time and circumstances."

K'Sor Brui looks thoughtful. "I am sad to hear these things. Your in-laws were wonderful people. They always treated us, um, my people, kindly and with respect. We all remember Bác Sau so well. Did you know him?"

"He died very soon after arriving in America following the communist take-over here. I was three months old at the time and with my parents in Singapore where I was born. My father says it is very sad I did not know grandpa. Grandma lived for many years after he died, and I loved her very much."

"Was Bác Sau sick? I don't think he was very old, and whenever I saw him he seemed strong. Do you think the change to such a different place had a bad effect on him? As you can see, I stayed in Vietnam after the communist victory, but many of our people tried to get out and some succeeded. They knew the communists would treat us harshly because we had been allies of the Americans – especially us, the Rhadé. After a long time we got news that many of our friends who managed to escape did not adjust to America and died."

"I did not know that. I am very sorry to hear it."

"Well, they were usually young men without families to hold them back. But if they had stayed, they would have been killed or treated brutally in re-education camps."

"I have heard that the camps were harsh, but many did survive them. Mr. Nam himself did."

"For our people things were different. First, a lot of our young men fled into the deep forest. Many of them had been part of what you Americans called the CIDG, Civilian Irregular Defense Groups. These had been created and trained by your Special Forces. They were excellent fighters. So these men formed back into an army and fought the communists. They knew that going to a camp meant death almost as surely as fighting did. But they were proud and brave and wanted to die in a fight, rather than quietly."

"You did not go? You faced the camps?"

"Yes. As a senator, the communists hated me, but they understood that if they did not treat me badly, they might be able to use me to subdue my people. I hated that, but because of Sénac, I tried to help my people without doing more than the minimum for the communists."

I take a moment to absorb this information. Then I say, "You are a very brave man." K'Sor Brui shakes his head. I continue, "I know a little about you and who you are. You are my father's dear friend. You named your son, Sénac because he was born shortly after you were elected to the Việtnamese senate in 1967."

K'Sor Brui looks both surprised and nostalgic. "How do you know that?"

"My father wrote about it in his journals." I look at Sénac. "You are nine years older than I. Because our fathers were so close, may I think of you as an older brother?"

Sénac is grinning. "Oh, this is wonderful. Of course." He gets up and gives me a hug. His father does the same. When we sit, each of us has tears in his eyes. The emotion is overpowering.

After a long silence, in which we collect ourselves, I say, "K'Sor Brui, you are the man who came from here to Saigon in March of 1975 and escorted my father back to the highlands to search for my grandparents. Without you, my father always said, they would not have been saved. I came to Việtnam to try to understand his life. I never hoped to find or meet either of you, but I have hoped very much to see the hamlet where he lived and worked."

"Do you have time now to come there with us? I still live there, and some of the very old men who knew your father and even fought battles alongside of him are still alive. They would be excited to meet you. If you have time, I can take you there now."

I look a question at Mr. Nam. He and Phùng have sat in silent attention to the conversation. Mr. Nam himself is obviously deeply moved. He nods. "We can follow K'Sor Brui in Phùng's car."

* * * * * * * * * * *

JJ has gotten comfortable with his new friends. They have treated him to a tour of Hồ Chí Minh City and to an excellent Vietnamese dinner. The only downside for him is that the city doesn't really resemble the one in his mother's old photos. It has changed so much that he can't feel he's walking in her footsteps and so he wonders how he will ever find her – and the man she selected to be his father. But he hides his disappointment in this regard because he is smitten with Thuy, the young lady Binh and Thien have brought into their efforts at helping. At age 22, she is many years younger than JJ, but she is whip smart – the brains of the outfit, in his mind – and extremely attractive. She has quickly recognized his self-doubt and low self-esteem and is making an effort at building his confidence in this search – and in himself. He, almost unwittingly, has responded by turning over to her instincts, the responsibility for finding out the identity of his father.

Thuy begins by deciding that they must physically visit every address JJ has from his research and his mother's files and papers. She quickly hits a wall in this effort because so many of the street names he has are unknown to her. But she is nothing if not methodical. She starts with Nguyễn Siêu, a street she knows. It's very close to JJ's hotel, and the address there is for his mother's employer of years ago.

They walk down Đồng Khởi Street, historic in its previous incarnations as Tự Do Street and Rue Catinat, towards the Saigon River. By the old Caravelle Hotel they turn left into Nguyễn Siêu. Thuy doesn't know it, but the street has a history. It is just one block in length and runs alongside the old Indochina Opera House, the seat of the lower chamber of the national assembly in the Thieu years. She finds the address they seek, but it is on the entry of a modern, high-rise building.

She had been hoping for something that reflected the wartime architecture. But that building, now obviously gone, had been torn down years earlier, obliterating forever the ambiance that told so much about those bygone times.

Seeing the modern building, and knowing it cannot possibly be the one that housed his mother's offices, JJ's shoulders slump. Thuy notices immediately and says, "We can't get discouraged by every failure. You told me you didn't think we would find much if anything."

JJ fears losing her support – and her company. He rallies immediately. "Right. I have to see this as a long road that might lead nowhere."

They all stand quietly before the shiny high-rise, collecting their thoughts. This is a melancholy and missed moment. If JJ knew that his mother's office building had begun life as one of two built at the behest of Ngô Đình Diệm to house provincial legislators when in the capital for official duties; if he knew that after Diem it had become an American BOQ and then, in 1974, when South Việtnam lived in an optimism of permanent independence from the North, was converted into the commercial space that housed his mother's offices; if he knew these things, he would at least have a very different sense of the environment that spawned his illegitimacy.

Thuy begins to walk over the area. Just around the corner, where not all the earlier buildings have been replaced, she comes upon an old woman sitting in front of an ancient-looking shop house. She greets her politely and, after a brief conversation, says to JJ, "She has lived right here for more than 75 years. Let me show her a picture of your mother when she was working here."

Thuy holds out the photo JJ has dug from his files. The old woman squints at it, taking it in her ancient hand and turning it every which way to catch the best light. After what seems an eternity, she gives a toothless smile and nods. Thuy translates. "I remember her. She was always around here, but many years ago. I have not seen her for a long time. Sorry, I don't know where she lives now." After a quick exchange, the old lady smiles. Thuy continues her translation. "She was always busy, busy. A skinny little thing, always rushing. She worked over there (she shrugs back in the direction of Nguyễn Sieu Street)."

Thuy asks, "Did she ever talk to you?"

"Oh, she used to have pho over there (indicating a still-operating soup stand) sometimes. That's how I met her. We were both eating and started to talk. She was not Việtnamese. Only part, and she talked very fast. She pretended to be a foreign lady, but her mother was Việtnamese, and her family was not so high like some other métisse girls. But she worked for a big American lawyer there (she again motions towards Nguyễn Sieu). She was smart. Not like a professor, like a gambler."

"Did she have a boyfriend that you knew of?"

The old lady laughs. "Her boss had important foreigners coming to see him for work. Many times she took them to eat during the siesta. And I could see that some of them liked her – and she liked them. Once she told me that she could tell right away which ones she could get favors from if she wanted to. You know, girls like her in those years, they all wanted to catch a rich foreigner and get away from here. They thought nothing of sleeping with many men."

Thuy stops her translation suddenly. She looks embarrassed. JJ says, "No, that's OK. I have heard some of my mother's talk with her friends. I loved her, but I know how she was. I am sad to say it, but she may well have used her appearance and her quick wit to try to catch a man. And she was not a very young girl when I was born. Perhaps she felt that she had to force things along. I think she may have been very forward with my father because she hoped to get him into marriage. The thing is, he was a man who was here for many years, so her boss's clients are probably not the right group."

Thuy thanks the old lady and is about to leave when she has a thought. She has listed out all the addresses in JJ's notes. She shows the list to the old lady. "Do you know any of these streets? I have never heard of some of them."

The old crone squints at the list and then laughs. She issues a quick comment and laughs again.

"What?" asks JJ.

"She says many of these names have been changed since the communists took over. Like Saigon is now Hồ Chí Minh City." The old lady is still talking, so Thuy continues to translate. "She says she can give me the new names of some of them."

Thuy scribbles down the names, as the old lady provides the information. Finally, she thanks her, and they go on their way. They travel by small Honda motorcycle, Binh and Thien on one, Thuy and JJ on another. JJ had at first felt very strange riding behind a female driver and grasping her around the waist for stability and safety. But as the day has progressed, he relaxes into the situation. Thuy is dressed in skinny jeans and a T Shirt. For JJ, the effect is breathtaking. She is slim, but by no means skinny. Quite the opposite. She has a mesmerizing figure that is highlighted by a prominent bustline, a shapely behind and long, silky black hair that hangs loose down to the level of her shoulders. Her face has an angelic beauty, and by the end of the day, JJ is hopelessly in love. He struggles to hide this from her but is sure he is as transparent as window glass.

It is a long, difficult day. They ride through the city ferreting out sometimes-tiny streets and then seeking in vain for anyone in these areas who can help in their quest. They take a break in a small café. As they sip cold drinks, with a few photos and old news articles on the table before them, an old man enters. As he passes their table, he takes a long look at the items, so much so that Binh gives him a slightly annoyed glare. Apparently, the man is too old to be disturbed by this. He has stopped cold and has bent forward to look more closely at one photo. Binh's expression turns to one of curiosity. The man nods to himself and moves on to an empty table.

Thuy and JJ go to him. Thuy says, "Do you recognize the lady in that picture?"

The man is apologetic. He introduces himself as, Hien. "Excuse me. The photo caught my eye. A girl like that lived near here years and years ago. Like so many others, she disappeared when the communists came. I have not thought of her or remembered her since those bad days. I was surprised by the resemblance between her and the picture."

"We will be interested in anything you remember about her. We want to find out about her, her life here."

The man looks at Thuy and then at JJ. He actually seems to study him for long moments. "Hmm, is he her son?"

The two are astounded. "Why do you say that?"

"He reminds me of the girl I remember. She was a busy little girl, and he (he nods towards JJ) is like her size, and, I don't know. It's a feeling he gives me. She was always going out at night. Sometimes by herself, but more times getting picked up by foreigners in their fancy cars. You know, those that had green plates with an 'X'."

Binh and Thien have now come to the table and are listening. Thuy says, "I don't know what you mean about the license plates." She looks at Binh and Thien. Each shrugs his shoulders in ignorance.

The man thinks for a moment. "Oh, I see. You all are too young. Those plates were for tax-free vehicles used by foreign-government contractors back during the war years. We Việtnamese had to pay a lot of tax if we wanted a car. The rich foreigners didn't, and many of us were angry. We thought our girls who rode around in those cars were…bad, easy."

"Do you mean that the car of a foreign business, maybe a lawyer's firm, would have a license plate like that?"

"Not unless it was doing business under an American Government contract. Maybe ship repair or even research studies would." Everyone looks disappointed. The man continues, "But a contractor company that was a client of a law firm could have a green plate. Why is this so important?"

Thuy explains their quest. The man says, "I can show you where she might have lived in those years. Like me, there are other old people around who might remember her and be able to answer some questions."

They treat the Hien to tea and a pastry and encourage him to share any memories he has of JJ's mother. He thinks for a bit and then shrugs. "I didn't actually know her. I just saw her around here a lot and saw her comings and goings. If I ever knew her name, I have forgotten it. I can just see her always being in a hurry. She would leave for work early like all of us. Sometimes she came home at the end of the day and went out wearing the kind of nighttime clothes young girls wore then. I think she would often come back late because neighbors talked about that."

JJ asks, "Did she have boyfriends?" Thuy translates.

"We should go to her street. I did not pay so much attention. Maybe you will find someone who remembers."

They walk through a warren of busy, narrow streets that run off one another at odd angles and with no evident pattern. JJ can smell the river. Thuy nods to him and says, the address you have is close to the water. They reach Bác Sī Calmette Street. Hien points them down the way. After a short walk, he stops in front of a shophouse. It has a grill that can be pulled across to secure the interior, but now the entry is open. Rice sacks are stacked on the floor. "Maybe here," he says.

Thuy is holding a weathered blue booklet – actually just a sheet of construction paper folded in half. On the front it says,

Tờ Khai Gia-Dinh, and the address of the shophouse is written by hand in a space below. JJ recognizes it as something from his mother's papers, but he does not know what it is. Thuy is showing the booklet to Mr. Hien. He has it opened and is reading and nodding. Thuy turns to JJ. "This is the family book for this address, the one that was current when your mother lived here. Each house had to have a book with the names and identity card numbers of each resident. I don't see, your mother's name here, but maybe she used a Việtnamese name. She did have the booklet."

Hien enters the house and calls out. A man appears. He seems several years older than JJ and looks like an accountant. There is a conversation with Hien pointing to the names in the booklet. The man nods. He disappears for a minute and calls to someone. When he returns, he points to a name in the family book and says, "This is my grandmother. She is very old but still strong. Maybe she can help you."

There is a shuffling sound, and an old lady steps into the front room. She is less than five feet tall, and she walks with the aid of a cane. When she smiles a greeting, Thuy is taken aback. Binh and Thien too react with obvious surprise. JJ is befuddled. Thuy says, "She looks a bit like you. Not an exact resemblance, but she has an air about her." JJ can't see it.

Thuy shows the old lady the picture of JJ's mother. She begins to cry spouting memories of his mother when she was young. She turns to JJ and touches his face gently. "You are her son. I can see it. You are the one she carried. That skinny girl and her big belly." She hugs him.

Thuy asks, "Did she live here all the time she was pregnant?"

The old lady cries harder. "No. Her father was very angry with her. He demanded to know who the baby's father was, but she would not tell. He threw her out. I begged him, but he threw her out."

"Did she go to stay with the baby's father then?"

"No. She stayed with a girlfriend and had the child at the French hospital. I visited her there. I hoped the baby's father would be there, but he was not. She said he didn't want the baby and would not visit her or see the baby or give it his name. He said she tricked him into bed; that he had never tried to make her his girlfriend and that he became affiancé to another woman several months after she had become pregnant."

"Did you have a guess about the father? Did boys come here to pick her up for dates?"

"Some did."

"Did they come by car?"

"Only one that I remember. He had a nice black car with a yellow number plate."

Thuy looks confused. "Do you mean green?"

At this point Hien interrupts. "No, I don't think so. Yellow makes sense. The green plates were for contractors. The yellow ones were for diplomats."

There is stunned silence.

* * * * * * * * * * *

The ride to the hamlet is taking longer than I have expected. But as time passes, and I know we are getting closer, I am seized by anxiety. More than any other place in Việtnam, this one, I feel, will reveal the core of my father to me. Everything that would explain the enigma of this man who so loved me but who had been able to be demanding and distant, will be found here. But the first thing I discover, as I wander the area at the side of K'Sor Brui, is wholly unexpected: I have been here before. In my dream!

K'Sor Brui senses my confusion, disbelief, fear, wonder. He asks if something is wrong, and I tell him of the dream. He does not laugh or belittle what I say. He nods! "I have been waiting before introducing you to our shaman. Perhaps I should not delay any longer."

I don't know what to say, and actually, I am afraid. I can't now deny that something far beyond my ken and understanding had, by some manipulation of time and space, earlier transported me to this place – a place that I had never been aware of or capable of imagining. Accepting this, combined with the fact that I am standing where my father stood fifty years ago, challenges my certainty of how the world is constructed and ordered. I am in the place where my father had lived major moments of his war, where, it now settles on me, he changed, from who he had been for the first twenty-one years of his life, to whom he became forever after that – the man I knew as my father. I am, in the place where, actually, he grew up.

K'Sor Brui has begun to walk on, but I have remained still. He looks back and sees, I am sure, the impact on me of this place and this moment. He comes and puts his arm around my shoulders. It is an intimate gesture to which I have no right, other than as my father's son. He wears a nostalgic smile as he waves with his free hand and says, "This is where we lived together, where we faced *everything* together." His voice is thick with emotion. He is remembering, and perhaps reliving, those irreplaceable days and challenges, shared with my father, when they were both so young, new to each other and so much lay ahead.

We walk through the hamlet. I count nine longhouses of varying dimensions. To my eye, the shortest runs to just over thirty feet. The longest appears to reach one hundred feet. Each house is elevated about five feet above the ground and sits on stout logs of more than two feet in diameter. The floors are log, the walls are made of bamboo. The roofs, which rise to a ridge some ten feet above the interior floor, are thatch laid over bamboo. Inside there are carvings on a cornice and on columns arranged near the entry and at a point where one section of the house is separated from another. Each building is arranged on a north-south axis and has a front entrance for men and a back entrance used by women. Notched hardwood planks, angled from the ground to the raised deck of the longhouse serve as ladders for entry. Each plank extends above the deck and has carvings at its top area. I am amused to see that in addition to a crescent moon and stars, there are also two breasts in carved relief.

K'Sor Brui watches me as I take all this in. He must see my reaction to the breasts because he chuckles and says, "Your father was surprised by that too. Originally, only the women's ladder bore that marking. Later, it began to appear sometimes on both the front and back ladder." When I continue to grin, he begins my education to Rhadé culture in earnest. "Women are very important in our society. For you westerners, families follow the line of the father. We are what you call, 'matrilineal'." He laughs out loud. "That is what your father called one of my 'fancy words'. When I first used it to him, he gave me a funny look and asked where I had heard it. I told him, from one of the anthropologists who had been coming to our hamlet since 1956."

He goes on and explains that descent is traced through the female line and that all property is controlled by the women and inherited from them. I have known nothing about any of this, although K'Sor Brui speaks as if he thinks my father would have told me. I don't say anything, but I am reminded that my father, at some point, just stopped speaking of his memories, when he saw I was not very interested in listening to him. In the presence of K'Sor Brui, and in this place, I feel again how disrespectful I had been. I promise myself henceforth to pay my father the honor owed him by his son and to which he had so much right.

We walk in the direction of a house that is distinctly different from all the others. It stands on stilts, perhaps eight feet above the ground. It has an unusual, sweeping, trapezoidal roof that is covered with woven matting rather than thatch and that rises to a total height of perhaps twenty feet. It stands at one edge of a large open area that has a stout pole fixed in its center. As we head for the house, a man emerges and nimbly descends the access plank. He smiles at K'Sor Brui and then leans forward to peer at me. K'Sor Brui has stopped us to wait for the man to approach. By the time he is just a few feet away, he is squinting at me intently. He is very old, wizened, but surprisingly spry. He stands nodding as he examines me. He reaches up and touches my face, feeling, with calloused fingers, its hollows and prominences. He says something in Rhadé and tears come to his eyes. I look to K'Sor Brui. He smiles at me. "This is our shaman, Y'Chorn. He says, 'You have come back'."

I don't know what I expected to hear. Surely not that. But I understand immediately what is going on, and I am struck physically weak by what my resemblance to my father has prompted. Y'Chorn continues his probing. He has passed his hand over the top of my head and touches the back of my neck gently. He then brushes a hand across my shoulders and, with one hand on each side of me, squeezes my arms at the top and then moves down their length to my hands. He takes each, in turn, in one of his and examines it carefully, tracing a finger across the various lines. When he finishes, he has tears in his eyes, as, unaccountably, do I. He steps back and nods. "You have come back," he says again.

I can hardly speak. I am choked up. I look to K'Sor Brui. He tells me, "Y'Chorn always said your father was one of us who had come to our years from generations past. He called him, 'Y'Keo', and insisted he would never leave us; that he was *dhut*, special. Much later, when your father knew our language better and understood our ideas, he said the word meant, 'charismatic'. He educated your father in our ways, traditions and beliefs and said he was, *khun hui*, destined for greatness, destined to lead us when the time came. He cried by himself when your father at last did leave."

Now, I am crying. I want to say something, to make things right, to apologize, but, how can I? What can I say? Coming from me, anything would be useless, meaningless. I say this to K'Sor Brui. "No," he tells me. "For him, you *are* your father, simply one generation forward."

This takes my breath away. I am shaken by the depth of emotion this old man felt – still feels – for my father. It is all incomprehensible to me. My father was…my father, not the reincarnation of a mountain tribesman from centuries past. I was – am--incapable of seeing him, knowing him or understanding him as such. But this man can see him in no other way. My father, to me, was a demanding, sometimes remote, native-born, highly educated American man. What was there about him that earned him the emotional friendship of so many Việtnamese and brought forth from this tribal shaman, profound emotion and the certainty that he was actually Rhadé?

When I share this question later with Mr. Nam, he says, "Exactly. Finally you have reached it. Finding the answer to that is why you are here."

In this moment, however, I know I must say something. I tell K'Sor Brui, "I am humbled and deeply sorry my father left. From his journals, I know what you did for him. I know he loved you; that he did not *want* to leave."

K'Sor Brui smiles. "I remember him writing in those books. He had to explain to me what they were. They survived him. He said they would."

Y'Chorn has been listening intently to our conversation. It is almost as if he understands. He interrupts. There is a quick exchange with K'Sor Brui who then translates for me. "Y'Chorn says you should not apologize. At first, he did not see things fully, but once your father had gone, he understood that he, your father, Y'Keo, was obeying Yang Rong, our leading spirit; that another would come. That 'other', he now knows, is you. That is why you are here."

Everything stops for me. Before my trip, I would have laughed off such a thought and such a possibility. But now, I don't. I am like the man who mutters, "This can't be," exactly because he feels the chilling certainty that, indeed, it *can*.

The mood is broken when Sénac, who has been showing Mr. Nam and Phùng around, comes to join us. It is almost noon. K'Sor Brui says he has planned for us to take lunch in the hamlet. He tells Sénac that he wants us to eat outside and asks him to let the women know. While we wait for the meal, we continue to stroll around the hamlet and its surrounding fields where the tribe grows vegetables and upland rice. Other staples include potatoes and cassava. The tribe also raises livestock: pigs, chickens, dogs and water buffalo. I begin, very slowly, to develop a sense of the place. I see a self-contained society that appears content to live on its land as, apparently, it has done for long years reaching back well over a century. I have a great deal to learn.

After lunch, Mr. Nam pulls me aside and offers a suggestion. "I think it is important for you to spend more than just a few hours here. Phùng and I can return to the city. I am not pressed to go back to Saigon, and you can stay here for a few days. I am sure that K'Sor Brui would drive you back to Banmethuot. If he does not have the time, we can plan for me to pick you up."

I have been thinking about asking permission to spend the night, but Mr. Nam's idea of a few days would surely be better. Sénac is with me now, while his father is discussing something with Y'Chorn. I can see them off by Y'Chorn's house, and I am amused watching the old man's animated quirks and gestures as he speaks. If he is indeed, "the village wise man," he does not present himself as if he bears the weight of the world and of wisdom on his shoulders. There is a certain lightness to him. I might even describe it as "charm."

Sénac watches me and tunes in on my thought. "He is a funny old man. My father does not like me to say that, and

I respect Y'Chorn for his knowledge and skills, but he does have odd ways."

"How did he come to be a shaman? I am guessing, but I don't think there is anyone here older than he or who would have been in the village when he took on the position."

"No, he is the oldest, but a person does not, as you say, 'take on' the position. Being the shaman is a serious matter. I will tell you, that we, our people, have been here in these mountains on this land for a very long time – much longer than the histories of many of the countries of your side of the world."

I give Sénac a look. It never occurred to me that he had a concept or knowledge of the Western world and its history. He seems to understand my thought. "For a very long time, my people – the tribal peoples, Jarai, Bahnar, Koho, Mnong, Sedang – they have lived in these mountains. There are stories about how we/they got here, but there is no clear history. I am lucky. By the time I was born, the tribes had been exposed, not only to the Việtnamese, but also to the French, who allowed us to have schooling. In my youth, school was readily open to tribal people. Because my father was a senator, he made sure to care for my education."

I am intrigued. "So you went to French school?"

"I should have gone to Việtnamese school. The government does not like us. They are even afraid of us. Many years ago, my father and others led a rebellion against the Việtnamese because they wanted to steal our land and kill us all. During the war, the Việtnamese were under pressure from the Americans to treat us better. They knew we could be useful in fighting the communists, so we were allowed to attend Việtnamese schools. But I went to French school. My father did not want me to learn lies about us from Việtnamese teachers."

"I see, but you had started to talk about being a shaman and living in these mountains for longer than anyone is sure of."

"Yes. Our elders tell stories which have been told again and again about our coming to these mountains. We believe these stories, although we cannot prove them, and we know that they have changed in the telling over so many centuries. But the basics are that we made a great journey from our original place to arrive here. We met many dangers and difficulties, and we overcame them. But we did not do that by ourselves. We had help from our primary spirit, Yang Rong. Over great expanses of time, we developed beliefs about rocks with spirits and forests with souls and woodlands inhabited by invisible imps.

I nod, listening carefully. I can understand this. It seems to me to be universal in primitive societies all over the world. Sénac smiles. I think he is pleased that I am paying close and quiet attention.

"We tried to understand the character of these spirits – even though, if you look at this today, you will say that we *created* these spirits. To us, that is not true. The spirits showed themselves to us, spoke to us – or to some of us. The people they spoke to helped us to understand them and how to keep on their good side."

"And Y'Chorn is one of these people?"

"Yes!" Sénac says this with great emphasis and apparent pleasure that I am following his thought. "The people who understand the spirits are special. Through their abilities to heal the sick, predict the weather, see into the future and past, influence events or the actions of others, and even exit their bodies, they give us-- a sense of security and solidarity. The shaman is one of these people. He helps us ward off sickness by prescribing and leading sacrifices. He harmonizes us with the spirits to assure the success of plantings and harvestings and the protection of our rice seed and stored harvests. He assures plentiful rainfall and a good growing season. He interprets signs to foretell future events, and he smooths the anger of the spirits if taboos are broken .We say these people are, 'pojau'. Y'Chorn is pojau."

I nod my understanding, but what he says next, without irony or affect, freezes me. "Your father was pojau, and – Y'Chorn belives – you are too!"

* * * * * * * * * * * *

JJ sits alone in his hotel room, idly fingering the remaining scraps of the file he had brought to Việtnam with such determination and hope. He is seated at a small desk. A mirror hangs on the wall in front of him. When he looks up for a moment, he catches sight of himself. He is saddened, but not surprised, by what he sees. It's the same disappointed, out-of-balance misfit he has seen all his life. He takes a deep breath and refuses to give in to the self-pity that has shadowed him since the end of this day with his new friends. He reflects. It is only their concern and kindness that stiffen his backbone and allow him to see the least glimmer of good in himself. If they care about him, and they surely seem to, there may be hope for him.

Thuy, Binh and Thien dropped him off two hours ago. They will return in just over thirty minutes to join him for dinner and plan next steps. The truth is, he has no idea at all what those might be. The big blow of the day for him was that the only real lead they got hinted that his mother's suitor might have been a diplomat. But he has no memory of her ever mentioning involvement with the diplomatic community. He thinks about that and decides that socializing on the diplomatic party circuit might have been normal for an attractive, young Eurasian girl in those days – surely not something to be spoken of exceptionally. The thought cheers him.

He steps out of the elevator and his eye is drawn to the strikingly beautiful silhouette of a Việtnamese girl a distance away, near the lobby entrance. He can see her from the back only. He angles towards her, hoping she does not leave before he can get a glimpse of her face. He is glad to have taken special care with his own appearance tonight. At least, if she notices him at all, it may be with a kind eye. All this is unusual for him. He is not 5'7" tall and has never had success with women. Indeed, he knows his flaws and weak points and has essentially given up hope of finding a wife. But tonight he has made a particular effort because he nurtures the dream that Thuy, who has been so very kind to him during the day, may, just by chance, have some small spark of feeling for him.

As he heads towards the girl, Binh and Thien appear at the hotel entry. They spot him and wave enthusiastically. At this, the striking girl turns in his direction. It is Thuy. His heart stops. She gives him a luminous smile. She is utterly beautiful in her evening-quality Việtnamese dress. He is so stricken that he stumbles slightly. He gives them all a smile. Binh and Thien shake hands with him warmly. Thuy leans forward and kisses him on either cheek in the French manner, which still survives in Việtnam, even after so many years of independence and communist rule. She can tell that he has tried to groom himself carefully. There is even a whiff of after shave. She holds him at arm's length and says, "Dẹp giai hóa." Binh and Thien chuckle and say, "Yes, yes, very handsome boy!"

JJ doesn't know that the Việtnamese often say this, with a slight undertone of good-natured jest, when they can see a man has made a special effort at dress or grooming. Even if he did know, he wouldn't care. The words have come from Thuy. They feed the very small flame of hope he holds for developing a relationship with her. He glows.

Thuy says, "We have planned a special dinner. You deserve it after the hard day we have had. Binh even borrowed a car. We are going outside of Hô Chí Minh City to a restaurant in Gia Dinh. You have never had anything like their food before."

They head over to Phan Thanh Giản street and follow it north as it leaves the city and joins the Bien Hoa highway. JJ is almost stunned by the heavy traffic that pours along the road. He had little idea of what to expect in Việtnam, but he surely did not anticipate this. He tries to remember if his mother ever described what Saigon was like when she lived there.

He draws a blank. The few photos he had happened on in her personal effects had the feel of the old sepia prints of late nineteenth and early twentieth century Australia. He never bothered to study them, but he does tell his friends, "My Mum had some pictures of the Saigon of her time. I don't think it was anything like this."

Thuy says, "We were all born well after those war years, so we don't know much about that time either. Actually, we were born even after the years of reeducation camps, boat-people-escapes and harsh communist repression. Our parents tell us that we are lucky to live in today's dynamic, modern Việtnam. But the place we are taking you gets us away from the rush of these days. It's a restaurant that serves game killed in our forests and jungles. It was around during the American war and even during the years of French control here."

They exit the highway just north of Thủ Đức and proceed down a road that eventually turns into a laterite track through a forested area. A spur off of this leads them to an outdoor restaurant that consists of several dining areas each set beneath an open-sided thatched-roof structure. Dim bulbs strung from thin, black wire provide the light. JJ is thrilled. He thinks he is, at last, seeing the real Việtnam.

The menu is posted on a chalkboard, and JJ has no idea of what is on offer. Thuy tells him, "The first thing on the list over there is porcupine. Then there is tiger paw, water buffalo steak, weasel and rhinoceros." She smiles as JJ blanches at the thought of eating any of this. She continues, "There are also a few kinds of snake and even snake wine."

That does it for JJ. He believes that these are real dishes, but he also can see that his three friends are watching his reaction happily. "No diced elephant foot or chopped trunk?" he asks with a grin.

"Oh, yes," says Binh. "Thuy loves elephants and doesn't like to think of their being killed for food, so she leaves that off her list. But if you want it, you can get it here."

"Aw, no thanks. I think I'll just have a hamburger."

They all laugh, but when dinner comes, it does indeed include porcupine, water buffalo steak, a stewed snake dish and a bottle of rice wine in which floats a very nasty looking serpent. JJ takes the bottle and shakes it. "Dead?" he asks. The snake twists in the currents he has induced in the bottle. "Crikey. Where's my hamburger and beer?"

As the dinner progresses, Thuy says, "Did we learn anything useful today?"

"I don't think so. I mean, that diplomat guy could have been anybody. Just a friend giving her a lift, maybe."

"It didn't sound like that," says Binh.

Thien adds, "I agree. I think there is something useful there."

JJ says, "Even if that's true, how would we ever find out who he is or was. That's a very cold trail to pick up after all these years."

Thuy steps in. "But isn't that true of anyone now? When we began the day, I was thinking that we might find someone who could say, 'Yes, I saw her with this one foreigner several times,' or, 'She used to visit a man at this house,' but even her aunt could not say that. I agree that our job is not easy, but I think we have to try until we exhaust all chances. That's why you came here, right JJ?"

JJ nods. For a moment, he can't speak because Thuy has said, "our job." He is so thrilled that he almost doesn't care if they ever learn anything, so long as he can be with her while they keep searching.

The conversation turns to next steps. JJ tells them that he has wracked his brain in an effort to remember if anything in the papers he lost would have pointed them in a productive direction. "I really don't think so. I mean now that we have done some actual leg work, you know, searching on the ground, I am afraid that I never had much truly useful information."

Everyone goes quiet. Binh, Thien and Thuy, eye each other around the table. They have thrown themselves into this effort, and now they are hearing that it might have been doomed from the start. JJ senses this. He is deeply embarrassed. He has grown used to people writing him off, but these three haven't. And he doesn't want even to risk that from them. Against all reason, they have been more friends to him than almost anyone else he can think of – ever.

It is Thuy who once again lifts his spirits. "Look, we all understand that coming here and doing this search maybe wasn't even an actual choice or decision for you. It was just something you had to do, even if you had no clues. I have had a growing sense today, and I think Binh and Thien have also, that you need this answer to add a missing piece to understanding who you are." She looks at the men. They nod.

JJ feels her comment in his heart. He realizes that even he did not know this. He does now, and all he wants at the moment is to be grateful to these three people, to be in their company where he is understood and respected. Sadly, it is Thuy who lets him know that might not happen. "We have at least one card left to play before JJ decides he has reached an end. We will go to see the two journalists who wrote about those days and who are still alive."

* * * * * * * * * * *

K'Sor Brui has joined us. "Mr. Nam says you are thinking of staying here for a few days."

"Yes. I would like to get a much better idea of life in the hamlet, how your people live. It seems so different from what I have learned of the Việtnamese."

"It is very different. I have mentioned to Y'Chorn the idea of your staying. He is excited by the thought, but he is quiet when I say you will stay for a few days. That is his way when he disagrees."

"Does he want me to stay longer?"

"Yes. He does not say it, but in his way, he *insists*."

I draw a breath. This is a delicate moment for me. K'Sor Brui senses my discomfort. I worry that I will say something insulting. I wonder how my father handled awkward situations here in his time. K'Sor Brui is silent. Finally, I say, "I think you and Y'Chorn hope I am the same person as my father was. Sénac has even told me that Y'Chorn thinks I am pojau."

K'Sor Brui breaks into a smile. "And you are afraid you will disappoint us, and maybe fail your father's memory in doing so."

I am surprised. He understands perfectly. "Yes."

He smiles again. "You will not disappoint us. Y'Chorn is a funny old man, but he is pojau. He does not guess at things. He understands them, sees them, if that is easier for you to grasp. The truth is that I was not in Banmethuot by accident. Y'Chorn asked me to go. He was certain that you, Y'Keo's son, would be there. He even 'knew' where you would be. And, of course, he would not expect – and does not think – that you are or can ever be the same man as your father."

He pauses for a moment, then says, "Y'Chorn is only one in our centuries of pojau. No two of them have ever been the same. Each is different, of course, and we recognize that as the wisdom of Yang Rong. Each brings unique ways of carrying the gift he was granted. Y'Chorn knows you are not your father, but he knows too that you are pojau. He is certain that it is you who will follow him when he dies."

There is nothing I can say. After a long silence, K'Sor Brui continues. "He touched you because that helps him to read you. Of course, he could see who you are – you do look very much like your father. But outward appearances have their limits. Y'Chorn is one of the rare people who can read the inner man. What he read in you is confusion, uncertainty, a desire to 'find' your father here, fear that who you find will not be who you have always thought your father was. Further, he read fear that you will not recognize the man you encounter here, that you will have to admit you can never be what he was, that you will have to leave us, feeling unworthy of him and forever after estranged. Y'Chorn, I will say it this way, sees that you will not leave us – that your place, prepared for you by your father, is here."

K'Sor Brui nods to me, touches my shoulder gently and walks back toward Y'Chorn's house. I am left standing alone by the pole at the middle of the large open expanse in front of Y'Chorn's home. I actually turn in a circle trying to find my emotional balance. After a minute or so, a tribal girl comes and offers her hand. I take it, and she leads me to a low wooden bench. She gestures. I sit, and she sits next to me. Soon, other young women come to join us. A few speak English. They are excited to have me visiting and want to practice their English. I smile and ask each her name and what she does. Two are married and mothers. The other two, still single, are students. One is in lycée. The other is studying in a course operated by Catholic Charities that teaches home economics, hygiene and childcare.

Soon other women come to join us. A few are leading young children, perhaps no more than two or three years old. Some of the others carry an infant on their hips. I ask about what they do. They all work hard, farming, weaving, cooking, tending chickens and even water buffalo, caring for the children, keeping house. They are curious about me, about where I came from, why I am here, do I know Y'Chorn, what is my job, do I have a wife. I tell them I am a lawyer from America. Several nod, but others do not seem to know where that is. There is a brief discussion in Rhadé in which, it seems, the older ones explain what and where America is. Eyes grow wide and, evidently, the interest in me grows. Do I have a wife? They ask again, amid giggles, shy eye-rolls and modest downward glances. But the modesty is only momentary. All eyes are on me. No, I don't have a wife. There are immediate smiles, nods, veiled glances, and many sad head-shakes. The girls chatter among themselves until one says that they are all sorry I have no woman to care for me. I say that in America it is not unusual for a man to be unmarried until he is thirty years old or more. The girls look sad. How can that be?

I start to answer, but one girl, she is perhaps sixteen, is arguing briefly with several of the others. Then there is silence. The group gives her a challenging look. For a moment, she is clearly embarrassed. Then, having gathered her courage, she tells me in hesitant English, "If you stay here, a lady will choose you. You won't have to be alone." She blushes slightly. The others are clearly delighted with the conversation. I am charmed by them all.

With smiles and giggles and shy glances, the group disperses. The girl who reassured me about a wife, tells me apologetically that they must prepare for evening. I watch them go, sad that the interlude is at an end. I sit alone feeling almost at home but also a bit lonely, so much had the women provided warm company. I begin to reflect on them and on the possibility that I have so far determinedly refused to consider: that I could ever make my life here. I drift into a reverie. I don't know how long I have been sitting like this, but suddenly I am aware of K'Sor Brui sitting beside me. He hands me a heavy, black-cotton shirt. It is open from the neck for about six inches. The opening can be closed with tiny, domed gold buttons that are affixed to a swath of red that runs the length of the opening and extends for perhaps three inches on either side of it. The shirt is a twin of the one I found in my father's closet. "Put this on, the sun is going down soon, and it will get cold."

I look around for Mr. Nam and Phùng. Surely, I have had no right to forget the time and keep them here so late. K'Sor Brui says, "I have asked Mr. Nam if he would like to stay the night with us. He and his grandson will go back to Banmethuot. If you wish to stay with us, they will return for you in the morning."

"I would like to stay."

Mr. Nam and I discuss how to handle things. He tells me not to worry. He will come back in the morning and then, if I wish to stay longer, he and Phùng can return to the city. He gives me an encouraging look, as if he has already understood that I may need more time here than just overnight. We agree on a plan. K'Sor Brui, who has given us privacy, now sees us look in his direction. He comes over.

"Have you made plans?"

Mr. Nam smiles at his former student. "Yes. Take good care of him. I have begun to think of him as *my* son. I will see you tomorrow, early." He shakes hands with K'Sor Brui and then turns towards me. He looks at me for a long moment. There is a warmth in his gaze. He shakes my hand, gives my shoulder a gentle squeeze and turns to leave.

K'Sor Brui gestures towards one of the longhouses. As we walk towards it he tells me, "This is where my family lives. You are welcome to stay with us. Y'Chorn may want you to stay in his house. If you stay with me, you will sleep on a bachelor's bed. If you stay with Y'Chorn, you may be invited to sleep on the Emperor's bed."

I give him a puzzled look. "I thought I would sleep on the floor, if that is normal."

"It is, but you, at least now, are not a *normal* visitor. If you stay, even one night, you must begin to learn about us." I nod.

We have reached his longhouse. It looks to be almost 100 feet in length. He gestures that I should climb the notched "stair". I do so and wait on the small "porch" while he climbs up. We enter the building. I find myself in a room that is perhaps ten feet deep and fifteen feet wide. There is a carved vertical column on one side that shows birds and an elephant. Where the high-ridged roof slopes down to join the walls, there is a beam carved with shapes and animals. "This part of the house is called a 'gah'. It is our," he hesitates seeking a word, "*salon*. The next space, just beyond this, is bigger. It is our bedroom...sleeping area."

"So that's where I will find the bachelor's bed?"

"Sometimes. Sometimes it is in a separate bedroom in the longhouse. A young man will sleep on that bed before his marriage. Maybe it is a test, to prove his respect or confirm his devotion. The bed is very narrow and made of hardwood."

"But I am not engaged to anyone."

He smiles with a twinkle in his eye. "Yes, but someday you will be." I give him a doubtful look. "Besides," he says, "the Emperor's bed is made of hardwood from our forests too, in case you are thinking it might be soft." He raises his eyebrows and gives a small laugh. I cannot resist and laugh with him. He continues, "It is a very old tradition. Each village has an Emperor's bed for the emperor himself if he visits. I have not heard that any ever has, but we continue the tradition, offering the bed to the most special guests only. After several months, your father was offered the bed."

"Whose decision is it to offer the bed?"

"That is hard to say, exactly. The women control the activity in the hamlet, and they have the greatest influence. But no one would make such a decision without Y'Chorn's agreement. But he would not approve the decision without a clear sense that it was acceptable to the women."

"It's complicated," I say.

"Not really. An understanding emerges over time."

The rest of the building consists of several of these gah-plus-sleeping areas in linear succession. K'Sor Brui explains that all the families descended from a mother's line live in one house. Each time a young woman of the line marries, the house is expanded by one "unit" (gah, plus sleeping area) to accommodate her new husband and family. Sénac, having married a woman of a maternal line different from K'Sor

Brui, lives in a different longhouse. Mischievous again, he says, "Perhaps you have already chosen your longhouse from among those that were clearly on offer when you spoke with the women today."

I am pretty sure he is making an idle joke, but if I am going to spend time here, I had better understand what my "friendly" behavior might suggest. I ask him about this. He replies, again with a gentle grin, "Don't worry. The woman will choose you, whether or not you have given her any signals!"

I tell him, "That is not a relief."

"Your father survived, and he was widely admired."

"Point taken," I tell him.

After dinner, which we have taken in the longhouse, we go outside to the open assembly area. The temperature has dropped sharply. It's cold. I am grateful for the shirt K'Sor Brui has given me. A large fire burns in the middle of the assembly circle. The tribal men sit in small groups on the ground along the circle's perimeter. Each group is clustered around a large earthen jar about thirty inches high and eighteen inches across at its widest point. The jar tapers to a base of twelve inches, the same diameter as its mouth. A long reed, threaded through a wood lath that has been wedged across the jar's opening, descends into its contents, a strong rice wine. Women are in the circle singing and dancing. Children, many of them bare bottomed, race everywhere. The tribe's livestock, chickens, pigs, dogs and ducks, scuttles around. Water buffalo lounge near the longhouses. It is a communal scene, as old as human settlement.

Already tired from the day, I am almost hypnotized by the dancing glow of the fire and the mingled rhythms of the women's singing and the men's droning voices. I have a moment in which I feel separated from myself and understand that this scene is not a show. It is reality, as the tribe lives it. I can see my father sitting in the same assemblage, fifty years in the past. I am absorbed into the understanding that tonight I will actually relive in his stead, these tribal, ritual moments and that he may sit beside in spirit form experiencing again what he so loved. I hear Y'Chorn tell me, "You have come back." Of course I have.

K'Sor Brui and I sit, joining Sénac, who offers me the drinking reed from his group's jar. I accept. I know the brew will be strong. I caution myself to drink little, but my hosts imbibe in deep, prolonged draughts. Instruction from Sénac confirms that the same is required of me. He points to a small, notched reed floating vertically in the wine and tells me to drink. He will watch the float drop with the level of the wine and indicate when I am to stop drinking. Until I get that signal, I must keep my mouth on the reed and drink. I will have to fight for air, breathing through my nose as I draw the liquid upwards – like siphoning gas.

Even with the family and community aspect of things, for the men, this is a drinking party. They are joking, challenging one another, and amicably competing to see who can drink more and stand it better. They are now all waiting for me to plunge ahead and, I am sure, get royally buzzed. I smile at them, make a face, shake myself as if I am greatly afraid. They laugh. Some make faces to show that the brew is sour to them also. All urge me on. I take a deep, theatrical breath and begin.

The wine is bitter, powerful, and instantly intoxicating. The fact that I am fighting for air as I drink, heightens this effect. The men are watching me, smiling, clapping in rhythm and laughing as they see me struggle to complete the draught expected of me. I mug a bit as if I am having more trouble than I actually am. A few yell and gesture that I must finish properly. Sénac gives me no quarter. When he finally taps my shoulder, I am dizzy. The reed-float has dropped considerably. In a jar of this size, that indicates I have imbibed a lot. I am already mildly drunk. Enjoying the camaraderie, I exaggerate the extent of my intoxication. One man reaches to take the reed from me and indicates that I should watch him to see how a real pro does things. Though seated, I execute an exaggerated, deferential bow and hand him the reed. There are smiles, good natured cheers and approving murmurs from the men. I breathe deeply and, silently within myself, thank Yang Rong, for the cold night air.

As the evening goes on, there is singing, group dancing and story-telling. Sénac and his father take turns translating for me. The stories are of the hunt, of battles fought in the distant past against other tribes, of hardships overcome in the tribe's migration into these mountains (they call them, "the long mountains") and of the repeated intervention of their great spirit, Yang Rong, to save, guide and protect them. Like the tribesmen, I am touched by the stories and feel their impact strongly. I am enthralled and more than a bit moved.

After several hours, when the women have withdrawn to the longhouses with the children and all the men are subdued and groggy with drink, Y'Chorn walks to the pole at the center of the circle. All goes quiet. The sounds of night are suddenly evident. With the others, I lapse into anticipation. The noise of the wind and the murmurs of the forest are ghostly, eerie. I feel spirits gathering, and I am frightened, afraid of being transported to a reality I have not before considered and never experienced.

Y'Chorn begins to speak, his voice little more than a whisper. Immediately, everyone turns and looks at me. Y'Chorn stops. I glance at K'Sor Brui, but his gaze has shifted from me to Y'Chorn. Long, silent seconds pass, and, under no conscious decision of my own, I find myself standing near the middle of the circle. Y'Chorn smiles. He nods emphatically, as if I have been a good boy. The men chorus approval. Y'Chorn then, in a loud, strong voice – that I doubted him capable of at his age – makes a declaration and extends his arm as if showing me off. Sénac whispers a rapid translation, "This is Y'Keo's son. He has come back to us." I shiver.

The sounds of approval grow louder. Several old men come forward to touch me, to feel the planes of my face as Y'Chorn had done earlier in the day. Like him, they have tears in their eyes. I find now that I do also. Y'Chorn nods and walks towards his home. The evening is over.

K'Sor Brui waits as the men present pass by, nod and touch me. When all have departed, he ushers me towards his longhouse and assists me, mesmerized and tipsy as I am, to climb the entry ladder. Inside, he leads me to a sleeping room where several young men doze fitfully. Against one wall, low to the floor, is a long, narrow bench with a slightly raised back in the manner of a sofa. I look at it and understand. "The bachelor's bed," I say.

K'Sor Brui, grins broadly. "Sleep well," he tells me and withdraws to his own quarters.

I do not undress. Despite the glowing coals in a brazier, the room is cold, and I am deeply tired. I settle myself onto the hard, narrow bed. Groggy and as drunk as I recall being after my first ever night of drinking heavily, I try to find a comfortable position. I fail. I lie on the verge of sleep but cannot still my mind as the extraordinary events of this day loop through it. At length, I succumb as my head echoes with, "Y'Keo's son," and, "He has come back to us."

I dream actively and vividly. In the dream, it's as if parts of me are separating. I continue to know I am me, but I am hovering alongside of my body. I become a bird, and I fly over all the long mountains. I am able to view the history of the tribe going back into the mists of time. I see the Rhadé and also all the other tribes. I meet their shamans, and I learn that all the wizards, witches, warlocks and witch doctors, shamans and sorcerers, conjurers and clairvoyants, wherever they might be or may have come from, trace their roots to the same source the stream of magic and mystery that courses beneath the surface of the world – primitive or modern. Wherever they were, whatever they were, the "pojau" were, at bottom, sensitives, able to communicate with that stream of magic through a rip in the veil that shields it from normal men.

It is an antic dream. I cannot call it, "prophetic." I settle on a more disturbing term, "clairvoyant." The ramifications of this are not lost on me, neither as I dream nor as I am awakened by the sun glinting through gaps in the longhouse wall. I ache from the bed, am groggy and a bit hung over, but I am sure of two things: Y'Chorn and his visions, knowledge, shamanic practices and magic are real, and, I no longer believe my life-long certainties about how the world is constructed. I understand that modern, "more advanced," cultures have done nothing but invent their religions and mythologies so they do not have to bear looking upon what men had in millennia past bravely confronted: the naked face of antic magic. I believe it possible that everything about me--my birth, my life, my father's life and the call I have felt to come to Việtnam and to this hamlet--was all put in motion, generations--and perhaps eons--ago. The masterwork of forces Y'Chorn reads and that I, now, with fear but also a certain joy, believe may actually lie behind the order of all life.

* * * * * * * * * * *

JJ has kept up a brave façade during their exotic dinner. He has enjoyed the food, the chance to get outside of the city and especially the opportunity to be with Thuy. The sole downer for him has been the prospect that if his search ends, Thuy will no longer be accessible to him. Until she essentially said as much, he did not realize how deeply attached to her – enamored of her, actually – he had become. Now, as they head back to town, he is searching his mind for a way to prolong the evening.

"I really don't know how to thank you all for your help and your interest in my problem. I never expected to meet people like you, people who would care about me so much." He stops, hoping that Thuy will use the opening to offer him kind words and lift his spirits. But it is Binh who replies.

"Thien and I were so very sorry to see what happened to you on the street. We just thought that we can't let a foreign visitor try to deal with something like that alone. And then, we have found out that you are a very nice man. Also, you give us the chance to speak English, and that is important for us. So, in a way, we should thank you too."

JJ nods, smiles, but does not reply immediately. Perhaps a bit more silence will allow Thuy to speak up. She says nothing, so JJ plays his next card. "I have an idea. Why don't we go to that club near my hotel and have a drink, a nightcap? There's maybe a new English word for you. He pauses to explain, but no one asks. The place has music too. I think I have heard Việtnamese songs when I walk by. What do you say? If you want, you can even dance."

The friends look at one another. Finally Thien says, I would like that. I think Thuy and Binh would too, but it's getting a little late. Even though we're going to be with you in the morning, each of us has to get to the office early so we can have our permission to take time off." The others nod.

Thuy can see JJ's disappointment, but she – gently-- drives a final stake into the idea. "We really would like to, but Thien is right. Actually, I'm going to have to ask you to let us go on quickly. I have some responsibilities at home before I go to bed."

They reach the hotel. JJ gets out of the car. The others do not Thien, behind the wheel, says, "Excuse us now. We'll be here by 9:30 tomorrow morning." Binh nods, Thuy blows him a very friendly kiss, and they leave.

At 9:30 the next morning, they meet once again at JJ's hotel. Each has gone to work and requested time off to help a foreign friend. Each request is granted, but the three had agreed to meet JJ regardless of receiving permission to be absent. They have become invested in his search, perhaps because their education has so conscientiously fed them one-sided information about the "American War" and the people who fought it on the losing side. Almost fifty years after the fall of Saigon, young Việtnamese have arrived at a point where they no longer care about being communists or a communist country.

Binh has been allowed the use of his borrowed car for an additional day. This is a good thing, as they have a distance to travel. By 11:00 AM they pull up in front of an attractive old villa in what used to be the Thủ Đức university village. Thien rings the bell by the gate. An elderly lady admits them and shows them to a large study that has floor-to-ceiling bookcases on two walls and five-drawer filing cabinets on another. A small, very old Việtnamese man sits behind a huge desk with a stack of old, yellowing newspapers by his right hand. He stands and offers them a smile. He has a full head of white hair. A thick moustache that turns down at the ends and frames his mouth makes him look a bit like a walrus. He gestures to a group of visitor chairs before his desk. "Please sit. I am Nguyễn Phu Vinh." Nodding at the papers on his desk, he adds, "I wrote under the name of Phi Bang."

The visitors introduce themselves, and Thuy explains why they have come. Phi Bang nods. "Yes, I understood that from our phone call. I am very happy to meet you all." He looks at JJ. "I am afraid, however, that I may not be of much use. I have looked through my files and old articles, and I have even discussed this with Qui, uh, Tran Van Qui, the other journalist, you told me, Miss, that you hoped to see also. Qui will be here shortly. I thought having both of us in one place would save you time and also that between us we might think of something we would have missed alone."

JJ thanks him for this thoughtful consideration and says, "My mum would never tell me who my father was. Through bits of conversation between her and her best friend – she died before my mum – I got the idea that my father lived in Việtnam for many years and was an important foreigner. Really, that's all I know, except that maybe he spoke Việtnamese."

The conversation is interrupted by Tran Van Qui's arrival. After Phi Bang makes introductions and brings him up to speed on the conversation, he says to JJ, "That should narrow things down a lot, but I am still doubtful. What do you think, Qui?"

"It's something to go on, but even so, there were several Americans, we are talking about Americans, aren't we, who did pretty well in Việtnamese."

"Well," says Thuy, "we did get some information that the man might have been a diplomat."

"How did you learn that?" asks Qui.

"We were told about a man who picked her up at her house in a black car with a yellow number plate. It seems that that color plate was for diplomatic cars."

Qui and Phi Bang exchange a glance.

JJ catches it. "What, what are you thinking?"

The two old men hesitate. Finally, Phi Bang looks at Thuy and says, "Please forgive me if what I say offends you." Thuy nods and smiles. "Back in those war years, Saigon was full of single young, foreign men. Even married men, for that matter, separated from their families by the American government policy of not allowing dependents to be here. Well, men, young or not, want female company. Our young ladies..." Qui has held up his hand. Phi Bang understands. "Yes, and not just our young ladies, are very attractive to foreigners." He looks at JJ for confirmation. JJ glances at Thuy and blushes deeply.

Phi Bang continues quickly, "So our ladies had many opportunities for a romance with an exotic or handsome or powerful foreigner. And they all knew that foreigners had money. For many of them it was either a temptation or simply a chance to have some fun and also to help their families by getting favors from the foreigners. Things like duty-free electronics or Martel cognac or food from the American commissary or free trips to places like Nhatrang and Hue and Dalat by Air America." He pauses.

Qui understands and shoulders the responsibility for saying, "So, it would have been normal for your mother to join this practice of dating a foreigner or even becoming his lover. Sometimes for fun or gifts, but often as a sacrifice for their family – or even for a loved, Việtnamese boyfriend."

The friends look at one another but say nothing. JJ speaks, "And you think my mum did this. That she had one, or maybe several, foreign boyfriends whom she used for whatever reason." It is not a question. The statement hovers and for long moments, looms like an elephant in the room.

Phi Bang says, simply, "Yes."

Silence reigns. Binh and Thien look too scared to speak. Thuy lowers her eyes. She is embarrassed. JJ knows he should feel shamed, but he does not. He has heard his mother speaking of such things to her best friend. He has seen how she transformed herself, cynically, he thinks, into the perfect Aussie wife, and he has gathered enough, over the years, to be almost completely certain that she lured his father to her bed to trap him into marriage. He knows that Qui's speculation is surely true. He knows too that the chance of identifying his real father from any name remembered by these old men and drawn from fifty years past, is a complete non-starter. He just nods.

They are subdued as they ride back to the city. There is not much to say, but Thuy puts the best face possible on the outcome. "We are so sorry that things have come to a blank wall. But you should feel proud that you have made such a complete effort – especially after a beginning that would have discouraged a less determined man."

JJ would love to take her comment as a statement of her admiration for his character, but he knows that it is born, in part at least, of pity. While he is bitterly disappointed by his failure to get the information he sought, he is far more affected by the fact that he must now leave Thuy forever. He rides in silence, trying to imagine a way to declare himself to her that will not put her in a corner or humiliate him. It's no use. All he can think of how desolate he will be without her and when he has to wake up tomorrow morning and know she is in the city but completely inaccessible to him.

With no ulterior motives, he invites his friends to lunch. They accept happily, grateful, no doubt, for the chance to break out of the gloom of the ride. It works. They have a relaxed lunch, such as would be between close friends, and JJ realizes that they have become precisely that. He is thrilled, and for the very first time, he sees himself as having developed a successful relationship with other people. He knows this is an accomplishment that may even obviate the profound need he has felt to discover the identity of his real father. If there is a tradeoff, this is a good one.

As the friends take leave, Thuy asks what JJ will do now. When he says he will go home, she looks sad. "Why not see a little of our country before you go? It would be a shame not to, especially when it is clear that you are beginning to be comfortable with Việtnam."

JJ considers this. "Well, would you all come with me?" The friends plead work and family obligations. "OK," says JJ. "Where do you suggest I go?"

"Easy," says Thien, looking for support to the others. "Go to Huệ, the ancient imperial city. Ride a sampan on the Perfumed River, with a beautiful Huệ girl. They are supposed to be the most beautiful in all of Việtnam. Visit the imperial tombs. See the Huệ citadel. You can't leave Việtnam without seeing Huệ." The others endorse the idea.

JJ says, "Do I have to take the sampan ride?"

They giggle. "Of course, it's tradition. All Việtnamese boys dream of doing that."

JJ looks at Thuy and gathers his courage. "Will you be the girl?"

"It wouldn't be right," she says. "I am not a Huệ girl."

Everyone laughs good naturedly. "OK, where else," asks JJ, hiding his disappointment.

The friends talk and decide, "You should visit our tribal people. How about this. Spend a few days in Banmethuot. It has modern hotels, and you can easily get a tour to a mountain tribe village."

Again JJ agrees and then says, "When I get back, will you all go for a day visit to the beach with me? As a goodbye party."

Binh says, "You mean at Vũng Tàu. Yes, good idea."

They agree on when JJ will return and then take leave of each other. There are genuine smiles, hugs, and not a few tears. As he watches their car pull away, JJ feels better than he has ever felt, and he has not given up on Thuy.

Chapter 21

I have been in the hamlet now for twelve days. I am not an accepted fixture yet, but I am less of a curiosity. The people who speak English or French look for chances to talk with me. They explain their work, introduce me to their children, ask many questions about me, America, my work in the States, my father and even if I am actually Rhadé. At night there is usually some communal activity. In this, I am learning a bit of the tribal dances, building something of a tolerance for "nam bay" (the rice wine) and beginning to get a small view of the tribal version of coquettishness. This last has me slightly off balance.

I am now housed with Y'Chorn, a move which has more than one rationale. When I departed Sénac's house, he asked me if I understood why Y'Chorn had invited me and what that meant. I said Y'Chorn had explained the need to move me because I had "no natural presence in a longhouse." I add my assumption that the proximity to him also would permit him to advance my instruction. Sénac got a look of great amusement on his face and actually shook with his effort at not laughing out loud.

"What?" I ask him. He is struggling too hard with his laughter to answer immediately. I wait, but he continues to shake with suppressed mirth. "WHAT?" I am getting frustrated.

He takes a deep breath. "He means, no natural presence yet." I give him a blank look, and he begins to rock with laughter again. "You will have a *natural presence* when you have been chosen by one of the women."

"I WHAT? You must be – *he* must be – kidding. Things don't happen that fast, and I have no interest in getting married. Even with all the time my father spent here, he did not marry."

"That was different. A different time and situation. As an American with official ties, he could not have become an actual part of us. We could not expect him to marry at that time. We expected him to do so when his situation made him available. You will stay here, follow Y'Chorn when Yang Rong decides, and guide us into the new times that surround us and await us. Of course you will be chosen by a woman."

I must look as stunned as I feel. Whether he actually misunderstands my thinking or is just having fun, he adds, "Do not worry. As a pojau, future tribe leader and successor to Y'Chorn, you are a great value, highly desirable. You will be claimed by one of the best women."

Before I decide that he is not serious in any way and give a joking reply, I pull myself up short. Exactly what did I *think* I was doing here? Going about my days as if I were not a visitor. Living under the shaman's roof and permitting him to teach me. So I nod and say, "I have not been here long enough to be thinking of that. Marriage custom is very different in America."

He smiles. "We know that in your life until now you are not a man of the forest. But we also know, Y'Chorn knows–*is sure*–you will discover this part of yourself." He touches my shoulder gently and leaves me, perhaps so I may reflect.

And I do reflect. I have been charmed by the people, their hamlet, their openness, their clear respect for my father and Y'Chorn's complete certainty that I am something

– someone – who I never, for even an instant, thought of being or thought I could be. I have felt enlightened by the Rhadé view of life and of how the world is structured. I have gotten drunk on local brew by drinking as if I were a fully integrated part of the tribe. I have had an extraordinary dream. I am enthralled by the idea that my father and I are actually an interwoven part of the ancient, mythic and mystical fiber of this tribe. I am further profoundly moved to think – to know, if I am able to believe wholly in Y'Chorn's shamanic wisdom – that the bond between me and my father was forged by magical forces back in the mists of prehistory and that it has survived time, distance, culture and even the animosity I bore my father for so long. Finally, I realize that I have somehow become alienated from/within my own life; that I came here, as Mr. Nam has said, more to discover who *I* am than who my father was; and that in Việtnam and here in this hamlet, I have discovered an ethos that contains all of these answers.

I have to catch my breath. Looked at all at once, these are enervating realizations. I now know that I must live my days here above a current of active evaluation, lest I make a disastrous error that harms not only me but, of more passionate import, this people.

There is still an enormous newness to everything for me, and I am trying just to focus on being here. Sénac and K'Sor Brui have been patiently teaching me the Rhadé language, mostly in the evening, when they and I have finished the day's business. Y'Chorn spends a good deal of time with me, teaching me the tribe's history and traditions. K'Sor Brui is usually my translator, but in recent days, I have made a small breakthrough. Because so much of what Y'Chorn tells me involves the repetition of the same phrases, "in the past," "our forebears," "you will soon feel Yang Rong's presence," I am building a vocabulary, beginning to understand things from context and catching on to the rhythms of Rhadé speech.

Y'Chorn takes me into the forest, walking for hours along tracks that I can hardly distinguish. He talks to me constantly about the trees and the animals we encounter, usually boar and weasels. He says there are tigers but that they hunt at night and are shy during the day. K'Sor Brui is usually with us so he can translate for me. The substance of these excursions is that I must learn to listen to the forest and its denizens. It has a soul and will never fail me if I learn to hear its knowledge. K'Sor Brui often names the trees and other flora that we see. He sometimes says whether a plant is edible. Y'Chorn points out plants and even tree bark which he says have medicinal qualities, the use of which he lectures me about. Some of the plants can be employed to treat pain, heal wounds or as tranquilizers. I am particularly interested by this information. I have known, of course, about medicines derived from exotic plants, but I am learning now, not as a pharmacy student, but as one being taught to respect the plants and understand their spirits. Y'Chorn tells me to learn to feel the spirit or soul of the trees and plants, again saying they will never fail me.

Time has been passing. It is just over two weeks now that I have been in the hamlet. I have been hoping that Y'Chorn would begin to instruct me in shamanic practices, but I feel that I am undergoing transition. I am now in no hurry at all to learn about shamanic practices – or anything else for that matter. I have been learning daily, about tribal farming practices, about hunting, about how these people see the world, how to craft and use a crossbow, and I am now content to take things as they come. I have begun to understand patience. I believe that there is somehow a right time to learn any given thing or start any enterprise, just as, for example, there is a right time to plant a particular crop.

At daybreak one morning K'Sor Brui asks me if I miss "my" world. "I mean," he says, "the one you have always and only known before joining us here."

I do not reply immediately. This in itself is a change for me, but I am actually *unable* to answer without careful thought. I understand that this is not a yes-or-no question. It seeks to learn if I have "integrated" anything in my short time here. K'Sor Brui looks at me carefully. He offers a small nod and walks towards a group of women who are preparing chickens for a meal. He seems to be joking with them, and, after a while looks towards me from the distance. I gesture that I can come to him if he wishes. He shakes his head, walks back to join me and stands in patient silence.

"No, I don't miss it. Maybe I will soon or sometime, but not now. That world is one thing. This is another. I am learning not to measure one against the other. I think I need to learn to be fully wherever I happen to be."

He smiles. "Well, let's see."

I look at him quizzically. "I have to go to Banmethuot," he tells me. Y'Chorn has suggested that I take you with me. If I know him, he thinks going there will be kind of a test for you; that it will teach you something about yourself or about being here that you don't yet know."

I smile. "Or, an indicator for him, of any progress on my part, and a way for him to see that his sense of me is correct."

"More the first part than the second. He does not doubt that he is correct about you because that judgment came not from him but from Yang Rong. Go and change. We have to leave ourselves the time we need in the city."

I realize that I am wearing a loin cloth and my tribal shirt. At Y'Chorn's suggestion, I have been dressing like this for several days to see if I can be at ease in such clothes. I must be. I did not even realize I was so garbed.

We make the trip to Banmethuot. I feel strange, as if I am a tribal curiosity headed for the city where I will be a foreign presence. We arrive at about 7:30 AM and decide to get breakfast in the market where, it seems like years ago, we met for the first time, not even a month in the past. I do not feel like the same person I was then, and indeed I am not. I am dressed in old camouflage fatigue pants that K'Sor Brui has loaned me and wear my heavy tribal shirt. My hair is getting long, and I have a developing beard. Western tourists, strolling through the market, look with open interest at both the locals and the occasional tribesman. I can't tell into which category they place me, although from the curious stares, I know that I am something they will talk about back home in Des Moines.

I am now fully used to the strong Robusta coffee, and I enjoy the buttery croissants set before us. As we talk, I look around, trying to imagine periodic visits to this very spot becoming a part of my life for however many years remain to me. Then the thought occurs that once Y'Chorn has died, and if he is right about me, I will become the shaman. I will be him. Do tribal shamans have coffee and croissant in the city marketplace? It's a disturbing question, one which throws yet another perspective on where I am heading. I will reflect on this. For the moment, I content myself with the answer: maybe they do, in the twenty-first century!

K'Sor Brui has noticed the slight smile come to my face. "What are you thinking?" he asks. Before I can answer, I catch sight of an unusual looking young woman. She is exotic, beautiful and clearly has tribal blood. Yet, there is an arresting difference. She is not stocky in the way of our village ladies, is clearly taller and moves with a different kind of grace. If things ended there, I would not be stopped in place. But this woman is identical to the tribal girl in my dream. Immediately I *know* she is from our village and that my life may, in this instant, have changed forever. I start to stand, seized by the thought that Y'Chorn wanted me to accompany K'Sor Brui today because he knew this girl would cross our path. K'Sor Brui is looking at me with concern but then sees the girl and himself starts to stand.

She has spotted me and almost at the same moment catches sight of him.

She breaks into a beautiful smile and comes to embrace him. It is not the normal tribal way. Now I am sure, both from her dress and her behavior, that she lives apart from the hamlet, perhaps here, but maybe even in Hồ Chí Minh City. I am disappointed. I stand smiling at her, waiting for K'Sor Brui to introduce me. I cannot take my eyes off of her. How can I possibly have dreamed her?

K'Sor Brui says something to her in Rhadé. I catch a bit of it. He has mentioned Y'Chorn, and then I hear my name. Her name is Ha Oum. She turns her beautiful smile on me and asks if I speak French. If not, she can manage English. I say French is fine. I glance at K'Sor Brui and gesture that she should join us. I offer her a croissant while we wait for more coffee. By the time it comes, I am hopelessly enthralled by her, although I take care not to interrupt her conversation with K'Sor Brui. After only a minute or so, she turns to me and says in careful Rhadé, "Did you understand our conversation? K'Sor Brui says you know some Rhadé."

I reply with my elemental Rhadé, "Only a word or two." She smiles and nods enthusiastically. "But," I continue in French, "I am only at the kindergarten level. I am glad you speak French."

She turns her full attention to me. I feel the power of her presence, of her beauty. "I am glad *you* speak French. My English is all right but not, *brilliant*." She pronounces the word in French."

I hesitate. I do not want to risk excluding K'Sor Brui from the conversation. But he is smiling and nodding encouragement. I am sure he can feel my reaction to her. He gets up, asks us to excuse him for a few minutes and walks off into the market.

Ha Oum says, "He likes you. He says he knew your father well during the war years and that he was a special man. He says you are a special man too and that your *real* name is Y'Dun. May I call you that?"

She tells me these things, all the while giving me a direct, frank look. I am almost hypnotized, but still manage to remember that in Rhadé culture, it is the woman who chooses the man. I am so very new to things that I want to chastise myself for even having that thought, but I recall Sénac's comment about my being chosen by a woman. A small part of me admits to being hopeful.

By the time K'Sor Brui returns from his conscientious absence, I have learned that Ha Oum is a nurse. She earned her degree in Hồ Chí Minh City after first completing a kind of paramedic course that was run up here and was open to tribal people. She practiced in the village, almost as a physician, for three years before she was able to gain admission to nurse's training at the old Saigon medical school. The teaching was in French, because her professors had learned in that language and in English because that was the language of the textbooks. After graduating, she got a job at the old French Grall Hospital, now Children's Rehabilitation Hospital 2, where she still works part of the time. The rest of her time is spent at one of the city's international hospitals. She comes to the hamlet once a month to assess the health of everyone and to minister to those needing treatment or to send them to town or to Hồ Chí Minh City for needed care. I have listened enthralled, without a word. When she has finished, I smile and say, "We, um the hamlet, are lucky to have you."

There is just a moment in which she reacts to my use of the word, "we." She says, "K'Sor Brui did say you are very special to Y'Chorn. Will you really be living in the hamlet from now on?"

I'm not sure how to reply. She waits me out patiently, all the while giving me her frank, open, perhaps all-seeing look.

She smiles, and it seems to me that a gentleness has stolen into her eyes as she waits. Finally, I manage to say, "The truth is, I don't know, but, yes, that may happen."

She surprises me. "K'Sor Brui tells me that Y'Chorn does know."

"He said that?"

She nods. "Y'Chorn is almost never wrong."

"I have been told that, and I am learning that. He is sure I was Rhadé generations ago."

She looks at me with her bottomless gaze. "Do you think that is possible?"

"Yes."

She nods slowly. "You have thought about what staying with us means?"

"I am thinking."

"Can you stay with us, and leave your friends, your work and the life you have always known?"

"That's a big question for me."

Again I am facing her bottomless gaze. "I think you know the answer already. You just have to agree to hear it from yourself."

This woman casts a spell, and I have fallen under it. Like a schoolboy, there is much I want to say to her, but I don't. I settle for, "I have seen the ladies in the village. I think you are not one hundred percent Rhadé."

She laughs. It is a charming, happy sound. "You are right. My grandmother was un peu fripon (she pronounces the words carefully), maybe coquine, you know?"

"Yes, in English we would say, 'coquettish' or a bit of a 'rascal'."

"Yes, yes." She giggles. "That is the word. She had a romance with a soldier in the French corps expéditionaire in the 1940s and birthed my mother. I guess the blood ran true, because my mother also took a French lover. I was the result. But neither father stayed with us."

I don't say anything, but she continues, with a mischievous gleam in her wonderful eyes, "We don't know yet whether that 'adventurous' blood has survived into the third generation."

I dare not say a word, but I am sure she is both teasing me and reading me like an open book. Her next question confirms this. "Are you married?" she asks.

* * * * * * * * * * * *

K'Sor Brui tells me that we have a series of errands to run. We will meet with a merchant to whom the tribe sells fine hardwood and another who buys our cloth, baskets and other handicraft items. Then, he tells me, we will go to meet with a lawyer who has handled disputes over land ownership for the tribe. "Here your lawyer training will be important. We are not certain that this man is always acting in our interest only. He is Viêtnamese, and can face pressure from the government to favor its positions. We do not have one our own people as a lawyer whom we can trust. Even if Maître Dien, the lawyer, is a fair man, if he must choose between us and protecting his business and family, it will be an easy decision to go against 'the moi'."

I remember the word. "The savages," I say. He nods.

We finish our business and take lunch at one of the modern hotels that have sprung up, in recent years, K'Sor Brui tells me. "Until a few years ago, Banmethuot was the dusty, provincial-capital backwater that it was in your father's time. Now it is very different. Even the tradition of the siesta is disappearing. Foreigners who come to make money don't like a two-hour lunchtime."

By 2:30 PM, we are ready to return to the hamlet. K'Sor Brui asks me to drive. I tell him I will need directions. He directs me to the market where, to my surprise and pleasure,

Ha Oum is waiting for us. K'Sor Brui gives me a sly smile. "I will sit in the back where I cannot hear what you two young people might say to one another." He steps out of the front passenger seat and repeats himself, this time for the benefit of Ha Oum.

Over the next two days, Ha Oum is completely occupied with examining the people of the hamlet. She begins with the children and works her way from there. I am taken up with my own activities and responsibilities, and I do not find time during the day to see her. On our first evening together in the hamlet, she sought me out and suggested we walk in the forest. I worried that this would be frowned upon but then remembered that it is the women who choose the men. In that environment, it is likely not inappropriate for a male and a female to walk and talk alone together.

Still, I have the thought that such a walk would signal, to any Rhadé, a seriousness in a couple's relationship. I push the idea aside, assuring myself that Ha Oum knows such seriousness would not be assumed in the case of one as new to the hamlet as I. Yet, I feel a thrill of hope – and a small touch of fear-- that her family's "adventurous blood" may be manifesting… just a bit.

That first evening passed quickly for me. I talked too much about myself. Before we parted ways, I apologized. I had wanted to learn so much more about her. "But you let me question you," she said. After a moment, she smiled and went towards her longhouse, leaving me with the feeling that I had been 'generous' to be so full of myself.

On the third day after our visit to Banmethuot, K'Sor Brui and I went once again to the city where I could meet with lawyer Dien and begin to gather documents about the land in dispute. Also, I was able to locate a few French translations about tribal law/custom law. Sénac was the one who had suggested I do this. He was, himself, very knowledgeable on the subject, which frequently became relevant to other legal disputes under Viêtnamese law. But, as he told me, he is not a lawyer. He can help me with customary law and its history, I am thinking that we would call it, "precedent," but he says my lawyer's mind will be a great advantage in cases where needed.

We again take lunch at one of the new hotels where I am greatly surprised to see JJ sitting alone, reading a guidebook. He looks up and spots me before I can make a move towards him. A smile lights his face, and he gestures asking if he may join us. I point towards an empty chair at our table. He looks different, happier. I introduce him to Sénac and then ask, "So, you found your father?" assuming this accounts for his happy look.

"No. That seems pretty much beyond possibility."

"I'm sorry."

"Well, some good came of it all. I met these Viêtnamese who were so kind to me. They helped me in my search. I never could have done that alone. We became friends. And here's the thing, one of them is the most beautiful girl you have ever seen."

"Wow, so dear old dad falls to the power of true love. Tell me about her."

He hesitates. "In a minute. First, what are you doing here? Really, how long have you been here? Must be a while because I left town after you did, and I spent almost two weeks between Huế and Danang. And hey, look at you, you look like you have moved in with the Montagnards. Longer hair, beard, tribal shirt." He nods at Sénac as if to indicate that he means no offense.

"It's a long story. But just let me say that this gentleman (I indicate Sénac) is a wonderful man, who has become a good friend. His father knew my father way back in the war years. Helped him save the lives of my mother's family. I'll tell you more later, but what are you doing here?"

"My Việtnamese friends suggested this trip that I am making. They told me not to return to Hồ Chí Minh City without doing a tour of a Montagnard area, so here I am. Hey, maybe you and Mr. Sénac can help me with that."

I look at Sénac. He says to JJ, "I'd be glad to help, but Y'Dun here might be your best guide."

JJ looks stunned. "Y' what, who? Is that a Montagnard name? *You* have a Montagnard name?"

"It's a long story."

"You said that already. I'll bet it is. Come on, tell me."

The waiter appears. JJ says he wants to treat us to lunch. Then he smiles and says, "Now, come on, sing for your supper." Sénac looks confused, but we order and spend the meal telling my story and deciding that we will return tomorrow to take JJ to the hamlet for a few days. He is so happy that the Aussie bursts out of him. "Good on ya!"

JJ has a great time in the hamlet. He meets K'Sor Brui and Y'Chorn. He joins us one evening around a jar of nam bay, which leaves him completely and happily drunk. But the highlight of all, he tells me is meeting Ha Oum. "She's a goddess, mate. I don't have to ask. You're lost. Good on ya." He picks up on my restraint. "Is something wrong? Did I say something bad?"

"No. But this isn't the modern world here. I haven't asked K'Sor Brui about this yet, but I am guessing that even when there is an attraction, things here happen in their own time. Anyway, it's not really up to me."

"No, huh? What do you mean not up to you? You gonna wait and make *her* ask?"

"Actually, yes. In this culture, the *woman* chooses the man."

He smiles. "It's a done deal then, mate. Are you so smitten you can't see how she is when she's with you?"

"So you're an expert on tribal women now?"

Chapter 22

JJ stays for three more days in the hamlet. He is delighted. "Hey, Y'Dun, (he has taken happily to calling me by my tribal name), I can't believe that I'm here and that I'm friends with the next shaman. I mean, really, mate, I'm just wondering what kind of magic goes on here. You're the next wise man, so you must know."

"JJ, I think the magic is that you got away from Australia and from that environment where things just were never right for you. Maybe you should make your life here in the hamlet too."

"Too? So you've decided? I knew you couldn't leave Ha Oum. But me, I'm crazy for this woman in Hồ Chí Minh City. If I would stay in Việtnam, it would not be out here. I have got to go back to see Thuy before I decide anything."

"Well, I haven't made any decisions. This is a really big thing, and I remind myself every day that if I decide to stay, I am taking on a sacred – yes, that's the exact word – trust that I will never have the right to go back on. Also, I have to be very careful of if and how anything may be developing with Ha Oum. I understand now, from the perspective of a Rhadé, what it means to a woman to choose a man and the obligation that being chosen places on the man."

JJ gets serious. "You're ready for some major decision, mate. I didn't know you almost at all in the city, and I don't know you that much here, but like me, you came looking for something, looking for *your* father, even though you know who he is. I can see that you are a little different now – maybe a lot different. I'm loving visiting here, but I am not bonding with this place the way I think you have. Crikey, even if Thuy decides she wants me, I think I would want to move us away from here. Maybe not right away, but someday. I don't see me living my life here."

"Jesus, JJ, where does all this thinking come from? A few weeks ago, you just wanted information, and, frankly, you were miserable, with, it seemed, no chance of ever having that change."

"Right, but, now that I look at things, I think I actually needed the beating I got at the airport, the bad treatment at the Ministry, the loss of my papers and the failure of my search. I had to hit the dead bottom, mate. I needed something to tell me that nothing outside of myself was going to change things for me."

"OK, so why not think about staying here? I mean just as an option. Seems to me that, even with the good change being here brought, you don't want to give it any more of a chance."

"So, look, mate, there's a story we tell in Aussie. A guy hits his fiftieth birthday. God comes to him and says, 'Mate, you've been a good bloke. As a special birthday present, even though you've got plenty of years left, I can arrange for you to spend a week in Heaven, just so you know what it's like.' So the guy says, 'great'."

"Where's this going JJ? If the punchline is that Việtnam is not Heaven, I know that."

"Nah. Just listen. So after two days in Heaven, the bloke is bored and St. Peter can see it. He offers to let the guy visit hell, just, um, for the hell of it."

I must look impatient, because JJ says, "Come on. Listen. The guy loves hell. Babes, golf, the devil is handsome and urbane, great chess player. Weather is fantastic. When he finally dies, St. Peter meets him in Heaven and says, 'You can stay here or go down below.' A no brainer. He points downward and in a flash he's in a sweaty, cavernous inferno below ground being snarled at by the hound of hell. He's treated like dirt, abused, starved, whipped. He demands to see his old friend, Satan.

"It takes weeks. When Satan finally shows up he is not the same guy as before. He's all red, with horns, a tail and trotters for feet and is one nasty dude. The guy says, 'What happened to all the wonderful people and things?' Satan says, 'Before, you were a tourist. Now you're an immigrant.'

"I'm a tourist right now, but I know me. If I become an immigrant, it won't be good. You're different – really different. I'm not sure you get it yet, but I do. You really are Y'Dun. I'll only ever be JJ."

* * * * * * * * * * *

JJ left for the city two days ago. Ha Oum has to leave tomorrow, and after discussion with Y'Chorn and K'Sor Brui, I have explained that I have much to do before I can commit to the hamlet – if I commit. To my surprise, this is no problem at all. Y'Chorn smiles, nods and tells me that of course I have much to do. He is not concerned. I will return. Sénac, Ha Oum and I make the trip to Banmethuot to see to errands before leaving the hamlet for an extended trip the next morning. In town, I call Mr. Nam and tell him that I will arrive at Tân Sơn Nhứt airport at 11:00 AM the next day. He says he will come with Phùng to meet the plane. He is anxious to see me.

Mr. Nam is waiting when Ha Oum and I exit baggage claim. He spots me immediately. A smile spreads on his face. I reach to shake his hand, but he gives me a fatherly hug and then holds me at arm's length. "There are some changes," he says and then turns to look at Ha Oum. "Please introduce me."

I make the introduction. He looks at the two of us. "This lady is from K'Sor Brui's hamlet?" We both nod. "Are you related to him? He was a student of mine many years ago. A wonderful man."

Ha Oum says she is not related but that she grew up admiring K'Sor Brui. Everyone in the village knew he had been a senator during the Nguyễn Van Thieu years, although for people her age, that was dusty history. More important was what he had suffered to protect the tribe during the years immediately after the North Việtnamese takeover in the south.

Outside of the terminal, Phùng awaits us. He straightens up and breaks into a huge smile when he sees me. Then he realizes that Ha Oum is with me, and he is clearly struck by her beauty. Mr. Nam notices with a twinkle in his eye. To Ha Oum he says, "This is my grandson, Phùng. He is a great help to me and a fine young man." Phùng looks embarrassed, but he does square his shoulders just a bit. He shakes my hand and then says, with obvious admiration, "Miss Ha Oum, I am very happy to meet you. Will you ride with us?"

Ha Oum gives him her beautiful smile. "And I am pleased to meet you. Yes, Y'Dun and I will ride together with you and your grandfather."

Phùng seems a bit confused and turns for a moment to look for the additional passenger named, Y'Dun. Mr. Nam grins and gestures towards the back seat. "I'll ride up front with Phùng. Ha Oum, the back is for you and *Y'Dun*."

After I have checked in at the hotel, we all sit out on the terrace for a light lunch. I tell about my stay in Banmethuot and in the Rhadé hamlet. Ha Oum gives her background. By the time lunch is over, we have agreed to have dinner together. I will invite JJ to join us. Phùng will drive Ha Oum to her apartment so she can drop her suitcase. He will then take her to her work at the Children's Hospital. It is near my hotel. She will be ready to meet us at the hotel in the early evening for dinner.

When Phùng and Ha Oum have left, Mr. Nam asks me about my situation with the Rhadé. As always, he is a complete gentleman. He begins with the courtesy of asking for the permission that he knows he has. "May I speak frankly with you?" I nod. "I did not expect – as I am sure you did not – for things to develop as they have with the Rhadé. It appears to me that you are either very much drawn to returning to the village to spend your life there or that you feel obligated because of the relationships your father had there." He pauses, but I do not comment. He thinks for a moment and then continues. "This is difficult for me to say. I think you know that I respect the tribal peoples and do not at all approve of the prejudice the Việtnamese have against them. But I must ask if you have considered the gravity of the decision you seem to be contemplating.

"I would tell myself that asking you such a question is none of my affair or responsibility, but we two have become close. I feel, in the absence of the sympathetic hearing and wise counsel your father would have offered, I can perhaps be useful."

"Of course," I say. "You never have to worry about limits in our relationship. You told K'Sor Brui that I am like a son to you. I was so happy to hear you say that, all the more so because I had come to think of you as a father."

He smiles, and we go into the lounge to sit and talk further. I explain in detail what took place in the hamlet, especially about Y'Chorn. I say that I truly do not yet know what I will decide, but confess that if I am to commit to the village, I will still have to have a way of earning some income for several years. At the moment, I have no idea about how I could do that.

Mr. Nam nods. "Perhaps I have some thoughts. But before that, let me ask about the relationship between you and Miss Ha Oum. She is very unusual looking. Tribal women are most often very solidly built. She is not as thin as our Việtnamese ladies, but she is quite beautiful and, I would say, elegant in appearance. I am sure you are attracted to her, and from the brief chance I have had to observe, she feels very comfortable with you. Is this a romance that will influence your eventual decision?"

I almost laugh. With a big smile, I say, "Well, from what I learned in the village, I, the man, am not the person who decides."

Now it is Mr. Nam's turn to laugh. "Yes, quite right, but I think I am seeing the direction her choice might take. If she chooses you, will that determine your decision?"

I hesitate, so Mr. Nam continues. "Well, we can leave that for now. You said you wanted to meet Judge Đao. I told him about you. He remembers your father fondly and is anxious to meet you. He said that he has few obligations these days, so if I phone him, he can likely see us immediately. He remains a greatly respected jurist. I am sure he will have some ideas about how you might earn a living while nevertheless serving the village."

I am thrilled. "Can we see him tomorrow morning?"

"I will arrange it. For now, if you are not too tired, we can go to the cemetery, or at least to where it was, to remember François Sully and many others, if their names will mean anything to you."

"Mạc Đĩnh Chi Cemetery," I say.

"Sadly, no longer that, but you remember the place name, and for those who believe that history, whether written by the victors or not, should never eradicate the past, that is important."

"Of course I remember the name. Who were some of the notables buried there?"

"There were so very many, starting with French military who died in the attack on the Saigon Citadel. There followed many senior French military people and later than that, many senior colonial administrators and wealthy Việtnamese. Perhaps the most notable were President Ngo Đinh Diem and his brother, Ngô Đình Nhu. François was buried there, as you know, and, as I recall, Nguyễn Van Bông, a fiercely independent nationalist scholar, politician and Rector of our National Institute of Administration."

Mr. Nam pauses and takes a moment to collect himself. I note his emotion and say, "You must have had friends buried there."

"Yes, but at the moment, I am thinking of Bông. In his role at the National Institute of Administration, he was my boss, but he was also a dear friend."

I am remembering something from my father's files. "I think my father knew him and respected both him and his wife greatly."

There are tears in Mr. Nam's eyes. "Yes, his wife was wonderful, very attractive and a less reserved personality than Bông himself. Everyone called her Jackie. I am not sure that even I knew her Việtnamese name. She loved him deeply, even though many people found the combination of his scholarly reserve and her open enthusiasm to be an unusual match. When Bông was assassinated by a bomb placed under his car, Jackie was distraught. At his interment at Mạc Đĩnh Chi, she cried bitterly and attempted to throw herself into the grave. That was something that was expected of widows, but she was genuinely grief stricken." He pauses, overwhelmed by emotion as if no time has passed.

"And it is people like Bông who were summarily disinterred and had their remains relocated?"

"Yes. And if the remains were not claimed, they were cremated and destroyed."

"Perhaps that is the fate that François met."

"Perhaps."

I am angry – as I know my father would be. He never forgave the Communists for their thuggery and failure to respect those elements of Việtnamese history and society that did not please them. "Let's go," I say. "Bearing witness is an act of respect and humility."

At the site of the cemetery, I believe I am surrounded by the ghosts of all the disinterred. I cry. When Mr. Nam asks how I can feel so deeply, I can only answer, "Les revenants."

Mr. Nam is momentarily surprised – as am I – at the French word that has popped out of me. "Yes," he says. "Ghosts. I hear and feel them always." He pauses.

I say, "I don't know why the French word came to mind."

He looks thoughtful. "There were so many French buried here. Perhaps Y'Chorn is perfectly correct. You are indeed a sensitive, able to feel and hear the spirits."

We walk around the perimeter of the park and stop by a section of its western wall. "Speaking of ghosts," smiles Mr. Nam. "It was here in 1971 that President Thieu directed that a section of the enclosing wall should be demolished. A Cao Dai priest, a renown clairvoyant – maybe like you," he adds with a sly smile, "Told Mr. Thieu that since he had been involved with those responsible for the assassinated President's death, the least he could do was to liberate his spirit from the cemetery."

"Ghosts," I say again. "I have always suspected they are real."

We return to the hotel almost in silence. When Phùng appears to pick up his grandfather, Mr. Nam says, "I am less worried about your decision now. Whatever it is, I am sure it will be the right one."

At 8:00 PM, we all meet at a roof garden restaurant on Nguyễn Huệ Blvd. near the river. It is a beautifully decorated place. As our group gathers and is seated, I get a chance to observe each one. I am curious, of course, about Thuy, who is accompanied by the two young men who originally stepped up to help the desperate JJ. They all seem to be fine people, but it is clear that none has experience of such a grand place as this restaurant. Still, looking around the table, it strikes me that no one in our group seems to feel naturally at home in this environment. Mr. Nam whispers to me that in my father's time here, there were famous restaurants, but none like this. He was comfortable in those places but feels completely out of his element here now. Indeed almost everyone makes some comment about never having eaten in such a luxurious place before. JJ's Việtnamese friends chuckle and say as a group, that they expect they will never again experience anything like this restaurant.

Thuy asks Ha Oum if she is used to places like this. She replies that being on staff at two hospitals, one of which has many foreign doctors, and being of tribal background, she does get invitations to join her colleagues in such places. Thuy smiles at her and says, "It must help also to be a very beautiful woman."

Ha Oum replies, "I am sure you know all about that."

Thuy looks embarrassed and says, "I am still just a student. I work part-time, but as a low-level office clerk."

JJ cannot help himself. "I know men." He grins and continues in a self-deprecating tone, "After all, I am one, and I can't believe that any man who sees you often would not want to take you to dinner."

It is a restrained, modest observation, but Binh and Thien stop their private conversation instantly upon hearing it. They give Thuy a long look. She is clearly uncomfortable. With lowered gaze, she says, "I am a traditional Việtnamese girl. My parents still teach and enforce the old values." She pauses and looks at Mr. Nam. He smiles and nods. "Also, my family does not have money for fine dresses, and I am actually not comfortable alone in the company of foreign men." She looks kindly at JJ. "Unless I have learned that they are honorable. It is very hard for foreigners to understand traditional girls like me."

There is a weighted silence. Ha Oum intervenes, "As a minority woman, I understand what you say, but I have had to get used to new ways. Perhaps Y'Dun (she glances at me) can sympathize about feeling out of place. He has lived for a few weeks in my hamlet and is very much a curiosity there."

Everyone laughs, and the conversation for the rest of the evening centers on my thoughts and experiences in the hamlet. There is other talk, but whenever it strays into potentially sensitive areas, all take refuge in the wonder of my tribal name and experience. All in all, it is a very enjoyable evening. When we part, JJ asks Binh and Thien to be sure to stop by the hotel tomorrow after work. He smiles at Thuy and says, "I would appreciate it if you can come also." She offers no reply, just a smile and, as she departs, a kiss on either cheek, which she also offers to me and all of the party.

Back at the hotel, JJ asks me to meet him for an early breakfast. He no longer wears the bright smile he has managed to keep in place during the entire evening. I can see his distress. "Would you like to have a nightcap and talk a bit?"

"Thanks, not now. I need some time to think."

* * * * * * * * * * *

The next morning, JJ and I have breakfast. I am waiting for him when he walks out onto the terrace. He sees me and comes over without hesitation. I can't help but notice the change in him. He is not tentative, maybe because we know each other a bit now, but I think the change goes deeper than that.

"Morning, mate. Very nice night last night. Great meal and really special people. I gotta tell you, mate, you're crazy if you don't dance a jig when Ha Oum gives up her girlish reserve and lets you in on the secret of how much she cares for you. Not that she is working hard at hiding it."

"Bridges we cross when we come to them," I say. "What about you? Thuy is as beautiful as you said she is, very bright also. She does have a charming reserve about her. Between the two things, I can easily understand why you are hooked."

"Yeah, right. Too bad she isn't."

"Have you told her how you feel?"

"Do you really think she can't tell? Crikey, I've got zero experience of women, and it seems I get them better than you do."

"Have you told her?"

"Well, no, but do I really have to? She can read me like a road sign."

"Yes, you *really* have to."

"Why? So she can laugh in my face and humiliate me? I've seen that movie far too many times."

"No, so with the sure knowledge of your feelings, she can examine her own."

"And what do I do when she has a laughing fit?"

I give him a slightly disgusted look. "Well, then, you begin to cry and immediately raise the intensity to tantrum level. Not content with that, you will through yourself on the floor, kick and punch it, swear that your life is over."

"Nah, knowing me, I'll put my tail between my legs, skulk off and brood alone for a week in the quiet of my room without eating."

"Sounds like a plan."

"Come on, mate, help me."

"JJ, you *have* to speak up. It's the only way you will know for sure. If she says anything other than, 'no,' you can work on the relationship. If she does say, 'no', you are free to pursue other opportunities when they arise. It's a win/win situation."

"Easy for you to say."

"Yes, and not easy for any man to do, but worth it."

Mr. Nam appears on the terrace and comes to join us. I

order coffee for him. He looks at JJ and tunes in on the vibe. "Do I have to remind you? Y'Dun is a future shaman, a wise man. He is the best possible counselor. Even he may not know that henceforth any advice he gives was whispered to him by Yang Rong, the Rhadé master spirit."

The ploy seems to work. JJ breaks out in a smile. "Right. I forgot for a moment. OK, wise man, I'll take the advice – not yours, mind you, Ya... um, Yang..., you know, *that* guy."

"Got it. But now Mr. Nam and I have a visit to make. We'll see you around lunchtime, if you're free. Will you be good until then?"

"Yeah, good. Really. Maybe you're getting the hang of this Y'Dun stuff."

* * * * * * * * * *

Phùng stops in front of the gate of a walled compound at 50 Đoàn Thị Điểm Street. It is one of many such houses in this beautiful residential area. Without our asking, the gate swings open. Phùng drives in on a driveway that sits to one side of a well-kept garden and beautiful, old, French, colonial-style villa. An elderly man steps from the house onto the large front terrace and smiles warmly at Mr. Nam. I immediately recognize him from a photo of my father's. Although he is decades older, his distinctive, happy face is unmistakable. I catch my breath, deeply surprised by the impact that seeing this man has. I recall him in his business suit in the old photo, smiling at my father and shaking his hand with obvious warmth and friendship. He does not wait for an introduction. He steps towards me but stops a slight distance away and looks me over. His expression changes to one of profound emotion. "You are his image," he says. He shakes my hand and at the same time grasps my arm at the elbow. After a minute of handshake, and with tears in his eyes, he steps closer and hugs me. "The son of my dear friend. A man who did so much for us Việtnamese jurists. A man who clearly loved us. He was the best of the Americans, of all those who came here in those days. To fight, to build, to help. He did all of those things. I am so very glad to meet you. To touch my dear friend once more before I die." He stops, overwhelmed by emotion.

Mr. Nam, himself, has been caught in this tide of feeling. The two ancient friends look fondly at one another for a moment and then hug. Judge Đao ushers us into the house. We are in a large salon that runs the width of the building. The cement tile floor is covered with a mat made of woven-straw squares. It imparts a certain warmth, while nevertheless leaving the feeling of the room cool under the slowly turning fans suspended from the ceiling some fourteen feet above. I cannot help myself, I gape at the surroundings.

Judge Đao smiles. "This looks familiar to you?"

"No. It's just that in the time I have been here, I have not been in a private home."

"Then perhaps you don't know. Your father lived here for a few years. I always loved the house. When its owner died, I bought it, happy to have my dear friend as a tenant and thinking that one day, if he left us, I would move in with my family."

I am stunned. This is a vital missing piece in my understanding of my father's time here. Judge Đao suggests that we do a walk through the house and around the property. As we do, I think I can feel my father's presence, and I savor my sense of how he was when living here. The house is wonderful. I am sure it became "home" to him. Was he torn between here and the Montagnard hamlet? How could he have left either place? I am overcome by sadness that he had to leave at all, had this taken from him, and, at the end, he became a single parent, lonely I think, but who loved me and raised me, even though, for so long, I bore him animosity.

Back in the salon, drinks await us, ice tea and orange soda. Judge Đao and Mr. Nam sit side-by-side on a sofa, two friends, as alike and as natural together as sections from the same orange. These are men of generous and sympathetic nature. They look at me and see my sadness. Judge Đao says, "You can imagine him happy here?" I nod. "He was sad to leave but accepted that. When we last parted, he hugged me and said, 'Đao, I shall never for even a moment in this life forget you'." He looks nostalgic and continues, "Soon, perhaps, I shall have the chance to talk with him about that promise – in the next life.

"But Nam tells me that you may complete the circle your father began, by returning to live among us – or the tribal people. He has told me a bit of your professional background. I will need more details, but I am now so old that I have advanced to the status of 'venerated jurist'. I am sure I will be able to arrange a position for you, both with one of our more internationally-oriented law firms and with a foreign firm. You have a background synopsis to send me?"

I have come prepared and take my resume from my inside jacket pocket. Behind the basics, it contains an appendix which sets forth several of the specific cases I have handled, briefly explaining the signal issues of each. Judge Đao scans it quickly, nodding occasionally. He looks up. "Thank you. This is excellent. Nam will reach you when I can arrange the necessary meetings."

We take our leave, with me thinking – hoping actually – that there is as much of my father in me as many wonderful people here think. And within, I berate myself, "He never told me. I never knew."

Mr. Nam drops me off at the hotel. I thank him profusely for arranging for me to see Judge Đao. "He is an extraordinary man," I tell him. He smiles.

"You know my history and friendship with Đao. Yes, he is a very special man. I think Americans might say, 'a special human being'. He is a gentleman and has the ability to empathize with almost anyone. He is virtually never dismissive of another person. Because he is such a genuinely caring man, people almost always feel they have been treated kindly by him. Yet, over so many years, I have come to understand that is something of an illusion. He is always gentlemanly, but it is very unusual for him to be so completely involved with someone as he was almost immediately with you today. I hope you will have the chance to develop a long relationship with him. You will be much the better for it – as I have been."

I am too humbled to say anything. After a silence, Mr. Nam adds, "I believe that Đao has something in common with Y'Chorn. Each senses in you something special, even extraordinary. You must now look within yourself, recognize your gift and find the courage to allow it to flourish."

Mr. Nam's comment fills my mind. I wonder if it was just an observation or something more: a criticism or maybe a challenge. I am so diverted that I don't see JJ, who has been waiting for me. He appears in front of me as if out of nowhere. I nearly bump into him. "Hey, mate, what's up? Didn't you see me waving from the terrace? Guess not. You look like you've been in another dimension."

"Sorry. I've got something on my mind."

"Yeah, I guess so. Must be serious. I was hoping we'd catch lunch and talk a bit, but if you're not up for that, we can let it go."

"No, that's ok. We've both got to eat, right?"

We go back to the table JJ had abandoned a minute ago, and his pal, Tran, the waiter, comes over immediately, all smiles. He greets JJ in Viêtnamese and holds a short conversation with him in the language, taking care, as much as I can tell, to introduce a few new words for JJ's growing vocabulary. "You're getting to be a native," I say.

"Nah, but I do like learning a bit of the language. I have been trying to practice it because I want to use it on Thuy when she comes by this afternoon. I want her to see how hard I'm trying to be worthy of her."

"JJ, you *are* worthy of her, and you should not doubt that."

"Yeah, that's the thing. I never thought I was worthy of anyone, but now, here, I'm thinking that maybe I'm on the way."

"Great."

"But I keep wondering what I'll do if she says no."

"Didn't we agree that whatever her response, you're a winner?"

"Yeah, I remember, but if she says no, I'll think I've only gotten second prize."

"There is no second prize. Each outcome is the top winner. The only difference is when you collect the trophy: right away or down the road a bit."

"You know, Y'Dun, you got a way of saying things and looking at things that's pretty good. Anyway, what was on *your* mind?"

"For now, let's just say, the future."

JJ shakes his head. "That's either a cryptic or an evasive response. Gor, I'm opening my soul to you, and you're either not doing the same for me, or you've been completely swallowed by the tribal, mystic thing." He gives me a questioning look.

"Yes."

He grins at me. "OK, OK. See you later."

I leave JJ and go out to walk. I don't go far. I want to stay around the hotel because I have come to realize that the enormous physical changes here since my father's years, have split the place almost into two 'cities'. One where I am able to experience the surroundings he lived within, and another that he would hardly recognize. I think of the former as Saigon and the latter as Hồ Chí Minh City. I have been in Việtnam for a month now and have begun to accumulate my own experiences and impressions. I feel the magnetic pull of the place, and I think again of my father and of François Sully, two men who bonded with the country and its people. Two men who, either let their guard down and permitted this place to seep into their blood and souls, or who felt the dust of the country upon them and wore it happily until it became part of their very beings.

The thought brings to mind numerous venerable names from my father's journals and from my reading of books in his library as I prepared to come here: Gerry Hickey, Robert Shaplen, Bernard Fall, David Halberstam, Denis Warner, Ellen Hammer. Some began as scholars studying this place. Others were journalists who began here "on assignment." All succumbed to its spell.

I am reminded of Ernest Hemingway's:

If you are lucky enough to have lived in Paris as a young man, then wherever you go for the rest of your life, it stays with you, for Paris is a moveable feast.

But it is Viêtnam that was their movable feast. Like my father, like François, like so many others who experienced this place and that era, it became a defining event – if not *the* defining experience--of their lives. Friends made here and dispersed by the Communist takeover in 1975 remained, somehow, the dearest of their days. Their deaths decades later and after long years of little or no contact, as I know from my father's journals, moved the survivors beyond words or tears.

What kind of country, what kind of people, what kind of shared experience creates such emotion and such a bond? I consider this as I walk back to the hotel and wonder whether I have the courage to "let my gift flourish" – because that will mean spending the rest of my life here.

When I get back to the hotel, I ask at the front desk if the name, Robert Shaplen means anything to anyone there. I am greeted by blank stares. The staff is too young even to have been alive in the days when "Bob" Shaplen, as my father called him, stayed at the hotel. I turn away from the reception desk and head for the elevator. I am almost back at my room when I hear my name being called. Approaching from down the hall is an older man in a business suit. I wait for him. He introduces himself and politely asks if I would join him downstairs for tea. He has something to tell me. I thank him, and a few minutes later we are sitting in the hotel's courtyard garden behind steaming cups of B'Lao tea. I inhale the familiar aroma, take a healthy sip and smile as I taste this special brew once again. "B'Lao tea," I smile.

My host, Mr. Khanh, looks surprised and pleased. "You are familiar with this tea?"

"Yes, I visited one of the plantations. My father, at one time, worked in Banmethuot, and he was close friends with François Sully, who had worked as a planter in Blao when he first came to Việtnam. But, excuse me. You had something to tell me."

"Yes, but you are sure? Your father knew Monsieur Sully? He was a famous man, and he loved our country."

"I am sure."

"Then perhaps that explains your question about Monsieur Shaplen."

I look at Mr. Khanh. He appears to be perhaps sixty years old, but his consistent use of, "Monsieur," pronounced properly and uttered respectfully, indicates that he was alive here when the French influence remained strong. "You attended French school here?" I ask.

He lowers his eyes and says quietly, "Yes, but perhaps you know that those times are not well regarded now."

I nod and ask, "Which school?"

His head snaps up, and he takes a long, measuring look at me. "Jean Jacques Rousseau," he says quietly.

"Near the Palace on Nguyễn Thi Minh Khai Street?"

"Now, yes. The street had many names before."

"When my father was here it was Hồng Thập Tự, and the school became Lê Quy Dôn, after it was Jean Jacques Rousseau."

He smiles broadly. "You know so much about the old times. These are beautiful memories for me."

"You must be older than you look, and perhaps you came to find me because you know who Robert Shaplen was."

"I am almost seventy. I am permitted to work here because I have known the hotel for so long and never had any record of political opinions. I was young then, but I did know Monsieur Shaplen. He stayed here very often. How can I help you?"

"I know he always stayed in the same room and that Monsieur Francini let him keep his private files there even when he was not in town. I am wondering if you can show me that room."

"Please wait. I will be right back."

He returns after a few minutes with what I assume to be a passkey. "I had to see if the room is occupied. It is free. Please come with me."

We walk down a hall on the second floor and stop before Room 236. He opens the door and makes a sweeping gesture that I should enter. "Please stay as long as you wish. I am sure this has a special meaning for you." I thank him, and he leaves me alone.

Of course the room has been completely renovated and surely does not resemble the old 1960s–70s room that Bob Shaplen occupied, by the kindness of the then-owner, Philippe Francini, paying rent only when in residence, but not when the room was held empty for his notes and files. I sit in a chair by a small desk, close my eyes and listen. I imagine Shaplen at work, codifying field or interview notes, thinking back over his years of experience in-country, forming the idea for his books, *The Lost Revolution* and *Time Out of Hand,* and writing his Letter from Asia that appeared regularly in *The New Yorker* magazine.

The ghosts of Indochina crowd the room. They tell the story of the Duke of Montpensier buying the hotel in the 1880s to serve wealthy colonials and other elites who would come to Indochina for jungle adventure and to hunt game. They relate how the Corsican, Mathieu Francini, later bought the hotel from its then-Corsican owners as they went bankrupt, and turned it into "the place to be." How Philippe Francini, son of Mathieu, took over the hotel in 1965 upon his father's death, and how the hotel became headquarters for Time and Newsweek and, of course, for Robert Shaplen.

The history of Indochina and of Việtnam lives in the room and is exhaled by the very walls of the building. With no justification, I feel a part of this history, and the room whispers to me, "You are of this place."

I exit the room with only one foot in the present, but aware enough to remember to thank Monsieur Khanh for his kindness. He tells me that it was his pleasure. I leave him, thinking that he too, surely far more than I, is "of this place" and did not even have a choice about accepting the selection that fell upon him so very many years ago. I wonder if I have a choice now.

* * * * * * * * * * *

Ha Oum has stopped by the hotel at the end of her workday, as agreed. We are sitting on the terrace making plans for the evening when JJ appears. He joins us. Ha Oum comments that he looks especially handsome. "Đẹp giai hóa," she says.

JJ recognizes the phrase. "Yeah, yeah. I've heard it before. I don't believe it for a minute, but a guy's gotta put his best foot forward."

We chat for a few minutes. Binh, Thien and Thuy show up.

Trân pulls another table over to ours, and we all sit together. After an hour, Ha Oum and I go off for dinner, leaving JJ to face his moment of truth.

"I guess he'll tell us when we get back," says Ha Oum. I nod. "What will he do if she says no?" She pauses, "Or if she says yes?"

"You know, I have no clear idea in either case. He does plan to leave here in a day or so. If she says yes, of course he'll come back, but after that, I don't know. If she says no, I suppose he'll go back to Australia."

Ha Oum is thoughtful. "I hope he doesn't do that. Not right away. He is a nice man, but he does not have much faith in himself. If he returns to Australia, he'll probably slip into his old ways."

* * * * * * * * * * *

Back on the hotel terrace, JJ and his friends are silent for a minute. Binh says, "That American guy is a little strange. Does he really think he's a Rhadé? And I have never seen a tribal woman away from her village. For sure not one like her who is with a foreigner."

Thien says, "Yes, but she is very pretty."

The other two laugh and kid him for a moment. Then they all are silent again. Finally, Thuy says, "I would like to talk with JJ alone for a minute. JJ, can we sit in the courtyard? It's quieter." Binh and Thien don't complain. It's almost as if they expected this.

In the courtyard, they order drinks yet again. When the waiter has gone, Thuy looks at JJ with a softness he has never before seen from her. It thrills him, lifts his hopes, but also scares him. He knows it's his play, but he just can't begin. Thuy says, "I think you wanted to talk with me."

JJ is suddenly scared stiff. He is anything but a lady's man or confident romancer. Thuy cocks her head. "It's okay, JJ."

God, he thinks, she sees right through me. I don't have to say a word. She knows. But he knows too that it is now or never.

He draws a breath. "I love you, Thuy. I didn't expect to. I tried hard not to, but you're so beautiful and so smart and so wonderful and so...you. I couldn't help it. And now I'm out of reasons to keep you coming to see me. And if I say goodbye, it will all be over, final."

She is listening intently, with her angelic face and with her beautiful eyes that he has known as being businesslike but which are now moist.

"I have to face that, but I could not face it without taking, maybe the only opportunity I will ever have to tell a woman that I love her and mean it completely."

* * * * * * * * * * *

As Ha Oum and I walk to dinner, I say, "I have my fingers crossed." She gives me a confused look. "Oh, that means that I am hoping for the best for him. We'll just have to wait and see what answer he has gotten."

We get diverted by being seated at the restaurant and ordering. Ha Oum comments at my selection of lamb for dinner. She says she has never tasted it. When the food comes, I immediately offer her some. She goes through a minor act – I *think* it's an act – of being afraid to taste this "exotic" dish. I make a show of being relieved that she likes it. We joke about the vast differences between what foreigners eat and what Rhadé usually eat. She destroys the whole idea of the frugal Rhadé diet, however, when she orders a Bombe Alaska (Baked Alaska) for dessert – and downs it all alone when I refuse her offer of sharing. We both laugh.

On our way back to the hotel, I say, "I hope JJ is OK."

She says, "I do care, but he'll survive no matter what."

I nod slowly.

"What about you, Y'Dun?"

"What *about* me?"

She smiles. "You know, at first I thought you were a tourist, but seeing you in the hamlet, hearing about you from K'Sor Brui and Y'Chorn, observing you and being with you, I don't think that any longer. I think Y'Chorn might be right about you. Because of my work, I know many Viêtnamese and foreign men." She looks at me with her bottomless eyes. "You are not like them, and you are waiting for something."

"Really? What am I waiting for?"

She gives me a smile that says, *you don't fool me.* As we walk, she takes my hand.

Back at the hotel, we find JJ sitting alone in the courtyard garden. One look at him tells the story. He is clearly disappointed, but he does not appear to be "devastated." The first thing he says to us is surprising. "You two look happy."

Ha Oum, still holding my hand, turns towards me smiling. "We are," she says.

JJ nods. "I'm glad."

I prod him gently. "Tell us about it."

He does, quoting almost verbatim, I think, what he said to her. Ha Oum and I are taken aback, surprised, maybe even a bit stunned. I look at her thinking that this is what I want so badly to say to her. She looks at me with tears in her eyes. After a moment, she turns to JJ. "Beautiful. Perfect."

"Yeah, well, it didn't do the job. I mean, when I finished, she was crying. I didn't know why, but I got hopeful. Then she told me things about herself. It was her way of letting me down gently. But what she said opened my eyes even more. It told me who she is, what character is packaged in that beauty, and what I was losing with her refusal. Still, I was glad that she could see things clearly, even though I could not.

"She began by saying that she's still a young girl, not really a woman yet. She's a traditional girl from a very traditional family, and even though there are not many of those left, she will never be different. She's had kind of puppy love things, but she has never even held hands with a boy because proper girls don't do that. She has been raised to be modest, and she is. She has become very fond of me, even has admired the way I have dealt with the disappointment of my search, but marrying me would be wrong for both of us. I can never be a proper Việtnamese husband – that is what she has dreamed of having, all her life. Also, she can never be anything but a traditional Việtnamese wife, and she knows that will not suit me. 'Still, JJ, I have love for you, and I will always be your special friend'."

He shakes his head sadly. "It would have been easier on me if she had just said to bugger off."

Ha Oum looks from him to me. "Really?" She asks him, but also me.

JJ says, "Sometimes too much kindness hurts more than a harsh word. She, Binh and Thien left a while ago. I've had some time. I'll be OK. I would not have said this even a week ago, but I get it. There are plenty of fish in the sea."

Ha Oum looks confused for a minute. She considers this and finally understands.

"Right? Asks JJ.

"Right," she says. Then, giving me a mischievous look, she adds, "But speaking as a Rhadé lady, I know the trick is finding and catching the best one. And all the 'fish' are not female."

Chapter 23

"Did you sleep OK last night?" JJ and I are having breakfast.

"It took me a while to drop off, but after that, yeah, fine," he says. "A good thing too because I've got a long trip ahead of me, back to Aussie.

"Don't you want to relax a bit before you head off?"

"Why? I've done the tourist thing, failed to get any useful information about my real father's identity and now have one major unrequited love in my portfolio. You can't say I haven't accomplished anything here in the last month. Nah, time to go home."

"Home? Back to your step-brothers and the pre-Việtnam JJ?"

"Ouch! When you put it that way, it doesn't sound so good, but I'll survive."

"Sure, but is that what you want, to survive? Didn't you find out something about yourself here? That maybe you're not that JJ anymore? That if you give yourself a chance – take a chance – your life can be, will be, different?"

"Yeah, well, I took a chance. See where that got me."

"Look, no matter what we think, we have possibilities that are waiting for us out there, maybe even that are intended for us, if we will open the way for them. Come on, JJ."

"Gor, are you doing your Y'Dun-shaman thing again? Do you really believe that jazz? I don't mean to rain on your parade, but that stuff is not possible. Look, you got a bit carried away, with that and with the emotional meetings you've had with your father's friends. And Ha Oum surely didn't act to dissuade you of anything. Now, with her on the scene, maybe you're backed into a corner. If you give up the Y'Dun stuff, you lose her. She is a full-on babe, mate. And don't tell me that sex isn't on your mind. For you, this is not a tough choice."

"I fell for 'that jazz', as you call it, before I ever knew of Ha Oum, and I'll make my decisions on what I see as the merits of things."

"Right, and she's one hell of a merit."

I don't like the comment or the tone, but I remind myself that JJ is hurt. He has said that he's OK, but how can that be? For the first time in his life, as far as I know, he fell hard for a woman and actually thought he might have a chance with her. And I am not unaware that whatever relationships he had in Australia never worked out at all. I take a breath and say, "JJ, I'm very sorry that things did not go well with Thuy, and, frankly, I did think, last night before falling asleep, that your timing with her was unfortunate. I thought about the things she said to you. They all rang true to me, but I thought also that if she were just a bit older and more experienced, some of her attitudes might have had a chance to soften. Then I thought how lucky I am that my timing with Ha Oum has somehow been right. I..."

He cuts me off. "No! You don't think that way, Y'Dun, or whatever name you want to use. YOU think that Rhadé spirit or spook has planned all this. What BS! You know who your father is. People here receive you like you're the second coming. Shit, they think you actually are the second coming – of your father anyway. Everything since you hit town, if I understand what you tell me, has been one big – and getting ever bigger – pleasure. Don't pretend to understand me. You have never lived the shit that I have, so bugger off."

That does not sit well with me. I retaliate. "Cut the 'oh-poor-me' shit, JJ. You figured out that you are in danger of having a real friend – me. You also figured you had a beautiful woman who could actually care about you. Now that the woman has had her life-long reasons for backing away, even though she has true feelings for you, you want to become the old JJ again. The fatherless son, the child whose mother was divided in her devotion, the guy who has no friends and who needs to hate and blame the world. You can't lash out at your mother, so you go after me. Screw you. I don't need that crap."

"Very wise and shamanic of you," says JJ. He flips me off and leaves.

I had thought I would spend the morning walking around the city, talking with JJ. We've talked a lot since our first meeting weeks ago, and I have gotten to like him. I thought he liked me. I'm angry. I don't need this aggravation just at the moment when I am about to go home, and just when I am painfully aware that I have a decision I must soon make. Fortunately, Mr. Nam calls to say that Judge Đao wants to know if I can meet him at a law office later this morning so he can make introductions. Yang Rong at work? I say, "I'll be there."

The law offices of Tran Van Phu and Nguyễn Thi Ly are located on the 12th floor of what looks to be a brand new building. I don't know exactly what I expected, but it was something less western-looking, less American-looking than this. A beautiful Việtnamese woman sits at the reception desk, which is crafted from fine Việtnamese hardwood. A name plaque says Duong Thi Ha, Receptionist, in English, beneath what I assume to be the same title in Việtnamese. She offers me a luminous smile that almost stops me in mid-stride. I give my name. She stands and begins to come from behind the desk. "Judge Đao, Lawyer Phu and Lawyer Ly are waiting for you in the conference room. Please follow me." I fall in behind her and am mesmerized as she glides down a hallway. I almost have to pinch myself. Can males really get any work done when creatures such as this are in the office? I snap to. It's time to get professional – as an attorney, not as a shaman. I smile to myself.

Judge Đao makes the introductions. Lawyer Phu is quite evidently the firm's senior partner. While it is never easy to tell the age of older Việtnamese, I guess Mr. Phu to be in his early sixties. This would mean that he might have been in his twenties when he met Judge Đao. Ms. Ly appears to be in her mid-thirties. She was not yet born when Judge Đao was working on modernizing Việtnamese criminal code. Both speak excellent English. As I sit, Đao says, "I see you have changed your look somewhat."

I touch my now-clean-shaven cheeks and smooth my neatly-trimmed locks. I smile. "I am not on vacation any longer. If I am going to practice law, I owe it to clients and to the dignity of this office to respect professional grooming standards."

Judge Đao relates my appearance when he originally met me. The two lawyers smile and inquire into the story behind my stay in the Rhadé hamlet. Ms. Ly asks how I expect to assist their firm and their clients if I am occupied with becoming a tribal shaman. I explain that I am a securities and transactions lawyer in the United States and, further, that I have strong knowledge and understanding of these fields in British and French law. I have made no decisions yet about remaining in Việtnam, but if I do decide to stay, it will be so I can see if I am indeed, as Y'Chorn insists, destined to lead the tribe in its Banmethuot location. While I understand that it will not be easy to serve two masters, I have worked out in my mind, a strategy that should permit me to honor the interests and needs of both.

The Việtnamese partners exchange a skeptical look. It occurs to me that if it were not Judge Đao who had introduced me, I might, at this point, be on my way out the door. "How do you expect to do this?" asks Mr. Phu.

"My plan is to spend Mondays through Thursdays here, working in the office and meeting with clients and others in Hồ Chí Minh City. I would spend weekends, starting on Fridays, in Banmethuot. In this way, I believe I could bill about thirty hours each week. If we allow that I would also work after office hours, which I am used to doing, I would bill in excess of thirty-five hours each week. While I am not present, I will make arrangements so that I can be reached by phone with only slight delay, even if I am in the hamlet where there is no service."

Mr. Phu looks at Judge Đao and Ms. Ly. "He has thought carefully about this." The statement comes out in a tone of approval.

Ms. Ly looks skeptical. "I understand that the plan as you describe it can work. Of course that is not a guarantee that it will. Leaving that aside for the moment, I must say I am not very much at ease with a foreigner, like yourself, with anyone for that matter, who actually thinks the pretensions of some tribal shaman might make sense."

Judge Đao looks uncomfortable. He is a consummate gentleman – of the old school, as the saying goes. I am guessing he does not approve of Ms. Ly's directness. Mr. Phu also looks a bit ill-at-ease.

I look at Ms. Ly and say, "I understand and sympathize that you are not at ease! How do you think I felt when I found myself tempted to believe something so utterly beyond my normal frame of reference and experience? Two things: I greatly appreciate your being direct, frank, confronting me. If there is even a remote chance that we will wind up as colleagues, we will want – and need – this honesty. Next, if you feel that you simply can't get comfortable with this, it is surely best that we go no further with the idea of your bringing me into your practice."

Judge Ðao and Mr. Phu smile at each other, each with a somewhat mischievous twinkle in his eye. I get the idea that they relish this conversation and are content to let its two antagonists "slug it out."

Ms. Ly glances at my resume. "And what is your Rhadé name? I assume you have one."

"Y'Dun."

"So, Mr. Y'Dun, are we to tell our clients that Mr. Y'Dun will serve them, or are we free to use this name (she taps my resume)?"

"That depends."

"Really! On what exactly?"

"On whether I am acting as a counselor at law or in a more general advisory capacity, where the guidance of Yang Rong will be most useful." I say this with a grin.

She gives me a broad smile. "I take it Yang Rong is a Rhadé spirit." She mimes clapping her hands. "Well done."

Judge Ðao and Mr. Phu are actually chuckling a bit. Ðao says, "Y'Dun has told me about how he came to accept the shaman's certainty that he is indeed destined to replace him one day. Do you want to share that with the skeptical Ms. Ly?"

Mr. Phu says, "Please do. I can hardly wait."

Ms. Ly, now smiling broadly, extends her hand, palm up, as if to say, "The floor is yours."

"I'll spare you the ugly details. Americans say it is better to see the final product of a sausage, rather than to watch it made. The first thing for me was to avoid confusing the tribe's 'basic, not to say, primitive', way of life, with ignorance. They hold beliefs that have stood them in good stead for centuries. The next thing was to admit that it is surely hard to believe in a world where spirits account for everything one cannot understand. But when I learned that the Rhadé believe that certain special men can contact the stream of knowledge and energy they say flows beneath the visible world, things started to look different to me. After all, most people acknowledge an all-powerful god or supreme being, especially when they need an explanation of, or comfort for, something that overwhelms them. This does not seem very different from the Rhadé belief in a universal energy."

There is silence. It clearly seems that 'my audience' is waiting for something more. I smile and say, "Now, to show you that I possess the good lawyer's ability to keep the client ready to pay for more, I will simply add, the rest of the story will be available if/when we become colleagues."

The two partners are smiling, but Mr. Phu returns us to the serious matter at hand. "Judge Đao's recommendation of you weighs heavily in your favor. Still, as a matter of diligence – and respect for you as a professional--we have reviewed your resume and paid special attention to the specifics of your securities practice. Based on what we see, you have considerable expertise in that area, as well as in transactional law. You would add considerable strength to our firm in both areas, but especially in securities, where we have very little capacity at the moment. Ms. Ly has looked up two opinions in cases where you were the lead attorney for the prevailing parties. We are impressed with the work and knowledge that must have led to the results achieved in those cases." Ms. Ly nods her agreement. "Would it be possible for you to request that your secretary in the States email us a sample of your writing so we may complete our consideration of your suitability for our firm?"

When I say that I will see to this, Mr. Phu again shifts our ground. "Please, Đao, Y'Dun, join us for a light Việtnamese lunch. We have a small dining room for staff, which we have reserved in your honor."

At lunch, Mr. Phu explains that the firm also has offices in Hanoi. Since Hanoi is the capital of Việtnam, that office is considered, the head office. I say that I have understood him to be the principal partner and question why he is not resident at the head office. He explains, "The simple reason is that while Hanoi is our capital, Hồ Chí Minh City is essentially our commercial capital. Beyond that, the actual, primary-level reason is that it is wise to have a principal in Hanoi who is regarded as 'ideologically reliable' by our political leadership.

"I am glad you asked that question because if you do join us, you would sometimes have to work in Hanoi – although usually only for several days at a time. In general, nothing that would interrupt the four-day, three-day schedule you have suggested."

"Will I, as an American, be acceptable to the communist leaders in Hanoi?"

"There are already many Americans living in Hanoi and working at the Hanoi offices of American companies and law firms. You will not be different from those people."

"Until," I say with a sly smile, "I become officially Rhadé."

Everyone chuckles. Ms. Ly says, "We assume that moment is not imminent and that if and when we come to that bridge, you, Y'Dun, will have the wisdom to guide us all across it. I have an important meeting after lunch and must excuse myself. It has been a pleasure – and interesting. We will talk more soon. If you have time now, Mr. Phu will introduce you to some of our lawyers, speak with you about our practice in general and the specifics of it that relate to your expertise. He will also be interested to learn more details of your professional experience."

I thank her. As she departs, Judge Đao says that he will leave me to Mr. Phu. I ask him if he is free around 6:00 PM tomorrow to join me at the hotel for drinks and to meet Ha Oum. He agrees.

* * * * * * * * * * *

I walk back towards the hotel through the center of the city's business district. I recall when I first set foot here just over a month ago. It seems longer than that, so much has happened. The area is no longer new or exotic to me. It does not yet feel like home, but there is a familiarity now. As I walk, I drift into a kind of reverie. I imagine my father walking and driving through here fifty years ago, as if it were his home. Then, I realize that it actually was his home; that he had so bonded with the place and the people, he felt as if he and the city belonged to each other. The thought stops me cold. I stand in the middle of the street and have to be brought out of my trance by a concerned pedestrian. He taps me on the shoulder and says something I don't understand. Thankfully, he takes me by the hand for a moment and then squires me to the sidewalk. "Are you all right?" he asks in good English. I give him an embarrassed smile and a nod. He waits a moment to be sure I am focused and then goes on his way.

I look around to get my bearings. I am standing on Hàm Nghi Boulevard, in front of the building that became the American Embassy in 1950, and I am almost submerged by a flood of memories. They are not my own, but my father's, as he dutifully recorded in his notebooks and journals. They begin with his love for the old French names of Saigon streets. From this one's beginnings at a landing known as Crocodile Bridge Creek; through its development as a center for Chinese emigrant traders from Canton, when it became Boulevard de Canton; to its selection as the site for the Hotel d'Annam, the "in place" of the times, when it had again changed name and become Boulevard de la Somme; to its rechristening as Hàm Nghi Boulevard in 1955, this street has a history that traces the rise of Saigon as a major commercial center and principal Việtnam city.

I stand in front of the old Embassy building, aware that it appeared in Graham Greene's 1955 novel, *The Quiet American*, as "The American Legation" and painfully aware that it was severely damaged by a car bomb in 1965. There is so much here, so much to know, and, unaccountably – because I have been here for but the briefest time – I feel emotionally attached to the city and to its spirit and history. I continue on my way, slowly coming back to the present, thinking about my recent meeting and the decisions I will soon have to make.

I decide to walk past the hotel. I head onward towards buildings that once housed the South Viêtnamese ministries of Economy, Defense, Social Welfare and Interior. I walk around the square where the Cathedral and the Post Office still stand and then go on to the old Thống Nhut Nhứt (reunification) Blvd, now Blvd. Lê Duẩn. At this vantage point I have but to turn in a circle to see key locations in the unraveling of the independence of the Republic of Viêtnam. To the south, at the head of Lê Duẩn stands the old Independence Palace, now Reunification Palace, an unoccupied monument, site of the iconic photo of a victorious North Viêtnamese Army tank crashing through the palace gate on April 30, 1975. To the west are Gia Long Palace, where President Diệm and his brother were captured by the 1963 revolutionary junta, the former Ministry of Foreign Affairs and the Reuters office of those days. Down Lê Duẩn Blvd. to the north is the site of the American Embassy that was attacked at Têt in 1968. It is now the US Consulate. Farther down is the Saigon zoo, which contains a botanical garden and the old headquarters of the Société des Etudes Indochinoises. I am surprised at the emotion these sights provoke in me. How can it be that, simply because these places and events, this history, meant so much to my father, they mean so much to me also? Incomprehensibly, I feel as if my blood and my being are intertwined with those of this place. And this brings an eerie and sobering thought. For all that I have been charmed by, tempted by and believed in what Y'Chorn has told me, can it truly be that I, as he said my father was, am actually of this land and this place going back into the mists of time? I return to the hotel.

Ha Oum arrives before 6:00 PM, earlier than I had expected her. "There was an emergency," she says. "I had to go in at 5:30 this morning and have only just now finished. I knew it would be a long day, so I took some 'civilian clothes' (she is in her nurse's uniform) with me. Can I go to your room to shower and change?" I nod and hand her the key. "Come with me, please. I am tired and will want to rest for a while up there."

She comes out of the bathroom wrapped in a towel. She is astoundingly beautiful. Her long hair is down. The towel is molded to her considerable curves, and her freshly showered, café-crème complexion glows. Thrilled by the sight of her, and still under the influence of my afternoon emotions, I don't dare move. I don't dare speak for fear of saying something wrong, perhaps irrevocable. I am sitting at the room's small desk. She stops by my chair and looks at me for a long, silent moment. I know something is happening. I feel somehow humbled. She continues to look at me in silence, but this is not an inspection or an assessment. I feel as if she is absorbing me. At length she kisses me gently. She steps back and with her bottomless gaze upon me says, slowly, clearly and with evident certainty, "I choose you."

* * * * * * * * * * * *

We are on the hotel terrace. It is very early. We skipped dinner last night and are starting on a large breakfast. JJ appears. He spots me and begins to turn away, but he does a double-take. His face softens, and for a minute he just looks at us. Then, with a huge smile, he comes over. "Got room for one more?" Ha Oum gestures that he should sit. Still smiling broadly, he says, "So, it's done, is it, mate?"

Ha Oum replies immediately, with a big grin. "You're asking the wrong person, *mate*."

"Right. I forgot. The man has no say in the matter." He looks happily at me.

"What can I say?" I ask with exaggerated self-deprecation.

"How about, 'finally,' or 'thank God', uh Yang…that guy, or just 'Wahoo'?"

I smile at him. "All of the above."

"Good on ya, mate. Look, about yesterday. You didn't deserve that. I'm really sorry."

"Shut up and eat your breakfast. I have important things to do, like just being here with this wonderful lady."

"Yes, please," says Ha Oum. "You two can talk once I have left for work."

She finishes her meal quickly and rises to leave. She gives me a kiss and then leans over to give the startled JJ a hug. For a moment, he doesn't know what to do. Then he hugs her back and stands as she departs. He looks after her and is clearly a bit flustered. "Gor, do I deserve that? I think she did that to make me feel ok, included, maybe even an accepted part of your circle." He is actually blushing. "You know, mate, I don't remember any female – surely not a young attractive one – ever doing that for me. Well, yeah, Thuy did give me that Frenchie, air-kiss on either cheek thing, but this was different. This was, 'You're one of us, JJ'. Am I right?"

"I think that was exactly the point."

"Did you tell her about our…ok, MY piss up yesterday?"

"Yes."

"And she still did that?"

"JJ, you're a friend. Friends don't stay angry forever. They get over it."

"Like I said yesterday, you haven't lived my life."

"OK, right. But that was then, and there and those people. This is here, and now, and me and her, and even people here who have been so kind to you. Do you think you can get used to that?"

He breaks eye contact, hangs his head, and is silent for long moments. When he looks up, it seems that he is fighting back tears. "Ya know, I'm not sure. No knock on you, mind you, but I'm not sure I trust it – trust me. I do know that I spent a very unhappy day yesterday. A lot of time reassuring myself that I was right and you were wrong. After a while, the more I reassured myself, the more I began to think that if I was so bloody right, I would not need the endless reassurance."

"JJ, I'm pretty sure that compared to you, I've had it easy. Kind of funny, really. I've had my father, but not my mother. You, just the opposite."

"Yeah, but you at least knew who your mum was."

"That's a big thing, even though she had her problems. Still, I had a lot of anger towards my dad. In a way I only started to really settle that after he died. That was tough for me, but walking in his footsteps here really opened my eyes. Who knows, maybe yet we'll find out something for you."

"I kind of doubt that, but maybe I should learn a bit from your Rhadé buddies. Maybe Yang…, you know, will step in." He laughs.

"OK, so now, what's your plan? Packing? Seeing your three Việtnamese friends one last time? What?"

"I'm packed and all. Truth? I kind of wanted to get right with you before leaving."

"Well, you've done that."

"Right, but something still doesn't feel good, finished. Know what I mean?"

"Not really. I understand the feeling, but I don't know what would remain for you to do now."

"Yeah. Tell you what. Do what you've got to do. I'm gonna go back to the Ministry of Interior and try to thank that guy who began by giving me a hard time on my first day and then softened up."

"That's a really nice idea. Do you think that's what's bugging you as unfinished?"

"Nah. It's just something I thought, all of a sudden, I want to do. The guy might go right back to his original behavior, but he, and Trân here (he gestures at the waiter) and Binh, Thien and Thuy, they all managed something I didn't usually encounter in Aussie. They got past whatever there is about me that turns people off."

I am silent, very surprised by what JJ has just said. He goes on, "Do you think that maybe, when you get out of, away from, your normal, life-long context, you somehow subtly change the way you present yourself to the world? I mean, it might not be something you do consciously. And these 'new' people, they see you that way, instead of how the people back in your usual context saw you?

"Look, you told me you were angry with your father for a long time, but finally, too bad it was after he died, you read his journals and began to see him differently. You saw him the way he appeared to himself. By the time you get here, you have changed. You are looking for information about him with love – not with anger. Everyone you meet picks up that vibe, and you have a great visit."

"So what about you? You got the crap kicked out of you from the get-go."

"Right, because I was still the Australia JJ. Resentful, angry with my mum and her lawyer, and more than half expecting and looking for trouble. Even up there in the Ministry, now that I think of it, only when I got worn down and gave up my attitude of 'what the hell goes on here, why are you doing this to me', did the officer change.

"Even with you. I couldn't get you angry with me until I went back to being the Australia JJ. You said the exact words about my 'oh, poor me', stuff. Right on. That was the Australia JJ."

There's nothing for me to say. JJ seems to understand. He looks at his watch. "Still early, but I want to get to the Ministry when it opens, so I can see that guy, Vien, before he gets tied up. I'll catch you back here whenever."

I watch him go and then return to my now-cold breakfast. As I gesture to Trân to at least get some fresh coffee, I catch sight of lawyer Phu and lawyer Ly. They are headed towards my table. I stand and gesture that they should sit. "You're out early," I say.

They sit. Mr. Phu says, "Just a bit, but we wanted to catch you outside the office, and Judge Đao told us that you usually start with an early breakfast here."

I nod. "Will you both join me? For coffee – or tea, if not for a full breakfast."

The two of them smile. Ms. Ly says, "We are not limited to tea. Coffee is fine."

"Right. I had the chance to see that Việtnam grows both and that the quality is excellent."

Mr. Phu glances at Ms. Ly. "Tell us about that," he says. She nods her interest.

I give them a brief on my visits to Bảo Lộc and Banmethuot. Mr. Phu says, "That's very interesting and relates to why we're here. Judge Đao thinks very highly of you. Some of that opinion, I mean no offense, comes no doubt from his high regard for your father. As Việtnamese, we pay attention to a person's family background, but as lawyers, considering bringing you into our firm, we must be circumspect. So we came to meet you in a less formal, less official environment and to see who you are behind your impressive professional credentials. We don't have doubts in that area. You are still young, still learning and rising in your profession in America. But it looks to us as if you will become a highly respected professional, a 'big man' in the American term."

This is not the moment for an American, 'aw-shucks' act. I say nothing.

"But we are looking to have you work here, in Việtnam. In relations with foreign clients, who would make up the majority of your practice, you will surely do well. But we remember that you will always be doing your job in the context of this country, with us and other Việtnamese as colleagues. Can you deal with that, with us and our ways, with the culture of this country? Also, by hiring you, we are making a bet that not only will you fit with us, but that we can build an in-house capability, instead of having to farm it out, as you say, to other firms. You are licensed to appear in court in America. You may have to do that in line with your work for us. If you do that, our firm can charge for that service directly."

"I understand."

Ms. Ly almost cuts me off. "Now you see why it is important to us to trust that you will not decide to leave us for a full-time tribal life before a decent interval has passed. That interval amount of time, for us, would be five years at the least."

"I very much appreciate your putting your cards on the table, as we say. So, let me ask, have you reached a decision on me? Are you making me an offer?"

"The lawyer in him," says Mr. Phu. "Yes, although at this moment, let us please call it a proposal. If you feel comfortable that you can accept the terms we are suggesting, we will formalize matters by turning the proposal into a written contract – with specified compensation – which you may consider for one month before having to reply. That will give you some time back in America while you try to decide."

I look at Ms. Ly and say, "The lawyer in him."

We all laugh. They say they have appointments, now that the workday has officially begun. I nod my understanding and tell them that I look forward to our planned evening together. "Judge Đao will be joining me for drinks here at 6:00 PM. Can you begin at that time? I will be introducing him to my fiancée. I would like you to meet her, and I will also invite Mr. Nam, a friend of Judge Đao, who has been so wonderfully helpful to me this past month."

Mr. Phu says, "We know Mr. Nam well." He glances at Ms. Ly. She nods. "Then we will both be glad to join you." They excuse themselves.

I finish my cold coffee and thank Trân for his kind service. I do this in Việtnamese because I know it pleases him and that he has appointed himself as language teacher to the two benighted foreigners he has come to enjoy serving each day. "Không dám," he says. "Tôi rất vui khi được giúp đỡ' bạn." (You're welcome. I am happy to help.)

I leave the hotel and walk down Đồng Khởi Street. I spend an hour looking in the fashionable shops for a suitable gift for Tom, my mentor back in the law firm. I take my purchase back to the hotel and am surprised to find K'Sor Brui waiting for me. We sit down for drinks, as if I needed more. He gives me news of Y'Chorn and of the hamlet and tells me, with a mischievous grin, that Y'Chorn has informed him Ha Oum has made her decision.

"How does he know that? Is this something he has planned all along with her?"

"No, he would not do such a thing. It is just, remember, he is Y'Chorn. But I am 'modern' enough to double check with you. I had to come down here anyway, and of course I would stop to see you before you leave."

"You know that there was no real need to double check. He is right. She will be coming to the hotel this evening at 6:00 PM. We're going to have drinks with Mr. Nam and several other people, including the partners in a law firm that may hire me to work if/when I return. Are you free to join us? Ha Oum and Mr. Nam will be happy to see you. If you say yes, I'll make a party of it and take us all to dinner."

"You say, 'if'. Is there any question?"

"I have to think things through carefully, so, yes, the final decision is not made."

"What happens to Ha Oum if you decide no?"

"I hope she would remain with me regardless."

K'Sor Brui is silent, clearly thinking. "Well, I don't need to worry – and neither does she – because Y'Chorn does not misread things. You will return. She will make you an excellent wife. You will be a good husband, and you will learn to be a Rhadé husband. I will drink nam bay at your traditional wedding in the hamlet."

"Aren't you getting ahead of yourself?"

"No." He says this with unshakable certainty and then adds, "And for tonight, it will be my pleasure to join you all."

JJ returns to the hotel as I am saying good-bye to K'Sor Brui. Apparently he has had a good visit with Col. Vien because he is smiling and has a spring in his step. The smile gets broader when he sees K'Sor Brui. He comes over and offers him a hearty handshake and a, good-to-see-you mate, greeting. K'Sor Brui looks a bit surprised but returns the handshake happily. "I've got to go now, Mr. JJ, but I hope I will see you tonight."

"What's doing tonight?" asks JJ.

"First tell me about that smile that Captain Vien left you with."

"Ah, yeah, right. Well, when I walked in, there was almost no one there yet. Even most of the personnel hadn't appeared. So I walked through to Vien's area, not seeing anyone along the way. When I stepped into his area, he was alone, already at work reading some poor bugger's file. I hesitated. After a moment, he must have sensed that someone was there, because he looked up. You won't believe it, mate. When he saw me, he got this big smile. He stood up and actually gestured me to sit in a chair before his desk. Then he says, very slowly and clearly in Việtnamese, 'Rât vui ông về'. So I kind of understood, something about being happy I came back. I know the happy bit from hanging with Thuy and the guys.

"Anyway, I say, 'Tôi về cảm ơn ông.' You know, 'I came back to thank you'. He laughed and got us tea and talked to me in English for maybe twenty minutes. He said he hoped I found my dad. When I said I didn't, he offered to help. When I said I was leaving tomorrow, he urged me to stay and if I could not, to be sure to come back so we could have a Việtnamese meal together."

"That's great, JJ. A real victory."

"Yeah. I couldn't believe it. I said I would come back. When I left him I was so happy, I just took off and walked around so as not to forget this place. Now, what's going on tonight?"

"Well, it started out with me planning on having my judge friend here for drinks this evening and to meet Ha Oum. He's a wonderful man, a dear friend of my father's, and I feel that having her meet him will be a bit like her meeting my old man himself. Then a bunch of things happened, and I wound up inviting the lawyers who might hire me if I come back, and…"

"Are you still on the 'if' stuff? Come on. You know you're coming back."

"We'll see on that, but I realized I should invite Mr. Nam. He knows the lawyers and the judge. Then K'Sor Brui showed up, and I invited him. Now here you are, so we can make it a goodbye party for you, along with everything else."

"Right. But about that goodbye stuff. I think I'm going to delay my departure. No rush, right? I'll go when you go."

"Oh ho! So now it's no rush, is it? At breakfast you couldn't get out of here fast enough."

"Hey, a guy can change his mind, can't he?"

"Yes, but the JJ I first met was pretty fixed on his ideas and positions. So, do we now have a new JJ? Nah, couldn't be!"

"All right, mate, get off the new JJ's ass and let him be."

"I'll let him be, if he'll think about coming with me to Hawaii, just for the hell of it. Just so he doesn't jump back right away to Australia and maybe fall back into being the old JJ."

"You really mean that?"

"Sure. I have plenty of room at the house. There's a housekeeper to clean up after us, an ocean to swim in and a few exotic flowers. Maybe even one or two who will make you forget the lovely Thuy."

JJ gets a far-away look in his eye for a moment. Then, he shakes his head. "It was a learning experience, a hard one. But maybe I can use the knowledge gained to my benefit...um to the benefit of the beautiful Hawaii girls."

"You'll really come?"

"Ask me tonight."

Chapter 24

*T*he dinner was an extraordinary affair. In retrospect, as Ha Oum and I bid our guests goodnight and went, as a couple, to our room, I was thinking of the dinner as if it were, in a way, like the last scene of an opera. The entire cast appears on stage, sings the final song, and the curtain comes down. It wasn't quite that simple, but the evening confirmed many things: the emotional friendship between me and the two older men, Mr. Nam and Judge Đao; the feelings of admiration Ha Oum generated in these men – and indeed in everyone; the conviction on the part of the lawyers that they need not worry greatly about whether I would be comfortable in Việtnam and be a fit for their firm, and finally that JJ had turned a corner and was becoming comfortable with himself in his new persona and outlook.

Mr. Phu and Ms. Ly left us as we all departed the restaurant after dinner, but the others returned to the hotel with Ha Oum and me and treated us to cognac in the courtyard. K'Sor Brui excused himself first. He had an early flight back to Banmethuot. He spoke quietly to Ha Oum, holding her hand in both of his. He hugged me and said Y'Chorn had told him Ha Oum and I were planned by Yang Rong. The old man was, he said, deeply moved when he declared this. As he turned to leave, he told me, "No if."

Judge Đao and Mr. Nam, the two friends of ancient years, looked on at us with obvious emotion. Đao told me that my father would wholeheartedly approve. Mr. Nam, seeing, no doubt, his own youth before him said simply that not everyone must give up his Hugette.

When they had taken their leave, JJ thanked us for the dinner. He then took out his cell phone and asked us to stand among the flowers and plants in the courtyard garden. "I think this might be the first of you two alone, posing as a couple. Tell the little ones that Uncle JJ took it on the night when everything was confirmed and before he booked his first flight ever to Hawaii."

I started to say something, but he cut me off. "See you in the morning."

The evening has finally ended. In our room, Ha Oum holds me. "You will come back, won't you?"

"Of course. I love you."

"To stay." She hesitates. "Forever, I mean."

"For you," I say.

She becomes deeply serious and tells me with intensity and also great love, "I can go with you anywhere, be with you anywhere, but at the last, I must always be here. Far from Việtnam, far from my hamlet and my people, I will not be the same. But you, as I believe – and as Y'Chorn knows--at the last, belong here.

"I call you Y'Dun because that's who you are for me. I did not choose the man who carries your American name. I chose Y'Dun. I love so much about you, but most of all, I love that you can so understand my people, care about us, that you can be Y'Dun. I know that we will have differences over our years. I will be able to deal with those because I will always know that inside of you, there is Y'Dun."

Ha Oum lies beside me now, wrapped in a sleep of peace. I have much to think about. At age thirty-eight, I am not a boy.

At least since my father's death, I have thought of myself as, "a man." But now, in the air conditioned dark of this hotel room, I wonder about that judgment. I have been confronted, by someone who is indeed "a woman," with the need to accept the responsibilities of what I have, perhaps, only been pretending to be. Quietly, I thank God for Ha Oum, her maturity, honesty and the challenge those represent to me. I think to myself that all males, on the edge of this decision – marriage, commitment to another – should have such a clear-sighted, courageous, waiting partner. I think my father did not.

The morning feels urgent. Ha Oum is as she has always been since she announced her choice. We have a continental breakfast, and she leaves for work. I take a quick walk around the area, trying to see it as it was in my father's time. I feel close to him and regret not knowing him in those days. When I return to the hotel, JJ is at breakfast. We discuss our plans for the day and then go about our business. Tomorrow at this time, we will be on a plane heading for Tokyo and then Hawaii. It is an exciting, but melancholy, thought.

The day passes. We three have a light dinner and retire for last minute preparations. Ha Oum and I talk as I fold clothes and pack my bag. There is none of the intensity of last night. She is relaxed but "taking me in" as if to remember everything. It is embarrassingly romantic of me, but I miss her already.

Morning. Ha Oum heads for work. "I will greet your return; not watch you depart." Phùng arrives to take us to Tân Sơn Nhứt. On the way, he stops just outside the airport where I had asked him to stop on my first day. He has memorized the words on the now-non-existent stele and repeats them to me. Then he says, But YOU will not be forgotten. And YOU will come back."

* * * * * * * * * * *

JJ and I are boarding our Hawaiian Air flight. Next stop, Honolulu. The flight attendants are dressed in Hawaiian prints, a few even in muumuus. JJ is excited. We are in first class. The "stewardesses" are very attractive, all slender, many with long, silky black hair and that extraordinarily exotic mix of ethnicities, Polynesian, Japanese, Chinese, even Portuguese, that marks Hawaii. "I could get used to this," JJ says.

"More beautiful than Thuy?" I jab him.

"Thuy who?" he grins.

We're home. It's been a long flight. We're both tired, but JJ is positively vibrating. As we approached the islands, he was glued to the plane window and kept up a running commentary on what he saw. "Gor, it's beautiful, Mate. I mean it sits down there like some kind of a miracle in the middle of nowhere, and we found it. Jeez, look at that. Is that Diamond Head? It's spectacular. The whole place is spectacular. Those tall, green cliffs and the land that runs up to beaches all around. Beautiful sunshine, and the water glittering like a jewel in the sun."

"Come on, JJ, I'm sure when you fly over the coasts of Australia, it looks somewhat the same."

"Nah. It's different. I mean this is a Pacific island. Maybe Fiji or Tahiti looks a bit like this from the sky, but this is special. And this is your home! Why would you ever leave it to go live in some backwards jungle hamlet with a bunch of people who are not too far out of the stone age? Really, mate. I mean I know you love Ha Oum, and she is beautiful and really one hell of a woman, but, gor, mate, bring her here!"

He draws a breath and looks silently out for maybe a minute. "Sorry, mate, I got carried away. I know you have your reasons. Don't mind me. I'm flying in my own plane right now – on a real high."

When we pull into the broad driveway in front of my house, JJ jumps from the car and stares out over the hedge of yellow hibiscus at the unobstructed view of Diamond Head. "It's real. I mean there it is, and you live here. It's like Diamond Head is just across the lawn. Hey, is that the house, down those steps and in the yard? Oh, God."

By the end of the day, JJ has explored the house and yard thoroughly and taken over the guest bedroom, my boyhood room, as if he is a permanent resident. He has been going through my boyhood mementos and asking numerous questions about them. Many of my answers involve information on or stories about my father. He listens to these with great attention. Finally, done in by the time change, we decide to sleep, with the determination to wake in time for dinner, after which we hope to go to bed at the normal hour, in an effort to get over jet-lag quickly.

Despite our good intentions, the jet-lag holds on for several days, and our activities are punctuated by early-hour wake-ups, which allow us to take long walks over Diamond Head in the morning cool and late-day swims when the sun is warm, but not unbearably hot. In the long hours spent uniquely together, we are getting to know each other well. We talk together constantly at these times and slowly share stories from our lives that reveal who we are and how we became so. Inevitably JJ's stories are about his sense of alienation and the feeling that if his real father had been present, he never would have suffered such torment. Equally inevitably, mine revolve around the opportunities my dad created for me by having our wonderful house, sending me to an excellent school and being able to pay for special things in addition to my education, such as foreign travel and sports team travel – both important given the isolation of Hawaii.

One night at dinner, JJ says to me, "You know, you're a very lucky guy. What I hear from you is that you loved your father enormously, even while you were angry with him and resented him. Do you realize that?"

"Well, it is actually only recently that I came to appreciate him and love him. Only recently that I discovered who he is and realized all he did for me, all the crap he took from me, all the things he forbore to say to me and all the pleasure I should, as a son, have given him but did not."

"No, no," says JJ. "I listen to you, and it's clear you loved him all along. What I hear is a sadness in you that you realize it only now and have not had the comfort of it for as long as you could have. To me, it's clear. That's one big reason why going to Việtnam, walking in his footsteps and meeting his old dear friends means so much to you. You feel that you are finally giving him what you withheld for so long and should have given at the time when it was due, and he needed it."

I am stunned. He has seen it all clearly and spoken it in a way that brings tears to my eyes. I fight them back.

He looks at me and nods. "It's OK. What a great thing to have that, even if it comes a bit late. Better late than never. You know, I think I get your dad, and some of those tears that you are obviously resisting, are welling up in me. Because I'm saying to myself, 'JJ, if you had his dad, you would have been happy from the get-go. You never would have suffered what you did. You wouldn't have so much ground to make up in your life'. But for me, as for you, better late than never."

Life begins to settle. I encourage JJ to drive himself around the city and the island, as the best way to familiarize himself with the place. "Do you feel ready to drive on the right side of the road?" I ask.

"Good thought. That's a bit dicey right now."

"Well, take the car and give it a shot."

"I'm afraid I might do exactly that: give it a shot, or a whack. How about this? I'm gonna need a car anyway. Why don't I rent one for now? That way you can do your stuff without worrying about me, and I can crack up a rental instead of your vehicle."

I laugh, but it makes sense, so by late morning, JJ has his wheels, and I'm on my way to the office, with the present for my mentor.

* * * * * * * * * * * *

As I exit the elevator, our receptionist can see me through the glass doors of our firm. She smiles as I walk in. "Well, look who's here. You came back. We all thought you got scooped up by some exotic beauty over there and would never be heard from again. Welcome home." I smile a thank you. "Tom has been wondering when you'd be back. He'll want to see you right away." She picks up the interphone. After a murmured conversation, she says, "He's waiting."

As I walk down the hall, Tom peeks out of his office, sees me and gets a huge smile on his face. "The prodigal son returns. Boy, is it good to have you back." We go into his office. He closes the door and gestures towards one of his visitor's chairs. "Once you sit down, it will be like you haven't been away at all." He looks me over. "You look different. Tan, thinner, maybe a bit more self-assured. Tell me everything."

I begin by giving him his gift, a lacquer portrait of a Cham princess. Her likeness is rendered completely in finely crushed egg shell, which is bonded to the black, base-coat lacquer of the tableau and then covered with two highly polished layers of clear lacquer.

"Is that really for me? Jesus, it's a beautiful piece."

"The subject is a Cham princess. The medium and technique are traditional in Việtnam."

He thanks me profusely and stands to try the tableau out against a few spots on his wall. "This elevates the whole place. Thank you again." I smile. "Now, tell me everything."

"That's a tall order. There's much more to tell than I ever expected."

He makes a gesture with his hand as if to say, come on, come on. I ask, "Have you got time?"

He looks at his watch. "Sure. We can order in lunch if we need to. Hit me."

I tell him the whole story – at least the key parts. At first he interrupts a bit to ask questions, but as I proceed, he is clearly so surprised, that he just sits back and listens.

When I'm done, he clearly does not know what to say or where to begin. Finally, "So this Y'.. something guy thinks you're the reincarnation of an ancient shaman and that you will return to his tribe and eventually replace him? Is he nuts?"

"No."

His jaw drops. He gives me a long, appraising look. "No? Just, no, nothing else, no explanation? Let me rephrase. Are you nuts? Good God, I might have expected anything, but sure as hell not this! Next thing you'll tell me that he got you married off to a tribal girl to cement the deal." He gives me a sarcastic and questioning look.

"No."

"Shit, just no again? Come on."

"It doesn't work that way. The tribe is matricentral and matrilineal. The women choose the man they want to marry, so Y'Chorn was in no position to marry me off to anyone."

"Well, that's something. At least we won't have to arrange an annulment. So, small blessing, you escaped with your bachelorhood intact."

"Not exactly."

"Not exactly! Will you please stop the monosyllabic and cryptic answers? What the hell does, 'not exactly mean'?"

I tell him about Ha Oum.

"Ha who? Is this some kind of tribal dream girl like the one in the weird dream you had?"

"Yes."

He erupts. "Stop it. Give me the whole f..ing story."

I do so, but I also mention that if I do go back to Việtnam, I will be working a few days a week with a Việtnamese firm that is growing and developing foreign clients who may have securities issues and needs. "I am thinking that we could cooperate with you guys, when necessary."

"You what? Listen, stop the baloney. Come down to earth. Go into your office and get to work. I've got lots for you to do."

"Not right now, please. You need to take me seriously on this."

He shakes his head. "Did you get bitten by the same bug your old man did over there? Busy during the day and shagging local maidens at night?" He has a thought. "And don't give me a one-word answer!"

"Tom," I say, as kindly as I can, "to you, my dad is my father, not my old man. And, understandably, you have no idea of what he did and what he experienced over there, but I now do. I can tell you that it was deadly serious, highly personal in certain aspects, and could not have been done by a lesser man than my father."

He takes a very deep breath. "OK, look, I'm really sorry for my attitude and for some things I've said. Even though I really don't get this change in you, I understand you are serious about it. I hope you will share everything with me – all the details, gory or not. You have been almost like a son to me, all the more so because of the close, mentoring relationship we've had. Clearly, you have grown beyond that, but if I can help you as you consider this, be a sounding board, anything, I want to do that. And I assure you of my good faith in doing so."

"Thank you. I don't doubt your concern, affection for me or good faith. This situation is actually beyond any reference point in my life up to now. We are both kind of flying blind, but I will value your thoughts."

He is quiet, clearly thinking, trying as hard as he can to wrap himself around this. Finally he says, "Well, did you bring the lovely lady back for a look at Hawaii – a look at your home and context?"

"No, but we will do that."

"Do you have a picture, so I can at least get a look at the lady who will be my calabash daughter-in-law?"

JJ has emailed me the photo from the courtyard garden. I show Tom the picture I have. "Holy guacamole. She is gorgeous. Give me her name again." I do. "Ha Oum," he repeats. "Listen, buddy, no matter what you do, don't lose her."

"I don't control that. Remember, she chose me. Tribal women do not make that choice frivolously. They make it before the tribe, and it is a sacred decision. If I were a fish, you could say that I am fully hooked."

"I am surprised to be saying this, but that seems like a good thing now. Listen, let me turn you loose. Carol and I will invite you to dinner so we can talk more and so you can get the benefit of her woman's wisdom. I'll call you as soon as she tells me a good time."

He comes around the desk, gives my shoulder a squeeze, shakes my hand warmly and then walks with me to the lobby. He stops. "I was looking forward to bringing you forward for partnership. Do you think that could make sense now?"

"Tom, I have been hoping for that, but I have to be honest. This, Ha Oum, the hamlet, the tribe, changes everything. I can't in good conscience let you raise this now."

He gives me a long look. "You're committed?"

"No final decision, but committed to Ha Oum, yes."

He nods. "Well, let's not burn any bridges yet, and one way or another, I will always think of you as a son who, maybe, outgrew his calabash dad."

* * * * * * * * * * *

JJ returns to the house at the end of the day. As usual, since we arrived in Hawaii, he is on a high. "Come on out and see what I rented. It's a Jeep. You know, off-road capability." He grins. "I thought I might just run off the road on my own as I tried to avoid some mess that I created on the wrong side of things. Not to worry. She's still pristine, the Jeep. Not a scratch on her – yet. Gor, I drove all over. Went completely around the island. Saw those waves on the North Shore. Beautiful, awesome. Some local guys out there told me they're much bigger in the winter. Told me too about some Eddie somebody guy, who disappeared on the ocean while paddling away from a stricken sailing canoe to get help. One or two of these guys had stickers on their old pickup trucks: 'Eddie Would Go'. This is one fantastic place – with fantastic people.

"Like, for example, these guys, they spotted me as a foreigner right away. They were sitting around on the grass by the beach, drinking beer, playing the ukulele and singing and having fun. They invited me over. We talked a lot. I downed a few cold ones they offered, along with some grilled steak in Teri...something sauce. Beautiful. I learned a lot. Like, I'm a howley. Is that how you say it?"

"Haole," I correct him gently. Actually, you are *hapa*. I am too. It means, 'half' as in half haole and half something else. "I'm glad they were nice to you. It might have turned out differently."

"Yeah, they said that there are, um, haoles they don't like. I gather that things get a bit wild from time to time, but they sure were nice to me. I mean, everyone I crossed paths with, on the beach, on the street, at the petrol (gas to you) stop. Everyone had a smile, maybe a nod, maybe exchanged a word. I could get used to this. Gor, it's so different from what I lived back in Aussie. Not that the Aussies are a pain. They're usually lots of fun, but back there, I was the old JJ. No more, mate. New forever, that's me!"

I can't help myself. I am laughing at his enthusiasm and at the dithyramb he has just delivered, almost without taking a breath. "What!" he says.

"Nothing. Just glad you are liking it here. Things will settle after a while, so when they do, don't feel too let down."

"Right. I know that, but I am thinking that maybe I might want to stay here. You know, not go back to Aussie or even Việtnam. What do you think?"

"Let's take that step-by-step. Of course, you're welcome to stay in the house here as long as you want. So let's see what happens."

"Really, in the house? Fantastic. I love this place. You said your father kind of created it. I mean redesigned it to his taste and all so that it shows who he was, right?" I nod. "I'd really like to see a photo of him if you have one. I keep thinking, like I said, I kind of get him. Seeing him would confirm or not the physical picture I have of him, just from hearing about him. If he fits what I think, maybe I'll ask you permission to 'adopt him' and pretend that he was my spiritual dad. That OK with you?"

I laugh. "JJ, anything that works for you is good with me. I really am happy to see the guy who has emerged from the JJ I first met. Let me see if I can find a picture."

I put away all the pictures I had lying around when I left for Việtnam – except the ones relevant to dad's time on the ground there. Those I took with me. We never had any proper photo albums, so I just stuck the other shots in a specific drawer. I rummage there now and bring out a fat pile of old black and white pictures and begin to file through them. JJ looks over my shoulder. There are all kinds of scenes: me as a baby in Singapore, me at swim meets with my boyhood swim team, mom and dad holding chubby me at age four months, and so on. JJ loves it. As I work through the shots, I flip by the one that I have sometimes wondered about. It's the chubby baby, maybe four or five months old, being presented to the camera like a teddy bear, held forward with one had around its belly and the other under its behind. Only the infant is visible.

JJ grabs my hand as I start to pass the photo. "Whoa, who's that?"

"I don't know. The child of one of Dad's friends, I guess. It was in a group with other photos of friends' children. I really didn't think very much about it."

JJ doesn't comment. All of a sudden, he's quiet. He continues to examine the picture.

"Something wrong?" I ask.

He shakes his head quickly. He doesn't want to be diverted from the shot.

I lean forward and try to look over his shoulder. He's not just looking at the picture, he's *studying* it, and for some reason this makes me uncomfortable.

He shuffles back through the full stack of pictures until he comes to the one of me, age four months. He holds it next to the unidentified shot he has been examining. "Looks a little like you," he says.

I peer at the pictures. There is a slight resemblance, but that could be because, at early ages, babies sometimes do seem to resemble each other. I have the feeling that if I disagree, we'll have an argument, so I say nothing.

"No?" he prompts. "Then maybe it looks like me, huh?"

I am shocked. The implications are too clear. Before I can say a word, he turns the picture over and sees the writing on the back: the Việtnamese question, "Của ai?" and the date. He gives just the smallest nod and turns to me. "Do you know what this means? The writing."

I shake my head. "Never thought it was especially important."

JJ glances towards the bookshelves where my fat, bright-green-covered English-Việtnamese, Việtnamese-English dictionary sits in glowing evidence. "You're way ahead of me on the language stuff. Can you look it up?"

By now I am actually scared. I can see where this might be leading, and I have the feeling that JJ already *knows for sure* the content of the revelation that is looming just a step or two ahead. I'm trapped. I can't refuse.

While I fumble with the dictionary and make a few mistakes seeking the translations that will make good sense in the circumstance, JJ waits, tapping the picture against the nail of his left thumb. Finally I have it. "Whose is it?"

"Huh?" I have caught him by surprise.

"Whose is it? The words mean, Whose is it?"

"Yeah, I thought it might be something like that."

"Really?"

"Yeah, because, you see, that's my mum's handwriting. No mistaking it. If you want, I can show you the letter she wrote to me that I was given only after her death."

I shake my head.

"And," he says, "this date here is four months to the day after my birthday."

The ramifications of all this plunge me deeper into shock. But now JJ himself seems awed – maybe even daunted – by what it all suggests.

He forges ahead and asks casually, "Any chance your dad knew my mum in those days?"

I knew something like that was coming. Now that he has asked, in my head I am screaming, "goddamn right it's possible."

I'm not sure he has even noticed my distress. He just continues, "And there is one more thing."

Oh shit, I think. Of effing course there is.

"You see the ring on the hand holding the baby?"

In honesty, I have never paid that much attention to this goddamned photo, but I sure as hell see it now.

"That's my mum's ring. No other like it anywhere. Her

grandfather had it especially made – from his personal design – as an engagement gift for her grandmother. The ring passed to her mother and then to her."

I try to recover my composure by answering his question. "Sure. I mean I don't – we don't – know for sure. It never occurred to me, even as you were finding out bits about her back in Việtnam. But now that you ask, sure. They were there at the same time, and you did find out that she moved in circles that he would have been part of. Yup. Why not?"

I do my best to be open and matter-of-fact in my answer. I have come to like JJ very much, to feel a closeness to him and to be glad of having maybe put him on a course that will change and improve his life and his view of himself. But I do not at all like this development – and its ramifications. Ugly thoughts I don't especially care for and never even dreamed of before, are now buzzing in my head. I know my expression has changed. Anyone looking at me will see it. JJ is looking. Given his troubled past with virtually anyone he has encountered, he does not miss the implications of what he sees.

"You ok, mate?"

"Yeah, sure."

"Right." He puts the picture down on the table. He doesn't exactly "slam" it down, but he flips a corner of the stiff paper so that it snaps as it hits the surface. Without a further word, he walks off to his room and closes the door.

I am stunned, angry at JJ's attitude and feeling uncomfortable in my own home. I'm breathing heavily, and my mind returns immediately to the note on the back of the photo. *"Whose is it?"* I know that I could never have attached any significance to this before now, but I'm pissed. I can almost see his mum as she wrote that. The tone is smug, snarky, taunting, "shitty," not to put too fine a point on things.

Memories of my first encounter with JJ come leaping back. "Don't worry about me. I don't count. I'm just a statue, a parked car." Snarky, self-absorbed, self-pitying. And, given what he has let slip about his mother, an indication of her less-than exemplary character that ties in with some of the nastiness I saw from him early on. He had no father, so there is no "like father, like son," but that does not rule out, "like mother like son." I snort and shake my head.

A while later, I hear the door to JJ's room open. I don't look up. In a dry voice, he tells me, "Going out. I'll be back. Don't worry about me." The door closes with a slight bang. The words, *I'm just a parked car,* hang in the air like a silent ghost.

I pick up the picture and study it. There is something in me that just doesn't want what seems obvious here to be true. But the more I look at the picture, the more it seems that it could be JJ. There is a definite resemblance to me, but that would make sense if my dad was his dad. I try to get my mind on all the things I have to do and decide. Just a few minutes ago, everything seemed great, simple, happy. Now, I am getting a look into myself that I don't like at all, and, God help me, a look at my father that threatens the picture I had of him as an honest, honorable, caring man.

Finally, I focus on what I have to do. I must decide if I will indeed return to Việtnam permanently, and if so, what becomes of this house. Back here, on the ground in Honolulu, the decision I have to make seems less obvious than it did when I was in Việtnam, more daunting. Am I really ready to cut myself off for good from where I grew up and from the life and career I labored to build? I'm not the same as JJ in this way. I have happy memories of my home, and at least a few good friends here. Also, I have to look into the requirements for obtaining a residence visa in Việtnam.

While I consider all of this, the phone rings. It's Tom. "I know it's short notice, but Carol wants to see you as soon as possible. She's pretty upset at the idea of your leaving us for good. Our house, 6:30 tonight. Can you make it?"

I hesitate.

"Any problem?"

"I have a house guest."

"Ha Oum?"

"No."

"Come alone. I get the idea from Carol that this will be a 'family' discussion."

By the time JJ gets back, I have learned what I need to know about getting a residence visa for Việtnam. I can start out with a six-month visitor's visa and apply to convert that into a multiple exit and re-entry, resident visa. I am not sophisticated in these things at all, but I decide that between Judge Đao, Mr. Nam and the lawyers, I will have the help and influence I need, should problems arise. I will tell JJ this and also alert him that he will have to dine alone tonight.

To my surprise, my good mood, at having learned that the visa question can be readily managed, dissolves when I hear JJ come in. "Back," he grunts and goes immediately into his room.

Before the door closes, I say, "JJ, we've got to talk."

"Yeah. Something is up with you." He comes into the living room and sits down. "Let's have it," he says.

"What the f..k does that mean?"

"It means that you're in a snit about something, and it pretty obviously has to do with that picture. Doesn't take a genius to figure out that you're putting two and two together and getting, 'half-brother,' and that has put you in a shit. It was all ok to have good old JJ around to buddy up with, but when he gets maybe too close, is maybe family, maybe the bastard of your effing beloved *daddy*, you don't like it one god damned bit!"

The first reply that comes to my lips is, "Fuck you." But I

choke it back. "Before I get into the meat of what I think and how I feel, I have one requirement."

Silence, but I say nothing more. Either he's going to ask what it is, or we're finished here and now, for good and ever.

More silence. I promise myself that I'll give him just 60 seconds more, and I check the sweep hand of my watch to keep track.

"Fuck it, okay. What's the requirement?"

"That you apologize to my father and to me for that comment."

"What? No goddamned way." He draws a breath. "OK, maybe to you. I mean this whole thing is disastrously sudden. It's OK for me because I can see immediately what I have to gain – emotionally, to say the least. But, in its way, if it's true, it screws up your happy, well-ordered, successful life and maybe even the future you have been planning with Ha Oum. So, OK, *Y'Dun*, I apologize. Really, I do."

"To my dad, also," I insist.

"No, sorry, honestly. But your dad – likely mine too – knocked up my mum and left her in the lurch. Left her to rot, to manage on her own, when he at least had the wherewithal to help her financially. Left her to have her bastard – me – alone, and then do all the messed up things she did to handle the situation he left her with. Left her to turn me into the alienated, fucked up guy you met in Việtnam and, I admit it, helped to straighten out. So, again, sincere apologies to you, but again also, fuck your – our – father."

That tears it. I punch him in the face and knock him almost out of his chair. "You son of a bitch. You don't know what you're talking about, but I'll lay it out for you. Your mum – your words – *hunted* my dad and seduced him when he was vulnerable, having just learned of his father's death, in hopes of embarrassing him into marriage. Fucking self-absorbed, grasping, duplicitous bitch! So, you hold this against *him*? Horseshit!

"But that's not enough for you. You blame him for the way she handled things after your birth, for behavior that was, obviously, part of her shitty, snippy, resentful character. For behavior that messed you up. Sorry, buddy, you're pointing the finger at the wrong person. And there's more.

"We both know how it was in Việtnam in those days. Beautiful Việtnamese women, some of them taking advantage of their beauty to screw any foreigner with money, either to marry and escape Việtnam and the war, or to get dollars and favors for their families – even for loved Việtnamese boyfriends. That's exactly what your fucking – no pun intended – mum pulled on my dad."

He straightens up in his chair and glares at me, but with a bit less rage than before. His cheek is cut, and his eye is black and swelling. I get up. He shies away, but I am just going to get a cloth and some ice for his face.

I'm still not fully under control. I toss the cloth into his lap and tell him, "I found stuff in his notes and files and journals that made no sense to me. So I just shrugged my shoulders and ignored it. But now some of it makes sense. There's a typed letter addressed to the American Ambassador in Việtnam of those years, saying that the writer was *impregnated* by a distinguished American and begs the help of his office in *resolving this matter properly*. The thing is, the letter in my dad's files is an original. That's one reason why I couldn't understand what was going on. Now, the answer can only be that your mum sent the letter to my dad to 'scare' him into marrying her. Right, JJ, as if it's *your* mum who deserves an apology. Bull shit. My dad, MY DAD, he's the one who got diddled. Ironic, right, because she wrote the letter about *her* getting diddled. He's the one who deserves an apology

"Forget it. Forget the apology. I don't give a shit who you

are, whose son you are. If you're the product of that woman, and if you can't see what's right and wrong here, screw you. Here we go again with, 'oh poor me.' Grow up, man up or, go fuck yourself!"

I want to leave the house and run until I drop. But it's MY house, and I don't owe JJ a god-damned thing. So I sit and fume in front of him, waiting, almost hoping for him to give me some more bullshit.

We sit opposite one another in uncompanionable silence. JJ does not disappear into his room. He holds the ice against his black eye and seems to be looking at nothing, somewhere in the distance, out of the other. I am not going to leave the field. I pick up a book I had been reading and try to get back into the story. After a while, I catch a glimpse of JJ moving around the room, but I am not focused on him, and I concentrate on not paying attention to him. I can feel my rage subsiding, but this is not over for me by any means.

"Y'Dun, will you give me a second here?"

I look up. JJ is leaning forward, holding the offending picture. He seems drained of his anger. The look on his face is almost pleading. "Look, JJ," I say. "This thing is major as far as I am concerned. I…"

He cuts me off gently. "I know that, and I am sorry I got shitty about it and then got you shitty. If you'll just give me a minute."

I shake my head. "Look, if I calm myself down, I understand completely what this all means to you. The thing is, I'm much more focused on what it means to me. I had no idea at all about any of this."

"Neither did I," he jumps in quickly.

I hold up my hand. He says, "Right, right, you don't give a shit about me. Sorry, please, go on."

"I was alone with my dad from the time I was four months

old. There was no one else – NO ONE. He played with me, loved me, read me to sleep, took me to the zoo, all those things. He even said to me, 'It's you and me, pal. Just the two of us.' As a kid that meant so much to me. It was my world, my safe harbor, my tangible assurance that I was loved. Shit, he cooked for me – every night. Cooked! No dinner out of a can or frozen, pre-packed stuff. He did what other fathers did – and what mothers did too. Can you imagine?"

JJ nods sadly

"Sure, there came a time when we went off the rails, and I began to resent him. Sure that became a major thing in my life, but I understand now that it operated against a fantastic luxury that I had: that he was always present, always there for me, that he loved me and that 'it [was] just you and me pal.'"

JJ nods again.

"And now, when I have lived through what I learned in Việtnam, when I have reached the wonderful point of understanding him and loving him without any limit, I find out that, maybe it wasn't just you and me, pal. That it was the two of us plus someone. He lied to me – not by commission, but by omission. OK, I get why. He thought I needed absolute certainty about how important I was. And, of course, he had no idea of where you were, and apparently no way of finding out. So I can forgive all that. Jesus, I love him so much.

"But now, maybe, I have to share him with someone – with you. I can't help it, JJ, I'm devastated. I know my dad would want me to 'understand,' to forgive him and to accept my half-brother, if I have one – if that's who you are. The truth is, I'm a grown-up. I can do that. I will, once I get out of my snit and over the shock. But for the moment, I need some space. And I sure don't need you bad-mouthing my dad!"

There is a long silence. JJ looks as sad and as lost as I feel. Finally, he says, "Y'Dun, I apologize with all my heart. I am so sorry. I owe you a lot, but most of all, I owe you your privacy and the right to live the life that stretches before you now. I'll do whatever you want. But I want to take at least part of the burden for that decision from your shoulders.

"You are right to have gotten angry and to have told me off. We Aussies always believe that holding it in does more damage than a good old, knock-down, drag-out punch up, because it's only after it all comes out that the healing can begin. I'm pretty sure you Yanks feel the same way."

He stops talking, but I am too drained to react.

"Look, if you want, I'll go get a room and get out of your life." I shake my head. "Or get a room and stay in touch for your advice in setting myself with a job and household stuff." I shake my head again. "Or," he says, fingering the picture, "we can try to pull things back on to the rails, if not all the way back to actual friendship."

I am silent, thoughtful. Finally, I manage to say, "What are you thinking?"

"Well, first, I think we need to get to the truth of this situation."

"So what? Do a DNA test?"

"We can, probably should, just so everything is clear. Whatever the answer is, it's just an answer and obliges neither of us to anything."

I nod an acknowledgement.

"OK," I say, "one day at a time."

In an effort to indicate that I mean it, I return to questions JJ raised to me just a day or so after he got here. He's a licensed civil engineer in Australia. He had a bunch of questions about whether the designation is accepted in the US. I don't know and told him to look up engineering firms operating locally, contact them and find out about that and about getting permission to work here. As an Aussie, that should not be difficult – especially as there is a shortage of experienced engineers. Now, when I tell him he'll have to eat alone tonight because of my command performance with Tom, it turns out to be a good thing – and removes any onus from my not being available.

"Yeah, well, about that," he says. "While I was in a funk over the picture and all, I did what you suggested, visited some engineering firms, more to calm down than anything, but you were right. Most of them need someone like me. I began just by asking the receptionists whether I could speak with anyone about work. You'd think I said I was going to drop big bucks on them. At each firm, I was promptly received by a senior partner. Wound up with three dinner invitations – for tonight. Good luck that the first one, which I accepted, turned out to be from the guys who sound the best for me. So, no harm, no foul. Probably for the best. See you in the morning."

I'm not good, but I'm cooling down, and I feel up to thinking through whether I stay here or go. By the time I get to Tom's, I'm as close to clear-thinking and composed as I'm going to get today. Prepared to deal with Carol, who considers herself my big sister, and has always been ready to give me a talking to and get me back on the rails, when she deems that I have gone haywire.

If that's what I expected from her, I'm not disappointed. Although I am surprised by the vehemence with which she attacks the subject. She greets me at the door, gives me a hug, takes a long look at me, searching, perhaps, for tell-tale signs of toxic change, puts a beer in my hand and points me to a chair on the out-door lanai. Tom is nowhere in evidence. "Where's Tom?" I ask.

"He's a coward. He'll come out when he hears a drop in the volume of my voice." I give her raised eyebrow. "First," she says, "show me the picture of your tribal beloved that you showed Tom. Boy, was he impressed!" I take out my cell phone and comply. She examines the photo, hands it back and not without a heavy sarcasm, says, "Jesus, Tom's right. The kind of babe men leave their wives for."

Her implication is clear. I am smitten, and this exotic creature is the incarnation of every oversexed male's, sophomoric, erotic fantasies. She and I have had these conversations before, but at those times I was much younger. Also, she had met the women, appraised them and found them a bad intellectual match and obviously using their sexual attractiveness to assert a hold on me. At those times, I let her straighten me out because I knew she was right, although I did taunt her by saying, "and where is the downside in all this?"

"You assume, Carol, that such is her game. Not this time. You haven't met her, and you have no basis to judge – her or my--motivation."

She is surprised. I have never hit back at her so forcefully. She absorbs this and appraises me. "You're different now, since you've come back. OK, tell me everything that went on, all of it, all the details. I need to understand."

Her voice has lowered to her normal tone. Just as she said, Tom appears and joins us. He brings me another beer, turns on the grill and sits down to listen. I give Carol exactly what she asked for. It's a long story. Tom has not heard the details before this either. Carol does not interrupt. This is unheard of for her. She holds up her hand only once so she can tell Tom to put on the steaks. Then, I continue. When I finish, the beef is surely ready. Tom gets up to serve. Carol draws a breath and says, "Wow."

During dinner she asks a hundred questions, but I can tell that she is just reassuring herself, and not seeking fodder for an argument to set me back on the tracks. It's very late when I leave. We have explored every nook and cranny of what I experienced in Việtnam and in arriving at the point where I have this decision to make. I have not said so to either of them, but the process has clarified much for me. As we walk to the door, Carol says to Tom, "You had better push through that partnership thing if you hope to keep any contact with him or to see him if and when he does visit."

Tom looks a bit surprised. "He hasn't actually decided anything yet." He looks to me for confirmation.

Before I can say a word, Carol says, "Oh yes he has. He'll figure that out in a day or two. Men are always the last to know." She gives me a hug. "God help me," she says. "I approve, and I look forward to meeting this lady who so charmed you – and who had the good sense to choose you."

When I get home, I am relieved to find that JJ is asleep. In the morning, however, almost as if nothing has happened, he asks me about my relationship with Tom and Carol. It's awkward. I am not inclined now to be open in sharing personal information with him. But, in the spirit of 'one day at a time', I give him a quick summary.

"So, Tom is a colleague, mentor and sometime father surrogate?" He reflects, "Yeah, I see it. But Carol she's the brains of the whole outfit. Always has been, I suspect. At a guess, she's why Tom climbed the ladder, and she has been in your corner all along. That's why she has always taken after you when she decided you need it. It's why now she's not fighting you. She must have watched you like a hawk, noted your gestures, body language and tones of voice and weighed your choice of words. Only after that did she put her seal of approval on things. You're lucky. You may have missed something in what went on over there, but she didn't. You're safe. Don't fight it."

I am frankly surprised, but maybe I shouldn't be. JJ picked up on my feelings about the photo in a second. Still, I say, "Where was all this perception when you were agonizing over Thuy?"

He laughs. "I'm an engineer, mate. I'm good with evidence and calculating. Only thing is, when I have a dog in the fight, all that goes out the window. I'm useless.

"Anyway, on the engineer subject, Mr. Hara, that's the name of the partner who invited me to dinner last night, brought two of the other partners with him, as well as two of the more senior associates so they could meet me and scope me out."

I give him a questioning look, well aware of his awkward history with people. He sees it. "Not to worry. Engineering is my element. I'm good when that's what's on the menu. OK, sorry. I've got to hurry up now. They're going to introduce me around the firm this morning and make me an offer, contingent on verification of my credentials and experience. He also says that the firm will assist me with immigration matters and with either converting my Aussie credential or getting course work and testing to get US certified. All good. I'm lucky – and so are you. You get away from me for the day; get the chance to think about important things. Me, I get both a job and some space."

He leaves, clearly feeling upbeat about his future. I'm left with the echoing aftermath of our nasty argument, my disgust at how I reacted to the whole half-brother prospect and still with the need to decide on staying here or going for good. At the moment, I have no idea at all of what to do. I'm like the donkey, Buridan's ass, who was dying of thirst and of hunger. Placed exactly midway between a pile of hay and a trough of water, he couldn't decide which to go for first. He died – of indecision. Not what I want for myself!

I'm trying to force things, and I know that's not a formula for success. I decide to back off, veg out. When my mind has processed everything, it will deliver the right answer to me. I can't suppress a grin. I hear JJ saying, in his Aussie way, "How very shamanic of you, Y'Dun."

Chapter 25

I have kept in close touch with Ha Oum. We speak three or four times a week. There is not much news from her end. She goes about her daily business as usual. The bulk of our "news" comes from my side, and it is this that is most on her mind. What am I thinking; when am I coming back; how long will it take me to wind up things in Hawaii? I have been honest with her from day one. I tell her that, as much as I love her and miss her, it is hard for me to just close the door on forty plus years of life in Hawaii.

She says, "Of course. I have been concerned about that. I have thought about it in terms of myself. And I remember, as I am sure you do, telling you before you left, that I would always have to come back here, even back to the hamlet. At that time I was just being honest, but when I remember that, I wonder why it did not occur to me that maybe you had some of the same feelings about Hawaii."

I am silent for so long that she thinks the call has dropped. "No, I'm here. Just thinking." And that's what I do. I think, in silence.

"Thinking what?"

"That, right at that time, I should have recognized the parallel between your connection to the tribe and to Việtnam and my attachment to Hawaii."

"Maybe, but I think you had to go back and be on the ground there to understand that and to judge it." I say nothing. "Now, I think I should have said to you, 'Go back and think about all this when you are far from me and far from all the strong feelings, uh, *les émotions*, that have come upon you here'. It was unfair of me not to have thought of that. I have an idea."

I say nothing, and there is a long silence from her end. Finally she continues. "If you agree, I will come to join you in Hawaii. I think I can get a visa without too much trouble. If you sponsor me, things will probably go quickly. I'll plan on staying as long as we both think is necessary."

"Necessary," I say. "You know what that means."

"I suppose it means, until we decide we are together or not together."

"Yes."

"Y'Dun, may I call you that in Hawaii?"

"Of course. That is who I am for you."

"The question we will decide, is not that. It is, who you are for you!"

* * * * * * * * * * * *

I talk with Tom and tell him that Ha Oum is applying for a visa so we can be together in the context of Hawaii. He approves, thinks this will help us – help me – to make a clear-eyed decision about my future. I suspect he hopes it will bring me to my senses. I ask him if he can talk with Whit Richards, a State Department attorney whom he assisted in a complex legal matter a few years back. He says he will make the call immediately. An hour later he phones me. "Have Ha Oum email you copies of her application and supporting documents. I'll get them to Whit, and he will expedite things. Does she even have a Việtnamese passport, or do we have to wait for that first?"

The time difference between Hawaii and Việtnam slows

me down. When I finally reach her, she tells me that she does have a passport. The Việtnamese government participates in all kinds of ASEAN* conferences. It had sent her to one in Singapore on rural health services. "Not that they are really interested in me or my people, but my going let them show how concerned they are about their aborigènes. The head of our delegation made sure to take lots of pictures of me. The final report on the conference, published by ASEAN, had a photo of me on the cover. I did not like that, but if it would help the tribal peoples, I would not complain."

It takes a few more days for her to get things together and send them to me. Tom sends them right on to Whit, and we wait. Not long. Whit comes back the next day and tells Tom, "Did you look at this woman? She is beautiful, exotic as hell. Not one hundred percent Việtnamese, I'd say."

When Tom reports this to me, he is a bit unhappy. "Jeez, everyone's taken with her – even Carol, as you know. What chance do I have of your giving her up? Well, maybe she'll decide to stay here. Anyway, while we wait, why don't you come back to work? I've got lots for you to do."

So, just like that, I'm back in my groove. Well, not quite. JJ and I are living in the house together now, each taking off for work in the early morning and returning home at night, so it's not fully my old life. And I, mentally at least, have one foot in Việtnam and the hamlet.

I speak regularly with Ha Oum, following the progress of her application. She gives me news of the hamlet, K'Sor Brui, Sénac and Y'Chorn. She tells me that K'Sor Brui and Sénac have asked her to keep them informed about me – about us. Y'Chorn does not ask her questions. She thinks he is completely certain that I will return. "I wish," she says, "that I felt as sure." She pauses and gives a little laugh. "You know, I think Y'Chorn is getting to be even stranger than he has always been. He gives out with his little characteristic squeaks

---

* Association of Southeast Asian Nations.

and head-nods more often. He's not getting younger. K'Sor Brui worries about him, that he may die before you return. He asks me to come to the hamlet each week and to check Y'Chorn's health when I do.

"I have to say that, quirks or not, the old man seems as strong and aware as he has ever been. I think he has set his own clock and has no intention of dying until he has taught you what he knows and helped you, as he thinks of it, to accept and understand who you are."

There is an awkward silence. Finally, I ask, "What about you? What do you think?"

I can hear her draw a breath. "I trust Y'Chorn. Asking you to have that same trust at this time, is unfair. So I am coming to you. I believe things will be as he says but that they must find their own way of getting there."

While awaiting Ha Oum's arrival, I am back behind my old desk, doing daily precisely the mind-numbing work I fled when I had my dream and decided I had to go to Việtnam. The work is no more satisfying now than when I left. I fight the feeling I have of wasting time, marking time. I warn myself that what I experienced in Việtnam was nothing more than a romantic adventure, the mid-life male's version of running away to sea. Nevertheless, I take the necessary steps to put my affairs in order, should I decide to depart. I set up a revocable living trust, name Tom as the successor trustee and place the house and all my other assets under the trust. If I leave, all bills and house expenses will go to Tom. His bookkeeper will pay them from an account I have established for the purpose.

In the evenings, I try not to dampen JJ's energy and enormous enthusiasm for eating out and experiencing Honolulu. But the city holds little mystery for me, and there remains a small distance between us in the wake of our argument. It's closing, but time still has some work to do in healing things completely. So JJ is happy to go off on his own with a few new friends from work. I am delighted for him. I am not so sanguine for myself. At the office, I keep my door closed and limit contact with colleagues to the necessary minimum. Tom notices. He tells me I have had a personality transplant and that I should sue the surgeon because the result is not an improvement. He needles me on this often until I tell him that I miss Ha Oum. "Ah hah," he says.

I don't really think that I have fooled Tom. Carol has convinced him that I will surely be leaving Hawaii and the firm, and so he lets me be. But in a way he is right. Not that I have had a personality transplant but that I am withdrawn, spending more time locked in my own mind than out among my colleagues – or anyone else for that matter.

Because JJ continues to pass his evenings with new friends, I am left alone at home where I am fully preoccupied with my decision. I spend hours wandering through the house, taking it in, looking at the certificates on the wall, sitting in my old room and enjoying that my dad had kept it as it was. I raise the floor over the "archive room," descend into its cool dark and sit there for huge blocks of time, often touching things that my dad touched, that were so intimately personal to him. And I remember the first time I did anything like this – with the books, as I took them off the shelves, discovered them and the letters some of them held and realized that they whispered to me. Now, this entire house whispers to me, this room especially. There is so much of my father here. I am moved to tears. And now, having experienced Việtnam, there is so much of me too. More than once, sitting here, in the quiet of the empty house, I fall asleep. When I awake, in the deep of the night, it is always the same. Can I really leave this? Then, I think of Ha Oum and wonder, can I really stay.

Finally the day comes. I am at the airport early with three beautiful leis – orchid, pikake and plumeria. I am nervous. I want her arrival to be perfect. Tom, with his connections, has gotten me permission to enter the secure arrival zone.

The door to the jetway opens and a few rushed passengers burst through it and sprint off towards immigration. Then Ha Oum appears. In spite of myself, I catch my breath. She is elegant, more beautiful than I have remembered. She wears a black, tribal sarong with bright colorful rows of stitching and embroidery at the bottom. On top she wears a fitted white blouse with a mandarin-style collar. It emphasizes her shape and is secured, from neck to waist, by a row of large, tooled silver buttons. The sight is so arresting that airport workers and passengers waiting for other flights take her in. There is a moment of hush before the drone of a hundred conversations resumes. She spots me and hurries forward. I slip the leis over her head and try to give her the traditional cheek kisses, but she has released her small, wheeled bag and thrown her arms around me. We hold each other tightly and share a prolonged kiss. She is so striking, and our reunion so intense that several onlookers offer a small, good-natured cheer and gentle applause. She laughs happily. When we turn to head for immigration and customs, Tom appears from wherever he has been hiding, along with Whit Richards. He steps forward and says, "Please introduce me." Then, smiling at Ha Oum, he says, "I'm Tom, Y'Dun's surrogate father." Ha Oum surprises him and me. She gives him a hug. He introduces Whit and explains who he is. Flushed with excitement, she gives him a hug also.

Whit is happily surprised. "Wow," he says. "Can we do this every day?" Then he asks for her passport and baggage claim stubs. "I'll take care of this. You go on ahead."

Ha Oum is thrilled. "It's so beautiful. I can understand why it's hard for you to leave. Does anyone who lives here ever leave? Why would they?" She is so excited. "Can you drive me all around. I want to see everything."

"There will be time for that. Now you must be exhausted."

"No, please, show me everything."

And so we drive completely around the island, stopping at Waimea Bay to watch the huge waves. We continue on, past the Crouching Lion cliff formation, to Kaneohe Bay and then on to Kailua. We get lunch at Buzz's Steak House across from Kailua Beach. By the time we get home it is late afternoon, and Ha Oum has been sleeping in the car as I drive. We pull into the driveway. She wakes up and catches sight of Diamond Head and jumps out of the car in excitement. When I finally get her downstairs onto the deck that has an unobstructed view of Diamond Head, Waikiki and all the way out to the western end of the island, she drops happily into a chair. "It's wonderful, every bit of it. You should have told me, talked more about this beautiful place and house. I would not have come thinking that I had even a chance of luring you away."

"If I was not serious about leaving, I would not have let you come thinking that I was or at least could be."

She stretches like a contented cat. "Y'Dun, I love you here, in Việtnam, in the hamlet, anywhere. Right now it seems easier to do that here." She gives me a mischievous smile.

There is a noise. She looks towards it, into the house and her smile grow bigger. "JJ. Is it JJ?"

"Yup. It's me."

"Are you visiting?"

"No. I live here now. Got a job and a car and a house to live in."

She looks confused for a minute and then pieces things together. "Here, in this house?"

"Yup."

"That's exciting. Nice for both of you." She looks at me. "You are... camarades de chambre?"

"Roommates," I translate.

JJ looks a question at me. I nod. I won't keep our argument from Ha Oum, and, regardless of my final decision, I have to let go. The matter has to be definitively put to rest sometime. Now seems best. If I am to start a life with Ha Oum, there can't be any shadows in our closet.

"A bit more than that," smiles JJ.

Ha Oum sits bolt upright. She shoots a confused look at me. "Do I understand? I know there are men like that, but you two..."

"Brothers," says JJ. "Well, half-brothers. I found my dad."

"Here?"

"Yup. Have a look." He goes and gets the baby picture of him.

"That's YOU," yelps Ha Oum. Then she completes the picture. "Y'Dun, you two have the same father?"

"Signed, sealed and DNA-test confirmed," I say.

She laughs happily.

We spend the next two weeks talking, being together in ways we had not before, deepening our understanding of each other. I take her carefully through the house. I show her the archive room, as I call it, and tell her the full story of the house and of my growing up here with my father. We stand in my boyhood room. The décor is still as it was when I was in high school. She inspects everything, asks questions about everything. She sits on the bed and gestures for me to sit beside her.

"And this is where you slept all those years? It's where your father became Field Marshall Von Tickle, she marvels with a giggle. Y'Dun, I want to cry. The poor man, he loved you so much but somehow got it wrong between you. I think he must have been wonderful. I know Y'Chorn thinks so and to this moment misses him."

"I have had many regrets about how I behaved towards him when growing up. Going to Việtnam was part of my attempt to understand who he really was. It makes me very sad that so many people there knew him better than I did and loved him far more.

"I started to figure things out when I finally moved back into the house and after I dreamed of you. I finally knew that if I wanted to find him, to understand him completely, I had to walk in his footsteps in Việtnam."

"And, now that you are back here, do you think you did that in Việtnam, in the hamlet?"

"I do, very much so. Shockingly so, really."

"And is that now, uh...un fait accompli? Over, no need to be thought of again?"

I know where the conversation is going. I shake my head. "No. It is actually a part of the process that answered questions for me and explained who I am and what I must do to, at last, keep faith with him. Keep faith with what in his life meant almost as much to him as I did. Maybe it meant even more, but he could not abandon me for Việtnam. He could only choose to abandon Việtnam for me. Raising me, as I finally realized a while back, was an act of love and self-denial – self-sacrifice, really."

She looks at me, with the bottomless gaze that knocked me sideways back when I first experienced it in the Banmethuot market. There is a calm in her but also a small, accepting anxiety. "I get it," I say. "I understand now."

She takes my hand and turns towards me. I can see that there are tears just behind her eyes. She leans forward and kisses me gently. I kiss her deeply. "I want to go back – for you, for myself, and surely, for him."

"And this house, this place, we abandon those?"

"Definitely not. We have an obligation to him and to the family we will have, to maintain this place that he worked to design and that so breathes his being. He was a man of two souls: one bound here; the other bound to Việtnam and your people. We will carry that forward – for generations. Two souls, two homes, united across time and distance."

We are silent. Ha Oum understands, I am sure, that we have crossed a kind of Rubicon. She knows all about me now. I have laid myself open. Then I realize that there is something else, that shadow that I swore would not loom in the depths of our emotional closet. "There is one more thing."

She looks at me. "JJ?"

"Yes."

"I have seen a change, small but there, between you and him."

"We had a fight when I, we, realized that my father might have been JJ's also. He was certain immediately and very happy to have his answer. I was angry immediately. I guess I felt betrayed by my father, that he never told me this – if it was true. Maybe I didn't want to share my dad with anyone – especially with JJ and his problems and his mother, of whom he had painted an unflattering picture. Things got nasty, very nasty. I got nasty. Finally, credit to JJ, he made it possible for us to calm down. Little by little, I became less upset. We've been returning to our close friendship, bit by bit."

"And now?"

"Pretty much back to normal. There is still a bit to go, but that will come in time."

"You accept what your father did with his mother?"

"Yes, because I understand the atmosphere, in those times, of almost free-for-all sex between foreign men and Việtnamese women. And because I understand how it happened; that he was 'hunted' by her and 'tricked' into bed, at a moment when he was deeply vulnerable."

Ha Oum gives me a small smile that hints she is thinking, "REALLY?" Maybe with a dose of, "Just like a man."

"Yes. I know what it sounds like, but I'll give you the details so you can decide for yourself."

She takes my hand. "If you wish, but I do not doubt you – or him. He will soon be my father too." She hesitates.

"What?"

"Well," she giggles just a bit, "I am thinking I had better be honest about this sort of thing, because sooner or later you will remember my grandmother and my mother, and my own mixed blood."

I smile.

* * * * * * * * * * * *

It has been a wonderful two weeks with Ha Oum here in Hawaii. We met and fell in love in her element. Now she has experienced mine, and we, having none of the newly-met and early-attraction tensions, have spoken to each other freely. I think I have told her absolutely everything about me – the good and the not-so-good. I have held nothing back, and I am sure she has been equally open with me. We have, of course, discussed the decision that lies before me. She has not pressed for an answer, seemingly relaxed and content to let me process things.

It's a beautiful, warm Hawaii evening. JJ, as he often does, has shared dinner with us and then departed to leave us our privacy. On this night, we both know it is time for my decision. Ha Oum takes my hand. She looks out into the soft darkness at the silhouette of Diamond Head and the distant lights of Waikiki. "It is so wonderful," she says. I nod.

"I never told you this," I begin. She stiffens slightly. "No, it's nothing terrible. There is an American author, Robert Louis Stevenson."

She claps her hands. "L'Ile de Trésor." I know that. She is so happy with her knowledge.

"Yes, Treasure Island. It's his best known work. But there is an essay he wrote that is wonderful and very special to me.

It's called The Lantern Bearers. It's about a group of boys who go out at night to get together. Each wears a long, dark coat. Under the coat he carries, attached to his belt, a small lantern with a lit wax candle. It is not visible to anyone, but when the boys meet up, each opens his coat and shows his lantern. Shows it to the chosen only."

"How wonderful," she says, her eyes shining.

"I have thought about that story many times, never sure I understood it very well. But since you have been here, I think I get it."

She looks at me expectantly.

"The hidden lantern contains each boy's unique, personal light, the light he holds within him that defines him, distinguishes him and contains his very soul, but which he takes care to reveal only to those he has chosen. I think, now that when you love someone, you reveal your light to her, and she reveals hers to you."

"Or maybe, what attracts two people is their ability to glimpse each other's light. And that tells them each is special for the other."

"Yes," I say, "but for your people, and for me, I think there is something else. I think Y'Chorn has the gift of seeing each person's light; that he saw the light in my father and then the same light in me."

She is enthralled, nodding enthusiastically.

"I think I will always be bound to Hawaii, but I believe that for me, as for my father, my light burns brightest in Việtnam."

"You have decided," she says.

I nod. She stands, pulls me to my feet and throws her arms around me. We hug, holding tight, cheeks pressed together. I can feel her tears, and I am sure she feels mine.

The die is cast. We begin our preparations for departure. I review all legal matters with Tom. We work together to draft clear instructions about how to manage my affairs in my absence. We take care to state my goals and intentions so that any "ambiguous" decisions that may confront Tom or his successor, can be made with a knowledge of my intent. JJ is free to stay in the home, although I encourage him to buy a property of his own as soon as he sees fit. While in the home, he will contribute to its repair and upkeep as he and Tom agree. Any disputes are to be resolved by JJ's preference. Everything in the house that belonged to my father or was there during his residence is to be kept and maintained in good condition.

Days pass. Things fall into line. I have ample time to reflect quietly on what I am about to do, but I am at ease with my decision. Carol has taken Ha Oum under her wing and is trying to get to know and understand her. They have lunch together a few times. Ha Oum says Carol wants to be sure she understands me as we two strike out on a life that Carol finds hard to imagine. At the second lunch, Ha Oum tells Carol that she has a few things to learn about me. That stops her for a moment. Then, as Ha Oum tells it, she nodded slowly and said, "I'm not worried anymore. You will manage him well."

Ha Oum replied, "You should come to our hamlet and see our ways. Remember, in our society, the wife chooses the husband. The men do not forget that."

There is a round of good-bye dinners. As it draws to a close, Ha Oum and I are simply anxious to leave. We both feel that we have reached an end and are ready for our new beginning. Two days later, JJ drives us to the airport in his new car. It's a club cab Toyota Tacoma. I'm amused. This is by far the most popular vehicle in Hawaii. I kid him about it.

"Right," he says. "Would have gotten one anyway, but I'm an engineer, and I work on job sites a lot. My company said they would pay a portion of the price if I got a pickup. So I did. If I was not one of the boys before this, I sure am local now."

At the airport, he is emotional. He hugs us both. "I don't want to get all gooey here. I mean, this is a big moment, but

283

we'll be talking, email or something, all the time, and you'll be back to touch Hawaii at least each year, right?"

"That's my plan, once we've settled down in Việtnam."

"Right. We're brothers, full-on brothers. No half-brother stuff. Closer than the real thing, right?" He hugs Ha Oum. "Give him boys so the family name goes on and Uncle JJ has guys he can teach Aussie Rules to. But be sure to have at least one girl. Someone as beautiful and wonderful as you."

He looks at me, tears in his eyes, unabashed as his voice falters. "You changed my life, mate – Y'Dun. I can never thank you in any way that says what I feel."

He turns to Ha Oum. "Don't get jealous now." He gives me a hug and then hugs her again, tightly. He's beginning to cry. "Ha Oum, you are the sister I never had. I love you so much. Take care of Y'Dun. He needs it. Make sure Y'Chorn teaches him well, and…He hesitates. "Aw, crikey." He struggles to suppress a sob and then says, "Yeah, right." He nods quickly and leaves us.

Chapter 26

*I*t's a long tiring flight. I have put us in first class. Who knows whether we will ever make this trip again. We must look like newlyweds because the flight crew is especially kind to us. They ask where we are from, although they surely know I am American. Ha Oum replies that we now live in Saigon. "Oh, Hồ Chí Minh City," says one of our flight attendants.

Ha Oum shakes her head emphatically. "To him, to us, it will always be Saigon. But we have our family home in a small Rhadé hamlet outside of Banmethuot." The flight attendant looks surprised but also fascinated. Ha Oum squeezes my hand. "This is who we are from now on." I nod.

When we exit the terminal in Việtnam, it is like nothing has changed. Phùng is waiting for us. He runs up to Ha Oum and gives her an enthusiastic hug. He no longer calls her, "Cô" (miss). Now she is "Chị," elder sister. It is an indication of his acceptance of and respect for her and of the fact that we now have a family. Mr. Nam stands by smiling. Ha Oum hugs him and speaks the traditional, respectful greeting from young to old, "Thưa bác, em moi về" (honored uncle, little sister is back). I do the same except I say, "Thưa bác, con moi về" (honored uncle, your son is back). It all feels good and right.

By the time we reach the hotel, it is as if we have never been away. Mr. Nam has caught us up on Judge Đao, K'Sor Brui and that the lawyers have prepared a small office for my use. As I check in, Mr. Khanh comes to the front desk and greets me with a smile. He inclines his head respectfully to Ha Oum and says to me, "I have prepared Monsieur Shaplen's old room for you. I think he will be glad that one who knew him and respects his memory will share the room with him."

Our first weeks are filled with moments like these. For Ha Oum, it is a homecoming. For me, I feel that I am more at home than I have ever been anywhere else. It's not that I have no moments of missing Hawaii. It's just that everything here seems so completely natural, as if it has been waiting patiently for me to discover that my place has always been here. There is, of course, much basic settling in to do. I have to begin processing for a residence visa, and Ha Oum and I, comfortable at the hotel but wanting a home, begin to consider what is available and whether we want an apartment or one of the old, French-era villas that still exist in residential areas just outside of downtown.

We find a wonderful villa on Ngô Thời Nhiệm Street. Ha Oum likes its large garden and walled isolation from the street. I am moved by its proximity to the Xá Lợi Pagoda and to what I know to be an old USAID office, which no longer exists. Ha Oum begins the job of buying furniture and making the unfurnished premises into a home. She confesses to me that doing this is difficult for her. Since leaving the hamlet for the city, she has lived in a small, furnished apartment. Her only familiarity with the kind of homes foreigners live in comes from our house in Hawaii and from dinner parties she has attended at the residences of doctors from her hospitals. She buys numerous decorating magazines and sets about educating herself. I comment only when asked, and when I am not at work, I spend time out of the house walking around the area.

"Where do you go on all these walks that you take? I would like to come with you, but between work and fixing up the house, I don't have the time."

"I go to places nearby that I read about in my father's journals."

"What places?"

"The Xá Lợi Pagoda for one, and the intersection of Cách Mang Tháng Tám (it used to be Lê Văn Duyệt) and Phan Dinh Phùng."

"What's so interesting there?"

"You mean you don't know?"

"I don't. Cách Mang Tháng Tám means street of the August Revolution, but I don't even know what that is."

"I forget that you were born many years after South Việtnam fell to the communists."

"You were too."

"Yes, but, but I have read my father's journals, and these have moved me to read history. It's fascinating. The August Revolution was a popular uprising led by Hồ Chí Minh and the Việt Minh against the remaining French military and Japanese army occupiers, in August, 1945, a time of unsettled control here in the south."

"Yes, they teach that in the Việtnamese schools. I forgot. In those years I was completely Rhadé. I did not think of myself as Việtnamese. I'm still Rhadé, of course, but I can't avoid being Việtnamese also. I do have to use a Việtnamese passport."

I smile. "You could consider getting an American passport – if you decide to marry an American."

"I'm thinking about that."

"I see. OK. Well, anyway, the Xa Loi Pagoda was the center of Buddhist resistance against President Ngô Đình Diệm, and the intersection I mentioned is nearby. It's where the monk, Thích Quảng Đức, burned himself to death on June 11, 1963 and set off the eventual overthrow of Diệm."

"They don't teach that in the Việtnamese schools. Well, yes, the Buddhist uprising, but I think they don't want to make the monks too heroic. This Thích Quảng Đức, he really did that?"

"Walked quietly from the pagoda to the center of the intersection, followed by a small number of other monks. One held a gas can. Quảng Đức seated himself in the lotus position. He prayed quietly. A monk poured gasoline on him. He waited without a sound. When the gas can was empty, a monk handed him a wooden match. He struck it and set himself on fire. He was quickly engulfed. He sat without a sound, in the lotus position throughout the ordeal. After a few minutes, his body began to list. Eventually, dead by then, he fell onto his back. The waiting monks covered his body with a robe and took him back to the pagoda. They discovered that his heart was charred but had not burned. We can go see it, on display in a glass case at the ground level of the Xá Lợi seven-tiered pagoda."

"You chose this house because it was in the midst of that horrible history?"

"No. Actually, we chose the house – because it is beautiful and quiet. But, yes, I knew the history of the area. There is another house nearby, on Bà Huyện Thanh Quan Street, that belonged to a friend of my father, Dr. Trường Văn Quỳnh. His brother ran off to join the Việt Cong and became a high ranking leader."

She looks at me. "You are very emotional about Việtnam and its history – even about the history of my people, I think." She offers me a mischievous smile. "I did not understand that completely when I chose you. Now that I do, I think I will keep you anyway."

Within a month, we are pretty much completely settled. Ha

Oum is back at the hospital, and I have begun work with the lawyers. After our first six weeks in country, we travel to the hamlet. Ha Oum's family is excited to see her. Y'Chorn, K'Sor Brui, Sénac and many others who have come to accept me, whether in the wake of that first night of drinking, or because Ha Om has chosen me, await the formalization of our marriage. By Rhadé custom, it is the wife's family that bears full responsibility for the wedding. Because they must ask permission of the prospective groom's parents, for their daughter to marry the son, Ha Oum occupies herself with planning, but nothing formal takes place. I spend much time with Y'Chorn. He is now focused on teaching me – language, customs, history and his arts.

Back in the city, our life takes on a form. We begin to make new friends and socialize at dinners and cocktail parties. We are a bit too busy for my taste, and when I come home one evening, a bit late and ready to rush to get ready for a cocktail we have accepted, I find Ha Oum in casual clothes. "You must be tired," she says.

"I am. Aren't you going to dress for the cocktail party?"

"What about you?"

"I have to hurry."

"Y'Dun, don't. Don't hurry." I look at her. "We are always rushing, always going somewhere. It was not like this before. We had each other and some close friends. We had time for things, for ourselves, for real friends. Don't you miss that? That was when I fell in love with you."

"Are you really suggesting that we should skip the cocktail party?"

She gives me a happy smile. "Are you really suggesting that we should not?"

We both laugh, hug and settle down for an evening together. Ha Oum is right. Things feel so much better – the way they did before, what I looked forward to coming back to when we returned from Hawaii. "You have gotten confused," she says. "I know what is happening, and I am sure you do too. Carol warned me that once you start working, 'practicing law,' she called it, you forget everything and just work."

"She told you that?"

"And much more. Really, I think, even though she considers herself as your big sister, she is a little in love with you."

I laugh. "You think everybody's in love with me."

She gets very serious. "No! Not at all. I love you avec mes yeux ouverts, um, with my eyes open." Her tone softens. "Carol wanted to meet me to see if you had to be protected from me. She told me that. She is a very honest lady. She said you are very serious, especially when you work. She was afraid that you had been, um, enchanté by some sirène Asiatique. Oh, she used a word..."

"Enchanted, bewitched?" She shakes her head. "Smitten? Yes, I can hear her, 'smitten by an Asian siren'."

"Yes, that's it."

"Well, I was!"

"No, be serious. I told her what you were like. She said that was good, and I must not let you change, change back to what you have always been when in Hawaii. She said she understands that you can believe Y'Chorn because she believes everything you discovered in the house after your father's death was planned somehow, somewhere. She believes that going to Việtnam could have worked in one of two ways. Either you would change, as you have, and live the life maybe your father hoped you would; or the experience would not touch you, and you would return to your old ways and old life.

"She said Tom could never be like you, and that is why he hoped so much you would remain in Hawaii and be the way you used to be, be like him. He thinks the only mistake you are not making is being with me because (she says this without a shadow of irony or self-consciousness) I am beautiful."

I grin. "That does help."

I am being a wise guy. She is still intense. "Of course, and you are a very nice looking man, and that helps. But there are many – many, many – nice looking men. I did not fall in love with your look! I am not like some of those not-serious Việtnamese girls. I am Rhadé. A Rhadé woman has the burden of choosing. She chooses a man – not a look!"

Silence reigns, but not for long. "And," she adds, "It is time for us to take care of the marriage, up in the hamlet."

When I do not reply to that, she brings everything together. "So, instead of running to cocktail parties and dinner parties with people we don't know, we should have our own dinner party. For our family. Will you see if Mr. Nam and Judge Đao are available this weekend? You could also invite Mr. Phu and his wife, since he knows both the judge and Mr. Nam."

I am amused and impressed. Ha Oum doesn't miss anything. She thinks things through carefully. Only when she has everything in order, does she declare her judgment – sometimes with considerable intensity. I reply to her, possibly with the lightest touch of humor, not to say sarcasm, "Yes, dear."

She gives me a look. "I don't know what that means. You say it some special way."

Actually, it means what it says, but I laugh when I say it because my father told me those two words were the secret of a happy marriage."

She laughs. "I understand. You say that. Sometimes you really mean it."

I hasten to interrupt, "Like now."

"And sometimes you say it to avoid a fight, calm me down." I smile. "We have something like that in Rhadé, but I will NOT teach that to you. I will also tell Y'Chorn, K'Sor Brui and Sénac that I will kill them if they teach you." Now, it is her turn to smile.

* * * * * * * * * * *

It turns out that the dinner has to wait. Mr. Nam is not available on the weekend. We learn also that K'Sor Brui will be in town on the following Tuesday and Wednesday. I check with everyone on their availability and, with Ha Oum's agreement, include Ms. Ly also. The dinner is set for Wednesday. Ha Oum is very busy preparing and very worried about the impression her self-furnished and designed home will make. I remind her of our agreement that going forward, we are the people we have to please. I also point out that the only guests who might possibly have a negative impression are the lawyers because we are not close to them at this point in time. I also slip in my opinion that the house looks wonderful. "Ngoại giao," she grins. "Cả môt bô ngoại giao." (Diplomat. You are an entire Ministry of Diplomacy all by yourself!)

Our guests are invited for 7:00 PM. I am ready to receive them by 6:15 PM. Ha Oum giggles. "Oh, Y'Dun, you know!"

"Yes, my father mentions more than once in his journals that Montagnards always arrive early. No harm. It will be good to have some private time with K'Sor Brui."

Experienced in dealing with foreigners and other non-tribal peoples, he arrives at 6:30 PM – a considerable concession, but still early enough to catch the unwary off guard. He laughs and shakes his finger at me when he sees I am ready for his early arrival. "I shall have to find other ways to surprise you. Of course, if I start showing up two hours early, you will invite me two hours late, and we may mix each other up hopelessly." I laugh. "Perhaps," he adds, "the best solution is for you to become Rhadé in your habits. Then we will have perfect understanding."

"Between you, Ha Oum and Y'Chorn, I am sure I am already on the way to that change."

Ha Oum enters while I am speaking. "What change?" K'Sor Brui explains. She throws me a significant and, I think, wifely look. "No need for you and Y'Chorn to work on that. He will learn. He has a sleep-in teacher!" She gives me a mock warning look.

"Yes dear," I say.

The others appear on time. Judge Đao and Mr. Nam arrive together. The judge lives nearby, and Mr. Nam has picked him up en route. When we are all settled, Judge Đao asks if I know the history of the area. I say that I do, but Ms. Ly says immediately that she does not. Judge Đao relates briefly what I have already told to Ha Oum. Ms. Ly says she knows of the Buddhist resistance to President Diem but did not know where Thich Quang Duc (she did not even know his name) had burned himself to death. Mr. Phu kids her, saying that perhaps she should worry more about her fit for Việtnam than about mine. It is taken in good humor. Our conversation covers many subjects and at last returns to the question of fitting in with or adapting to an alien environment. The specific question is, will I find a way to adjust to Rhadé culture and practices.

Ha Oum mentions that formalities surrounding our marriage must be observed and that chief among these is that the bride's parents must ask permission of the groom's to conduct the marriage. I add that I am hoping Mr. Nam will agree to serve in the place of my father. He smiles happily but glances at Judge Đao. I catch the look and ask immediately if Judge Đao would also agree to serve. This will provide me with the normal complement of two parents, and I could not feel closer or more like a son to any other men in the world.

Ha Oum says I will have to observe all the traditions and customs. I say that I have heard it is not uncommon for tribes to marry across tribal groups and that the differing customs of both tribes involved are often respected. I especially like the Hmong custom of chasing and spanking the prospective bride. K'Sor Brui breaks out in a broad smile. He nods enthusiastically and says he approves of my careful research into tribal customs. Mr. Phu seems especially amused. He looks at his partner, who remains unmarried and says, "Perhaps our new associate can find you a Hmong husband." She blushes.

Ha Oum remains businesslike for just a few more minutes. She checks with Mr. Nam and Judge Ðao that they would be able to remain in Banmethuot for at least the two days that Rhadé custom requires for celebrating a marriage. The two men reply that all she need do is give them two weeks advance notice of the dates, and they will gladly serve. Assured, she takes her shot at me. She thanks them by saying, "Of course I will do so. There may be a problem, however, if my parents decide to follow the customs of other tribes, as Y'Dun has hinted may be his preference. The Tai require that the prospective groom live for three years in the home of his in-laws to be, before the marriage is allowed."

With a big smile, I say, "Point taken."

"No, it's not that easy. Carol wanted to make sure I could manage an American man…"

I interrupt. "Carol is the wife of my boss in Hawaii. She has always considered herself my big sister, but I am learning that the female sisterhood may be a stronger tie. She gave Ha Oum all kinds of advice for handling me."

"Yes, and she taught me some sayings to remember. One is, 'be careful what you wish for; you may get it'. (She gives me a significant look.) Another is, 'What's sauce for the goose is sauce for the gander'. I told her, no. In Rhadé culture, what's sauce for the goose is sauce for the goose."

At this last, there is a sage nodding of all the experienced male heads in the room. Ms. Ly looks especially interested. She says to Ha Oum, "Perhaps we should become better friends."

After our guests leave and we retire, Ha Oum slides into bed next to me. She hugs me and says, "It was a good evening. We must keep these people close."

* * * * * * * * * * * *

Exactly one month later, we greet all of our guests from that dinner at the airport in Banmethuot. Ha Oum and I have been in the highlands for three weeks, concluding preparations for the marriage. We are both slightly different people when in the village, each a bit more reserved and slowed to the pace of life in an environment that still retains many elements and behaviors of its ancient past. Ha Oum is living in her family's longhouse, and I am lodged with Y'Chorn, who teaches me traditional lore and custom continuously. I have made progress in understanding the Rhadé language, but either Sénac or K'Sor Brui is always nearby to assist as needed.

At night, when we are alone, before we sleep, Y'Chorn shares memories of his life and even of his marriage (his children died young, and his wife passed away more than twenty years ago). He cautions me that these things he does not share with others, but I must know them. This revelation has enormous impact on me. I would say it sobers me, but I have been serious about what is taking place, since our arrival. There is a difference between contemplating from a distance what one is about to undertake and living in the full presence of the reality of that undertaking.

I think of my father. It occurs to me that ultimately he departed the hamlet precisely because he knew he could not, without reservation, honor the proposed undertaking before him. Perhaps I have sensed, since first coming here, that the responsibility for doing so had, in the way the world completes the unfinished, fallen to me. I am humbled to be so chosen and by the line I am being initiated into.

Four days before the wedding, as Y'Chorn and I are on one of our early walks in the forest, he stops in a small clearing and looks me over with an appraising, all-seeing eye. He touches my shoulder and, as in the past, feels the planes of my face. He nods emphatically and pronounces, "Good." We go on our way. He has marked a moment. I think I know what it is. I have been feeling different recently. He has confirmed the change, approved it. Any doubt that I have disappears when Ha Oum, later the same day says, "You have changed."

The next few days are busy. Finally, the time comes. Sénac brings Mr. Nam and Judge Đao to the hamlet, and Ha Oum's family completes the formality of requesting of them, my parents, permission for the daughter of their house, to marry the son of theirs. It is a deeply moving moment, for me of course, but also for the two ancient friends who have lived long lives, known and loved my father, shared emotional life-changing decisions and now, as they tell me later, live what they understand is a life-culminating moment. Mr. Phu and Ms. Ly are also present and obviously impressed and affected by the event.

That night, there is feasting, drinking, dance and song outside in the cold, just as I experienced many months earlier. Ha Oum's family has taken care to provide warm wraps for the visitors, and special quarters are allocated within their longhouse. Each of the old men is offered a draught of rice wine through the familiar long reed. Each bravely takes his drink, far less than is expected of a younger male, but the tribal men cheer approvingly. Lawyer Phu is greatly amused by the festivities and himself gets promptly tipsy by slugging down a considerable quantity of the potent nam bay. When we finally retire, I am surprised, and not especially thrilled, to see that a bachelor's bed has been provided for me in Y"Chorn's house. Unlike all the other nights, we do not talk at length before going to sleep. Y"Chorn lies down on one side of the glowing brazier and, gesturing at the hard, narrow bed, says simply, "It is the last time, my son. Sleep well."

The hamlet, as always, is awake at dawn. As always, since we are in the mountains, it is cold. As always, there is much to do, but today is different. The guests are given breakfast in the longhouse of Ha Oum's family. Two young men stand outside of Y'Chorn's house, awaiting his bidding. I am sent to wash and prepare. The young men climb the ladder to Y'Chorn's home. In the large room where the old man receives people to hear their concerns, the men lay fresh matting on the polished floor, set flowers along the perimeter walls and place a crossbow on the floor towards the back end of the room. At ten o'clock, Mr. Nam and Judge Đao are escorted from their quarters and assisted up the ladder into Y'Chorn's dwelling. I await them there, clothed in tribal dress, a white loin cloth below a black chief's shirt with red piping around the bottom and cuffs and at the open placket below the neck. When we are ready, Ha Oum's family escorts her across the distance from their house to Y'Chorn's.

The procession is not as solemn as one might expect. Rather, there are smiles and even a few giggles. The women wear traditional dress, black sarong and blouses, each highlighted by colorful, patterned stitching. Ha Oum wears a fitted black sarong with bright blue stitching at its bottom and a fitted white, V-neck blouse secured with silver buttons along a black placket. He hair is pulled into a tight bun, setting off her wonderfully shapely face. She carries a small wooden box in her hands that are clasped in front of her.

I have attended many weddings and seen many brides looking radiant and beautiful in their wedding gowns and proceeding with stately step to echoing organ music. The effect is always powerful. But I have never seen a woman of such beauty, poise, radiance and confidence. I am shaken by the sight of her, and in an instant I have a vision of what my life will be from here forward. It will be nothing like I have ever thought or dreamed or hoped for. How could it? I will have children here who will know this forest and live with the tribe. I shall grow old in this hamlet, perhaps resembling

Y'Chorn if the years allotted me rival his. And I shall have this extraordinary woman at my side always.

I emerge from my vision. Ha Oum has entered the room. Her parents stand a few feet behind her, as Mr. Nam and Judge Đao do behind me. We face each other and sit on the floor with perhaps two feet separating us. I take a brass, tribal-worked bracelet from the small wooden box I have been holding and place it on the floor in front of me. Ha Oum does the same, drawing a bracelet from the box she has carried. There is complete silence. We look at each other. I have never felt such intense emotion, such love for another, nor have I ever felt so much love reflected back at me. I sense my father by my side. I shiver with emotion. After perhaps a full minute of silence and each of us being aware of nothing but the other, I pick up the bracelet Ha Oum has placed before me. She smiles in satisfaction. Her family moves slightly behind her. Then she picks up the bracelet I have placed in front of her, and her smile animates her whole face. I hear Mr. Nam and Judge Đao exhaling behind me. It is done. We are married. As we leave the house, Sénac gives me a sly smile and points to the crossbow on the floor at the rear of the room. He winks. "It is there to assure that you have sons."

* * * * * * * * * * * *

It is already four months since the wedding. Life has settled quickly into a routine, and Ha Oum and I, nurse and her lawyer/shaman husband, are almost used to thinking of ourselves as husband and wife – and not as newlyweds. I have been faithful in keeping to my four-day/three-day schedule and am feeling ever more integrated into the life of the hamlet. In addition, I have several clients at the law firm and have been working long hours regularly to represent them as they deserve. Mr. Phu, the only one of our city guests who remained in the hamlet for the entire, rather wild wedding celebration, pulls me aside. "You and Ha Oum have not taken a wedding trip. I have thought it not my place to speak of this with you, but now I worry that all your work may be keeping you from that, um…honeymoon."

"Well, it has been very busy, between work here and time in the hamlet."

"If you can get your 'boss', the old shaman, to give you some time off, I am sure that we can allow you whatever vacation you may want."

He giggles a little, and I am sure he is remembering the wedding festivities: the water buffalo sacrifice, being sprinkled with the animal's blood in a purification ritual, and getting totally drunk. This last, as a result of consuming heroic volumes of nam bay, in the company of the tribesmen who enjoyed him enormously and whom he still considers his great friends.

That evening, I mention the prospect of a honeymoon trip to Ha Oum. While we are discussing the idea, we get an excited phone call from JJ. It's eight months since he landed in Hawaii, and he is feeling like a native. He is almost bursting with news.

"So, mate, you won't believe it. You remember Mona, your dad's housekeeper and then yours, telling you she would retire within a year? Well, she has, but she's also sent me her youngest daughter as a replacement. Name's Shevaun. I said, fine with me. Just show her the ropes and tell me how much to pay."

"Sounds good, JJ. You will have an honest, reliable housekeeper. One less thing to worry about."

"Yeah, yeah, right. But here's the thing. She's been working now for six months. I'd never clapped eyes on her. She leaves me notes if we need anything, and I leave her money and notes about anything that needs attention. Never gave her much of a thought beyond that. I have taken care to be flexible, if she needs to change work days sometimes."

"So, is there a problem?"

"Well, no. But a while back I forgot something I needed for work and went home to get it. When I arrived, the front door was open, and I hear the vacuum going. I went to get my stuff and just about scared this kind of tiny, cute little lady to death. I apologized and introduced myself. Turns out that she's Shevaun, and I'm looking at her and thinking, Gor, where did she come from? Cute as a button, and a dynamo.

"I say, 'Don't mind me, I'll be gone in a minute'. She says, 'Don't rush, Mr. JJ. I am happy to meet you'. And she extends her hand, which I hardly look at because I am so taken with her. When I do grasp her hand, it is soft and delicate and, God help me, beautiful."

"JJ, are you in love, and after just five minutes of exposure?" Ha Oum is now listening in intently.

"Yeah, you could say that. But it's not after five minutes. I mean, it was love at first sight, but for months now we've spent all our free time together. It works. Put on your Y'Dun hat and tell me what's gonna happen. She's perfect for me. At 5'1" she's the right size, and she's this incredible, Chinese, Filipino, Latina mix."

"What's going to happen," I say, "is that you're going to find a way to introduce her to your brother to get his blessing. Remember, I am a shaman, and I can do such things."

He laughs. "Well, that's kind of why I called. I want her to meet my family – you and Ha Oum. So I have a proposal for you. I'm gonna take her to Aussie, to the region where I was born."

"Sounds great. What's the proposal?"

"Meet us there. Neither of you has ever been, and it will be a thrill for me to show all of you around. I can meet my step brothers in the company of my real brother and others who love me. I can't wait."

Ha Oum is smiling and nodding. She whispers, "A good place for a honeymoon."

* * * * * * * * * * *

The trip is wonderful. Shevaun is clearly in love with JJ, and, as Ha Oum comments, he has been transformed by his time in Hawaii and his relationship with this young lady. He is brimming with confidence. He carries himself differently, and even his step-siblings comment on the change in him. They are happy for him and suggest they establish the custom of yearly family reunions. JJ is delighted. He suggests that Ha Oum and I join him and Shevaun to travel a bit around Australia, but we tell him we want some time alone. He is gracious. "No problem, mate, as long as you will join us for a farewell dinner upon your return to Sydney."

Ten days later, we are back, relaxed, restored and ready to return and settle into what will be our life hereafter in Việtnam. At dinner it's just the four of us. As we sit late at the table in a harbor-view restaurant, JJ looks at Ha Oum and says, "Take care of my brother. I owe my entire new life to him." He's getting a bit misty and immediately tries to stifle the emotion. "Well, maybe not to him. To Y'Dun, really."

I smile and start to say something, but he gently cuts me off. This is his moment. "Look, mate, we kid ourselves. We think we have forever to say loving things to those who mean so much to us, but we don't. And one day we find that they are gone and we are left with a mouth full of – a soul full of – unuttered words and boundless regret. Look at us. You traveled halfway around the world to find your father, at least the essence of him, because you did not love him openly enough when he was alive. Me, my mum never leveled with me, even after her death. She raised me and left me as a truncated human being. She was a hard one, my mum. She's gone now, so maybe she's beyond regretting what she refused to say, to tell me. But I will not make her mistake."

He draws a breath and goes silent for a long, reflective minute. "Ha Oum, you have done something extraordinary. You have stepped outside your culture and traditions to give your life to this strange, bifurcated soul here at the table with us. As for him, I should have little praise. After all, what courage does it take to commit himself to the strong, beautiful, wonderful lady you are? But, of course, it's not that simple. So, as we are on the verge of separating into the lives that fate (I give him a look.), um, OK, Yang um, that guy, has laid down for us, I want you to know that I (he smiles at Shevaun) we, will always love you. We will care for the home that your – our – father created, and we will never be out of touch."

* * * * * * * * * * * *

Upon our return to Việtnam, we feel that our life together is at its true beginning and that our future will unfold from now. Fourteen months later, Ha Oum, heavy with our first child, joins me in the hamlet, where I am spending an extended stay. Y'Chorn is ailing, and K'Sor Brui has suggested I request leave from the law firm so I may spend as much time as possible with him. I have been in the hamlet for just over two weeks. It has, for many months already, become like home. When I arrive, I immediately meet with Y'Chorn and also with Ha Bai, who is a kind of hamlet executive, manages hamlet operations and is a first resort in settling disputes or disagreements. Y'Chorn, as shaman, operates at a level higher than she and steps into the practical, day-to-day, business and commercial situations, only when they involve tradition or religion or when the intervention of the spirits is needed. His job as shaman is, most essentially, to assure that everything the tribe does is harmonized with, pleasing to, the spirits. In this way, good harvests are insured and plague, illness, famine and other disasters are avoided.

My arrival is greeted with pleasure, and as custom dictates, I stay in the longhouse of Ha Oum's mother. I have gotten fully used to the Rhadé way of life and to tribal customs. I no longer feel strange in these surroundings or in my role when required to offer advice or render judgment. Y'Chorn had begun to accustom the tribe to accepting my more prominent role in matters as his surrogate. When Ha Oum arrives, I am delighted, but I have the rather strange experience of relating to her both as my wife and in my role as a tribal authority. In Hô Chí Minh City, we are a modern, urban couple. In the hamlet, we live much like any other tribal husband and wife. This is fine with me until Ha Oum goes into labor, and I am shooed away from the longhouse while the women of her family attend the midwife who manages the delivery. For years I have promised myself that I would stand by my wife as she delivered our children. As a tribal husband, I have no such privilege.

Like any other occidental husband, however, I worry and fret as her labor proceeds, well removed from my sight. At length, one of Ha Oum's aunts emerges from the house. She is smiling broadly as she holds aloft a crossbow. I can't help myself. I shout, "It's a boy!" Before I can run towards the house, Ha Oum herself, with her mother at her side, emerges onto the longhouse woman's porch. She holds a swaddled infant in each arm. People cheer. She hands one child to her mother and reaches out to me. I climb the ladder quickly and hug her gently. "Twin boys," she says. "One for each part of you."

Chapter 27

Our boys are now almost five years old. We take care that they spend at least four months a year in the hamlet. There they are Y'Keo and Y'Prun, the former named for my father, the latter with the Rhadé name given Ha Oum's French father. Their western names are Ben and Paul respectively. They are good boys so far, active and, in the hamlet especially, into everything. I am bemused by the facility with which they shift languages: English and Vietnamese at our home in Ho Chi Minh City, Rhadé and French when in the hamlet. The only confusion I have noted so far is, as Y'Keo has asked, why am I treated differently by people in the city than I am in the hamlet. It is, for the moment, difficult to explain.

With the passage of time, we have developed a family here. The boys have four living grandfathers: Mr. Nam, Judge Đao, Y'Chorn and Ha Oum's father. Lawyer Phu enjoys taking them places and is an excellent surrogate uncle. What we would call in Hawaii, a calabash or hanai uncle. JJ, of course, is their real uncle, and he seems to love the role. He sends numerous gifts from Hawaii and tells us he can't wait to have the boys spend a summer with him and Shevaun in Hawaii, in the home their grandfather created and, as I have told him and he has taken to heart, he intended to be theirs when the time came.

Our circle tends to be small and intimate, with strong bonds between all. It is expanded by a few of Ha Oum's professional friends and some of my clients, who live here for more than just a year or two before moving on to other assignments with their companies. There is one member of our group whose outreach to us especially pleased me. I thought it had come about by chance. I should have known better. My excuse is that it slipped in through my law office where, I am sorry to admit, my Y'Dun radar is not always engaged.

One day, our beautiful receptionist, Miss Ha (how she remains unmarried is one of the great mysteries I have yet to solve), came to my office when she surely could have rung on the intercom. "Mr. Y'Dun (she prefers that to my American name, which, to be honest, is not used often by any who know me. Y'Dun has become a kind trademark, distinction and even term of endearment), there is a gentleman who is asking to see you."

I know I have a client meeting in fifteen minutes. "Is there anything urgent?"

"I think this might be personal. He is an old man, someone who comes from the days when the city was Saigon. He seems a gracious gentleman."

"Then, please send him in."

To my great surprise, she reappears with a clearly aged Mr. Khanh, from the Continental Palace Hotel. I am taken aback and delighted. I come around the desk, shake his hand warmly and usher him to a chair in my sitting area. He is wearing his traditional black suit. Perhaps it is the same one he wore when we first spoke at the hotel more than five years ago. He stands awkwardly, waiting, it seems, for me to sit before he would dare take such a liberty. I am touched by his visit, that he remembers me and by the definitely old-world, pre-communist, perhaps even pre-American-presence and gentility that he embodies. "Mr. Khanh, this is a great pleasure. Please sit down, and thank you for coming." I say this to him in French, knowing that it is his preferred language.

He sits and smiles at me. "One does not hear the language very much anymore. It is part of the past, like me. A thing that has little use in today's city."

I ask gently, "Is this a personal visit, or is there something I may do for you as an attorney?"

"Oh, no, not personal. I would never permit myself such an imposition. You are now an important man, a lawyer and, I hear, a personality among our tribal people."

This is the kind of comment, the kind of courtesy, that was once common in Vietnam. It has, sadly, fallen out of use, out of memory, since the days of the harsh reeducation camps men like Mr. Khanh were subject to after the communist victory in 1975. I smile to encourage him to continue.

"My wife has died. She was the last thing I had in this world."

"I am so very sorry. You have children?"

"I did, two sons. One, Jean-Pierre studied in France. He became an engineer. He begged us for permission to remain there. It was best for him. We agreed. Before he could come home for a visit, he was killed in an auto accident. We had not seen him for six years. All we have of him is his remains, which were buried at Mac Dinh Chi. We had to move those when the communists destroyed the cemetery."

"I am sorry. What about your other son?"

"Philippe. He was drafted. (Without apparent irony, he uses the French term, 'appellé sous les drapeaux', called to serve beneath the flag.) He became a marine and was killed in a skirmish when our navy disputed Chinese incursions onto Hoang Sa."

His reference is to the Paracel Islands, which both countries claim. I am appalled by his misfortune and by the waste of life over such disputes. "I am deeply sorry. These losses must have been very hard on you and your wife."

"Yes. We were just two old people who no one cared about. Monsieur Francini gave me a special bonus to help pay for funeral expenses and assured me I could work at the hotel for as long as I wished. That has been a blessing. My salary there, all these years, has helped greatly. But after the deaths, my wife gave up. She was living only until le bon dieu would allow her to join her children. She was glad when the end came. She did not fight it. But now I am completely alone, and I am too old to continue working."

"How may I help?"

"I would like you to be my advisor, my lawyer and mon exécuteur testamentaire."

"If you have no one else, I would be honored to serve you."

"I want no one else. You knew of Monsieur Shaplen and cared about him. You understood, understand, those old days. To me, you are not un avocat commercant (the implication is a lawyer driven purely by mercantile considerations). You are someone who has come to belong to this country. More, I think, as what it was rather than what it has become. I will tell you my wishes, but you will understand them even before I speak. When I am gone, you will remember me, perhaps even keep the ancestors' altar for me."

He goes silent. In voicing these thoughts, he has been carried away by great emotion. I too am deeply moved. "It will be my pleasure to serve you. I will do my best to honor your wishes and expectations."

I see him to the reception area. Miss Ha nods towards my client who has been waiting patiently. She looks at me and, I am sure, sees the emotion I feel. She asks my next client if he can give me a few minutes before meeting. He smiles his assent. I have a moment of being certain that a less beautiful receptionist might not have gotten such a prompt agreement.

That night, I relate the meeting to Ha Oum. She remembers seeing Mr. Khanh at the hotel all those years ago. "The poor man," she says. "He chose the right person to confide in. I have always believed you are special. Maybe that began with Y'Chorn's certainty about you, but you have grown far beyond what and who you were in those days. We should invite Mr. Khanh to dinner and have grandpa Đao and grandpa Nam present. They will understand him."

As usual, she is right. Mr. Khanh is not of the education or status that Mr. Nam and Judge Đao have achieved, but he is of a personality well known to them and much respected. He is the kind of Vietnamese who, apart from them, can hardly be found anymore. In a few years, all such men will be gone, part of a history that will increasingly gather dust, dim and recede into an ever-more-distant past. These are men who grew up under French domination; who learned French in French schools; many of whom, like Nam and Đao learned their professions studying at French universities and then returned home, nurturing their nationalist pride and cherishing the generous and humane values of traditional Vietnam. These are the men on whom "free Vietnam," The Republic of Vietnam as it was once known, built its hopes and institutions, who suffered when it failed, who remained behind after the fall and faced harsh reeducation in communist camps and who have lived on as moral examples to subsequent generations.

We hold the dinner a week later. Mr. Khanh has been most reluctant to accept the invitation. He insists that he is not worthy of such an honor. I am sure he means what he says, but I now have abundant experience of gentlemen like him. I am able to convince him. Đao and Nam immediately put him at his ease. Mr. Nam recognizes him from the hotel. When I mention that Mr. Khanh knew Bob Shaplen, many barriers come down. By the end of the evening, it is as if the old men have been long-time friends. Mr. Khanh leaves first, still too new to our group to dare to overstay his welcome.

In bed after the dinner, Ha Oum tells me she is concerned for Mr. Khanh and for Judge Đao. "I don't remember very well how Mr. Khanh looked when I saw him on occasion at the hotel, so I am not certain. But he does not look healthy now. Would it be wrong if I suggested that one of our doctors would be glad to examine him?"

I tell her that I will speak with him in my role as his adviser. I expect that he will at least appreciate the concern. Then I ask her about Judge Đao. "He is failing," she tells me. It is important that he be examined immediately. I know him well and can see small changes that, especially at his age, can quickly become grave."

We are successful at getting each of our "grandpas" to see a doctor. Mr. Nam is aging but remains in good health. Ha Oum is right about Judge Đao. He invites us, Mr. Nam and our boys to an early dinner where he informs us, the adults at least, that his health is declining. "I have thought so for a while now, but I did not want to cause any of you unnecessary concern. Still, we all know that there is an end, and I have had a long, healthy and happy life. It will come one day, perhaps not far from now."

Mr. Nam looks at his old friend with great sadness. Judge Đao says, "You must go on, old friend. These boys (he gestures towards our sons who are playing across the room) need at least three grandfathers, and these two (Ha Oum and I) still need and want your guidance and wisdom."

When Mr. Nam starts to reply, the Judge raises a hand to delay him. "But for you, and of course this young family, I am alone. My wife, as you know, is long gone, and I am so old that I have outlived my two children. We all shall enjoy each other until my time comes. Then, you will, I hope, remember me fondly and continue as the family we have become."

Judge Đao dies peacefully just over a year later. Our boys have already been introduced to death through their experience in the hamlet. There it is a sad event, but not a tragedy. They cry for grandpa Đao and draw closer to grandpa Nam. In the hamlet, they talk with Y'Chorn about death and, to Ha Oum's horror, ask him when it will be his turn to die. He laughs gently at the question, but Y'Keo perseveres. "Our daddy can do your work when you do, so you don't have to worry."

Another year passes, and our once-large family is further diminished by the death of Mr. Khanh. He is ill for several weeks before dying. As his counselor and executor, I see him daily and spend several hours making sure his affairs are in order. He will not leave a large estate, but he has instructed me that it is to be for the benefit of his "nephews". When I suggest that he may wish to have me manage the estate for the benefit of Vietnamese street children, he is adamant. "You gave me dignity, family and friends at the end of my days. I will never know how to thank you for that."

Mr. Khanh is cremated after an appropriate visitation and mourning period. We are all deeply sorry. Mr. Nam has now lost two contemporaries within the space of fourteen months. When we return home, to the house at 50 Đoàn Thị Điểm Street that Judge Đao left to me, we set Khanh's ashes on a small altar which also bears the ashes of Đao and his wife. Mr. Nam is quiet. Finally he says, "I am glad Đao wished to leave you this house. For many years he considered it yours because your father had loved living here. But I think too that he anticipated the person you would become in this society and that, in time, you would place his ashes on the altar beside those of his wife. Soon, I will have the honor of your being the custodian of my ashes and of placing them on that altar alongside of my oldest and dearest friend."

The boys have been listening. They beg him, "No, grandpa. Don't leave us."

Mr. Nam smiles. "I will not leave. I will be right there (he gestures towards the altar), and you will be able to visit me and talk to me and care for me whenever you wish."

* * * * * * * * * * *

Many years have passed. Y'Keo and Y'Prun are grown men and have gone to follow their interests. As JJ had hoped, growing up, they visited him yearly. He even served as their surrogate father when we sent them for education at Hawaii's Iolani School, where I, myself, had been a student. Ben, Y'Keo, studied architecture at the University of Texas and now lives in his grandfather's house in Honolulu, which he continues to refine with certain thoughtful additions. He has his own architectural firm, which works closely with the engineering firm that JJ joined so many years ago and where his son and daughter have recently begun their careers.

Paul, Y'Prun, a graduate of Cornell Medical College, is an internal medicine physician. He lives at our first home on Ngô Thời Nhiệm Street but spends much time in the hamlet. Ha Oum and I have raised our family and had, she says, a wonderful life. "We have been blessed, with family of our making and family of our choosing, and you have proven Y'Chorn's wisdom." She hugs me and then, with a twinkle in her bottomless, beautiful eyes, tells me, "I chose well."

I give a short laugh. "And I, at least, had the good sense not to resist."

She offers me a mock exasperated look. "You had no choice," she says.

EPILOGUE

My father and mother are old now. They have come to Hawaii from Vietnam for what may well be the last time. The entire family is together here, an event that has not taken place since the birth of my first son, fifteen years ago. On that occasion, we all gathered in the hamlet where my mother, my brother and I were born. As tradition required, a midwife delivered the child, and my father, the shaman of our hamlet, presided over the celebration of the birth, his first grandchild. In the ensuing festivities, he sat on the ground in the cold night, in the glow of a huge bonfire and drank great quantities of our rice wine, nam bay. To the delight of all our people, he and my mother danced briefly, alone together, while our women and children chorused in delight and our warriors laughed and gamboled drunkenly. The hamlet sacrificed a water buffalo, and my father, in accord with ritual practice, collected the blood, sprinkled the assemblage with it and painted me, my wife and the newborn in a rite of purification and blessing. From that day, he lived almost without absence in our hamlet. There is joy and a shadow of sorrow that he and my mother have journeyed to Hawaii now.

My mother decided that they had to make this trip. My father is an old man. He appears to be still vigorous, but he is not without some of the ailments of considerable age, and my mother says she sees signs of frailty. That my brother is here to care for him if need be, has greatly eased my mother's fears about traveling. She wanted to bring the family and uncle JJ together, and to permit my father to stay, one last time, in the home where he grew up and which meant so much to him.

It has been a busy day, a bit trying for my father. He has gone to nap in his boyhood room, which even now remains as he left it when he departed for college more than seventy years ago. I am surprised to hear him giggling, almost like a boy, but there is surely pleasure for him in being where he began.

Later in the day, my mother returns from an outing with uncle JJ. She asks about my father. I tell her he is sleeping in his boyhood room. She smiles. "Let him rest. It has been a long trip and a long day. We will wake him in time for dinner."

Shevaun and my wife set the table on the deck grandpa built. It is a lovely, warm evening. We will dine watching the sun set over the Pacific beyond Waikiki. My mother smiles dreamily as she sips iced tea and looks out past Diamond Head. "I am so happy we came. He loved this. Through all our years in Vietnam, in the hamlet, this view was never more than a blink from his vision."

She gets up from the table. "I'll wake him."

"Sit, mom," I say. "I'll get him."

But she is already halfway up the stairs to his room. She is smiling, in anticipation, I think, at the prospect of seeing her aged husband, asleep in his boyhood bed. They love each other deeply, but it has always seemed to me that my mother took a special, woman's gratification in the deep pleasures of her man.

I have stopped at the foot of the stairs and watched her enter the room. What seems a long moment passes. There is no sound of conversation, and she does not emerge. More time goes by. "Mom?" I call in a stage whisper.

She comes to the doorway and gestures me up. She stands just inside the door waiting for me. My father is on the bed, a smile on his face. He looks happy and completely at peace. "He is gone," she says. There is a tear in her eye but also a gentle, loving smile on her lips.

"You're sure?"

"I am. Remember that I'm a nurse and recognize these things."

"But he looks so happy, peaceful and relaxed, and except for the giggling when he first entered the room a few hours ago, there has been no sound at all."

"The Field Marshall came and sat with him. He was a boy again, dearly loved by his father, the man he spent his entire mature life, loving and thanking. This was not a death. It was a reunion."

* * * * * * * * * * * *

A month has passed. In that time, we have taken my father's body back to the hamlet so our people could pay their respects, in accord with tradition; so they could bid farewell to the shaman whom they loved, all the more because he was clearly brought to them by Yang Rong. As he wished, although it is not tribal practice, my father was cremated here, in 'the long mountains', amid the timeless trees. A burial site was selected, and although no body was interred, a small funeral house was placed at the spot in accord with Rhadé tradition.

Now, back in Hawaii, I hold in my hand, a small box made from the wood of our mountain forests. It is the box from which my father drew the bracelet he offered my mother at the moment of their marriage. It now holds some of his ashes. My wife and son are with me, as are JJ, Shevaun and their children. We are in a small motor launch at the water's edge in Ala Moana Park, looking out at the surf break called, "Big Rights," that he loved as a boy. We push off and find our way to the deep water beyond the reef. There, I open the box and spread his ashes on the waves of the Pacific.

By arrangement, at the same moment, my mother holds an identical wooden box, the one which carried the bracelet she placed before my father in Y'Chorn's dwelling, so many years ago. She and Y'Prun, my brother, along with Y'Brahim, our shaman, spread my father's ashes in the forest to which Yang Rong and my grandfather had brought him before he ever dreamed that he was Y'Dun.

The breeze takes the ashes and makes them dance and fly about. They become one with the forest, just as they are doing here with our wonderful ocean. I know my mother is watching them there, as we watch them here. Over the great distance, her thought carries. I hear her say, "Y'Chorn, he has come back."

Acknowledgements

Finding Father has been a deeply felt project for me. I want to offer my special thanks, appreciation and profound respect to the Vietnamese people, especially to the many friends I made during my ten years in-country. I treasure how very close we became during those times and how so many of those acquaintances evolved into friendships and feelings of brotherhood and even love. I want to single out Pham Ngoc Kha, my first Vietnamese friend. Fifty-five years later, we remain close.

I also want to thank my in-laws, for their acceptance, love and the understanding they made possible for me. My heart is also extended in gratitude to all my wonderful Montagnard friends. Knowing and working with them was a privilege.

There is a legion of others, each of whom taught me something about this extraordinary country – about its history, culture, character, strengths, weaknesses, sense of humor, and its capacity to love, forgive and form enduring friendships. Dr. Gerry Hickey, Lawyer Tran Van Tuyen, Prof. Ton That Thien, Senator K'Sor Rot, Minister Pham Kim Ngoc, Mr. Nguyen Van Buu, were prominent social and political figures who took the time to befriend and educate me, and share their personal knowledge of important moments in recent Vietnamese history. Their gift to me was an abiding understanding of their country and events that shaped it, which made this book possible.

Also, I would be remiss if I did not acknowledge that cadre of challenging and beautiful young Vietnamese women who provided their own wisdom and insights and made those unusual times in that stressed place almost normal. I wish I could name them all here, but that is impractical.

I offer special thanks to retired US Attorney, Dan Bent, a dear friend of long years who patiently read drafts, listened while I floated ideas and discussed problems with him and offered thoughtful comment and criticism.

Finally, I thank my editor, Michael Bowker, who taught me to be an author. I had no idea of how exacting a process it is to turn a story into a proper novel. With patience and great skill, Mike taught me and ushered me through the process.